Heidi Stephens has spent her career working in advertising and marketing; some of her early writing work includes instruction manuals for vacuum cleaners, saucepans and sex toys. Since 2008 she has also freelanced as a journalist and, on autumnal weekend evenings, can be found liveblogging *Strictly Come Dancing* for *The Guardian*. Her debut novel, *Two Metres From You*, won the 2022 Katie Fforde Debut Romantic Novel Award. She lives in Wiltshire with her partner and her Labrador, Mabel.

By Heidi Stephens

Two Metres From You
Never Gonna Happen

HEIDI STEPHENS

NEVER GONNA HAPPEN

ACCENT

First published in 2022 by Headline Accent
An imprint of HEADLINE PUBLISHING GROUP

1

Cataloguing in Publication Data is available from the British Library

ISBN 978 1 4722 8585 0

Typeset in 11.6/15pt Bembo Std by Jouve (UK), Milton Keynes

Printed and bound in Great Britain by Clays Ltd, Elcograf S.p.A.

Headline's policy is to use papers that are natural, renewable and recyclable
products and made from wood grown in well-managed forests and other
controlled sources. The logging and manufacturing processes are expected
to conform to the environmental regulations of the country of origin.

HEADLINE PUBLISHING GROUP
An Hachette UK Company
Carmelite House
50 Victoria Embankment
London EC4Y 0DZ

www.headline.co.uk
www.hachette.co.uk

To Sam and Emma, with love

CHAPTER ONE

If she squinted intently at the bedroom ceiling, Emily Wilkinson could still see the outlines of hundreds of glow-in-the-dark stickers. Stars and crescent moons, tiny planets, spaceships shaped like chubby lipsticks with fins. She could clearly remember the day her dad had stuck them up for her, perched on a wobbly ladder, cursing his daughter's art direction. *Not THERE, Dad. You've got the spaceship flying into a planet. Point it towards the MOON. No, the OTHER way.* She'd bought half a dozen packets with her pocket money in the hope of replicating a school trip to the London Planetarium, but the abiding memory was her dad telling her to sod off and leave him to it.

The haphazard distribution of the stickers had annoyed Emily when she was nine, and it still grated on her nerves twenty years later. Half of the biggest stars were piled up in one corner like they were waiting for the headline act at a cosmic festival, and the section of ceiling by the window had no moons or planets at all. One of the spaceships was aligned exactly behind another, like it had broken down and was being towed to the Martian branch of Kwik Fit. Her attempts to relocate them by standing on a flimsy bookcase had given her several torn stickers and a trip to A&E. It turned out to be nothing more than a sprained ankle, but her dad had breathed furiously through his nose in the car the whole way there.

It was eight years since Emily had left home, the last of the Wilkinson children to fly the nest. All that remained as evidence of her former occupation were the stickers and the greasy Blu Tack marks on the faded pink walls. Now the bedroom was what Mum called her 'craft room', which was clearly secret Mum code for a place where abandoned hobbies go to die. Emily supposed she should be grateful it still had a bed, even though it had been rammed against the wall and festooned with brightly coloured fake-fur cushions that made her itch. Instead of Emily's swimming certificates and *NSYNC posters, the walls now featured a cross-stitch sampler in a frame which read 'Home is Where the Wine Is' and a foil scratch art picture of a timber wolf howling at the moon. Emily knew how it felt.

She took a deep breath and mentally offered up her current situation to the luminous papery heavens. *I'm twenty-nine years old, living back at home with my mum and dad. My ex, who is also my boss, has gone back to his wife. Which means I need a new job AND a new place to live, because also my room in my crappy shared flat has been destroyed in a hair-straightener fire, along with all my belongings. Everything in my life is a burning pile of shit.*

'Moomin!' yelled a voice from downstairs. She'd repeatedly requested that her dad stop using her childhood nickname, but her annoyance only encouraged him. 'Dinner's ready!'

Talking of burning piles of shit, it was Dad's turn to cook.

CHAPTER TWO

'So what are your plans, love?' asked Emily's mum, not for the first time this week. They were gathered around the dining table, which seated four in its normal state and six if you put the flap up. At Christmas her dad added a piece of plywood balanced on an old camcorder tripod to make it seat eight. You couldn't tell with a tablecloth on, and it just about worked as long as somebody sat in the doorway to the lounge and nobody made any sudden movements. There'd been talk of knocking the wall down and making downstairs open plan, but it had never come to anything. Most of this house hadn't changed much since the Wilkinson family moved in when Emily was seven, which she found oddly comforting.

'Leave her alone, Carol,' muttered her dad, squeezing the ketchup bottle so it farted a torrent of red sauce over his food. Emily wafted her hand for him to pass it over. Today's dinner was something that may once have been breaded fish, but several years of cooking had turned into some kind of carbonised brittle. She poked it with her fork and frowned as it snapped in half, resigning herself to the reality that even ketchup couldn't save the most dehydrated piece of haddock in West Sussex.

'I'm still waiting to hear about the insurance on my stuff,' she said, 'then I'll find a new flat and get a new job.'

'Why do you need a new job?' asked Carol, her voice shrill with alarm. 'The one you've got pays more than your dad's ever earned.' Emily was Personal Assistant to Mark Thompson, Managing Director of a big architecture firm in London, but she was currently on two weeks' compassionate leave to deal with the aftermath of the fire in her flat. By all accounts her housemate Lucy had helped herself to Emily's hair straighteners, then left them plugged in on her bed. They'd set fire to Emily's duvet around the time Mark had taken her hand in a bougie wine bar and said, 'I need to try to make my marriage work, Emily. For the sake of the children.'

'No need to rub it in, Carol,' Emily's dad said tetchily. He'd worked his entire career as an administrator for Chichester District Council, currently in the Planning and Building Control Department. Emily's mum was a school dinner lady and could make a bag of potatoes and a pack of frozen mince feed a family for a week. Neither of them earned much, and sadly you couldn't pay a mortgage with vocal opinions on cowboy-builder loft conversions and Jamie Oliver's war on Turkey Twizzlers.

'I'm just saying, Martin,' said Carol. 'Jobs like that don't come along every day, and she can't stay here for ever.'

'I've literally been here four days,' said Emily through gritted teeth, giving up on the fishy charcoal and attacking the cremains of the chips instead. 'My flat has burnt down, my boyfriend has dumped me, everything I own has gone up in flames.' *Including this dinner.* Maybe she was being a bit dramatic – in truth Mark had never been a proper boyfriend, even though their secret fling had gone on for two years. As for the fire, the smoke alarm had alerted her housemates to the blaze and the fire brigade had been there within a few minutes. All her stuff was gone, either burned or smoke-damaged beyond repair, but the building would be fine.

'Your boyfriend has dumped you?' asked Carol. 'I didn't even know you had a boyfriend. Why didn't you say?'

Emily shrugged. 'It's why I need a new job. He works at the firm.'

Carol crossed her arms in outrage. 'Well, I don't see why YOU should have to leave, just because he's finished with you. Why can't HE leave?'

'He's more senior than me, Mum,' Emily explained. *Just a bit.* 'It's complicated. I've been there three years anyway, it's a good time to move on.'

'Are you not going to eat that?' said Carol, standing up to clear the plates.

'I'm all done,' said Emily, patting her rumbling stomach. 'Just a bit unsettled at the moment.'

'We've only got the one loo,' said Martin. 'Let us know if we need to give it ten minutes.' He chortled to himself as Emily wondered how on earth her life had come to this in the space of a week.

'I love having you home, Moomin,' said Carol, patting Emily on the shoulder, 'but you can't have that room for ever. I need it for my crafts.'

Emily thought about the paper sack of unused knitting wool, the sewing machine that had seized up from lack of use, the sealed box of glitter and pipe cleaners and rainbow pom-poms. 'Then why can't I have the other room?' she asked. Number 22 Grove Street had three bedrooms; her parents had the biggest and the middle one was a guest room, having previously been shared by her two older brothers. Emily had always occupied the box room until Hobbycraft had launched a hostile takeover.

'I need to keep that for guests,' said Carol with a shrug.

'Simon could come home at any time, or David might want us to look after the grandchildren.'

Emily rolled her eyes. 'Simon's in Hamburg and David's in Newcastle, Mum. You're hardly round the corner.'

'I'm aware how far away my sons live, thank you,' said Carol, her voice giving a tell-tale wobble.

Give me strength, thought Emily. 'I've got a call with the insurance people tomorrow, and I'm planning to look at jobs this evening,' she said, standing at the sink and pulling on a pair of yellow rubber gloves. She'd actually been planning to watch a cheesy romcom on Netflix, but anything to get her mum off her back. The Wilkinsons were a close family but living at home at twenty-nine was far from ideal.

Her parents headed into the lounge to watch *EastEnders*, so Emily rinsed the ketchup off the plates and plunged them into soapy water while she considered her CV. She'd been in secretarial roles for eleven years, five of which had been at personal assistant level. She could organise diaries, plan parties, haggle travel deals and defuse all manner of professional and domestic crises. She was never late, always discreet and typed so fast her fingers were a blur. She was brilliant at shorthand, liked dogs and children and could sniff out bullshit artists from a hundred yards. Why wouldn't anyone want to give her a job?

Not that it didn't grate a bit that she needed to leave. She liked her job at Thompson & Delaney, and she'd loved working for Mark. To her credit, Emily had never chased him, and she'd fought the head-over-horn battle for months before the conference in Dubai, when the lift to their rooms had taken long enough for Mark to lean against the gilded wall and give her a look that liquefied every inch of her body from her neck to her knees. By the eighteenth floor Emily had known for sure that, when the doors opened on the thirty-second, she was going to let Mark take her hand and lead her back to his suite. It felt like something that she had no control over, and it was hard to worry about consequences when she was being banged into next week against a backdrop of fireworks over the Burj Khalifa.

And actually, when it became apparent that the Dubai trip was never going to be a one-off, it had worked out OK. Mark wasn't needy or demanding; there were no cheeky office winks or sleazy texts. They simply devised a series of subtle signals that indicated he was free if Emily wanted to stay at his flat. Sometimes she went, sometimes she didn't. Sometimes she went but they didn't even have sex; they just sat and drank wine and watched a film or chatted like two people who enjoyed one another's company. It had been two years of no-strings fun between two consenting adults who knew the score.

Which was why Emily had been surprised at how shaken and upset she'd been when Mark had delivered his soap-opera speech about giving his marriage another chance. Not that she'd let him see her distress at the time; a deadpan face is an essential weapon in the personal assistant's armoury. But before she'd had time to think through her response, she'd had a call from one of her flatmates saying her room was on fire, which had taken the evening in an unexpectedly stressful direction. Other than a bunch of company flowers delivered to her parents' house, Emily hadn't heard from Mark since. *Sometimes the silence speaks volumes*, she thought, yanking off the rubber gloves and taking Rudy the ancient family hound upstairs to help her look for a new job.

7

CHAPTER THREE

'It's good to see you, Emily,' said Mark with an attempt at a warm smile. His right foot was crossed over his left knee, jiggling frantically. Emily could tell he was nervous, which was no big surprise. She'd asked for a meeting with him and the head of HR at Thompson & Delaney, so he was probably wondering what kind of hell-hath-no-fury truth bomb she was about to drop.

'How ARE you?' asked Laura from HR, making zero effort to conceal how little she gave a shit. Laura had never liked Emily, who prevented her from gaining unfettered access to Mark to offload her daily list of petty grievances.

'I'm fine.'

'I'm so sorry about the fire,' said Laura, in a tone that suggested she'd be more sorry if she broke a nail or lost a fake eyelash. 'That must have been such a shock.'

'It was,' replied Emily. 'But nobody was hurt, which is the main thing.' The corners of Mark's mouth twitched in response to Emily's dead-eyed platitude, but it washed over Laura.

'Well, quite. Awful to lose all your belongings though. I hope there was nothing precious.'

Emily briefly considered making some random things up. Her childhood rocking horse, a collection of PVC gimp masks, a signed picture of Justin Bieber. Mark would know she was taking the piss, but perhaps now wasn't the time.

'Not really, mostly just clothes and stuff. A couple of gifts with sentimental value.'

She saw Mark's eyes flicker in her direction as he registered what she was referring to. For her twenty-ninth birthday in March he'd bought her a beautiful notebook from Smythson of Bond Street. It was covered with the softest sea-green leather, monogrammed on the cover with 'EW' in gold lettering. Later she'd sneaked a look online and seen that it would have cost Mark nearly £200 – an insane amount for a notebook, but still the loveliest gift she'd ever received. Emily had kept it in the box for seven months, unable to bring herself to use it. Now it was a pile of ashes.

'So are you ready to return to work?' asked Laura, clearly keen to move things along so she could get back to her day job of making staff feel like they were only one social media infraction away from her office guillotine. 'I assume that's why you've asked for this meeting?'

'Yes,' said Emily, sitting up straight and putting her clammy hands on her knees, 'but only to work my notice. I have a new job.'

Laura froze and Mark held Emily's gaze for a long moment, the jiggling foot slowing to a stop. 'Oh,' said Laura, glancing at Mark and clearing her throat, clearly waiting for him to say something.

'I'm really sorry to hear that,' said Mark quietly, looking like he genuinely meant it.

'I think the fire and everything just gave me a chance to re-evaluate,' said Emily, keeping her voice strong and her head high. 'You know, think about what's next for me.'

'Mmm,' said Laura tightly. 'But sorry, why did that require a meeting? Usually you would just write a resignation letter.'

Emily took a deep breath, letting the lie take shape in the back of her throat. 'Because I'm going to work for one of your competitors. I can't say which one at this stage, but I thought I should let you know.'

Mark's eyes bored into Emily's, but she didn't look away. She knew exactly what he was thinking – *is she lying to secure a quick exit, or actually that petty and vengeful?* She watched the cogs chunter in his brain as he arrived at the inevitable truth, his face softening into an expression that looked almost like admiration.

Laura shuffled some papers. 'Well, I'm not really sure your contract . . .'

'I've checked,' said Emily, with the calm certainty of someone who did attention to detail for a living. 'There are no restrictive covenants or non-compete clauses.'

A glimmer of a smile played across Mark's lips. 'Emily, could you step outside for a few minutes? This is obviously something Laura and I need to discuss. We won't keep you waiting long.'

Emily nodded and stood up, willing her knees not to knock together. She closed his door quietly and sat in the familiar chair behind her desk, taking a bottle of water from her handbag and downing half of it in one go. A few of her colleagues spotted her through the glass wall and waved, so she lifted the handset on the phone and swiftly dialled 123 for the speaking clock. As a softly spoken Scottish man informed her that the time was four-fourteen and twenty seconds, her friend Kirsten from the Finance team swerved in her direction on the way to the kitchen. Emily pointed at the phone and rolled her eyes, holding up her hand to indicate she'd come and talk to her in five minutes.

Emily knew this approach was risky; it wouldn't take much for Mark to find out that her competitor job offer was a lie, and she needed a good reference. But she was also sure of two things – firstly that she definitely couldn't go back to working for him now her compassionate leave was up, and secondly that he would almost certainly let her go without any fuss. Mark liked things clean and simple.

By the time Laura opened Mark's office door and nodded at her to come back in, the time was four twenty-seven exactly. Emily took a deep breath, smoothed down her skirt, and went back into the fray.

'Wait, are you saying you're on full pay for a month, but you don't have to go to work?' Shona's eyes boggled as she took another sip of wine. They were in a pub a few hundred metres from their shared flat in Stratford, all oxblood leather booths and oversized Edison light bulbs. Emily liked it because it was quiet and classy and not in Westfield Shopping Centre. There was something deeply unsettling about having a relaxed drink with friends while people nearby had their eyebrows threaded.

Emily nodded. There had been very little resistance in the end, although Laura's mouth had puckered itself into the tightest of cat's bums as she supervised Emily's desk clearance. There wasn't much; just the usual things every good PA keeps to hand – tissues, deodorant, hairbrush, sewing kit, tampons, spare pair of tights, plasters, various hangover cures and painkillers, a compact umbrella. She extracted the nude heels that lived under her desk, kept permanently at work so she didn't have to commute in them, then shovelled everything into a Tesco bag for life.

Within five minutes she was following Laura down the back stairs, avoiding the open-plan office so there wouldn't be any drama. That had been the deal – just leave quietly, no drama. Laura had given her a look of purest loathing in reception, then said, 'I'll email you details of what Mark agreed,' before stalking off, her heels clacking on the tiled floor. What Mark agreed, not Laura. Like Emily gave a shit either way.

She was sure that some people would have done a full Bridget Jones, bad-mouthing Mark then sashaying out of the office to Aretha Franklin like an absolute sass queen. But Emily wasn't the type, and Mark really didn't deserve it. She'd got what she came for, and the look on Mark's face had told her that he understood why she needed to go. Maybe he'd get in touch later, maybe he wouldn't. For now, Emily needed to leave him behind and get on with the rest of her life.

'They've already got somebody there who can take my job, so they didn't see the point in keeping me around,' she told Shona. This was the second big fat lie she'd told today, but it kept things simple. Shona and Eddie shared her flat, along with Lucy of the burning hair straighteners, but they'd never known much about Mark. They all got on fine as flatmates and often went out or watched a movie together, but it wasn't like they were best mates who disclosed all their secrets over late-night cocktails. They knew Emily had been seeing someone, but didn't press for details.

'You lucky bitch,' said Eddie. 'A month off on full pay.'

Emily shrugged. 'I'll be spending it looking for another job. Wait, where's Lucy?'

'She said she had bad cramps,' said Shona. 'I don't think she can face you, to be honest. She still swears blind that she'd turned your straighteners off at the wall, even though the fire inspector guy showed her the melted remains.'

'I didn't know she was borrowing them,' said Emily. 'What was she even doing in my room?'

Eddie shook his head. 'She used them all the time when you weren't there. I thought she'd asked. Sorry.'

'What's the hotel like?' asked Emily. The landlord's insurer had moved Shona, Eddie and Lucy into a hotel until Emily's room was repaired and the flat was repainted. The window and carpet had been replaced and they were now redecorating before the new furniture arrived. Emily had been offered the hotel too, but had decided her parents' house was marginally preferable. It would be nice to have her room back while she was doing job interviews though; commuting from Chichester was a faff.

'It's fine,' said Shona, topping up her wine. 'Annoying not to be able to cook, but the insurance guy said only one more week.'

'Did they manage to save any of your stuff?' asked Eddie.

'Two pairs of silver earrings and a photo frame,' replied Emily. She supposed the upside of not having much was that you didn't have much to lose.

Shona sloshed the rest of the wine into Emily's glass and put the upturned bottle back in the ice bucket. 'So what's next?'

'I've already got two job interviews lined up and I've just heard about another one,' said Emily. 'It looks interesting.'

'What kind of interesting?' asked Eddie.

'Another personal assistant role,' she said, sipping her wine. 'But working for a retired businessman instead of a firm.'

'What does he need an assistant for if he's retired?' asked Shona, plucking an artisanal cracker from the jam jar on the table and munching the end off.

Emily laughed. 'He's retired from business, Sho, not from life. Maybe he's got lots of other interests, or likes to travel a lot, I don't know. I'll find out more when I go for an interview.'

'Will you be staying in London?' asked Eddie.

Emily shrugged. 'No idea. I expect so. It's a live-in job, so it could be anywhere.'

Eddie looked horrified. 'What, you live in his house?'

'I don't think I'm going to be on the sofa bed in the spare room, Ed,' she said. 'I'm guessing it's a pretty big house. Or maybe he travels all the time, so I'd live in hotels.'

'That sounds super-weird,' said Shona, her brow furrowed as Eddie nodded emphatically. 'Are you sure he's legit? What if he's a sex trafficker and this whole thing is a scam?'

Emily rolled her eyes. 'It's been organised by a specialist agency,' she said. 'They only deal with high-end assistant jobs, so I'm pretty sure they've checked he's not a sex trafficker.'

'Still sounds weird to me,' said Shona.

'It's no different to being a nanny or an au pair,' laughed Emily. 'Loads of people do live-in jobs for rich people. It might be really interesting.'

'Until he murders you and dissolves your body in his acid-filled swimming pool,' said Eddie, nodding ominously at Shona.

'Oh my God, you're both insane. I'll let you know after I've met him.'

'Bet he's a sex trafficker,' said Shona.

14

'Murderer,' said Eddie.

Emily sighed and shook her head. It was a live-in job that had nothing to do with architecture and offered little in the way of dating opportunities. Right now that ticked a lot of her boxes.

CHAPTER FOUR

Emily stood in front of the full-length mirror in her freshly painted Stratford room, doing a final sweep for missed details. Her only surviving suit was the one she'd been wearing on the day of the fire, but it was also her favourite – a tailored blazer from Reiss in a pinky-beige colour, paired with a matching pencil skirt that fell just above her knees. Dresses didn't really work on her, because even though she was five foot seven, her top half was a size ten and her bottom half was a twelve or fourteen, depending on the time of the month. She'd inherited her mother's classic pear shape – no boobs and a curvy bum – and whilst the gym and running and swimming stopped her edging from pear to butternut squash, there was nothing she could do about her proportions. Suit separates in different sizes were her salvation, but there was no point buying anything new until she knew where she would be working next. Some places expected PAs to be fully suited and booted; others were fine with jeans and trainers.

The insurance company had paid out £2,000 for everything she'd lost in the fire, but she hadn't mustered the energy to go shopping beyond pyjamas, underwear, some basic gym gear and a few casual bits to mooch about in at home. Her make-up bag and phone had been in the handbag she was carrying on the evening of the fire, and other than the melted ghd hair straighteners they were the most valuable things she owned. Once she knew where she was working and living next, she'd go on a shopping trip – work clothes, shoes, the lot. Maybe she'd take her mum and buy her something nice too. They drove each other round the bend sometimes, but there wasn't much spare cash at home for Carol to treat herself.

Emily turned sideways to look at her profile. The suit was a good fit – she'd neither gained nor lost weight in the three weeks since the fire, which was a miracle considering how inedible her dad's cooking was. Mum cooked lunch for over a thousand secondary school children every day and regularly couldn't face the kitchen when she got home, so Dad did his best. Emily had offered to cook on a few occasions, but Martin had declared her stuffed courgettes 'too much pissing about for not nearly enough actual food', so that was the end of that.

She'd had the suit dry-cleaned and asked her dad to polish the heels she'd rescued from under her desk, just to make him feel useful. Her mum had insisted on giving her some new tights, even though they were a foul gravy-tan shade and made her legs look like hot dogs. Her long brown hair was pulled into a tidy bun, a few strands left loose around her face so it didn't look too severe. Minimal make-up, pale pink nails, tiny silver hoop earrings. She would have to do.

The alarm on her phone told her it was time to go, so she threw the heels in her bag, put on her coat and trainers, then headed for the tube and her appointment in Mayfair with Mr Charles Hunter.

Emily watched Mr Hunter scan her CV and wondered what he was thinking. Probably disappointed that she went to a bog-standard comprehensive rather than a fancy private school, or maybe pondering why she'd never gone to university with those A-level results. The answer was a simple one, really. She hadn't fancied being saddled with a hefty debt, even though at the time the fees were nothing compared to what students had to pay now. And she'd wanted to start earning a living and saving to get her own place, since there wasn't any money at home and she definitely didn't want to stay there for ever.

She'd worked a summer temp job at her school since she was fifteen, helping out with all the admin for the new September intake. Not only had she enjoyed it, but she'd been really good at it. She looked at ads on online job boards and saw that top executive assistants for law firms and management consultants in London could earn £70k or more, so why not aim for that as a career goal? She'd got an entry-level secretarial job at a building firm in Southampton and started doing evening courses at the local college to gain more qualifications, and by the time she was twenty-one she had enough experience to move to a shared house and a new job in London. Lots of her friends had gone off to uni, but now she was earning more than most of them without the student loan payments. Most of the time she had no regrets.

Charles Hunter was a handsome and powerful-looking man in his late sixties, Emily guessed. Tall, full head of salt-and-pepper hair, well dressed in a shirt and tailored suit but no tie. His handshake was firm and his smile was kind. He looked a bit like Pierce Brosnan and was what her mum would call a 'silver fox', a term that was usually followed by 'get in my box'. Carol could be quite the poet when the mood took her.

They'd already talked about her qualifications and work history, the kind of stuff she'd been doing for Thompson & Delaney. She'd answered all his questions confidently and felt sure that she was more than qualified for this job. So now it all came down to whether she was the right fit.

'Well,' said Mr Hunter, putting her CV on his desk. 'I'm sure you have some questions for me.'

'I do,' said Emily with a smile. She'd pre-prepared some simple but smart questions, stuff that was easy to answer but suggested she'd given it some thought. 'I've never worked for a private individual before, so I'm interested to know what kind of work it might be.' It was hard not to put on a posh accent in a place like this; it felt like the kind of thing you should do to fit in with the fancy furnishings and the huge wooden desk. But she swallowed the mouthful of fake plums and decided he could take her as she was, or not at all.

'It's very broad,' said Mr Hunter. 'Technically I'm retired, in that I've sold my business and I don't currently run a company. But I still have lots of other commercial interests, and I'm a very busy man. Most of the work will be very familiar to you – travel, correspondence, managing my diary, organising events, getting rid of people I don't want to talk to. That sort of thing.'

Emily smiled; she was no stranger to getting rid of annoying people. 'And why do you need someone to live in?' She glanced around the office, which was part of a large and imposing private house, and wondered why she couldn't commute. It was only a five-minute walk from Bond Street tube, which was twenty minutes on the Central Line from Stratford.

'The job isn't based here,' said Mr Hunter. 'It's at my main property in Norfolk.' Emily tried to hide her surprise, nodding politely instead. 'It's a little remote,' he continued, 'which makes it hard to find top-notch staff locally. I spend most of my time there and prefer to work face-to-face. Not very fashionable, I know.'

She paused, wondering if he was whisking her off to some haunted castle, and scrambled for another question. 'Do you have other live-in staff?'

'Just my housekeeper and my driver,' said Mr Hunter. 'Everyone else is local – gardeners, cleaners, estate workers, that sort of thing. Various members of my family come and go.'

She tried to process this unexpected location, feeling like her train of thought had been derailed. Ooh, here was a good question.

'Will the job involve much travel?'

'As much or as little as you would like, really,' said Mr Hunter. 'My previous assistant preferred to stay behind and work according to whatever time zone I happened to be in. But if you're the travelling type, there will be opportunities for you to accompany me. I'll make sure you have some free time and provide you with a local guide if necessary. I'm a great believer in immersing yourself in interesting places, rather than just passing through.'

Emily nodded appreciatively, like she was the kind of person who had extensive experience of global travel. In reality her only trip out of the country other than the fateful trip to Dubai was a weekend in Amsterdam with a former pothead boyfriend. He'd left her to explore the Rijksmuseum while he baked himself in a coffee shop, then slept the rest of the weekend. Emily's family had never done foreign holidays when she was a kid – what was the point when the beach was down the road? There'd been loads of day trips to Brighton or London, and once a week on a narrowboat in North Wales, but never abroad.

'What happened to your previous assistant?' she asked, then immediately wished she could take it back. It was a question she'd idly asked herself in her head and really hadn't meant to say out loud.

'I'm sorry?' asked Mr Hunter, looking confused.

Emily scrambled for a recovery. 'You mentioned your previous assistant didn't like to travel. I just wondered why she isn't your assistant any more.' *Oh God, it sounds like I think he's a terrible boss.*

'I killed her with my bare hands and fed her to my dogs,' said Mr Hunter, his face deadpan. Emily pressed her lips together to stop herself laughing, holding his piercing gaze along with her nerve. *I'm not afraid of you.*

'Fine,' said Mr Hunter, rolling his eyes theatrically. 'Her name was Andrea and she worked for me for twenty-five years. She and her husband lived in one of my estate cottages, but they recently returned home to Somerset to care for Andrea's mother, who is rather unwell. We speak regularly; I've arranged for her mother to be treated privately. Is there anything else you'd like to know?'

Emily gave her head a tiny shake. *Nice work, Wilkinson.*

'Andrea left a couple of months ago, and I thought I'd see how I got on without an assistant for a while. It turns out I get on very badly indeed.'

They were both silent for a moment, sizing each other up. Charles Hunter was hard to read, but he didn't look bored or uncomfortable. In fact he seemed to be rather enjoying himself.

'Do you have any other questions?' he asked.

'I don't think so,' said Emily, rearranging her hands in her lap and deciding it was time to put her cards on the table. 'The job sounds very interesting, but it's not an environment I've ever worked in before. It's hard to know if I'm suited to it, if that makes sense.'

'It makes perfect sense,' said Mr Hunter, gesturing at the CV. 'You have the skills I'm looking for, so it all rather comes down to whether we can tolerate each other. What's your gut instinct on that?'

The question took Emily by surprise, but her gut instinct was as clear as a bell. 'I think we might tolerate each other pretty well, actually.'

'So do I,' said Mr Hunter, sitting back in his chair and looking triumphant. 'Now. I have a question for you.'

Uh oh, thought Emily, sensing incoming danger. She smiled and tried to look calm. 'OK.'

'I've read your CV, and now I've met you in person,' said Mr Hunter, his eyes boring into her like an airport scanner inspecting every item of emotional baggage. 'And it seems to me that you could have your pick of every professional services business in London – any one of them would snap you up in a heartbeat.'

Emily accepted the compliment nervously, not sure where he was going with this.

'And yet here you are,' he said, gesturing vaguely around his office, 'interviewing for a PA job that wouldn't even register on your radar unless you had specifically asked the recruitment agency to tell you about jobs that were live-in.'

Here it comes, thought Emily.

'So my question is,' said Mr Hunter, making a steeple out

of his fingers and tilting his head to one side, 'why are you really here?'

Emily said nothing for a long moment, organising her thoughts. There was nothing to be gained from not being honest, and everything to lose. She took a deep breath and cleared her throat. 'I've recently come out of a relationship. The person involved works at the place where I used to work, so I really need to work somewhere else.'

'I see,' said Mr Hunter, waiting for her to continue.

'Also my flat burned down in a hair-straightener fire,' Emily added, hoping that a dramatic comedy twist might lighten the mood, 'so I don't have anywhere to live. Pretty much all that survived was this suit.'

'It's a very nice suit,' said Mr Hunter, his mouth twitching as he tried not to smile.

'Thank you,' replied Emily, instinctively smoothing down the skirt. 'I guess a lot has happened in the last few weeks, all of which has led me to look for a new challenge and a fresh start. Somewhere I can focus on my work and my well-being.'

'Hmm, I can see that.'

Emily decided she'd said enough, so she looked at him expectantly and waited. Mr Hunter tapped his forefinger on his lips, evidently deep in thought.

'Well, this has been very interesting,' he said, his face soft and friendly, like they'd just had a very pleasant date. 'I think I have everything I need. The agency will be in touch.'

CHAPTER FIVE

Emily left Charles Hunter's house in Mayfair with a thousand butterflies in her stomach, wondering if she'd done enough, and if maybe this was the beginning of a huge and exciting opportunity. Everything about the interview had felt right – the job description, the distance from her mess of a life, Mr Hunter himself. There was something about him that she'd really liked; a sense that he wasn't your usual self-absorbed rich person, that maybe he had his feet in the real world. It was hard to explain, but it had felt like the same kind of connection she'd had when she first met Mark. Not the physical attraction, obviously – more a sense that they got each other without either of them having to say very much.

She swapped her heels for trainers in the street, then walked south towards Green Park, stopping at Starbucks on Berkeley Street for a coffee. She needed to regroup and think about her next steps – the recruitment agency was already hassling her for a response to a job offer from one of the other interviews, but now she wanted to buy herself more time. It was assistant to a South Korean businessman who travelled for a large part of the year, so she'd be based wherever he was, which seemed to be mostly very expensive hotels. The interview had been conducted by his London lawyer, with Mr Lee popping in for the final five minutes to introduce himself. He'd been polite and friendly, but impossible to read in such a short time. She didn't have the smallest idea if she would enjoy working for him.

The other interview had been at a very expensive boys' school in Surrey – a combination of PA to the headmaster and general administrative dogsbody. She definitely wasn't keen on that one, but they hadn't been in touch yet anyway. Her suspicion was that they wanted someone a lot posher than her, who understood how the public school system worked and could rally the staff and governors with a bit of ra-ra-jolly-hockey-sticks energy. Not her scene at all, never mind living in a crumbling old building with hundreds of feral teenage boys.

She sipped her coffee, wondering how long it would be before Mr Hunter made his decision, and if she could fob off the agency on the job for Mr Lee until then. But he didn't seem like the kind of man who liked being kept waiting, and the idea of ending up without any of these jobs and going back to the drawing board was not very appealing. Perhaps she should call the agency this afternoon and explain her dilemma. Maybe they could chivvy Mr Hunter along and get a decision early next week.

Her phone buzzed with a WhatsApp message, so she put her cup back on the saucer and scrolled her finger across the screen. To her surprise, it was from Mark.

Can we talk? I'm at my flat.

She stared at the screen for a moment, considering her options. There was nothing on her list today other than getting the tube to Victoria then taking the train back to her parents' house in Chichester. It was Friday, and she really didn't fancy spending the weekend in her empty room in

Stratford. But 'I'm at my flat' was very clear in its intent. It screamed *I'm alone in my flat in London, not at home with my wife in Oxford.*

Emily gave her head a tiny shake and tapped her reply. *I'm in Green Park, best I can do is a phone chat.*

There was nothing for a minute, then three dots appeared to show that Mark was writing a message.

Mildreds in Kings Cross in half an hour? Please?

Emily couldn't help but smile. In sixty seconds he'd checked where was a sensible meeting point on the Victoria Line between Emily in Green Park and his flat in Highbury, and pinpointed a half-decent restaurant within walking distance of the tube. She'd taught him well.

Fine, she replied. If it was a choice between a proper sit-down lunch or an M&S sandwich on the Southern Railway Helltrain, she was willing to spend some time in Mark's company.

There was no advance booking for tables at Mildreds, but she and Mark arrived early enough to miss the main lunch rush and get a table more or less straight away. Emily had been to the Soho branch a few times with her best friend Kelly after a West End show, but this one was much more airy and spacious. Kelly identified as vegetarian but fell off the chicken wagon on a regular basis. The food at Mildreds was entirely veggie or vegan, and good enough to make you wonder why anyone bothered with meat.

'You look smart,' said Mark, kissing her on both cheeks. Emily couldn't tell him she'd been for an interview because they were still pretending she already had a job.

'A meeting with my new boss,' she said vaguely, smiling

at the waitress as she handed over menus and put a jug of water on the table.

'Do you have any plans to tell me where you're off to?' said Mark, filling Emily's glass. He was wearing designer jeans and a pale blue shirt, custom-made by a man in Hong Kong. Emily recognised it as one she'd ordered a year before, along with four others in different pastel shades. He was almost fifteen years older than her but definitely didn't look it; aside from his tailor, Mark spent an eye-watering amount on personal trainers and male grooming to keep the years at bay.

'No plans at all,' she said with a smile.

'Not many architects in Green Park,' Mark mused, tapping his manicured fingers on the table. 'Why didn't you want to come to my place?'

'I didn't want to see you,' she said calmly. 'I quit my job so I didn't have to see you.'

Mark smiled. 'But you're still here.'

Emily shrugged. 'Girl's gotta eat.'

Mark watched her for a while as she pretended to read the menu, clearly not done with his interrogation just yet. 'But you're not going to work for one of my competitors, are you?'

'I'd rather not say,' said Emily. She knew Mark would find this infuriating, but it felt important not to just roll over and give him exactly what he wanted. She'd been doing that for two years.

They both sat in awkward silence while the waitress took their order for fake chicken burgers and a glass of wine each – red for Mark, white for Emily.

'You know, I would have handled things differently if I'd known you'd take the news so badly,' said Mark, ducking his head down to catch her eye. 'I didn't realise you'd become so attached.'

'Neither did I,' said Emily, pulling a stupid face to break the tension. The last thing she needed was for this to become a declaration of deep feelings.

Mark smiled. 'It's nice to know that you WERE attached, though.'

Emily realised she was here to massage Mark's ego, in the absence of her willingness to massage anything else. Her wine arrived, so she slugged half of it. 'So what's this all about?' she asked. 'Why the message?'

He gave her his best lost puppy face. 'I wanted to see you. I miss you.'

Emily nodded thoughtfully. 'What you actually mean is you wanted to fuck me. Right?' The couple on the table next to them looked up from their Tofu Pad Thai with raised eyebrows, but Mark didn't waver for a second.

'I won't lie,' he whispered with a seductive smile, leaning in close enough that she could smell the woody, citrusy scent of his aftershave. Aventus by Creed; she'd seen it on the shelf in his bathroom many times. 'Watching you sit in my office in that tight skirt and screw me over for a month's paid leave made me really, really want to fuck you. And now you're wearing the same skirt and I'd take you over this table if you gave me half a chance.'

Emily didn't know whether to laugh, cry or scream. He was such an arrogant shit, but he knew exactly how to push every one of her buttons. A reprieve from the growing warmth in the pit of her stomach came in the form of her phone vibrating in her handbag by her ankle. She quickly leaned down to fish it out – the screen said 'private number'.

'I have to take this,' she said quickly, standing up and walking briskly out into the street as she swiped the screen to answer the call.

'Miss Wilkinson? It's Charles Hunter.'

Emily's stomach fizzed with nerves and wine. 'Hello, Mr Hunter.'

'Is now a good time to talk? You sound like you're outside.'

'I am, but it's fine,' said Emily. 'I'm just surprised to hear from you, I thought the agency would call.'

'They're calling the other candidates, but I wanted to call you myself.'

Emily squeezed her eyes shut and crossed her fingers. 'OK.'

'I'd like to offer you the job as my assistant.'

Fuck, thought Emily, but managed on this occasion not to say it out loud. Instead she went with 'gosh', which she was pretty sure she'd never said before in her life.

'I don't expect you to decide now, I'm sure you have lots more questions,' he said. 'So I have a proposal. I'd like to invite you to visit Bowford Manor on Monday if that's convenient for you. I'll send a car for you, all very casual, no need to dress up. It will give you some time to think about things over the weekend, then come and see what you think of the place. If you decide it's not for you, I won't take it personally.'

Emily's insides were dancing a happy jig. 'Thank you, Mr Hunter,' she said. 'I'd like that very much.'

'You look like you've had some good news,' said Mark as she sat back at the table, her cheeks flushed from the October chill and her thoughts a million miles from his offer to screw her over the table.

29

'I have,' said Emily, opting not to elaborate. The less Mark knew about her future plans, the better.

'Whatever it is, are you sure you don't want to come back to mine and celebrate?' he asked, trying to recapture the playful mood from earlier.

'I'm absolutely sure,' said Emily, looking at him intently. She loved flirty Mark, but it was time to draw a line, one way or the other. 'Look, Mark, I know I wasn't very happy about your decision to end things, but now I've realised it was definitely for the best.'

'Oh,' said Mark, his eyes wide with surprise.

'I hope we can be friends, but that's all I can offer.'

'I see,' he said, chewing the inside of his cheek. It was something he did when he was annoyed but trying to keep a lid on it. Emily had seen him do it a hundred times.

The waitress put two burgers in front of them and rattled through the usual offers of sauces and condiments. Emily picked hers up with both hands and took a huge bite. Mark stared at her, his face confused and uncertain. Clearly this lunch hadn't gone the way he'd hoped.

CHAPTER SIX

'No sign of the car yet,' Carol called through from the lounge as she peeked through the net curtains. 'Do you think he'll send a Rolls-Royce?'

'For God's sake, Mum,' said Emily, 'it's not due for half an hour, and of course he won't send a Rolls-Royce.' She paused with a slice of Marmite toast halfway to her mouth, realising she had no idea what kind of vehicle Charles Hunter would send. She'd assumed it would be a normal taxi, but what if it was a fancy limo? They lived in a seventies cul-de-sac with beaky neighbours who would wet their pants in unison.

'I prefer a Bentley, personally,' said Martin, with all the authority of a man who'd driven the same Ford Focus for over a decade.

'Are you sure you're going to be safe, Moo?' asked Carol, plucking a few dog hairs off the back of Emily's jumper. They'd gone shopping together on Saturday and Emily had spent £150 on a pair of skinny black jeans, a slouchy fawn roll-neck and some brown suede ankle boots with a cowboy heel. It was the kind of outfit she'd wear any weekend, so it felt like a good investment. Her mum had loved the jumper so much Emily had ended up buying her the same one in blush pink.

'I'll be fine, Mum,' said Emily, for the umpteenth time.

'It's just you hear things, don't you?' said Carol, wringing her hands. 'About rich men using their power, taking advantage of innocent girls. Before you know it one of the servants has given birth to his bastard child and gets kicked out on the street with barely tuppence to her name.'

'Bloody hell, Carol,' said Martin. 'You really need to stop reading those books.' Emily's mother was a voracious reader, and her tastes leaned towards bodice-ripping period bonk-busters and true-life tales of people who had survived terrible circumstances, like being locked in an attic or giving birth in a puddle outside a workhouse.

'I think one of us should come with you, Moo,' said Carol, 'just to be on the safe side.'

Emily stood up and rinsed her plate in the sink, taking solace in the knowledge that by the end of the day she'd have a job, either for a Korean steel magnate called Ye-jun Lee, or a Norfolk software millionaire called Charles Hunter. 'You and Dad have both got work. And anyway, I'm twenty-nine. I've spent eleven years in this kind of job, I know what I'm doing.'

'I just wish your brothers were here,' said Carol, like they were the Mitchell brothers rather than a structural engineer and a media executive. Emily took a deep breath and went back upstairs to clean her teeth and fetch her handbag.

While she wrestled her hair into a plait, a hairband clamped between her teeth, Emily mentally went through everything she'd learned about Charles Hunter. A quick google had established that he'd sold his online gaming empire to a huge US corporation three years before, in a deal that had been worth hundreds of millions of dollars. She'd found press pictures of him at various charity events and conferences,

32

accompanied in the less recent shots by a glamorous blonde of indeterminate age with unfeasibly perky boobs. Further investigation had revealed she was his ex-wife Tanya Hunter, who had rinsed him for millions in the divorce and now lived in LA. Mr Hunter had a son too, a dark-haired, pale-skinned property developer called Adam who had mean, piggy eyes and razor-sharp cheekbones.

Emily had stopped short of finding out everything she could about Charles Hunter's Norfolk house, Bowford Manor, even though she was tempted. Being chauffeured to a country pile wasn't the kind of thing that happened to women like her every day, so the least she could do was let some parts of it be a surprise.

The car turned out to be nothing more than a sleek black Audi saloon, albeit one that was immaculately clean with buttery leather seats. The driver was called Leon, a bearded, olive-skinned bear of a man in his mid-thirties who was originally from Croatia. He told Emily that he'd been Mr Hunter's driver for three years and lived in an apartment above the garage at Bowford Manor, although he'd stayed in a very nice pub in Chichester last night so he could pick Emily up.

They chatted companionably as Leon navigated the Chichester ring road, about how he drove Mr Hunter everywhere and maintained all the vehicles on the estate. He'd been a car mechanic in Zagreb before he moved to the UK and worked as a taxi driver in Norwich, then one day he'd picked up Mr Hunter's son from the station and they'd got chatting. Leon had given him his card so he could book his taxi whenever he was in the city, and when Mr Hunter was looking for a new driver his son suggested Leon apply for the job. *Perhaps Mr Mean Piggy Eyes isn't so bad after all*, thought Emily.

She asked Leon if he ever had to wear a full chauffeur's outfit with a hat, and he thought that was very funny. It was very casual at Bowford Manor, apparently – none of the staff wore uniforms. He knew Andrea, Mr Hunter's former assistant, very well, and described her as a 'very nice lady'.

'Are you going to be the new Andrea?' he asked Emily, beaming at her in the rear-view mirror.

She couldn't help but return the smile, although she felt the flutter of butterflies in her stomach again. 'Maybe. Today will help me decide.'

'They are very interesting family, but Mr Hunter is a good man, a good boss. That is all I will say.'

'Thank you, Leon.' She quietly registered the 'but' in Leon's comment and resolved to get to the bottom of what made the Hunters so interesting before the day was out.

The drive to Norfolk was four hours of tedious motorway, from the South Downs to the M25, then north-east through Cambridgeshire, Suffolk and finally into Norfolk. It was a part of the country that Emily didn't know at all, and at first glance it didn't seem to have much going for it unless you liked miles and miles of flat, featureless farmland. After a couple of hours they stopped for a quick break at a service station, and Emily took the opportunity to move from the back of the car into the passenger seat – it made her feel less car sick, and it was easier to chat to Leon.

As they drove deeper into Norfolk and left the motorway for slower roads, she began to notice some of the small details of the landscape – the pretty farms, the clusters of red-brick houses, the churches built from flint. The towns and villages signposted from the main road seemed strange too – Snetterton, Hethersett, Spooner Row, Cringleford. They sounded like place names from a children's story book.

Once they left the Norwich ring road, the car weaved through several pretty villages before arriving at the gates of Bowford Manor. Emily's experience of stately homes had been limited up to this point – a school trip to Uppark House when she was eleven or twelve, a family day out to Petworth when she was a bit younger, the abiding memory of which was being stung on the eyelid by a wasp and having to go to A&E looking like she'd been punched in the face. It was only a few months after the cosmic sticker incident, and her father had done the whole furious nose-breathing thing again.

Beyond those, the only posh houses she knew were the ones she'd seen in films or on TV, with hundreds of identical windows in neat rows. Grand, symmetrical places like Chatsworth and Highclere that reared out of the grounds like stone monoliths after a carriage ride down an interminable driveway, past a huge lake or an island with a Grecian temple.

The entrance to Bowford Manor was through ornate black metal gates, then down a winding, tree-lined drive that took them past ploughed fields and grassy paddocks. Emily waited patiently for a massive country pile to appear, but instead was rewarded with something a good deal more interesting. The manor house itself was built from red brick with a hodgepodge of windows and chimneys and towers in different shapes and sizes. It looked like a house from a fairy tale – on one side was a steeply gabled section that resembled an alpine chalet, and on the other side was a round tower shaped like a castle turret, on top of which was a huge weathervane decorated with a golden horse. The whole effect was chaotic and confusing to look at, but also entirely magical. Emily was instantly smitten.

A stern-looking woman waited on the steps outside the front door as Leon brought the car to a halt on the crunchy gravel. She was in her mid-sixties, Emily guessed, wearing a plain navy dress and sensible heels, with short, iron-grey hair that had clearly been cut for ease of maintenance rather than any kind of style. She opened Emily's car door with a disdainful look that suggested she hadn't been expecting much, and Emily had managed to confirm her opinion before she'd even opened her mouth. 'You must be Miss Wilkinson,' she said with all the warmth of a church crypt in January. 'I'm Anna, the housekeeper.'

Emily climbed out of the car into the sunshine and shook the woman's hand, determined to make a good impression. 'Call me Emily. Lovely to meet you, Anna.'

'Have a good day, Emily,' said Leon with a cheery wave through the car window. She smiled at him and watched as he drove off. She'd agreed with Mr Hunter that she'd get the train back later, since she was only going as far as her flat in London, so at least Leon didn't have to drive her all the way home again.

'Come on then,' said Anna impatiently, walking back up the steps towards the huge front door. 'We've got half an hour before you're due to see Mr Hunter; he's asked me to give you a tour of the staff quarters.'

'Thank you,' said Emily, hoping there was a bathroom

and a hot drink in that plan; it was two hours since they'd stopped for a break and she was desperate for a wee and a cuppa. She took a final glance at the outside of the house before heading inside, feeling a strange combination of being out of her comfort zone and oddly at home. She thought about what her dad would say if he was here. *Chin up, Moomin. Knock 'em dead.*

CHAPTER SEVEN

Emily's tour of Bowford Manor began in a grand entrance hall, which had a wide staircase on either side that swept up to an ornate gallery. It reminded Emily of the stairs on *Strictly Come Dancing*, as long as you ignored the walls lined with paintings of fields and horses and people in powdered wigs. But before she could imagine herself doing a waltz in a chiffon dress, Anna disappeared into a doorway hidden in the wooden panelling under one of the staircases, like Alice down the rabbit hole.

Emily followed down a flight of narrow stairs and found herself in the kitchen. It was a massive open space broken up with columns instead of walls, bigger than her parents' entire house. At one end was a gleaming steel range and glossy modern kitchen units with a huge granite island, and at the other was a comfortable lounge area with squashy sofas and an open fireplace, over which was mounted a giant TV. In the middle was an old wooden dining table that could easily seat twenty people.

'Mr Hunter's chef is called Sam; he comes in at noon each day to make his lunch and dinner,' said Anna briskly. 'We keep all the leftovers in the pantry freezer; staff can help themselves or prepare whatever food they like. Sam doesn't work on weekends unless there's an event, so it's not unusual for Mr Hunter to eat down here, particularly on a Sunday evening. He likes to pretend he knows his way around an oven.' Anna pursed her lips disapprovingly, as though Mr Hunter didn't belong in his own kitchen.

'There are no fixed mealtimes for staff,' she continued, 'so you'll be expected to sort yourself out. Nobody's going to run around after you.'

Emily nodded, wondering what kind of princess Anna thought she was. 'Fine.'

'Shall we go upstairs?' asked Anna.

'Can I just use the bathroom first?' asked Emily, realising that a cup of tea was an unrealistic expectation.

'Yes, of course,' snapped Anna, like Emily was already a colossal drag on her day. 'Why didn't you say?'

The various flights of back stairs were connected by narrow corridors that bypassed all the interesting bits of the house, other than Anna pointing out closed doors that led to the dining room, Mr Hunter's office and the family bedrooms. 'There's an identical set of stairs and corridors on the other side of the entrance hall; they were designed so the servants could access most rooms in the house without being seen.' Emily raised her eyebrows and Anna gave her a dead-eyed glare. 'You can use whichever stairs you like, obviously. But the back stairs mean you're less likely to meet Mr Hunter's family and get another job added to your list.'

'What's the family like?' Emily asked quickly.

'A mixed bag,' muttered Anna, hurrying up the stairs. Emily waited for her to elaborate, but apparently that wasn't happening any time soon either.

The stairs ended in the attic, in what had presumably once been the servants' quarters. 'There used to be a dozen servants' rooms up here,' said Anna, reading Emily's mind. 'But they've been knocked together over the years and now there are only four. Only one is currently in use, by me.'

Emily nodded but said nothing, sensing that Anna had no time for stupid questions.

'These would be your rooms,' said Anna, opening a door. 'They haven't been used since Mr Hunter's previous assistant moved into one of the estate cottages, so I'll have them cleaned and the mattress replaced.'

Emily had half expected a poky cell like servants' rooms on TV, but it was actually a suite of two low-ceilinged rooms with a row of tiny dormer windows looking out over the higgledy-piggledy roofline. The view beyond was spectacular, with ploughed fields and paddocks of grazing horses. The furniture in the bedroom was all made from a dark, heavy wood, and even though there was no bedding or curtains, it was easy to see how cosy it would feel up here in the dead of winter. A door led to a small lounge with an ancient squashy sofa in faded burgundy, an old-fashioned TV on a small table, and a bookshelf. It felt snug, and Emily couldn't help but imagine it with plants and blankets and a few family photos on the shelf. Her own little space.

'It's lovely,' she said, smiling at Anna. 'I like it a lot.'

'Just as well,' Anna said snarkily. 'There's internet up here, but I'll ask for the TV to be replaced – that one went out with the ark. There's a mini fridge and a kettle in the cupboard so you don't have to walk down four flights of stairs for a cup of tea.' There was a note of bitterness in her voice, like at some point she'd gone to war over this small luxury.

'The bathroom is on the landing,' she continued. 'There are two up here, so for now it would be all yours.'

'I'm very used to sharing,' replied Emily, thinking of growing up in a house of five with only one bathroom, then moving into her first shared flat and discovering nothing had changed other than extra leg hair in the bath and much less frequent cleaning.

'Hmm,' said Anna, giving her another top-to-toe inspection and apparently not liking what she saw. 'I'll take you to see Mr Hunter now.'

Emily nodded, pushing stray bits of hair behind her ears and wishing she could have a cup of tea to calm her nerves. Or a gin.

They went down the back stairs, stopping by the door to the first floor. 'Mr Hunter's office is the second room on the right,' said Anna. 'Don't go in without knocking.'

Emily wondered what she'd done to deserve this frosty reception, or whether this was Anna on a good day. She mumbled a weak 'thank you' down the stairwell, but Anna was already gone.

'So what do you make of the house?' asked Mr Hunter. They stood by an enormous bay window that looked out over the back of the house. Emily could see a stone terrace that led down to an immaculate lawn, with a fenced meadow on one side and some kind of walled garden on the other. A black Labrador was asleep in a tartan dog bed in the corner of the room, snoring peacefully.

'It's incredible,' said Emily. 'Nothing like I expected. How long have your family lived here?'

'Hmm, let's see,' replied Mr Hunter, drumming his fingers on his chin. 'Just over four hundred years, I should think.'

Emily laughed, then realised he wasn't joking. 'I like the

41

style of it, or the mix of styles, anyway.' Her voice faded as she realised she had no idea what she was talking about.

'Yes,' said Mr Hunter, 'it's joyfully quirky. My ancestors were an eccentric bunch – it was extensively renovated in the Arts and Crafts period, and after that each custodian added a new feature that purposely bore no resemblance to the last. But now of course it's protected by all manner of rules and regulations, so even if I wanted to honour the family tradition of whimsy and nonsense, I wouldn't be allowed. Do you know much about architecture?'

'Not this kind,' said Emily. 'The firm I worked for before specialised in sustainable offices and eco-homes.'

'Ah, you'd need to talk to my son about that,' said Charles. 'Adam is the king of glass and steel and concrete. He doesn't really appreciate history or heritage; he'd probably bulldoze this place and replace it with triple-glazed bungalows.'

Emily smiled politely and made no further comment, not sure she liked the sound of Adam Hunter. He may have helped Leon get a job, but he still sounded like a bit of a dick.

'So, I've drafted you an offer letter,' said Mr Hunter, gesturing for her to sit in the leather chair in front of his desk. 'A three-month trial, what do they call it these days? Probation. Then a full contract if we can still stand each other.'

Emily's fingers twitched, desperate to pick up the notebook and pen that she'd put on the desk earlier. Mr Hunter noticed and nodded, so she flipped it open and started jotting down notes in tight, efficient shorthand.

'Your weekends will be your own,' continued Mr Hunter, 'and I'll provide you with a car so you can stay here or go elsewhere as you please. As I mentioned, there's a swimming pool and a tennis court, and we have excellent stables if you like to ride.'

Emily gave him her best 'oh, how interesting' face, wondering what kind of life Mr Hunter thought she led where tennis and horse riding were regular weekend pursuits.

'I value openness and honesty, Emily,' he continued. 'May I call you Emily?' She nodded, already a bit sad that she wouldn't be Miss Wilkinson any longer. It had a Miss Moneypenny quality to it that had some old-school class. 'This kind of role isn't for everybody, I know. So if you hate it, just help me get through the horror of a family Christmas, then you can leave with no hard feelings.'

He reached over and handed her a folded sheet of paper, but Emily resisted the temptation to read it immediately, even though she was itching to get into the details. 'Apologies for my spelling and grammar – you'll see why I need an assistant.'

Emily laughed and tucked the paper into her notebook.

'There's some lunch in the kitchen for you, then feel free to take a look around the grounds, mull things over. Come back when you're ready to chat, or if you have any questions. How does that sound?'

'That sounds great, Mr Hunter. Thank you.'

Emily leaned on the fence overlooking the paddock by the stables, the offer letter in her hand. The salary was pretty much the same as she'd been earning at Thompson & Delaney, but that was in London. She'd had to pay rent and bills and food and travel. Here she wouldn't have to pay for any of that, which meant the difference in her disposable income would be insane. She could save a fortune, maybe send a bit home to help out Mum and Dad.

On the downside, she was twenty-nine and would have little or no social life. No dating was fine, that was all part of the 'focus on Emily' master plan. But no nights out with friends, no cocktail bars or last-minute picnics, no gym round the corner. Her weekends would be either spent here with Anna's resting bitch face, or a two-hundred-mile slog back to Chichester to see her family.

She watched as a large white horse ambled across the paddock to say hello. Emily didn't know anything about horses, but this one seemed calm and friendly enough, even though she'd never appreciated how massive their faces were close up. The horse stopped a few feet away and they sized each other up for a minute, then Emily instinctively held her left hand open for the horse to snuffle. It moved closer to investigate, then chomped the offer letter out of her right hand and chewed happily.

'HEY,' shouted a voice. Emily turned to see a man running across the paddock, waving his arms. 'Be careful!'

He stopped at the fence and breathed heavily. 'Sorry, didn't mean to shout. She's an absolute bitch and can bite, didn't want you to lose a finger.'

'She ate my job offer,' said Emily, attempting to give the man a once-over without shamelessly checking him out. Tall, broad shoulders, floppy brown hair that fell into his eyes, a light stubble on his chin. Handsome, not much older than her. The accent was definitely a bit posh, but not the awful braying drawl of the City bankers and stockbrokers she'd avoided like the plague in London.

'I hope you're not taking that as an omen,' said the man

with a smile, wiping his hand on his jeans, then holding it out. 'I'm Jamie.'

'Emily. Nice to meet you, Jamie.' The handshake was strong and firm, and she could feel the rough skin and callouses on his hands. She instinctively glanced at his hand for a wedding ring, then gave herself a mental slap. *Irrelevant, Wilkinson.* 'Do you work here?' she asked.

Jamie nodded. 'I do some estate work, help look after the horses.'

'Ah, OK.' She looked back at the white horse, who had finished eating her letter and was now yanking clumps of grass out of the ground. 'Does that mean you live on site?' She tried to convince herself she was only asking to get a better picture of the estate set-up, whilst also noting that his shirt had two buttons missing and his sleeves were rolled up to reveal strong, tanned arms.

'Most of the time,' said Jamie, clearly not keen to make eye contact. Emily couldn't decide if he was being enigmatic or annoying, or just didn't want her to know his business. Not a great start, either way.

The horse wandered over and biffed Jamie on the shoulder with its muzzle. 'So are you going to accept the job offer?' he asked, patting the horse on the side of her neck. 'Even though Luna has eaten it?' He smiled fully this time, revealing two rows of perfect teeth. *Either good genes or a very good orthodontist*, thought Emily – thankfully she'd been lucky; her parents would never have been able to afford braces.

'I don't know,' she said, taking a deep breath. 'I think so. It feels like a big decision.'

'They're an interesting family,' he said, raising his eyebrows.

'Interesting how?' Emily asked quickly.

'Oh, you know,' said Jamie vaguely. 'Lots of characters. Like all families, I guess.'

Clearly Jamie wasn't one for specifics, so she was going to have to help him along. 'I know Mrs Hunter lives in LA now,' she said airily, trying to make it sound like a casual observation rather than an invitation to gossip. 'She's very beautiful.'

'Yes, she is,' said Jamie with a small smile. 'Well, I need to get on. Nice to meet you, Emily. Good luck.' His eyes sparkled; the colour was somewhere between blue and grey but it was hard to tell from this distance. She watched him stride back towards the stables with Luna mooching after him, feeling a little hot and bothered. She should have worn a less chunky jumper; it had been cold in Chichester when she left, but here it felt considerably warmer.

Emily took another stroll along the path that followed the red and gold trees lining the driveway, then headed back towards the house feeling determined and full of purpose. She'd decided it was too good an opportunity to turn down – another string to her bow professionally, and an opportunity to save money for the future. She didn't have to do it for ever and she could always move back to London if things didn't work out. As she reached the bottom of the front steps, Charles Hunter emerged from the door followed by the man she'd already mentally dubbed 'cute horse guy'.

'Ah, there you are,' said Mr Hunter. 'I'm just off to look at a sick horse, so I hoped we could have a chat first.' He paused for a second, then turned to Jamie. 'James, this is Emily Wilkinson. I'm trying to persuade her to be my new assistant.'

James? thought Emily as she gave him an awkward smile. *Why so formal?*

'Emily, this is James, my youngest son.'

'Jamie is just fine,' he said, offering his hand as if their encounter over a horse-chewed letter had never happened. Emily shook it, feeling mildly discombobulated. *There's a younger son? Why didn't he say? And what did I just say about his mother? Oh God.*

'I'll see you over there whenever you're ready, Dad,' said Jamie. 'Nice to meet you, Emily.' He gave her another perfect-teeth smile and disappeared round the side of the house towards the stables.

'So!' said Mr Hunter, clasping his hands in anticipation.

Emily shook off her distracted thoughts and dragged her attention back to the job in hand. She took a deep breath and nodded her head emphatically. 'My answer is yes, Mr Hunter. I'd really like to accept the job.'

'Splendid,' he said, giving Emily a beaming smile. 'Can you start in two weeks?'

CHAPTER EIGHT

Emily queued at the counter to place their Nando's order while Kelly waited at their table, no doubt texting her mum to check that her four-year-old daughter Beth wasn't wrecking the house. A double chicken pitta for Emily and half a peri-peri chicken for Kelly, chips and coleslaw to share. Refillable Diet Coke for both of them to offset the custard tarts they'd have for pudding. Emily wondered how many times the two of them had eaten this exact menu over recent years, and whether Deliveroo would bring Nando's to Bowford Manor.

She fiddled with her hair while she waited, enjoying the freshly cut softness and bounce of it. Kelly was supposed to be having a day off from the salon today, but the promise of a bonus Nando's lunch had lured her in to give Emily a balayage colour treatment. Her long hair was now artfully faded from its natural brown at the roots to ice-blonde at the ends. It smelled of apples and hung in soft beachy waves down her back. She felt like one of those women in a shampoo ad.

'So let me get this straight,' said Kelly as Emily arrived at their table with the drinks. The salon had been busy so they hadn't been able to talk much there, but Emily had been bringing Kelly up to speed since they left. 'You've landed a job as assistant to some old rich guy with a massive house in the country, and it comes with food and accommodation paid for, and a free car. But you still get normal pay.'

'Something like that,' said Emily, nodding happily. She and Kelly had met on the first day of primary school and had been best friends for twenty-five years. There was nothing they didn't know about each other, although Emily had never been entirely straight with her about Mark. Kelly knew that Emily had been seeing somebody who was technically still married, but not that it was her boss. Had she been a little bit ashamed, or was the secrecy part of the appeal? Emily couldn't really say, but it hardly mattered now.

'You jammy cow,' said Kelly, twisting her mass of scarlet hair into a knot the size of a grapefruit and securing it with the hairband round her wrist. 'What are you going to spend all that money on?'

Emily shrugged. 'I don't know. Petrol so I can drive home and see my best mate and my goddaughter now and then? Presents and nights out for my favourite people? Or maybe I'll just save it all so I can buy my dream house.'

'Dream houses are boring,' said Kelly quickly. 'But prezzies and nights out are good. There must be a catch, though. Is he a creepy old sex pest?' Her eyes widened and she gave a short gasp. 'Or maybe the house is haunted?'

Emily rolled her eyes. 'Why does everyone think that rich men are sex pests? He's not even that old.'

'Haunted, then. I bet that's why his old assistant left, scared half to death by ghosts in the corridors. When are you going?'

'Tomorrow. My new car is being delivered at some point today, so I need to pack tonight. I spent all day yesterday shopping with Mum – it's nice to have clothes again.'

'I've spent my entire adult life worrying about starting a fire with hair straighteners,' said Kelly. 'I can't believe you actually did it.'

'It wasn't me,' said Emily indignantly. 'It was the silly cow in my flat.'

'Getting a whole new wardrobe though,' said Kelly dreamily. 'Almost worth burning the house down for.'

'It was a nightmare. The shops are already playing wall-to-wall festive shit. And my mum was absolutely on one, trying to get me to buy really bright colours.'

'What's wrong with bright colours?' Kelly was wearing purple dungarees and a green T-shirt that made her look like Barney the Dinosaur. While Emily was tall and flat-chested, Kelly was the exact opposite – petite with elfin features and enormous boobs.

'Drawing attention to myself isn't part of the job description,' Emily muttered. It sounded ridiculous, but it was true. Good PAs were like wallpaper; they blended in.

'Pah,' said Kelly dismissively. 'Have you looked in the mirror lately?'

Emily wafted her away. 'Anyway, I've now got clothes and shoes and towels and stuff, and a new suitcase. And a new haircut.' She tossed her head, enjoying the feeling of her hair swinging like a glossy curtain.

'I hate you,' grumbled Kelly, wrinkling her adorable nose. 'I'm so jealous.'

A waiter arrived with their food and dumped it on the table. Kelly immediately drowned her definitely-not-vegetarian chicken in half a bottle of garlic sauce, then attacked it like a woman who hadn't eaten since Beth's left-over Cheerios for breakfast. Emily watched her for a second, then reached for the bottle. It wasn't like she was planning to snog anyone any time soon.

They ate in silence for a few minutes, Emily wondering why anyone would go to a fancy restaurant when they could have this instead. 'It's going to be hard work though, Kel,' she said eventually through a mouthful of chicken pitta. 'Could be long hours. And probably pretty boring in the evenings.'

'What, all alone with your feet up in your rent-free room?' said Kelly sarcastically. 'Instead of wrestling a four-year-old into bed after a long day on your feet? Honestly, my heart bleeds.'

'Yeah, OK. Sorry.'

'When are you back next?' asked Kelly, mopping sauce off her face with a paper napkin.

'Not sure. A few weeks, I should think. I want to get settled in first.'

'Maybe you'll get swept off your feet by a rich neighbour. The guy in London is all finished, right?'

Emily nodded glumly. 'Yeah. Went back to his wife.'

'They always do, mate,' sighed Kelly with the weary perspicacity of a woman who had been round the block several times in her twenty-nine years. 'Let's cross our fingers for single, rich and undamaged.'

'I'm completely off men for a while,' said Emily. The memory of Jamie's twinkly eyes and warm handshake popped into her head. Not for the first time in the past two weeks. Or today, for that matter. Considering her vow of singledom, it was actually incredibly inconvenient.

Kelly put her knife and fork down and blew out her cheeks. 'I could eat that all over again.'

Emily's phone buzzed and she picked it up: her mum had posted a message in capital letters on the family WhatsApp group.

'Looks like my car has arrived.'

'Do you need to go?' asked Kelly, looking slightly bereft.

Emily smiled at her best friend, her heart as full as her stomach. 'Not until we've had a custard tart.'

Carol had clearly been watching from the upstairs window, waiting to spot her daughter walking home from the bus stop. By the time Emily was halfway down the street, her mum was already waiting outside the house in her slippers, bouncing from foot to foot like she needed the loo.

'Look at it, Moo!' she squealed. 'It's brand new! Your dad's already had a peek and it's only got sixteen miles on the clock. A man from the garage in town dropped it off. Dad signed for it for you.'

Emily circled the car, peering in through the window. A black V W Polo with grey patterned seats. Automatic, by the looks of it.

'Look at you, not even thirty and you've got a company car,' said Carol. 'I've already taken a picture and sent it to your brothers.'

'I know, Mum. We're all on the same WhatsApp group. I was in Nando's with Kelly.'

Carol's eyes lit up. 'Ooh, did you bring me a custard tart? Your hair looks lovely.'

Emily fished a paper bag out of her handbag. 'One for Dad too.'

'You're an angel. You got a package in the post too, I put

it on your bed. Are you going to take the car for a spin? Are you even insured yet?'

Emily nodded. 'They sent me all the details last week.'

'Let me get some proper shoes on, you can take me for a drive. Your dad's watching the football.'

Emily had hoped to go out for a drive on her own first, but she didn't want to dampen her mother's enthusiasm. She'd sold her battered Nissan Micra when she moved to London, so the only driving she'd done in the past eight years was occasionally getting weekend insurance on her dad's Ford Focus, and a trip away to a caravan in Lyme Regis with Kelly and Beth in a hire car. But since she had a two-hundred-mile drive tomorrow, maybe a few laps round the block would be a good idea. She had a flash of inspiration.

'I'll drive us to M&S and we can pick up some fancy pizzas for dinner. My treat.' She mentally totted up the calories she'd have consumed by the end of the day and vowed to adopt a rigid exercise regimen the minute she arrived in Norfolk. If she carried on like this, none of her new clothes would fit.

Carol beamed. 'Sounds lovely. Give me two minutes, I'll just put my face on.'

The drive to the M&S Food Hall put a further four miles on Emily's car, driven at a glacially slow pace so she could get used to the feel of the car. It drove smoothly and quietly and the automatic gearbox made everything easier, especially with her mum attempting maximum distraction by flicking through every radio station in search of Magic FM.

'I love Michael Bublé,' said Carol, swaying along happily to 'Everything'. 'It smells so lovely in here. Your dad's car stinks of dog and that pine air freshener. Go back the long way round, will you? The only thing waiting for me at home is the ironing.'

Emily smiled and turned right at the traffic lights towards the ring road, vowing never to hang a magic tree from her rear-view mirror or fill the door pockets with coffee cups and empty crisp packets.

By the time they pulled into Grove Street, Emily had taken the car up to the speed limit on the Chichester ring road and put a further eleven miles on the clock, but she was also conscious that the day was ticking on and she still hadn't started packing. She handed her mum the shopping and headed upstairs, trailed by Rudy. He was some kind of spaniel mixed with some kind of terrier, giving him the look of a wiry old man with big ears. He scrambled on to the bed with a little help from Emily, then settled down to watch her fold her new clothes into her new suitcase, then pack a cardboard box with books and stationery and photographs, and a brand-new set of ghd hair straighteners.

An hour later she was pretty much done and couldn't ignore the parcel any longer. It was a thick padded envelope with the address written in black marker pen, and Emily had known straight away from the flourish of the capital E that it was from Mark. She'd moved it to her mother's craft table, not wanting whatever was inside to spoil the nicest day she'd spent in ages. But eventually there was nothing more to do but open it, so she sat on the bed and took a few deep breaths.

Inside was a sea-green leather Smythson notebook in a tissue-lined blue box tied with a ribbon, identical to the one that had burned in the fire. Emily traced the monogrammed EW on the cover with her finger, hating how much she missed him. Mark was the first time Emily had properly fallen in love, even though she'd never been stupid enough to tell him. She'd known from the first few months working for him, and that night in Dubai had been inevitable, like a magnetic collision after nearly a year of edging towards each other.

She opened the front cover and found a plain white card tucked inside. On one side he'd written 'I'm sorry. Mx', in the same black pen, but the other side was blank. Emily wondered what Mark was sorry about – that his original gift had been cremated, or that he'd got under her skin enough that she'd opted to leave her job rather than look at him every day? Or did he regret finishing things, and wish he could take her back? Or maybe he regretted propositioning her in King's Cross a few weeks before? It was the most ambiguous apology of all time, and that was almost certainly not an accident. Her yearning turned to frustration that he couldn't be straight with her, that he'd floated out a vague apology to establish which way the wind was blowing.

She stuffed the card and all the packaging back into the envelope, clutching the notebook in her hands. Mark wanted her to make the next move, but she'd never been any good at chess and was done with playing his games. She ran her hand over the soft leather cover for a final time, then slid the book into her handbag. This time she wouldn't keep it in a drawer – she was going to use it. Tomorrow was the start of a new chapter, and Emily had no plans to repeat the mistakes of the past.

CHAPTER NINE

'I've made you some sandwiches,' said Carol, opening the Asda carrier bag to show Emily the foil parcels inside. 'Ham and cheese. And a flapjack, just in case. And a carton of apple juice.'

Emily bit her tongue, deciding that now wasn't the time to point out that she wasn't eight years old and off on a school trip to Marwell Zoo. Her mum meant well and liked to feel useful. 'Thanks, Mum.' She gave her a final hug then got into the car and pressed the button to lower the window.

Her dad slid the cardboard box into the boot and slammed it shut. 'You drive carefully, Moo,' he said. 'Take lots of breaks and call us when you get there.'

'I will,' said Emily, feeling a sudden rush of warmth and love for her parents. 'I'll be back for a weekend soon.'

'Get yourself settled in and let us know how you're getting on,' said Carol. 'Don't let your boss bully or exploit you. You still have human rights.'

'Bloody hell, Carol,' said Martin, rolling his eyes.

'What?' said Carol. 'I'm reading this book where this woman is trafficked into modern slavery and there's this gang of men who . . .'

'Not now, eh?' said Martin, patting the roof of the car. 'Get on your way, Moo.'

Emily smiled and gave them a final wave. Her parents

stood on the pavement and kept waving until she disappeared round the corner, at which point Emily let out the breath she'd been holding in for several hours. She relaxed into her seat, then turned on Radio 1 and headed for Norfolk.

Emily followed the route she'd travelled with Leon two weeks earlier, stopping at the same motorway services on the M11 to eat her lunch and stretch her legs. She popped into M&S to stock up on Percy Pigs, crisps and cans of G&T to keep in her room; they'd be something to look forward to after work, a way of passing the long evenings while she was settling in.

The second half of the drive took her through the same hundred miles of dual carriageway through unremarkable countryside to Norwich, then west on the ring road and fifteen minutes of narrow country lanes to the imposing gates of Bowford Manor. Anna had sent her a remote control to open them, presumably previously owned by Andrea, along with a key to the delivery door on the side of the house. So she took the fork off the main drive and followed the road round to the left past the stables and the garage, then parked up in the delivery yard and started unloading her belongings. The weather was cold but dry, so there was no hurry. Nobody seemed to be around, but it was Sunday and presumably even Anna was allowed a day off.

As Emily piled her belongings by the back door, Leon appeared from the garage and gave her a wave. He opened his arms a little like he was going in for a hug, which Emily deflected by grabbing her suitcase and wrestling it over to the door. Leon seemed nice and maybe that was normal in Croatia, but she wanted to get to know him a little better before they moved their friendship into the hugging zone.

'Let me take that,' said Leon, grabbing the case. Hugs or no hugs, Emily definitely wasn't going to turn down an offer to help her lug all this stuff up to the attic. She smiled and thanked him, then went back outside to grab the carrier bag of snacks and her rucksack instead.

By the time she'd puffed her way up to the attic Leon was waiting outside her room, so she propped the door open with her rucksack. She turned to walk back down the stairs, but Leon held up his hand. 'No, is fine,' he said. 'You stay here, I will bring up the rest. Is good exercise for me.'

'Thank you, Leon,' said Emily, wishing he didn't look at her with quite such a dazzled expression. She stood for a moment and appreciated the room. The bed had been made with crisp white sheets, and pale blue curtains had been hung at the windows. The dust was gone and everything smelled of lemony furniture polish. She walked through to the second room, which now had a flatscreen TV on the table. She peeked into the cupboard and there was a mini fridge with a kettle, a mug and a teaspoon on top, but the fridge was empty. *What else were you expecting?* she thought. *Champagne and chocolates?*

By the time she walked back into the bedroom Leon was waiting with the cardboard box, breathing heavily and looking a bit pink in the face. She dragged it into the room, then returned to the door. 'Thanks, Leon. I wasn't sure how I was going to manage that.'

'You are welcome. I just saw Mr Hunter, and he said to tell you that he'll be trying to roast a chicken in the kitchen later if you want to join him for dinner at six, but please don't feel obliged if you are tired.'

'OK, thank you,' she said.

'Well,' said Leon, looking a little awkward. 'I'll leave you to unpack.'

'See you later,' said Emily. He was still staring at her as she closed the door, with an expression that had more than a touch of hope about it. Emily had seen that look before, and definitely didn't want to encourage it. Even if Leon was her type, which he definitely wasn't, a romance at work was the very last thing on her to-do list right now.

By 6 p.m. Emily had called her parents, unpacked all her belongings and made her two little rooms feel like home. There was an odd kind of joy in tidying stuff away and arranging plants and books and photographs. But then she rationalised that the only previous times she'd moved house had been to a shitty flat in Hammersmith at the age of twenty-one, then a different shitty flat in Battersea a couple of years later, and then a final shitty flat in Stratford when she started working for Mark. Every one of them had been a bleak experience: trying to fit her belongings into a flimsy chest of drawers, putting a sheet on a stained mattress, discovering the bathroom door didn't lock and you had to wedge a chair under the handle.

This felt entirely different – the clothes in the big wardrobe were mostly unworn, the mattress and bedding were new, and it was the first time in nearly thirty years that she didn't have to share a bathroom. On that basis alone it felt like a five-star hotel.

Her arrival in the kitchen prompted a hearty 'hello!' from

Mr Hunter, who was pummelling a saucepan of mashed potatoes. 'I'm so glad you're here, Emily,' he said jovially. 'Here, grab a plate and pull up a stool, you're just in time.' A fire was crackling cheerfully in the fireplace by the sofas, making the room feel warm and cosy.

She sat on a stool on one side of the granite island as Mr Hunter arranged the saucepan of mash alongside a plate of chicken covered in foil and a tray of roasted veg. He poked a serving spoon into each, then grabbed a small pan of gravy from the hob and plonked that on the island too. Emily helped herself, thinking that her mum would be deeply disappointed at the lack of matching serving dishes, linen napkins and fancy candlesticks; this wasn't at all how she imagined the landed classes eating. Mr Hunter immediately tucked in, so Emily grabbed her fork and followed suit.

Just as she had taken her first mouthful, the back door opened and Jamie wandered in. He smiled at them both as he took off his muddy boots. 'Do I smell chicken?' he asked, grabbing a plate from the cupboard and sitting on the stool next to Emily.

'You're almost too late,' said Mr Hunter. 'We're already thinking about seconds.'

Jamie smiled but said nothing as he scooped a mountain of mashed potato on to his plate, and Mr Hunter turned back to Emily. 'Is your room all OK, Emily?'

'Yes, thank you. I'm all unpacked and settled in.'

'And is the car running fine?'

'It's perfect, thank you.'

'Well, if there's anything you need, just ask Anna.'

Emily nodded, having already decided not to ask Anna for anything unless she was bleeding to death. She ate another

mouthful of mashed potato, trying not to watch Jamie leaning over to stick his fork into a chicken leg. He smelled of
horses, sweat and straw, a combination that made Emily feel a
bit heady. She was used to being in close proximity to men in
suits and designer shoes; men whose tools were mechanical
pencils and drafting boards and tracing paper. She'd never
come across anyone so classically handsome but still manly;
she hadn't even realised that men like him existed outside one
of her mum's bonkbusters. He reminded her of someone famous, an actor maybe, but she couldn't think who.

'Do you ride, Emily?' he asked.

Emily choked on a slice of chicken. 'I'm sorry?' she asked,
her eyes watering.

'Do you ride?' he repeated, pushing a glass of water
towards her and looking mildly amused. 'Horses.'

'Oh.' She took a sip of water and tried to calm her breathing. 'No. I've never actually ridden a horse.'

'That's such a shame,' said Mr Hunter. 'It's a wonderful
way to explore the countryside. You should have lessons. I'm
sure James can teach you.'

'Oh no, I couldn't possibly . . .' said Emily, as Jamie looked
away.

'That reminds me, Dad,' he said, quickly changing the
subject. 'The vet came earlier to take a look at Tucker. He's
going to try a steroid injection.'

Emily carried on eating and tuned out the horse chat. She
felt a flicker of disappointment that Jamie had deflected his
father's suggestion so quickly, not that she had the smallest
inclination to learn to ride. She'd ridden a donkey on the
beach in Brighton when she was about six, then many years
later drank too much WKD Blue in a bar in Bognor and

had a go on a bucking bronco. She'd deeply regretted both experiences and couldn't imagine that riding a real horse would be any less awful.

Once dinner was finished, Emily and Mr Hunter loaded the dishwasher while Jamie covered all the leftovers and put them in fridge, before putting his boots back on and heading off with a smile and a wave. Emily wondered if he had a room above the stables, or if he returned to a grand four-poster bed in the house after he'd finished his work for the day. It occurred to her that he was probably the son who had recommended Leon to Mr Hunter, not Adam, so she happily went back to suspecting that Mr Hunter's eldest son was a bit of a dick.

Once the kitchen was wiped down, Emily thanked Mr Hunter for dinner and made her excuses to leave. It was still early, but a quiet evening in her little lounge with the TV, a can of G&T and a bag of Percy Pigs was calling, followed by a bath before bed. It would be one of the few times in her life that she'd be able to soak in the bath without someone banging on the door and telling her they needed the loo, and right now that felt like the high life.

CHAPTER TEN

By 6 a.m. on Monday Emily was wide awake, and no amount of mindful breathing or counting imaginary sheep was going to get her back to sleep. She dragged herself out of the warmth and comfort of her cosy bed and put on a pair of leggings that had escaped the fire by being abandoned at her parents' house for being too old and baggy to take to London. She pulled the labels off a new running top and a waterproof jacket, then laced up a box-fresh pair of trainers. Making as little noise as possible on the creaky landing floorboards, she crept down the back stairs and out into the yard.

The sun hadn't risen yet, but it wasn't completely dark either. Emily wasn't sure of the word for that – was twilight just an evening thing, or did it apply to morning too? Either way it was a strange kind of milky darkness and stillness that she'd never experienced before, unbroken by streetlights and traffic noise. She put her hand against the cold brick of the house and did a few half-hearted stretches, then began a slow plod around the side of the house and down the drive.

Once her eyes had adjusted to the light and her legs had stopped feeling like they belonged to a ninety-year-old woman, she started to relax and enjoy the peace and solitude of plodding through the local lanes, her breath forming clouds in the still air. She'd purposely left her phone and earbuds behind so she could stay alert to what was going on around her, not wanting to be the idiot who was entirely oblivious to tractors and bicycles and flocks of sheep. At one point she spotted a stile leading on to a public footpath and headed across a field, then immediately clagged up her new trainers with heavy mud and wished she hadn't. But she figured there was a limit to how muddy they could get and kept going.

Half an hour later, Emily was forced to face up to the reality that she was hopelessly lost. Somewhere along the way she'd accidentally deviated from the footpath, and an attempt to double back and retrace her steps had landed her on a bridleway by a field that looked exactly the same as every other field, with no hills or rooftops in any direction to help her get her bearings. Her feet were caked in mud up to her ankles, she had a bramble scratch on her leg that she could feel was bleeding under her leggings, and her watch told her she had precisely ninety minutes before she was due to present herself in Mr Hunter's office for her first day in her new job.

She put her hands on her hips and forced her brain to engage. The sun was just rising in the east, so she now knew which way that was. But it had been dark when she left the house, so she had no idea which way she'd been running to start with. She thought about the day she'd come for her interview, walking through the garden and seeing the back of the house bathed in autumn sunlight at lunchtime, so that must face south. Which meant the driveway headed north, but the paths she'd taken had twisted and turned, so knowing which way was east was entirely useless. Her head felt muddled and she cursed herself for not bringing her phone.

Pull yourself together, she told herself, rationalising that the track must lead somewhere. So she turned left and jogged along it as fast as she could, hoping she'd come to a road junction or a farm or something that looked vaguely familiar. She was so busy silently berating herself for being so stupid that she didn't notice the thing in front of her until it was huge and terrifying and about two feet from her face.

'Jesus FUCK,' she yelled, backing away into the crumbling wall at the edge of the track.

'Emily?' said a voice. She looked up in horror, realising that the huge and terrifying thing was actually the white horse she'd met in the field, which Jamie was now sitting on.

'Oh shit, you scared me,' she said, her heart thudding in her ears. The relief at meeting someone who could help her get home was countered with absolute mortification that it was Jamie. Literally anybody else on the planet would have been preferable. A group of angry nuns, farmers with pitchforks, the ghost of a Victorian child. Anyone but him.

'Are you OK?' he asked. 'Has something happened?'

'No, I'm fine,' she said, unable to meet his gaze. 'I was out for a run but I got a bit lost. Am I going the right way?'

Jamie sat back in his saddle, clearly relieved she wasn't hurt. 'Yes, it's not far. Keep going, turn left on the road at the end of the track. The gates are about half a mile up the lane on your right.'

Emily nodded, trying not to imagine what she must look like to Jamie. Red-faced, covered in mud, unwashed, bed hair stuffed into a ratty ponytail. A stupid townie who couldn't even navigate the countryside. 'Thanks,' she said, edging past him and starting to sprint. She kept going and didn't look back, blinking away tears of fury and relief and humiliation. She definitely should have stayed in bed.

*

65

Emily felt infinitely better after a shower and some breakfast, which was a mug of coffee and a slice of toast in the kitchen with Anna. Leon turned up but sat at the end of the dining table and said nothing, apparently not a morning person.

Anna didn't say much either, other than to politely acknowledge Emily's thanks for how nice her room looked, and to ask if Emily had everything she needed, the tone suggesting that nothing further was available so don't bother asking. Once she'd finished eating, Emily headed back upstairs to clean her teeth and fetch her notebook. It felt strange not to wear a suit for work, but Mr Hunter had been insistent that smart casual was fine. So today she was wearing a new pair of dark jeans with her brown suede boots and a pale blue Nicola Farhi shirt. She scrutinised everything for price tickets and labels, keen to ensure nobody knew that the shirt had cost £28 in TK Maxx.

Mr Hunter's office was just as she remembered it, apart from there now being two identical black Labradors squashed into the tartan dog bed by the window. He opened the door to a small side office that contained a desk, as well as access to a bathroom, a tiny kitchen and a windowless room with filing cabinets and a photocopier. 'Andrea set this office up,' he said, 'so the way it's organised might not suit you. Feel free to change anything you like.'

Emily glanced at the desk, which had a shiny new laptop on it. 'I got you a new one, Andrea's had seen better days,' he said. 'I've set it all up for you, it should be ready to go.' Emily's eyebrows must have betrayed her surprise, earning her a slightly caustic smile. 'I made my money in software, Emily, I'm not a Luddite.' She kicked herself for her overly expressive face, then filed a mental reminder to look up what a Luddite was later.

Mr Hunter gave her a tour of the filing system, showing her where all the estate records were kept along with paperwork for his various business and charity ventures. He had two sets of accountants and even more lawyers, all based in London. She scribbled shorthand notes as she started to piece together the various threads of revenue – a timber yard on the edge of the estate, tenancies for properties and farms, a wider property portfolio and various investments. The sums involved were mind-boggling; she'd never been this close to the money in any of her previous jobs, and the files felt heavy with responsibility.

Once the tour was over and Emily had established how Mr Hunter liked his coffee (black, strong, no sugar), she took her notepad and sat on the opposite side of his desk.

'So,' he said, 'a lot for you to get your head around.'

Emily nodded, trying to look more confident than she felt. 'I'm sure I'll get the hang of it.'

'I'm sure you will,' he said. 'The good news is I've got estate meetings all week. I'll be out every afternoon, so you can use the time to get your bearings. I've emailed my lawyers and accountants and told them to expect a call from you; they'll help you get a clearer picture of my affairs and let you know what you can do to make their lives easier.'

Emily made more shorthand notes as Mr Hunter continued. 'Go through the active files and my diary, make a list of any questions you have. Also find Andrea's file for the estate Christmas party, we'll need to talk about that tomorrow.' She nodded and kept scribbling.

'Let's do a ten a.m. catch-up every day, after you've

opened the post. Bring all your questions. Sam will give you some lunch in the kitchen at one; make sure you finish at five thirty whether I'm around to send you home or not.'

Emily nodded, remembering her first visit to Bowford Manor, when Anna had told her she'd have to make her own lunch. Apparently the kitchen rules weren't quite so rigid after all.

'Have you found the swimming pool yet?' asked Mr Hunter.

'No,' she replied.

'Ask Anna or Leon to show you; it's covered and heated, so you can use it all year round. Do you play tennis?'

'No,' said Emily, 'I like to run, though.' She tried not to blush at the memory of her disastrous run that morning and hoped Jamie wouldn't say anything. 'And I'm a good swimmer.' This was absolutely true; she had been a competitive swimmer at school and kept it up as much as she could through her twenties, usually in the sea at West Wittering or Bognor.

'Well, help yourself to the pool,' he said. 'I can't guarantee other members of my family won't be in it, but it's big enough for everyone.'

Emily nodded, wondering what she could say that might prompt Mr Hunter to talk more about his mysterious family, but her thoughts were interrupted by the phone ringing on his desk. She raised her eyebrows enquiringly – *should I get that?* He nodded and sat back in his chair.

'Charles Hunter's office. How can I help?' said Emily, quelling the jitters in her stomach. She'd answered a thousand phones in her time, this one was no different.

An angry male voice responded. 'Put Charles on the phone, right now.'

Emily paused for a moment. 'I'll just see if Mr Hunter is here. Who shall I say is calling?'

'Don't fob me off, young lady,' snarled the voice. 'I know he's there.'

Emily smiled to herself; this was familiar territory. 'I'm sorry, sir, I didn't catch your name.'

'For God's sake,' he muttered. 'It's Arthur Morley.'

Emily wrote down the name. 'Bear with me, Mr Morley, I'll just check if Mr Hunter is available.' She raised her eyebrows across the desk, but he wrinkled his nose and shook his head. She pressed the mute button and put the handset on the desk. 'I'll give him a minute to calm down,' she said. 'Is there anything else I should tell him other than you're not available?'

Mr Hunter thought for a second. 'Arthur's one of my tenant farmers,' he said. 'Tell him he's a crotchety old miser who cheats at poker.'

Emily smiled and pressed the button to unmute the phone. 'Sorry to keep you waiting, Mr Morley. I'm afraid Mr Hunter is in a meeting for most of the morning, but I'll let him know you called.' It was an old PA trick, that one – agree to pass on the message, but never promise that your boss will call back.

'Now listen here . . .' said Arthur Morley.

'Have a good day, Mr Morley,' Emily interrupted, then pressed the button to end the call. Mr Hunter beamed.

At 1 p.m. Emily went down to the kitchen for lunch and met Sam, Mr Hunter's chef, who was a large man in his sixties with a booming laugh and a ready smile. She propped herself up on a stool and ate a chilli prawn salad that was just about the best thing she'd ever tasted, and listened while he told her about how he'd met Mr Hunter in Mauritius almost forty years before; apparently the Hunter family had a house there, which was news to Emily. Sam's parents had both been chefs, his father in India and his mother in China, and they'd met working in a hotel on the island. They'd opened their own restaurant after they were married, and Sam was the eldest of two children who grew up chopping vegetables in the hotel kitchen. As soon as he was old enough he took everything he'd learned and opened a beachside café, which just so happened to be a short drive from the Hunter beach house. It became a home from home whenever the family visited the island, and 'Mr Charles' told Sam that if he ever wanted to move to the UK, he'd give him a job.

Ten years later that was exactly what happened – Sam met a British yoga teacher he wanted to marry, so he called his friend Mr Charles in the UK to ask if he'd keep his promise. For the first twenty years Sam worked full-time at Bowford Manor and managed a team of cooks, feeding a houseful of Hunters and all their friends and guests. But now it was mostly just Mr Hunter, so for the past decade Sam had worked three or four hours a day, five days a week. His wife Gabrielle taught exercise classes to people in care homes, whilst Sam spent his spare time tending his beloved garden and seeing their three children and four grandchildren. He was sixty-two now and enjoying the change of pace.

Emily thought he was wonderful and was entirely transfixed by his deft hands chopping and slicing chicken and vegetables for Mr Hunter's dinner. He made fresh salads and stir fries for lunch, usually traditional Mauritian or Asian fusion recipes, but dinner was something he could pre-prepare so Anna could put it in the oven or serve it from the slow cooker – usually a curry, a stew or a traybake of some kind. Emily thought of the freezer of leftovers Anna had mentioned and decided she could get used to this kind of diet.

'It's nice to have a new face around,' said Sam, his eyes twinkling. 'Especially one like yours. Leon told me you were a beauty.'

Emily blushed and stabbed a prawn with her fork, catching sight of Leon out of the corner of her eye. He looked mortified, which made Sam burst into fits of hooting laughter as Anna's lips disappeared into their joyless burrow of disapproval. Emily decided now was probably a good time to leave, so she put her plate in the dishwasher, thanked Sam for lunch, and went back to work.

When she got back to the office, Mr Hunter was just heading out to his meeting, so she held his leather briefcase and hat while he put his waxed jacket on. 'I'm glad I caught you before I left,' he said. 'I've just had a message from my son, Adam. He's coming here this weekend.'

Emily put the bag and hat on the chair and nipped through to her desk to get her notebook. 'He's bringing his wife and their children,' Mr Hunter continued as she made shorthand notes. 'They'll stay in Wedmore Cottage, but can you let Sam and Anna know they'll be here for dinner on Saturday night.'

'Anything else?' she asked.

Mr Hunter paused for a second. 'Just a heads-up for you, really. Adam can be . . . difficult. He hasn't always treated my staff with the respect they deserve, and he may take advantage of your arrival to tap you for information about

71

my business dealings. My advice would be to stay out of his way as much as you can, tell him nothing, and let me know if he gives you any trouble.'

Emily raised her eyebrows as she handed over the briefcase. 'Is that likely?'

Mr Hunter gave a deep sigh. 'I have three children, Emily, and they all manage to disappoint and delight me in various ways. It's rather embarrassing to have to warn you about my eldest son on your first day, but here we are. I have no doubt that you can put him firmly in his place; but forewarned is forearmed and all that.'

Emily nodded as Mr Hunter put on his hat and left, trailing both dogs. She stood on the spot for a minute as questions rattled around in her head. Firstly, what kind of trouble was Adam Hunter likely to give her? Secondly, what did Jamie do to disappoint his father? And thirdly, since when was there a third Hunter child?

CHAPTER ELEVEN

'Catherine,' said Anna, her lips pursed into a pucker of dislike that Emily was relieved to note wasn't reserved exclusively for her. 'The middle child. Lives with her mother in California. They'll be here for Christmas.'

It was Saturday morning before Emily managed to pin down Anna without Leon or Sam earwigging, so she took advantage of the opportunity to make casual enquiries about the more colourful elements of the Hunter family. Google had been rather vague on the daughter, referring to her as a 'socialite and influencer', but with very little by way of specifics. She also appeared to be twenty-six, thirty-one or thirty-four, depending on which tabloid you got your facts from.

'Mrs Hunter will be here for Christmas?' asked Emily. 'Even though they're not married any more?' She was treading carefully with her questions, not wanting Anna to rat her out to Mr Hunter for gossiping.

'She comes most years,' she huffed. 'It's her way of getting to spend Christmas with her children with minimal effort or inconvenience.'

'Doesn't Mr Hunter mind?' Emily asked.

Anna shrugged. 'It's a big house, and anyway she's usually only here for a few days before they go to the Hunter chalet in Switzerland.' She gave Emily a suspicious look, like somehow she'd been tricked into saying too much. 'I'm visiting friends for the rest of the weekend,' she added, 'so don't leave this kitchen in a mess.' Emily nodded, getting the distinct impression that question time was over for today.

After breakfast Emily headed back upstairs to call her parents, reflecting on her first week working at Bowford Manor. It had been a fast-track education in country estates and personal wealth, but she was starting to get to grips with the whole Hunter operation. She was also settling into a personal routine, going for a run on dry mornings (sticking to the lanes only, avoiding bridleways and men on horses), and a swim after work on the days it was pouring with rain outside and she opted to stay warm in bed for an extra hour.

The pool at Bowford Manor was bigger than she'd expected, almost as big as the kind you'd get in a leisure centre, but SO much fancier. It was nestled under a timber and glass structure on the far side of the walled garden, next to the tennis court and a tiny single-storey cottage that nobody appeared to live in. There were huge glass doors down either side that looked like they folded back in the summer, but in November Emily had the whole pool to herself. The water was heated and clean and free from bombing children and floating plasters, so she took the opportunity to swim one hundred lengths in an hour, her mind empty of lists and appointments and the strange and alien rules of upper-class country living.

She and Mr Hunter had come to an unspoken agreement where he didn't assume she knew everything, and she wasn't afraid to ask. It started with him saying, 'Adam wants me to go beating with him at Holt on Sunday – can you ask Leon to check over the Defender,' which sounded like Swahili to Emily. So she asked for clarification and discovered that beating was something to do with shooting pheasants, Holt was a town about thirty miles away, and a Defender was a type of off-road vehicle. But after that Mr Hunter had waited for a nod after each item on his list, so Emily had an opportunity to ask questions. He seemed mindful of her background without ever making her feel stupid or unworldly, and she reminded herself that if she ever said, 'I'm off for a balayage then a Nando's and a wander round TK Maxx', Mr Hunter probably wouldn't have a clue what she was talking about either.

Other than updating her parents on her first week and reassuring them that she hadn't been abused, trafficked or otherwise violated, the main reason she was calling was to invite them to the Bowford Estate Christmas party in a few weeks. Emily had been in two minds about whether she wanted her two worlds to collide under the influence of free prosecco and mulled wine, but then reminded herself that her mum and dad rarely got to do anything really fancy, and they'd probably be over the moon about it.

'We're invited?' asked Carol incredulously.

'You are. It's a party for all the estate workers and their families. Mr Hunter has invited you to stay so you can get ready here and go home on Sunday.'

'Blimey. Will all the family be there? Is it going to be really posh?'

'No and no. Mr Hunter will be there, but not the rest of the family. And it's not formal, so just a shirt for Dad and a dress for you. Nothing too glitzy.' Her mum's party outfits had a tendency towards short, tight and heavy on sequins, like she was about to do a cha-cha with Anton Du Beke on the *Strictly* dance floor, but on this occasion Emily was hoping for something a bit more low-key.

'I can't wait. The girls at Aqua Zumba are going to be so jealous. I might have to get my nails done.'

'Go for it, Mum,' said Emily with a smile, inspecting her own hands and wondering if there was a walk-in nail bar in Norwich.

'Look at us, staying in a fancy house and going to a party,' said Carol dreamily.

'I'm not sure you'll be staying in the house itself,' said Emily quickly. 'You might be somewhere else on the estate.'

'Still, nicer than we're used to. I'll speak to your dad about a new frock.'

Emily wrapped up the conversation with a promise to take her mum shopping when she was home in a couple of weeks, knowing full well that she'd end up paying for the dress and probably some matching shoes, and really not minding at all.

Emily's plan for her first Saturday in Norfolk was to drive to Norwich, get her nails done, top up her store of in-room snacks and maybe buy some running shoes that were designed for off-road. None of this was urgent, but she was itching for a mooch around the shops and maybe some lunch in a nice café.

But when she left the house via the back door into the delivery yard, her car wasn't in its usual space next to the wheelie bins. She scratched her head for a moment, trying to remember if she'd actually parked it somewhere else, but it had definitely been there when she went to bed last night.

Then she remembered that Leon had the spare key, so perhaps he'd moved it for some reason. She wandered over to the garage, which was part of the same complex of old buildings as the stables, but there was no sign of Leon or her car.

Feeling a little perplexed, Emily walked back round to the yard, thinking maybe she'd do some laundry then look for Leon and her car again in an hour. She didn't immediately register the man smoking a cigarette and watching her from outside the delivery door until she was a few metres away. She stopped and eyed him nervously, wondering if he knew anything about her car. Then she realised who he was. Adam Hunter.

'About bloody time,' he snapped. 'I was starting to wonder if anyone lived here. Nobody ever answers the fucking phone. Where's Anna?'

Emily supposed Adam was quite handsome in a square-jawed, thin-lipped kind of way, although his eyes were definitely piggy and his attempt at a winning smile was more of a sneer. He was a slighter, more angular version of Jamie, and she felt compelled to take a step back to avoid getting any closer than was absolutely necessary.

'It's the weekend,' she said, holding her head up and keeping her voice strong. 'Anna doesn't work weekends.'

Adam made a huffing noise as he threw his cigarette end into a puddle. 'I'm aware of that,' he drawled lazily, 'but she also knew we were coming so the least she could have done is check in. Never mind, you'll do. Are you new?'

'I'm sorry?' said Emily.

'Are. You. New. Here,' he said, enunciating the words loudly and slowly, his tone dripping with sarcasm. 'I don't think I've seen you before, and I'm pretty sure I'd remember.'

He looked Emily up and down appreciatively, making her shudder.

'I'm Emily Wilkinson, Mr Hunter's assistant.' She didn't offer a handshake, deciding she'd rather not touch him.

'Aha, the new Andrea,' he replied with what he clearly thought was boyish charm. 'Quite the upgrade on the old model, I must say. I'm Adam Hunter, I'm sure the old man has told you all about me.'

Emily held his gaze but said nothing, wondering how this repellent man could possibly be related to Jamie and Mr Hunter.

Adam looked away, clearly already bored of this conversation. 'I need some things bringing over to Wedmore Cottage,' he said, inspecting his fingernails. 'Food, mostly, but also some spare sheets, Hugo has wet the bed.'

'Right, well, I'm actually on my way out,' said Emily. Another PA trick – never apologise for something you're not remotely sorry for.

'Jesus,' said Adam, plucking a pack of Marlboro Gold out of his shirt pocket and hanging one out of the side of his mouth as if he was James Dean. 'Do any of the fucking staff in this house do any work?'

Emily folded her arms. 'I work for Mr Hunter from Monday to Friday,' she said coolly. 'But not at weekends.'

'I understand that,' he said, a steely edge creeping into his voice. 'But I'm also Mr Hunter, and I'm asking for your help.'

'I'm sure Anna won't mind if you help yourself to food,' she said with the least fake smile she could muster. 'And there are loads of spare sheets in the linen room.'

Adam lit the cigarette and observed her through narrowed

eyes. 'You're quite a piece of work, aren't you? I can't say I appreciate your tone.'

'You don't appreciate anyone's tone unless they're doing exactly what you want,' said Jamie, appearing from the front of the house. He was wearing black jodhpurs, a sleeveless puffer jacket and brown riding boots, like some kind of Disney prince.

'Ah, my little brother to the rescue,' sneered Adam. 'I just want some fucking food and clean sheets, is that really too much to ask?'

Jamie put himself between Adam and Emily, uncomfortably in Adam's face. He was a solid three inches taller and considerably more beefy. 'You lived in this house for over twenty years, Adam,' he said. 'Go in and take what you need, the staff aren't at your beck and call.'

Adam huffed furiously, then thumped his cigarette across the yard and disappeared through the back door, slamming it behind him. Jamie turned to Emily and smiled awkwardly. 'Sorry about my brother, he still hasn't fully evolved from when he lived in a cave.'

Emily laughed, relieved that Adam was gone and a bit proud of herself that she had stood her ground. 'Don't worry about it, I'm fine.'

'Yes, I can see that,' said Jamie appreciatively. Emily wondered how women usually responded to Adam's bullying; clearly they hadn't grown up with two older brothers in a house that was a bit like *The Hunger Games*.

'I seem to have lost my car,' she said. 'Have you seen it anywhere?'

Jamie nodded. 'I saw Leon driving off in it earlier, I think he went to fill it up for you.'

Emily's eyes widened in surprise. 'You pay for my petrol too?'

Jamie shrugged. 'Not as a rule, but Leon hates Adam's guts and likes to find excuses not to be here when he's around.'

'Hmm,' said Emily, hoping her face was doing the job of expressing all the sentiments she didn't think she should say out loud.

Jamie paused for a few seconds, like he was wrestling with a decision. 'I'm going for a ride tomorrow,' he said. 'Avoiding a family pub lunch after Dad and Adam get back from a shoot. Do you want to come?'

Emily was momentarily rendered mute. 'I . . . oh . . . I don't know. I've never . . .'

'Ridden a horse, I know,' said Jamie. 'I'll teach you. It's just a walk, you don't have to do anything other than sit there. You can ride Rupert, he's very steady.'

Her mind rattled frantically through the reasons to say both yes and no. 'I don't have the right clothes,' she offered feebly.

'Do you have a pair of leggings and a waterproof jacket?' he asked, tilting his head knowingly. Obviously he'd seen her in both when she was running in circles around the countryside.

'Yes,' she replied, trying not to blush.

'Fine, I can lend you boots and gloves and a hard hat,' he said.

Emily was all out of excuses. 'OK, then,' she said with a nod and a nervous smile.

'Good,' said Jamie cheerfully, turning to walk towards the road. 'Ten thirty in the stable yard.' He walked a few metres, then raised his voice so Emily could hear him even though he didn't turn around. 'I can show you all the best running routes.'

She could hear the smile in his voice and felt a frisson of anticipation, even though the idea of riding a horse wasn't remotely appealing. Then it occurred to her that Adam could reappear from the house at any moment, so she hurried off to wait for Leon by the garage. He arrived just before she did, giving her an enthusiastic wave as he parked up.

'I filled up your car,' he said, leaping out of the driver's seat.

'You really didn't have to do that, Leon. But thank you.'

He beamed at her, and Emily decided he was actually very good-looking in a hairy, uber-masculine kind of way. Kelly would have him for breakfast then go back for seconds at lunch. 'I can clean it too,' he said.

'There's no need,' said Emily with a smile. 'I'm off out now anyway.'

'I wanted to ask you about tomorrow,' he said suddenly, as if he was forcing the words out like air from a balloon.

'What about tomorrow?' she asked, feeling confused. Jamie had only just spoken to her – what did Leon know about it?

'I am going for a drive up the coast,' said Leon, blushing crimson. 'I was thinking you might like to come with me.' He looked hopeful and also a little broken, as though he'd already played this conversation out in his head and decided she would say no. 'We can take a picnic,' he added forlornly, separating out the two syllables like he'd never said the word out loud before.

'Oh. I'm sorry, Leon. But I already have plans for tomorrow.'

Leon looked at his feet. 'Is OK. Maybe another time.'

Emily smiled apologetically, wishing she was better at telling guys she didn't want to date them. While Mark was on the scene she'd justifiably been able to say 'I've got a boyfriend' without having to elaborate, but she wasn't going to invent one to protect Leon's feelings. She'd have to bite the bullet and be honest with him, but maybe now wasn't the time.

'Thank you for looking after my car,' she said, dropping into the driver's seat and starting the engine. She waved and pulled away, noting that he was still watching her when she reached the end of the driveway.

CHAPTER TWELVE

Emily arrived at the stables the following morning feeling jittery and nervous, trying to convince herself that it was more about getting on a horse than seeing Jamie again. She was also wearing a new pair of black leggings, having bought some decent ones in Norwich yesterday. The old ones were all plucked from the brambles and had gone a bit baggy in the crotch, so they were now stuffed in the wheelie bin.

Jamie was waiting in the yard, leaning against the wall and squinting into the autumn sunshine. He said good morning and gave Emily a smile that made her want to throw up and also snog his face off, although probably not in that order.

'This is the tack room,' he said, showing her into a dark space at the end of a row of stables. 'We keep all the important stuff in here.' The room smelled of leather and soap and damp wool, the walls lined with saddles and bridles and blankets. Emily fished through a row of riding boots until she found a pair in her size, then turned to face Jamie so he could give her some gloves and she could try a helmet on. It wasn't like the fancy black velvet riding hats she'd seen in pictures – more like a plastic scooter helmet with a small brim. His brow knotted in concentration as he adjusted the strap under her chin, making Emily feel a bit sweaty. She clamped her lips together in the hope that he couldn't smell the Marmite on her breath, and noted that his eyes were definitely grey rather than blue and the chin stubble was trimmed and tidy. Her thoughts drifted to him lying in bed, then him in bed naked. He didn't seem the pyjamas type.

'All done,' said Jamie, booting Emily out of her lustful day-dream. 'Come and meet Rupert.' He grabbed a helmet off a peg and led Emily out the other door to the yard, where a brown horse was tied to a metal railing, already saddled and tacked up.

'He's a lovely steady chap,' said Jamie, patting Rupert on the side of the neck. 'I promise he won't carry you off into the sunset.'

Emily shoved aside the inappropriate direction of her thoughts and gave Rupert a pat. He was reddy-brown and shiny like a conker, with kind eyes and a white stripe on his nose. He nudged Emily's hand and made a whickering noise.

'Who usually rides him?' she asked.

'We've got a few grooms and stable hands who help out,' said Jamie, untying the reins from the railing. 'Keep the horses exercised and looked after. We also work with a local charity that offers riding lessons for adults with disabilities. Rupert is the star of the show, everybody loves him.'

Emily relaxed a little, thinking that Rupert sounded ideal for a novice like her. She stopped stroking his nose and he biffed her shoulder, like a dog demanding belly rubs.

'OK,' said Jamie, holding out the reins. 'Time to climb aboard.'

Emily looked doubtfully at the height of the saddle and wondered how the hell she was supposed to get up there.

'Fine,' said Jamie, rolling his eyes. 'You can do it the easy way, just this once.' He led Rupert over to the stone mounting block in the middle of the yard and nodded at Emily to climb up. 'Hold the reins in your left hand, put your left foot in the stirrup, then push up and swing your right leg over. Easy.'

Emily took a deep breath and replayed the instructions in her head as she worked through each step. *Hold the reins, left foot in, push and swing.* She looked down at Jamie and started to laugh nervously. 'Fucking hell, I'm on a horse.'

'Yes, you are,' said Jamie with a grin. 'Now you just have to stay on.' He fiddled around for a while, tightening the strap under the horse and adjusting the length of her stirrups. Rupert didn't move, and Emily wondered what all the fuss was about.

Jamie disappeared into the stables for a minute, then returned with the white horse who'd eaten her offer letter and scared her on her run. 'This is Luna,' he said. 'She's a bitch, but she's also my favourite.'

'How many horses do you have?' Emily asked.

'Currently twelve,' said Jamie. 'Chester and Lucifer, who belong to Dad and Adam. Rupert and Luna. Tucker, another steady fellow that we use for disabled riders, but he's currently lame. And Star, who belongs to my mother, but she never rides him. The other six all belong to locals; we just provide livery.'

Emily had no idea what livery was and decided not to ask, instead watching Jamie pop his foot in the stirrup and leap on to Luna's back without bothering with the mounting block. Just watching him made her thighs hurt, amongst other sensations.

'Are you ready?' asked Jamie. 'Just sit up straight and hold the reins loosely.' Emily nodded, so Jamie set off towards the gate that led to one of the estate paths. Rupert followed without Emily having to do anything, which took her by surprise. The swaying movement was a lot more side-to-side than she'd expected, and it felt quite unnerving at first. But after a couple of minutes she got used to it and tried to relax.

'Where would you like to go?' asked Jamie, turning in the saddle to look at her as they followed the main estate road away from the house.

'What are my options?' she replied.

Jamie held up two fingers. 'I can show you the estate, or we can head out and see the countryside.'

'I'd actually really love to see the estate today,' said Emily, hoping the unspoken *you can show me the countryside another day* wasn't too obvious.

'No problem,' said Jamie. 'Sit tight and I'll take you on a tour.'

Emily grinned excitedly, enjoying being so high up and plodding along at such a gentle pace. It reminded her of the narrowboat holiday they'd taken when she was little, relaxing into a new pace and rhythm until it began to feel perfectly normal.

'Am I doing this right?' she asked as the path widened and Jamie pulled back so he could walk alongside her.

'You're a natural,' he said, with a smile that made her feel warm inside. 'It's nice to go riding with someone – my girlfriend absolutely hates it.'

The fire in Emily's stomach fizzled out instantly, replaced by a sick feeling of disappointment and then a wave of relief. Of course Jamie had a girlfriend, men like him were never single. *Oh, thank God, this makes life SO much easier.*

'What does she do for a living?' she asked lightly, betting she was a doctor or a human rights lawyer or something incredibly worthy and important.

'She's a physiotherapist,' he replied.

Bingo, thought Emily.

'She's done a lot of work with wounded servicemen returning from Afghanistan.'

Ugh, double bingo.

'She lives in London so we don't see a huge amount of each other. I hate being in London, but she likes it here and comes up when she can. She's here in a couple of days, actually. Her name's Louisa.'

Of course it is, thought Emily. She immediately pictured Louisa in her head – willowy and beautiful, expensive hair and teeth, healing hands that also played the cello.

'What about you?' asked Jamie. 'Do you have a partner?'

She briefly considered making up a boyfriend who was an aid worker in Sudan and also an underwear model, then thought better of it. 'I did,' she replied, 'but we split up last month. It's part of why I took the job here.'

'Oh dear,' said Jamie with a nervous laugh. 'Sounds ugly.'

'Not really,' said Emily, not wanting him to think her love life was a hot mess. 'I just needed a change, a chance to put myself first for a while. I think it was the right decision.' He didn't say anything, so she decided to seize the opportunity to go fishing. 'Tell me about your family,' she asked. 'They seem . . . interesting.'

Jamie smiled at her recall of their first conversation. 'Well, you've met my charming brother,' he replied. 'His wife Victoria is very much along similar lines, and their two sons are little monsters. Anna has to lock up anything fragile when they come to the house.'

'Wow, OK,' said Emily, thinking of her brother David, who she adored, and her two gorgeous nephews. She couldn't wait to see them at Christmas.

'I probably shouldn't be telling you all this,' added Jamie, 'but you did ask. My sister Catherine lives in LA with my mother. They're both very . . . LA, I guess.'

'What does that mean?' asked Emily. The closest she'd been to LA was her former flatmate Paul, who transformed into a drag queen called Beverly Hells at the weekends and owned a wig that had allegedly once belonged to Joan Collins.

'Catherine has a new face every time I see her, but no job that I know of. As far as I can tell, she and my mother spend their time shopping, lunching and doing yoga.'

'I mean, it's one way to live,' said Emily.

'Sometimes I wonder if I was switched at birth,' said Jamie with a laugh. 'But then I spend time with Dad and realise how alike we are. Although I think he wishes I'd done more with my life by the age of thirty, had some of his ambition.'

So that's what's disappointed Mr Hunter about Jamie, thought Emily. *Could definitely be worse.*

'What are your family like?' Jamie asked.

Emily smiled at the thought of them. 'Oh, pretty ordinary really. My mum is a dinner lady at my old school in Chichester and my dad works for the council.' She glanced at Jamie to see if he had tuned out, but he looked fascinated.

'Any brothers or sisters?' he asked.

'Two brothers, both older,' she replied. 'David lives in Newcastle with his wife Joanne and their two kids, he works for an engineering company. Simon lives in Hamburg with his husband Eric, he does something in advertising.'

'Simon, or Eric?' asked Jamie.

'Simon,' said Emily with a smile. 'Eric works in a museum. Curating, conservation, something like that. He's German and lovely.'

'Why do I get the feeling you like your family a lot more than I like mine?' asked Jamie.

Emily laughed, realising how much she missed them all. 'Yeah. They can be a bit much sometimes, but I love my family a lot.'

'Will they all be back for Christmas?' he asked.

'David and his family will,' said Emily happily. 'Simon and Eric are staying in Hamburg. Mum and Dad's house is . . . pretty small, it's really hard for us all to get together.' She wondered if Jamie had ever been in a house like the one her parents lived in. Probably not.

'I envy you,' he said, looking back across the fields to the house. 'We've got a huge house and we spend most of our time avoiding each other. I'd give it up for a proper happy family any day of the week.'

'Really?' asked Emily, gesturing at the landscape. 'All this?'

Jamie nodded, his eyes blazing. 'In a heartbeat.'

After twenty minutes or so they rode past a large, red-brick cottage with a thatched roof and white-framed windows. The front door was sage green and flanked by two bay trees in huge pots. It looked like the quintessential English country cottage from a picture book, and Emily was instantly smitten.

'That's Wedmore Cottage,' said Jamie, pulling his horse to a stop. 'It's Adam's house whenever he's here.'

'It's beautiful,' she said. 'What about when he's not here?'

Jamie shrugged. 'It stands empty. He's officially the heir to Bowford Manor, so he thinks he's entitled to live in the nicest property on the estate. But it saves him living up at the main house so I'm not complaining.'

'And what about you?' she asked. 'Where do you live?'

'I've got a little apartment above the stables,' he said. 'It's nothing fancy, but I like it.'

Emily nodded. 'How many properties are there in total?' She'd already been through the estate files and knew the answer, but she wanted to keep Jamie talking. He had a nice voice and it gave her a good excuse to look at him.

'Fourteen,' said Jamie. 'Most have tenants, a few are working farms. There's a little place by the pool that gets used for guests when the main house is full, which isn't very often.'

'I saw that, it's really pretty,' said Emily.

'It used to be the party house when we were teenagers,' he said with a wistful smile. 'It was a great place to hang out with friends, have parties by the pool.'

'Hmm,' said Emily breezily. 'I used to hang out with friends by the pool too, except it was a stagnant pond on the caravan park where my best mate lived.'

Jamie gave a bark of laughter, then blushed to the roots of his hair. 'God, I'm sorry,' he said. 'I must sound like such a wanker.'

'It's fine,' said Emily. 'Just interesting, that's all. When was your thirtieth birthday?'

'October,' said Jamie, looking at her questioningly.

'OK, so we're pretty much the same age; we'd have been in the same year at school. But we grew up in completely different worlds.'

'We're not friends with dukes and duchesses, Emily,' he said with a soft laugh. 'Dad has a title, but he never uses it. His best friend is the local GP. We're not exactly high society.'

'I suppose that depends on your perspective,' she said,

then realised that sounded a bit chippy. 'I'm sorry, I'm not having a go. This is all just new to me, I guess. Takes a bit of getting used to.'

'Yeah, I'm sure,' said Jamie. 'Do you fancy some lunch?'

'I'd love some.' Emily had been too anxious to eat much breakfast and was now starving. 'What did you have in mind?'

'I know a pub that has valet parking for horses,' replied Jamie.

She turned to look at him, wondering what other services were provided to rich people that nobody else knew about. 'Really?'

'No, Emily,' said Jamie, rolling his eyes. 'But we can tie them to the fence and sit outside.'

She grinned as her stomach rumbled. 'Sounds like a plan.'

They sat on a wooden picnic bench outside the pub, Luna and Rupert loosely tied to a gatepost so they could chomp on the grass verge. The waitress didn't seem terribly thrilled about serving food outside in late November until Jamie gave her a killer smile, at which point she looked like she'd have happily delivered it on a silver tray whilst wearing roller skates.

'What's the best thing about living round here?' asked Emily.

'Apart from being able to take your horse to the pub?' asked Jamie.

'Mmm,' said Emily, chewing on her cheese and pickle sandwich.

'It's quiet, I guess,' he said. 'There's a different pace of life in Norfolk, nobody ever seems to be in a hurry.'

Emily swallowed the sandwich and washed it down with a gulp of cider. 'I really like it,' she said. 'I didn't think I would.

The countryside feels quite different; I'm used to the Downs and everything being more hilly, but Norwich is actually a lot like Chichester.' She realised she sounded incredibly naive and unworldly, and hoped he wasn't judging her.

'It's a beautiful county – the beaches on the north coast are stunning. You should get out and explore.'

Emily thought momentarily of Leon, then repressed a guilty thought about whether Jamie might also offer to be her tour guide. But he finished his sandwich and stood up, brushing the crumbs off his jacket on to the grass.

'Right, Miss Wilkinson,' he said officiously. 'Time for you to learn how to get on a horse the proper way.'

Leon was buffing a battered Land Rover as Emily did a bow-legged walk out of the stable yard, his face set into a mask of bleak judgement. She briefly considered just going back to the house and having a bath before her saddle-sore thighs seized up entirely, but this issue wasn't going to go away, so she might as well deal with it.

'How was your ride?' Leon asked as she approached the car, rubbing the door so hard he was at risk of removing the paintwork.

'It was nice, thank you,' said Emily. 'My first time on a horse – Jamie kindly offered to teach me.'

'I'm sure he did,' said Leon through gritted teeth, now down to the bare metal.

'Look, Leon,' Emily said gently, turning her palms upwards in a gesture of openness. 'I'm sorry about today, but I need to be honest with you.'

Leon stopped buffing and looked at her, his face more hangdog than ever.

Emily took a deep breath. 'I feel like maybe you want to be more than just friends. Am I right?'

Leon looked away, his shoulders slumped in defeat. 'I think you are very beautiful,' he mumbled.

'I'm really flattered,' said Emily, 'but I've just come out of a relationship and it was very difficult. Taking this job was a way of focusing on myself for a while.'

Leon lifted his head a little, eyeing her doubtfully.

'I'm not interested in a relationship with anyone,' said Emily. 'I just want to do a good job here.'

Leon gave her a watery smile. 'Is OK, I understand.'

'Can we still be friends?' she asked.

Leon shrugged. 'Of course.' He stood up straight, his pride temporarily restored now he knew he hadn't been usurped by Jamie. 'You should wash. You smell of horses.'

Emily punched him playfully on the shoulder and headed into the house for a bath, wondering if she'd have said the same thing to Jamie if he'd just told her he thought she was beautiful. Absolutely she would. Definitely.

CHAPTER THIRTEEN

Jamie's girlfriend Louisa arrived two days later, and as expected she was tall, thin and flame-haired, like a human matchstick. She had shiny white teeth, a tinkly laugh and the breezy confidence of someone who'd sailed through life on a superyacht of privilege, but Emily had to grudgingly admit that she and Jamie made a ridiculously gorgeous couple. Louisa was inclined to walks in the grounds layered against the cold in cashmere wraps and fur scarves, but always with her long hair flowing in the breeze like Rupert's tail; in less charitable moments Emily watched her from her office window and hoped her ears were cold. When Jamie was with her, Louisa gripped his hand like he was a toddler who might run off at any moment. Emily wondered why she didn't go the whole hog and put some reins on him; there were plenty in the tack room.

Louisa left the estate after only a few days, which left Jamie mooching around with a doleful face, like a hungry basset hound. Emily had only seen him a handful of times since her arrival at Bowford Manor, but now he seemed to pop up everywhere, hanging out with Sam in the kitchen at lunchtime, or loitering around Mr Hunter's office for no particular reason. She assumed he must be at a loose end if he was offering to help her wrap festive food hampers for the tenants or put Mr Hunter's Christmas cards in envelopes, but she was too busy to let herself get distracted by him. He was undeniably handsome, but even if he hadn't been her boss's son and dating someone else, she was resolute in being off men right now. That said, it was nice to have company and somebody to pass her bits of sticky tape.

Adam's family had also returned to London after a long weekend at Wedmore Cottage, without Emily ever having seen Victoria Hunter up close. She definitely heard the children, however; mostly being told off by Anna for running in the hallways, climbing on the furniture or tormenting the dogs. Under different circumstances Emily might have offered to help, but Anna was sour-faced and disapproving about everything Emily did, so she decided to leave her to it. It was easier to stay in her office and let chaos reign in the corridors.

Even though his family had gone, Adam was still holed up in Wedmore Cottage two weeks later. Emily occasionally saw him driving around the estate, but otherwise had become very adept at dodging him. She familiarised herself with all the side corridors and deep doorways in the house where she could duck out of sight if she heard him coming – he had a tendency to clear his throat loudly and repeatedly, which was both irritating and extremely useful. Occasionally he'd pop in to see his father and make a great deal of theatre out of closing the door to Emily's side office, as though whatever he had to say wasn't for her untrustworthy ears. Not only did she not give a shit, but it didn't make any difference – the partition wall was wafer-thin and she could hear every word of Adam's entitled whining.

She'd mentioned it to Mr Hunter during her first week, not comfortable with eavesdropping without his knowledge.

It turned out that he was well aware, to the extent that he and Andrea had devised a secret code. 'Can you pull the door to' was an instruction to actively listen in and take notes, whereas 'can you close the door' meant that it was fine to listen in, but not essential if she was busy with other things. Finally, 'can you close both doors' meant it was private and could she please leave her office and take a break.

So far the final option had never been requested, which meant she had the joy of listening to Adam's bleating. The theme was always the same – he wanted money for some 'dead cert' business opportunity, and Mr Hunter didn't want to give it to him. She had to admire Adam's persistence; he definitely didn't have any other redeeming features.

On one occasion Emily went to the pool for a swim after work and found Adam ploughing up and down in mini flippers and webbed gloves, like a pale toad in turquoise Speedos. The idea of sharing a body of water with him filled her with horror, never mind doing it in a swimsuit that showed her nipples in the cold air. So she immediately about-turned and ate a bag of Wotsits in the bath instead.

Luckily Emily didn't have much time to brood about Adam or Jamie or anyone else, because her weekends had been consumed by Christmas shopping for her family, and her working hours were tied up with planning the Bowford Estate Christmas party. It was scheduled for the following weekend with over a hundred guests confirmed, including all the staff and tenants and their families. The party was a Bowford tradition that went back a hundred and fifty years, and Emily didn't want to be the first person to mess it up.

The good news was that Andrea had left a folder stuffed with detailed plans and checklists and contact details from previous years, and Anna had spent nearly thirty years being in charge of the food. This party was on too big a scale for Sam the chef, so instead they hired a local catering firm who would prepare all the food in the Bowford kitchens, then bus in a team of staff to serve at the tables.

Emily had overseen the delivery of a huge Christmas tree, which was now standing in the entrance hall between the two staircases. Leon had retrieved crates of fairy lights and beautiful glass baubles from the attic and they'd decorated it together, Leon telling her about Christmas traditions in Croatia and Emily wondering whether drinking prosecco in your pyjamas before breakfast counted as a British tradition. At one point Jamie appeared and helped them drape garlands along the gallery and down the bannisters, seemingly in high spirits and keen to get involved. Leon was polite but watchful, as though he resented Jamie interrupting his time with Emily and suspected him of having some kind of ulterior motive. Emily tried to focus on the job in hand, ever aware of Jamie's proximity despite her best efforts not to look at him.

The drinks reception would be held in the entrance hall, then guests would eat a three-course dinner in the adjacent grand dining room before returning to the hall for dancing. Emily had hired a live band who would play ninety minutes of floor-filling cover versions from the gallery, then a DJ who'd take over until the small hours. Leon had regaled her with many tales from previous years, confirming Emily's suspicion that the whole thing could get incredibly messy and all the other rooms in the house would need to be sealed off. Apparently last year two people had passed out on the sofas in the kitchen and somebody had been sick in Anna's knitting basket.

The previous weekend Emily had gone home to Chichester to take her mum shopping for a party outfit. The electric-blue dress Carol chose was eye-wateringly sparkly, but at least it featured considerably more fabric than she would normally consider. Somehow Emily had also ended up buying her shoes and a clutch bag, and a shirt and trousers for Dad, but she'd been so thrilled and it felt nice to be able to treat them both. Emily had also bought a cocktail dress for herself, with capped sleeves, a low back and a skater skirt that skimmed over her hips and fell just above the knee. The bodice was made from thousands of tiny multicoloured sequins, and when she tried it on at Kelly's, her goddaughter Beth had gasped and said she looked like a magical fish.

It was a week before the party when Adam appeared in the doorway of Emily's office, only ten minutes after Jamie had popped in to see if his father was around, then hung around making small talk about Emily's plans for the weekend before drifting off again. She needed to do a sweep of Norwich's shops to finish her Christmas shopping tomorrow, but if members of the Hunter family didn't stop bothering her, she was never going to get out of the office. Mr Hunter had gone to the dentist to deal with a raging toothache that had been making him cranky for days, until Emily had lost patience and booked him in with the first local private dentist she could find on Google. He'd bitched and grumbled about it not being his usual dentist in London until Emily had given him her best hard stare and he'd mumbled his assent.

'All by yourself?' asked Adam, leaning against the door frame like he was too raffish and sexy to support his own weight. He was wearing dark blue jeans paired with a tailored pink shirt and tan shoes; the whole look screamed 'BMW city boy wanker'.

'Not any more,' she replied, forcing herself to smile even though he made her skin crawl. 'Can I help?'

'I wonder if I might borrow your photocopier,' he said, waving a large brown envelope.

'Of course,' said Emily breezily. 'Would you like me to do it for you?'

'Nope,' said Adam, 'I'm sure I can press the button all by myself.' He gave her his interpretation of a winning smile, which made him look like a ravenous shark.

'Just through there,' she said, gesturing to the windowless room where all the filing cabinets and stationery were kept. 'Shout if you need anything.'

Adam disappeared, so Emily carried on with her emails as the photocopier hummed and whirred. He returned a minute later, still holding the brown envelope along with some loosely folded sheets of A3. He gave Emily a wink as he headed back into the corridor, calling 'Have a good one!' from the doorway without bothering to turn around.

Emily shuddered and carried on working for a few minutes, then headed into the filing room to check a date on a contract in one of the filing cabinets. She spotted the sheets of paper in the photocopier feeder straight away, and quickly checked Adam hadn't returned before taking a peek. They looked like the plans a land surveyor would create; Emily had handled these kinds of documents all the time at Thompson & Delaney. She lifted the top sheet to look at the one below – they were clearly plans of the Bowford Estate, with certain areas shaded out in pink and blue.

Instinctively she pressed the start button, her heart thumping as she drummed her fingers impatiently on the edge of the machine. The pages whipped through the feeder at high speed as the copies appeared underneath. Emily snatched them off the tray and left the originals exactly where she'd found them, then hurried back to her desk and stuffed the papers into the bottom drawer of her desk. She took a few calming breaths and carried on with her work.

Adam reappeared a couple of minutes later, looking a good deal more flustered than he had before. Emily focused on her computer screen, determined to look like she hadn't moved an inch and everything was exactly as he'd left it. Adam glared at her suspiciously but said nothing.

'Is everything OK?' she enquired, her hands frozen over the keyboard.

'Yes,' said Adam, a little defensively. 'I just left some papers on the photocopier.'

'Oh, right,' said Emily, going back to her typing. Adam didn't move, so she stopped again. 'Do you want me to fetch them for you?'

Adam softened his glare a little, clearly realising his behaviour probably seemed a bit weird. 'No, of course not. I can get them myself.'

Emily nodded and returned to her task, ignoring Adam as he went back into the filing room. He stalked back out with the plans and left without saying goodbye.

She breathed out slowly, her heart pounding out of her chest. Espionage was definitely not her strong point, and now she really needed a cup of tea.

CHAPTER FOURTEEN

Carol and Martin Wilkinson arrived after lunch on the day of the Christmas party, full of stories of their epic drive and the parlous state of the garage toilets on the A11. Emily was happy to see them and determined to make them feel at home, even if it was just for the weekend. She showed them to the little guest cottage by the pool, which was just as delightful and cosy on the inside. Apparently Anna was too busy to deal with greeting guests as lowly as the Wilkinsons, but that was fine by Emily.

'This is lovely, Moomin,' said Martin, opening the cupboards in the tiny kitchen. 'There's tea bags and everything.'

'I put some milk in the fridge for you too,' said Emily, delighted that they liked it. 'You can come over to the house for breakfast tomorrow.'

'Listen to you,' said Carol, checking out the bathroom. '"You can come over to the house,"' she echoed in a singsong voice. 'Too posh for the likes of us now.' She smiled indulgently at Emily, then lifted the lid on the toilet to check it had been properly cleaned. 'Look at the loo, Martin. You could eat your dinner out of that.'

'Listen, I know you've just arrived,' said Emily, 'but if you want to see the kitchens we'll need to do it now before the caterers take over.'

'Ooh, yes please,' said Carol excitedly. 'I bet it's just like *Downton Abbey*.'

Emily laughed, not wanting to ruin her mum's fantasy of bubbling copper pots and Mrs Patmore yelling at kitchen maids. She'd walk them through the walled garden to show Dad the greenhouses, then round to the yard.

Even though Emily could only show them the kitchen and the entrance hall, her parents were entirely enchanted by Bowford Manor. Martin insisted on doing a full lap of the outside of house, pointing out unusual period features and things that you'd absolutely never get planning permission for these days, while Carol huffed and eye-rolled, clearly itching to pass dinner-lady judgement on the set-up below stairs.

Emily showed them the two hidden staircases in the entrance hall, each leading to a different end of the kitchen. Carol declared this 'genius', and also gave her seal of approval to the range cooker, the pantry and the huge granite island with the induction hob. Emily made them both a cup of tea, hoping that Anna wouldn't turn up and treat them like dog poo, but there was no sign of her.

When the caterers arrived with huge crates of plates and glasses, they made themselves scarce, bumping into Jamie in the delivery yard. He was looking entirely edible in his jodhpurs and puffer jacket and gave Emily a smile that made her thighs tingle.

'These are my parents, Carol and Martin,' she said quickly, nervous that Jamie would announce himself as a Hunter and fluster them both.

'Pleased to meet you,' he said, shaking both their hands. 'I'm Jamie.'

'Do you work here as well?' asked Martin.

'I look after the horses,' said Jamie, glancing at Emily.

'Moomin's not one for horses,' laughed Carol. 'The closest she ever got was a donkey in Brighton.'

'Thanks, Mum,' said Emily, trying not to blush at Jamie's raised eyebrows. He was either wondering why she hadn't told them about her riding lesson, or more likely enquiring as to the origin of the nickname 'Moomin'. *Embarrassing.*

'Are you coming to the party later, Jamie?' asked Carol, ever the matchmaker. It occurred to Emily that she had no idea if Jamie was coming or not.

'Oh,' he said. 'Well, yes, I expect so. I'm sure I'll see you there.' He said a polite goodbye and headed through the back door and down the stairs to the kitchen. Emily wondered why he hadn't told her parents who he was, but then remembered that he'd withheld that information the first time she met him too. He wasn't one to flaunt his Hunter credentials; unlike Adam, who could probably wank out the family crest.

'He's handsome, Moo,' said Carol. 'Lovely eyes.'

'Lovely girlfriend, too,' said Emily, keen to kill the conversation dead before her mother started planning for a spring wedding and a Christmas grandchild. 'Come on, I'll walk you back.'

Emily did a final check on the entrance hall just before the guests were due to arrive and found everything laid out and ready. The band were setting up their gear in the gallery, ready to sound-check while everyone was having dinner. The DJ had popped by earlier to set up his decks and lighting rig in front of the Christmas tree and was last seen on the

103

sofa in the kitchen watching the football. Emily hadn't checked on the food because that was Anna's department, but the delicious smell wafting up the back stairs suggested everything was under control. She could hear the bar staff in the morning room popping corks – they'd stand by the front door with trays of glasses until everyone had arrived, then man the free bar until the booze ran out.

'You look lovely, Emily,' said Mr Hunter, appearing down the main stairs. He was wearing a dinner jacket with an unexpectedly exuberant bow tie featuring penguins in Santa hats.

'Oh, thank you,' said Emily, enjoying being properly dressed up for the first time since she'd arrived at Bowford Manor. She'd bought a pair of silver heels to match her dress, and also forgone her usual sensible bun in favour of wearing her hair down, letting it fall in soft waves down her bare back. She'd used her new hair straighteners to create the effect and had checked they were unplugged four times before leaving her room.

Mr Hunter checked his watch. 'Time to open the doors, I think,' he said. 'Funny how people are always on time when there's a free bar.'

Emily nodded and retreated into the shadows by the Christmas tree, crossing her fingers that everything would go to plan.

Anna found Emily an hour later, happily chatting to her mum at the bottom of the stairs. Emily was on her second glass of fizz and the pink spots on Carol's cheeks suggested she was probably on her third. Anna looked like she could do with a couple herself, but at least she'd swapped her uniform of grey, black or navy for a burgundy velvet dress.

'I need to speak to you,' she snapped at Emily, not bothering to introduce herself to Carol.

'This is my mum, Carol,' said Emily, refusing to stoop to Anna's level. 'Mum, this is Anna. She's the housekeeper.' Carol gave her a slightly squiffy smile and raised her glass in greeting.

'We have a problem with dinner,' said Anna impatiently, entirely ignoring Carol.

'What kind of problem?' asked Emily.

Anna sighed heavily. 'The caterers have been and gone and all the food is ready, but the minibus with the waiting staff has broken down,' she whispered, glancing at her watch. 'They should have been here half an hour ago and be serving up the main course by now.'

'Can't we send a couple of cars to rescue them?' asked Emily.

'Yes, of course we can,' Anna replied crisply, 'but they're twenty minutes away. By the time they're ready to serve it will be gone nine o'clock. The band are due to start at half past eight, we'll have to completely reschedule the whole evening.'

Emily thought for a moment, visualising the running order for the evening in her head. It wasn't a disaster, but it was less than ideal.

'Can I make a suggestion?' said Carol, draining her glass.

Anna looked at her like she'd just been sick on her shoes. 'I'm sorry?'

'I wondered if we could serve the food from the kitchen.'

Anna's eyes narrowed into tiny slits. 'I don't follow.'

Carol smiled like this was the most obvious plan in the world. 'Lead everyone down to the kitchen,' she said, 'then line up all the hot food on that huge table. The three of us could serve it straight on to their plates, which they can carry back to the dining room.'

Anna was silent for a moment as she worked through the suggestion. 'What about the starter?'

'Forget the starter,' said Carol, wafting her hand dismissively. 'Nobody gives a shit about the starter.'

Emily coughed. 'It's not a bad idea, Anna,' she said. 'We could send everyone down the left stairs and back up the right, keep the traffic flowing. Then when everyone's finished their mains we can all go back down for dessert. It might be fun.'

Anna looked doubtful, glancing from Carol to Emily. 'Fine,' she said. 'I'll organise some taxis to take the waiters home.' She glared at Emily. 'It's your fault if this goes wrong.'

'Leave it to me,' said Carol enthusiastically. 'I'm a champion dinner lady. Anna, we'll go down and start laying out the food. Do you have a plate warmer?'

'Yes,' said Anna, clearly affronted at the suggestion they might not. 'The plates are already in it.'

'Lovely,' said Carol. 'Moomin, you go and let Dad and Mr Hunter know the plan, then come and join us in the kitchen. Ask them both if they'll start hustling everyone down the left-hand stairs in ten minutes.'

'I'm on it,' said Emily. 'Thanks, Mum.'

'Don't you worry about a thing,' said Carol, giving Anna's arm a squeeze. Emily smiled as the housekeeper snatched it away, but Carol didn't even notice.

Dinner ended up being something of a triumph, with everyone enjoying the novelty of queuing for their food, requesting exactly which bits they wanted, then heading back upstairs to sit anywhere they liked around the tables in the dining room. After the mains were done, the guests hurried back downstairs to grab a spoon and pile into a table of puddings. Most people didn't even bother going back upstairs to eat them, instead standing around in the kitchen eating sticky toffee pudding and profiteroles until the band struck up in the gallery and Mr Hunter led an impromptu conga to the dance floor. Anna managed a grudging thank you to Carol as they stacked all the plates and bowls for the caterers to collect in the morning, although Emily didn't even get an acknowledgement.

Later Emily stood by the Christmas tree watching the dance floor, feeling tired and happy and a bit drunk. Her parents were dancing to Chaka Khan's 'Ain't Nobody' as if they both had a family of small animals living in their underwear, and Mr Hunter was throwing shapes with a couple of the stable hands, looking like he was fighting off a swarm of bees. Jamie appeared next to her with two glasses of fizz, which immediately caught the attention of Carol. She gave Emily a theatrical wink and a double thumbs up, which thankfully Jamie didn't see.

'Not dancing?' he asked, handing Emily a glass.

She smiled and took a sip. 'I'll dance with my dad if you dance with yours.'

'Hmm,' said Jamie, raising his eyebrows as the DJ segued into 'Disco Inferno' and his father cranked it up a notch. 'Might give that a miss.'

'No Louisa this evening?' she asked, trying to sound relaxed and breezy. He was wearing a blue suit with an open-necked white shirt and smelled of a woody, masculine aftershave, which made Emily's imagination drift in the direction of mistletoe and log fires and festive shagging.

'No,' said Jamie, staring into his glass. 'She's back in London.'

Emily nodded, noting with a flurry of pleasure that he didn't sound terribly gutted about that. She could see her mum dancing in their direction, thrusting her hips back and forth as Martin went into a short routine of disco moves. Emily turned to face Jamie in the hope that she might distract him for at least three minutes.

'What are you doing for Christmas?' she asked.

Jamie shrugged. 'Not sure yet. The family are all off to Switzerland.'

'You don't sound very keen.' Emily tried to imagine not wanting to spend Christmas in snowy Switzerland, but then remembered Adam would be there and decided she'd rather spend it working double shifts in a slaughterhouse.

'I'm sure it will be lovely,' said Jamie. 'When are you going home?'

'Next Saturday,' she replied. 'I've finished all my shopping so I'm pretty sorted.'

'Of course you are. Would you like to dance?'

The question took Emily by surprise; she hadn't seen it coming and suddenly it felt like the biggest decision she'd ever make. She looked away so he didn't see her blush, and noticed Leon watching them from the other side of the dance floor, his face bleak. Behind Jamie's head Carol was making a heart symbol with her hands and waving it in their direction. Emily suddenly felt very hot.

She took a deep breath and met Jamie's gaze. The way he looked at her made her feel dizzy, and she realised how much she wanted to say yes. But she also knew how easy it would be to fall head over heels for Jamie Hunter, and what common sense remained told her that was only ever going to end in tears. She'd been reckless with her feelings over Mark, and she was determined not to make the same mistake again. 'I won't, but thank you,' she replied. 'I really need to go and check in with Anna.'

He looked disappointed at the obvious rebuff, but also like maybe he understood. 'That's OK,' he said. 'Enjoy the rest of your night.' As Emily turned away, he brushed his hand lightly on her arm. 'Just so you know,' he whispered, 'you look incredible in that dress.'

Emily's face burned as she dashed for the back stairs, feeling dizzy and flustered. She drank a glass of water from the tap in the kitchen, listening to the thumping music overhead and cursing her body for getting hot and horny for a man she absolutely couldn't have and definitely didn't want. And what was Jamie doing flirting with her and asking her to dance? It didn't seem fair, somehow.

Once she'd pulled herself together, she headed back upstairs to join the party, letting her dad drag her on to the dance floor to the opening bars of 'Into You' by Ariana Grande. She danced in circles as she sang 'I'm so into you I can barely breathe', and by the end of the song she'd scanned the room enough times to be pretty sure that Jamie had left.

CHAPTER FIFTEEN

Emily woke up with a woolly head on Sunday, which was no surprise considering she'd danced until 3 a.m., helped Mr Hunter hoof out the stragglers, then accepted his offer to escort her and her absolutely bladdered mother back to the pool cottage so Emily didn't have to walk back to the main house on her own. Martin had headed off to bed around 1 a.m. but Carol had decided she would be the last woman standing. Or in her case, doing the 'Macarena' up one flight of stairs, along the gallery and down the other.

Breakfast was a largely silent affair, with a green-tinged Carol chewing her toast like it was the insole from an old trainer and wincing every time the caterers carried off another crate of plates and let the kitchen door slam.

'Are you OK to drive, Dad?' Emily asked.

'Yeah, I'm good,' he replied. 'I stopped drinking early doors, unlike your mother.' Carol gave him the finger and drained her coffee mug.

'What are your plans today, Moo?' she asked, trying to battle her way out of her hangover like a zombie hauling itself out of a grave.

'Not much,' Emily said. 'Might go for a swim later, have a nap. Mostly just staying out of the way so I don't get roped into cleaning up.'

'Good plan,' said Carol, covering her mouth to mask a

huge burp. She looked like death warmed over, but she'd be telling stories about this party for months. 'Time to head off,' she added, taking a banana from the fruit bowl and putting it in her handbag for later. 'Might have a snooze on the way home.'

'Sod that, you're navigating,' said Martin, who didn't believe in satellite navigation and refused to give up his spiral-bound AA Road Map from 2008. He'd read too many stories about coaches following the recommended route and ending up dangling off the edge of a cliff.

'I can't even see, let alone navigate,' said Carol.

'Christ alive,' muttered Martin, hauling Carol out of the chair and half-carrying her out of the kitchen.

Jamie appeared from the stables just as Emily was walking back to the house after waving her parents off. She briefly entertained the possibility that he'd been watching out for her, then decided that was unlikely. She'd fallen asleep thinking about him, and the sudden memory of the subsequent wine-fuelled dream she'd had made her blush.

'Did they have a good time?' he asked, rubbing his hands against the cold. It was a beautiful December day – cold and frosty, but windless under a cornflower-blue sky.

'They really did, thanks. Mum is absolutely hanging.'

Jamie laughed. 'I'm off for a ride in a bit. Do you want to come?'

Emily hesitated, knowing it was a bad idea but also acknowledging that she couldn't avoid Jamie entirely, and riding lessons were about as chaste as it got. 'I'd love to,' she replied. 'I'll just go and get changed.'

Jamie gave her that smile again, making Emily wonder if

she had time to deal with the ache between her legs before she had to sit on a horse and make it FAR worse.

'So, Moomin,' said Jamie with a grin. 'What's that all about?'

Emily laughed, relaxing into the sway of Rupert's plod along a bridleway towards a distant windmill. 'I had a Moomin toy when I was little – you know the white cartoon trolls?'

Jamie nodded. 'I thought they were hippos.'

'They look a bit like hippos, but they're trolls. Swedish or Finnish or something. Anyway, I had this Moomin toy and I carried it everywhere, wouldn't leave the house without it. My brothers started calling me Moomin and it stuck.'

'Does that mean I call you Moo?'

Emily gave him a look. 'Only if I can call you Jimmy.'

'Yeah, not so much.'

They carried on in comfortable silence for a few minutes, with nothing but the occasional sound of birdsong and the heavy crunch of hooves in the frosty grass. The landscape was flat and endless and vast, punctuated by little stands of trees and the grey tower of a church. Emily couldn't think of a better way to tackle a hangover, although she definitely wouldn't say no to an egg and bacon sandwich.

'Is Louisa joining you for Christmas?' she asked casually, imagining her in head-to-toe designer ski gear, flame hair blowing in the wind.

'Ah, no,' replied Jamie, looking off into the distance. 'Well, we're not actually together any more.'

Emily's stomach gave a swoop that had nothing to do with hunger. She turned to look at him until he met her gaze. 'What happened?'

Jamie shrugged. 'Nothing dramatic. I just realised we were never going to want the same things, and it wasn't fair to let Louisa think I might change my mind.'

'I'm really sorry,' lied Emily.

Jamie held her gaze. 'Are you?'

A hot feeling crept up her neck; this whole conversation had taken an unexpected turn and she felt wildly out of her depth. 'Yes,' she said, doubling down on the lie because the alternative was too mortifying. 'You made a nice couple.'

'Right,' said Jamie, looking away. 'I was kind of hoping you might not be THAT sorry.'

Emily's heart started to pound; common sense told her to change the subject now, but her curiosity got the better of her. 'What do you mean?'

Jamie sighed. 'Oh God, you're going to make this really difficult, aren't you?' He laughed awkwardly, blushing to the roots of his hair. 'I thought maybe you might consider us . . . spending more time together.'

'What, like dating?' asked Emily, trying not to sound shrill.

Jamie looked at her and nodded, his face open and very clearly not winding her up.

'Why would you want to date someone like me?' she asked, hating how needy for validation she sounded.

'Why wouldn't I?' he asked.

Emily thought about it, feeling like she was tackling a jigsaw where none of the pieces fitted together. She shuffled all the elements in her head and tried to make sense of them. Fact 1: Jamie, who she fancied the pants off despite her best efforts and had filthy dreams about, was asking her out. Fact 2: He was Mr Hunter's son and dating him was absolutely against all her rules and could result in her losing her job. *Do NOT lose your head over this one, Wilkinson.*

'I'm not sure,' she said. 'I guess I just never imagined I was your type.'

'And what is my type, exactly?' he asked, the tiniest edge creeping into his voice.

'I don't know. I guess I'm just really different from Louisa. She was beautiful and successful and . . . willowy.' Emily guessed it sounded like she was fishing for compliments, but she was genuinely taken aback that last night's flirting was more than just the heat of the house and too much prosecco.

'What the hell does willowy mean?' asked Jamie with a laugh. 'And since when were you not beautiful and successful? You've whipped this whole house into shape in less than a month AND put my bellend of a brother back in his box. You're funny and smart and . . .' His voice petered out as Emily felt a warm glow in the pit of her stomach.

'And . . . what?' she asked.

'I was going to say "hot", but it felt like it undermined the other two.'

Emily laughed, struggling to believe she was about to do this. 'I'm really flattered, Jamie, but I can't go out with you.'

He was quiet for a moment, his mouth set into a hard line. 'Is this a money or a class thing? Because that would be pretty disappointing.'

'No,' Emily replied quickly. 'It's not that.' She sighed heavily, knowing that the only way to explain this was to lay her cards on the table. 'The relationship I was in before I came here was with a guy called Mark. He was my boss, and we had a thing for two years before he decided to give his marriage another go.'

114

'I'm sorry,' said Jamie. 'But I really can't see how that's relevant.'

'After that, I made a promise to myself to keep work and private life separate.'

Jamie shrugged. 'OK, but I'm not your boss.'

'No, but you're part of the family I work for,' she said. 'It's a conflict of interest.' They were passing Wedmore Cottage, so Emily gave Rupert's reins a gentle tug to get him to stop. She could stare at that house all day.

Jamie said nothing for a minute, letting her admire the house while he searched for loopholes. 'Do you really care that much?'

'I do, I'm sorry,' said Emily, desperately wanting him to understand. 'I really like this job, I want to make a go of it. I don't want to have to sneak around, I did that for two years.'

Jamie blew all the air out of his cheeks and shifted in his saddle to look at her, his eyes searching for an answer. 'If things were different, if I was just the guy who looked after the horses, would you say yes?'

Emily gave him a sad smile, feeling like she'd been kicked in the guts but also sure this was the right thing to do. 'Of course,' she said shyly. 'I fancy you rotten. If things were different, I definitely would.'

Jamie laughed. 'But it's never gonna happen.'

'No,' said Emily, holding her head up with absolute certainty. 'I'm sorry.'

He nodded slowly. 'OK, I understand. Gutted, though.'

'Yeah, me too,' said Emily. 'Will you still teach me to ride a horse?'

Jamie sucked air through his teeth and stared at the sky. 'I'm not sure I can bear the pain.'

'Ah, fuck you,' laughed Emily. 'Do these animals go any faster?'

'Oh, thank God, I thought you'd never ask. Ready to learn to trot?'

Emily returned from the ride feeling happy and exhilarated, having quickly got the hang of rising out of the saddle in rhythm with Rupert's trot. It had forced her to focus and use her strong legs and core, with the added bonus of shaking off the remains of her hangover. Her backside was going to hurt like hell tomorrow, but hopefully in a good way.

When they got back to the yard, Jamie took the opportunity to give Emily a lesson in untacking a horse. She enjoyed the methodical logic of it, the removing and cleaning and learning of names of different parts. Once everything was back in its allocated space in the tack room they moved on to grooming, washing and brushing Rupert to get rid of all the mud and sweat. Even though she was cold and tired and hungry, it felt good to be working rather than just handing Rupert over to one of the grooms and expecting them to do the hard bit.

She hadn't even begun to get her head around Jamie's revelation that he was now single and was interested in her; that seemed like something from last night's dream. Somehow knowing that he had feelings for her was enough to put her on cloud nine even if she was resolute about not getting involved. Spending time with him at weekends, learning to ride and look after the horses, being friends while she lived and worked at Bowford Manor – that would have to be enough.

'I'm starving,' she said, fishing her phone out of her jacket pocket and taking a selfie with Rupert, his face hanging over the door of his stable with a blue blanket over his glossy back. She uploaded it to WhatsApp and sent it to Kelly so she could meet the new love of her life.

'Me too,' said Jamie. 'What do you fancy?'

'A bacon and egg sandwich and a mug of tea.'

'That sounds perfect,' laughed Jamie, joining Emily on the other side of Rupert so she could take a selfie of all three of them. 'There's absolutely nothing in my fridge, so let's try the kitchen.'

They left the stables and crossed the road towards the delivery yard, but it was impossible to miss the huge black limo parked at the front of the house. Leon was unloading Louis Vuitton luggage from the boot with his face set into a thunderous scowl, watched dispassionately by a chauffeur in an immaculate grey uniform who was checking his manicure.

'Oh crap,' said Jamie, making an emergency stop. 'My mother and sister are here.'

'What should I do?' asked Emily. 'Offer to help, or hide?'

'Definitely hide,' replied Jamie. 'Sneak in the back and keep your head down.'

'OK,' she said, peeling off towards the delivery yard. 'Thanks for the ride.'

'Come and say goodbye before you disappear for Christmas.'

Emily turned and nodded, giving him a smile that she hoped communicated a million unsaid things.

CHAPTER SIXTEEN

By Thursday Emily had managed to avoid any direct contact with Tanya and Catherine Hunter, mostly by starting work early and staying holed up in her little office as much as possible. There was plenty still to do – Mr Hunter was leaving with the family for a ten-day trip to Switzerland tomorrow and was determined to put work aside until the new year so that Emily could do the same.

But even though Emily hadn't physically met the Hunter women, she could hear them bellowing through the house – both Tanya and Catherine had those mid-Atlantic accents that wavered between upper-class British and Hollywood starlet, depending on who they were talking to and how demanding they were being.

After work she walked over to the pool for a swim, thinking this would probably be her last one before she went home for Christmas. She mentally ticked off her to-do list for tomorrow on the way, starting with a final call to the charter flight company at Norwich Airport to check everything was on schedule, before hustling the family out of the house in three executive cars that would collect them and all their luggage. It was a whole new world to Emily, and she had checked the details a hundred times to make sure nothing had been missed.

Mr Hunter was happy to fly commercial airlines for most

of his trips, but for a family holiday of nine people including Adam's two children and their nanny, it was far easier and less stressful to charter a private jet. One of Tanya Hunter's most vocal complaints this week had been that Mr Hunter didn't own his own plane so she and Catherine could fly back and forth to LA without using Virgin Atlantic, which had apparently been 'unacceptably busy, even in first class'. Listening in the safety of her office, Emily's eyes had rolled so far back into her head she'd wondered if they might get stuck there for ever.

She'd also booked two helicopters to transfer the Hunters from Sion airport in Switzerland to Verbier, which would apparently take about fifteen minutes. Jamie was on the list for both the charter plane and the helicopter, so it looked like Mr Hunter had persuaded him to join the family for the festive break. She'd found pictures of the family chalet in Verbier online; Mr Hunter rented it out for a breathtaking weekly fee whenever the family weren't using it. It was ridiculously swank – an eight-bedroomed wood-clad Alpine palace with a sauna, Jacuzzi and log fires everywhere. Emily thought of her tiny bedroom in Grove Street, her mum's Iceland turkey for Christmas dinner and the fake plastic Christmas tree with decades of homemade decorations. She couldn't wait to get home.

The pool was quiet and empty as usual, so Emily left her clothes on the bench and slid into the warm water. She tucked her hair into a red silicone hat and adjusted her goggles, making an early New Year's resolution to make time every weekend to drive to the beach for a swim. The pool was great, but it was no substitute for freezing cold salt water and a biting January wind. Swimming in the sea in summer was fine, but winter was only for the hardcore, and you were much more likely to have the beach to yourself.

She emptied her mind and focused on the rhythm of her front crawl, turning her head to breathe every other stroke. She was twenty lengths in when she heard the echo of voices and realised she was no longer alone. When she finished her length she took a break, lifting her goggles up on to her forehead so she could see who'd arrived.

'Who are you?' asked a tall, thin woman in a gold velour tracksuit, her hair wrapped in some kind of turban. She was followed by a carbon copy who only appeared to be a few years younger, which was clearly testament to the talents of Tanya Hunter's plastic surgeon.

'I'm Emily, Mr Hunter's assistant.'

'Ah, the famous secretary!' trilled Tanya, putting her enormous handbag on the bench. 'We've heard SO much about you. Sorry to cut your swim short.'

Emily said nothing, realising she was being dismissed. The pool was eight metres wide and plenty big enough for three, but apparently sharing the water with staff wasn't acceptable. She hoisted herself out of the pool and grabbed her towel, feeling humiliated and furious.

'Are you, like, busy right now?' asked Catherine Hunter in a breathy, singsong voice. 'I'm, like, SO behind with my packing. There's literally a mountain of clothes on the floor of my room – could you be a sweetheart and pack them for me?' She looked at Emily expectantly, with the same grey eyes and square face as Jamie and Mr Hunter. Adam had Tanya's heart-shaped features, although Tanya's nose had definitely been upgraded at some point.

Emily gave a short nod. She pulled on her clothes as

quickly as her wet skin would allow, desperate to get away from these two women as soon as possible.

'Be super-careful with the red silk dress,' said Catherine, unveiling a microscopic silver bikini that barely covered the world's most gym-honed body. 'It's Dior.'

'Ooh,' said Tanya, 'that reminds me. There's a green Versace shirt on the back of the chair in my room, it has a lipstick mark on it. Can you see if you can get it out? Anna might have some ideas, I'm sure you'll think of something.'

Squirt of hairspray and some warm water, thought Emily, biting back a thousand versions of 'Fuck you, I'm not your servant.' She grabbed her bag and hurried back to the house, figuring she could get this job done then avoid being the Cinderella to their Ugly Sisters until they'd left the country tomorrow. It was tempting to complain to Mr Hunter, but he had enough on his plate and she didn't want to bother him. She could pack a suitcase and clean a shirt in half an hour, it was hardly a huge ask.

She dumped her swimming stuff in her room, then jogged down to the second floor. She wandered the corridors for a minute, realising she had no idea which rooms belonged to Tanya and Catherine.

'Emily?' said a male voice. 'Is everything OK?'

She turned to find Mr Hunter standing outside one of the rooms, holding a pile of clean laundry that was clearly destined for a suitcase.

'Oh,' she said, frantically trying to come up with a legitimate reason why she might be loitering outside the family bedrooms at 7 p.m., 'I'm looking for your daughter's room. And Mrs Hunter's.'

121

Mr Hunter's eyes narrowed. 'And why might you be doing that?'

Emily hesitated, wishing the carpet would swallow her up.

'Oh, for goodness' sake,' said Mr Hunter, rolling his eyes. 'What have they asked you to do?'

Emily sighed. 'Catherine would like me to pack her suitcase, and Mrs Hunter needs a stain removing from a shirt.'

'Hmm,' said Mr Hunter. 'And where did they find you, exactly? Did they come up to your room?'

'No,' she said emphatically. 'I was in the pool.'

Mr Hunter nodded, his lips clamped together and his nostrils flared. She'd seen Jamie doing the same thing, and it struck her how alike they looked. 'And were you already on your way out of the pool, or did they ask you to leave?'

Uh oh, thought Emily, clearing her throat awkwardly. 'It was implied that I should leave.'

Mr Hunter exhaled through his nose, his mouth set into a furious line. 'Just so I'm clear, my ex-wife kicked you out of my swimming pool and asked you to do my daughter's packing and her laundry?'

'Technically Catherine requested the packing herself,' said Emily, 'but yes to everything else.' She couldn't help but smile at the ridiculousness of it all, which made Mr Hunter start to laugh.

'Honestly, the bare-faced cheek of those two,' he said. 'Sorry about your swim. Go and dry off and I'll deal with it. Could you pop into my office in an hour?'

Emily nodded and scurried back to her attic room, marvelling for the millionth time how a man like Mr Hunter could have ended up with so many awful relations. Every family had a bad egg, but you could make a rancid omelette out of the Hunters.

'Apologies for earlier,' said Mr Hunter, smiling at Emily over his desk. 'I've had a word.'

'Thank you,' she said. 'I wasn't sure on the boundaries.'

'Hmm,' said Mr Hunter. 'Sadly, boundaries are a concept my ex-wife and my daughter don't really understand.' He smiled and steepled his hands under his chin, and suddenly Emily wondered if she'd read this all wrong and she was in trouble.

'I just thought it was a good time for us to have a catch-up,' he said. 'You've been here over a month now, so I wanted to check you're happy with everything before you head home for a break. Make sure you're planning to come back.'

'I'm really happy,' she said. 'I love the job, and I really love working here.' The words took her by surprise; she'd never consciously thought about how attached she'd become to the house and the estate.

'I hear my son is teaching you to ride,' he said with a smile.

'Yes.' Emily hoped that was all Jamie had told him. 'I love it.'

'He says you're a natural,' said Mr Hunter. 'If you're planning to keep it up, get yourself some proper cold weather riding gear. You'll be glad of it in the dead of winter.'

Emily nodded, already looking forward to shopping for all the right clothes. Maybe Jamie would help her make a list.

'Anyway, I'm glad you're happy here,' continued Mr Hunter. 'You've made my life considerably easier. And I've got you a Christmas present.' He opened the top drawer of his desk and picked out a flat box wrapped in silver paper.

'Oh,' said Emily in surprise, 'that's really kind.' She turned the box round in her hands, not sure if she was supposed to open it now or take it home for Christmas.

'You can open it,' said Mr Hunter, wafting his hand. 'It's not very original, I'm afraid.'

Emily pulled off the wrapping and opened the box. Inside was a black and silver Montblanc rollerball pen with *E. Wilkinson* engraved on the cap.

'I don't know what to say,' she stuttered. 'It's beautiful.'

'I bought Andrea a similar one the first Christmas she worked here, and she's still using it twenty-five years later. I hope you like it.'

'I love it,' said Emily, genuinely touched. 'Thank you.'

'You're very welcome,' said Mr Hunter. 'Is there anything else we need to talk about before I head off tomorrow?'

Emily hesitated, thinking of the photocopies in her desk. She still hadn't shown them to Mr Hunter, and on a number of occasions she'd considered putting them through the shredder.

She took a deep breath. 'Actually, there is one thing.'

Mr Hunter pored over the pages, his brow knitted into tight furrows.

'When did you photocopy these?' he asked.

'Two weeks ago,' said Emily. 'I would have shown them to you sooner, but I wasn't sure if I should have them at all. And I didn't know if it was something you already knew about. I guess Adam's behaviour seemed a bit strange, but I'm sorry if I've overstepped the mark.'

'You did the right thing,' said Mr Hunter, looking up at her with a reassuring smile. 'I appreciate it.'

Emily nodded and stood to leave. 'I'll see you in the morning to go through all your final travel arrangements,' she said.

Mr Hunter nodded. 'Thank you, Emily.' She wandered back up to her room, clutching the box containing the pen and wondering whether it was her travel planning skills he was grateful for, or her quick thinking when faced with a son who was very clearly up to no good.

CHAPTER SEVENTEEN

On 23rd December Emily loaded up her car with her suitcase and bags of presents for her family and Kelly and Beth, enjoying the peace and tranquillity of a completely empty house. The Hunters had departed the previous day with only the minimum of last-minute chaos, mostly involving Catherine not being able to find her Chanel sunglasses and refusing to leave without them in case there were paparazzi at the airport. The idea that the paps would slog to Norwich Airport a few days before Christmas to get a long-distance picture of Catherine Hunter seemed laughable to Emily, but she seemed to be under the illusion that she was Kim Kardashian. Emily was despatched to look for them, and by the time she returned empty-handed ten minutes later the whole family had left.

Luckily private jets don't leave without their passengers, so later Emily was able to confirm with the charter plane company and the helicopter transfer firm that the Hunter family had been safely delivered to their chalet in Verbier. For the next ten days they were not her problem, although she'd been disappointed that she and Jamie hadn't managed to say goodbye before he left. She had a little Christmas present for him, but it could wait.

She'd also made Leon an origami sports car out of Christmas wrapping paper; a skill that her brother David had taught her when they were children. He'd taken the box like it was a precious jewel and thanked her with tears in his eyes, before heading off to Stansted to fly home to Croatia. Later she found a badly wrapped parcel outside the door to her room, with a note saying not to open it until Christmas Day. It felt soft and squidgy, but beyond that she didn't have a clue. Anna had also left this morning to spend Christmas with a friend, not bothering to elaborate and giving Emily a 'Merry Christmas' that was distinctly lacking in festive cheer.

None of them were expected back until 2nd January, so Emily had wrapped up all the final bits of office admin, put Mr Hunter's Out of Office on, and messaged the Estate Manager so he could pop by and lock the house up. Now all that remained was to drive home and immerse herself in several litres of Wilkinson festive spirit.

'Oh good, you haven't left yet,' said Jamie, popping up behind her and making her scream.

'Fuck, you scared me. Why aren't you in Switzerland?' She tried not to panic, wondering if she'd messed up some of the arrangements.

Jamie shrugged. 'I decided not to go. Really not my scene.'

Emily rolled her eyes as she breathed a sigh of relief. 'Yeah, sure. Snow, mountains, hot chalet girls as far as the eye can see. I can see why that wouldn't be your scene.'

'Well, maybe under different circumstances. I'm just not sure I can do ten days of intensive family time.'

Emily couldn't really argue with that. With the exception of Mr Hunter, Jamie's family were absolute horrors.

'So who are you spending Christmas with?' she asked,

wondering which local family had offered to take him in like a Dickensian orphan.

Jamie didn't say anything for a moment, and Emily looked at him as the penny dropped. 'You're kidding.'

'I'll be with the horses, and the stable hands will be back on Boxing Day. They love Christmas hours, we pay triple time.' He laughed at Emily's horrified face. 'Don't look all sorry for me, I really don't mind.'

But Emily did mind. She minded a lot, as it happened. In her world Christmas was about togetherness and laughter and spending time with the people you loved. Jamie being here alone just wasn't right, so the words were out of her mouth before she could stop them. 'Why don't you come home with me?'

'I've been thinking,' said Emily as they drove down the A11. She was on a hands-free call to Jamie, who was in a blue VW Golf behind her; it was another Bowford car that any of the staff could use for running estate errands. He'd easily found festive cover for the horses, but he still needed to get back for Boxing Day and there were no trains. So they were driving to Chichester in two separate cars.

'Have you changed your mind? Should I take the next exit and go back?'

'No, of course not, you idiot. But I think you need to pretend to be my boyfriend.'

'Wow,' said Jamie with a short laugh. 'I feel like this is all moving too fast.'

'Ha ha,' said Emily sarcastically, overtaking a coach that was crawling down the inside lane. 'I just think you being a friend feels more weird.'

128

'More weird than you arriving home for Christmas with a boyfriend they didn't know about.'

'Even more weird than that, yes. Anyway, we've only been dating a week.'

'OK, I'll be your pretend boyfriend. Have we slept together yet or is it still early days? Just in case your dad asks.'

'You're SO funny. It's early days and I'm not that kind of girl,' said Emily, blotting out memories of teenage blow jobs on the ancient stone bench in Chichester market cross. 'You'll be on the air bed in the lounge anyway.'

'Oh well, in that case I'm not coming.'

'Also you mustn't tell them you're a Hunter. They think you work in the stables.'

'I do work in the stables. That's my actual job.'

'I know, but if they find out who you really are, Mum will lose her shit.'

'Fine by me. I'll be Just Jamie. Like Prince, or Madonna.'

'Thank you,' Emily laughed. 'This is the maddest thing I've ever done.'

'I know, but I promise to be the best houseguest ever.'

'We'll stop at the next services. I need a coffee and you need to raid M&S for foodie gifts.'

'You're the boss.'

Emily smiled and pressed the button on the steering wheel to end the call, then took a few deep breaths to ready herself for the call with her mum. She was banking on Carol's inability to resist a stray with a sob story, and the fact that Jamie's unexpected arrival would be offset by the breaking news that Emily had a handsome new boyfriend.

'Hey, Mum,' she said.

'Moomin? Are you OK?' said Carol, her voice panicked. 'Have you broken down?'

'No, I'm fine, Mum. I'm on the A11.'

'Is it busy? Are you stuck in traffic?'

Emily rolled her eyes. 'No, everything's moving nicely. The satnav says I'll be home by five.'

'God, don't tell your dad you're using that, he'll think you're on your way to Aberdeen. Your brother's due around five too. I'm all on edge, I can't relax until you're all here. I haven't even had a drink yet.'

Emily glanced at the clock on the dashboard; it was barely 2 p.m. She took a deep breath and plunged in. 'Listen, Mum. You remember the guy you met last weekend? Jamie, who works in the stables?'

'How could I forget?' asked Carol. 'Very handsome, lovely eyes.'

'That's the one. Look, I can't give you the whole story, but he and I are kind of seeing each other, and he doesn't have anywhere to go for Christmas so he's coming home with me.'

There was an extended silence. 'What, today?' squealed Carol. 'You're bringing Jamie home with you today?'

'Yes,' said Emily, crossing her fingers on the steering wheel. 'He's in the car behind me right now. He's got to be back by Boxing Day.'

'Bloody hell, Moo,' said Carol. 'It's a bit short notice. I'm not sure I've got enough Kievs.'

'I can pop out to Iceland later,' said Emily. 'I'm really sorry, but he was going to spend Christmas on his own.'

'Where are his family?' gasped Carol, her voice full of concern.

Emily crossed her fingers to offset the incoming lie. 'He hasn't really said, but I think he finds it very difficult to spend time with them.'

'Oh, poor lamb,' sighed Carol. 'It must be bad if he was planning to spend Christmas alone. Well, of course we'll make him welcome. I'll ask your dad to get the other airbed out of the loft.'

'Thanks, Mum,' said Emily. 'He's brought his own duvet and pillow. Please don't ask him about the family thing, I think it's a bit complicated.'

'I wouldn't dream of it,' said Carol, who was almost certainly already dreaming of it. By the time they arrived she would have honed a fictional narrative that involved a childhood with an evil father who locked him in a coal shed and a mother who drank to dull the pain of her cursed existence.

'We'll see you in a few hours,' said Emily.

'All right, love. I'm glad you and Jamie have got together. He seemed a bit smitten at the party.'

Emily laughed. 'How would you know? You were so pissed you could see through time.'

'I know, but what a night we had.'

'Moomin, you're home!' yelled Carol three hours later, pulling her into a huge hug. 'Oh, this is just lovely.'

Emily lugged two carrier bags of M&S food and drink inside, wondering what must be going through Jamie's head right now. Surprised by how small their house was? Horrified by the rainbow fairy lights and the knitted elves hanging from the bannisters? Emily couldn't look at him, just in case.

'Thanks for having me, Mrs Wilkinson,' he said. 'I'm really sorry it was such short notice.'

'Don't be daft and call me Carol,' she said, wrapping him into an unnecessarily lingering hug. 'You're a bonus Christmas treat. Come on through and I'll get the kettle on.' He turned and gave Emily a grin as her mother dragged him off, and Emily allowed herself to breathe.

'You all right, Moo?' said Martin, appearing from the kitchen. 'Mum stolen your new man already? Come on, I'll help you get your bags in.'

Martin swapped his slippers for a pair of black Crocs that lived by the front door, then followed Emily back outside. Everything felt different here; Emily couldn't explain it, but even the Chichester air smelled like home.

'All OK then?' said Martin, which was Dad code for 'Is your new man treating you in a way I would approve of?'

'Yeah, I'm good,' said Emily, handing him the bags of presents. 'Really good, actually. Happy to be home.'

Martin nodded and pulled her into a hug. 'That's all right then.'

Jamie eased himself into family life at the Wilkinson house as though he was entirely comfortable in this world, giving no indication that he'd spent his life in a huge house on a two-thousand-acre estate. If he was taken aback by the gaudy Christmas tree and the shabby furniture in the tiny rooms, he didn't let on. Instead he drank Carol's tea, then switched to beer when Emily's brother David arrived with Joanna and their two boys, nine-year-old Billy and seven-year-old Charlie. Emily hadn't seen her brother's family since the summer and felt the happy anticipation of proper time together to catch up. It was a shame Simon couldn't make it, but the house already felt like it was full to bursting.

Emily cornered Carol in the kitchen to discuss the sleeping arrangements, worried that Jamie's arrival had made things difficult. 'Where are Billy and Charlie sleeping, Mum?' she asked. On previous visits they'd shared the second bedroom with their parents, but they felt a bit old for that now.

'They'll have to go in with David and Jo,' said Carol, 'unless you have a better idea.'

'Why don't they take my room?' suggested Emily. 'Billy can have my bed and Charlie can sleep on the airbed on the floor. Give David and Jo a bit of space.'

'Where are you going to go?'

'I can sleep on the sofa down here, and Jamie can have the other airbed.'

'Ohhhh,' said Carol with a theatrical wink. 'I see what's going on.'

Emily blushed. 'No, it's not that. We haven't . . .'

'What, you haven't done it yet?' whispered Carol.

'No, of course not,' said Emily, trying to look scandalised at the suggestion. 'We literally got together last week.'

'All right, blessed Virgin Mary,' said Carol, holding up her hands. 'If you don't mind being downstairs, that would be lovely for David and Jo. And better for the boys too, I expect.'

'No problem,' said Emily, plodding back upstairs to retrieve her suitcase. Somehow she'd managed two Christmases dating a man she couldn't tell her parents about, and now she'd brought a man home who was only pretending to be her boyfriend. *Nice work, Wilkinson, you've really got your shit together.*

'Jamie,' said David over dinner of chicken Kievs, chips and peas, thankfully cooked properly by Carol rather than cremated by Martin. 'Is there any chance that you can play chess?'

Jamie nodded. 'I can, actually. My dad . . . used to work for a software company that had an online chess game. So I played a lot as a kid.'

Emily smiled to herself. She was pretty sure Mr Hunter had owned the company that created one of the early versions of online chess.

'FINALLY,' said David, holding his beer aloft in celebration. 'After a lifetime of these philistines, there's a chess player in the family.'

'Steady on,' said Emily, not wanting to make Jamie run for the hills.

'Do we still have a chess set, Dad?' David asked.

Martin nodded. 'In the cupboard under the stairs, next to the KerPlunk.'

'This chicken is lovely, Carol,' said Jamie, polishing off the last bit of his Kiev.

'It's from Iceland,' she said.

'What, the country?' asked Jamie, his brow furrowed in confusion.

'No, the shop,' laughed Carol. 'He's funny, this one.'

After dinner Carol and Martin headed into the lounge to watch a Disney film with their grandsons, while Jamie stayed in the dining room to play chess and drink beer with David.

Emily and Jo went into the kitchen to open a bottle of prosecco and wash up.

'He's an absolute catch, Em,' said Jo. 'Proper dishy.'

Emily had always liked Jo; she'd met David at university and now worked as a primary school teacher in Newcastle. David had been a bit wild in his youth, but Jo had convinced him to settle down and have a family. They clearly adored each other and their boys and seemed to have a happy life up north. Emily had been up to visit them a few times and loved the city; she just wished she could go more often.

'Yeah, he's great,' she said vaguely, 'but it's early days.'

'What does he do again?'

'He works on the estate where I work. Looks after the horses.'

'What do you know about horses?' asked Jo with a grin.

'Not much, but I'm learning. Jamie's teaching me to ride.'

'I bet he is,' snorted Jo, and they both fell about laughing until David came in to ask them to be quiet because he was attempting the Scandinavian Defence.

Emily sat cross-legged on the sofa in her pyjamas, hugging her pillow. It was nearly midnight and the house was finally silent, David having gone off to bed once he'd finally claimed a chess win. Jamie was lying on his side on the airbed, propping his head up on one elbow. He was wearing a fitted white T-shirt and it took all that remained of Emily's self-control not to crawl over and lick him.

'Sorry if my family are a bit much,' she whispered.

'I think they're amazing,' said Jamie. 'I've never really spent time with a family like this, where everyone actually likes each other.'

'We don't have much, but there's plenty of love to go round,' said Emily. 'Sorry, that sounds really cheesy.'

'It's true though, they're brilliant. I'm really glad I'm here.'

Emily smiled, her heart full. 'I'm glad too. And as an added bonus, you get to meet Kelly tomorrow.'

'I can't wait,' he said, punching his pillow and settling down on his back.

'I have a question for you,' said Emily.

'Go on,' he said, sounding nervous.

'Did you let my brother win at chess?'

Jamie laughed. 'Yes. He's really not very good, and I wanted to go to bed. I don't think he noticed.'

'Incredible deception skills. Goodnight, Jamie.'

'Sleep well, Moomin.'

'Get out.'

CHAPTER EIGHTEEN

Christmas traditions were a big deal in the Wilkinson household, and Christmas Eve had followed the same schedule for as long as Emily could remember. It started with sausage sandwiches for brunch, then into town in the afternoon to pick up any last-minute gifts or have a couple of pints of festive spirit. There was a carol service in the local church at 6 p.m., then home for a takeaway Indian or Chinese, decided by a family vote. If there was an equal split, the decision was taken on the flip of a chocolate coin.

For Emily, the festive trip into town was an opportunity to meet up with Kelly and Beth and give them their presents, although in pre-Beth years they'd often spent it drinking in a pub that was a go-to haunt for old school friends who were back for Christmas. This year Beth was four, so old enough to be off-the-wall excited about Christmas, and Emily couldn't wait to see them both.

She explained all this to Jamie as he deflated his airbed and packed his bedding away behind the sofa, worried that he might be finding all the organised fun a bit overwhelming.

'It's fine,' he said, 'I'm really happy to go with the flow. Just point me in the right direction.'

Emily smiled. 'You make a good fake boyfriend, Jamie Hunter.'

'Just Jamie, remember? I'm like Prince. Also, what did you

tell your mum about my family situation? She keeps talking to me like I'm a battered child from a broken home.'

'Ah,' said Emily awkwardly. 'My mum is prone to melodrama. Have you seen her bookshelf?'

'Yes,' said Jamie, 'she told me to help myself last night, and particularly recommended a story about a child who was forced to live in a cold stable until he finally escaped. She wouldn't give away the ending, but I sensed he might have murdered his family.'

'That sounds festive.'

'It was either that or a steamy saga about a nymphomaniac duke who seduces virgin kitchen maids.'

'Oh, those are her absolute faves. Never ends well for the kitchen maids, though.'

Jamie raised his eyebrows. 'Never?'

Emily gave him a significant look. 'Never.'

Emily met Kelly and Beth by Chichester Cross and gave them both a huge hug. Jamie hung back to chat with the rest of the family while Emily swung Beth up on to her hip and expressed absolute shock and awe at how big she'd grown in the few weeks since she'd last seen her. Kelly stared at Jamie openmouthed until she caught his eye and got a smile in return.

'Is that him?' asked Kelly. 'Fuck me, he's absolutely gorgeous. Proper hunky. He looks like Jamie Dornan.' Kelly was wearing an acid-green bomber jacket with denim shorts, opaque tights and platform trainers. The green jacket and scarlet hair made an oddly festive combination, like a punk elf.

'Ssh, he'll hear you,' said Emily, the penny finally dropping on who Jamie reminded her of.

'Why didn't you tell me?'

'We've literally been on two dates. Both horse riding, there's been very little . . . other stuff.' This was technically true, which made Emily feel better about not being entirely honest with Kelly. She'd tell her everything once Jamie had gone back to Norfolk.

'And you've brought him home for Christmas,' said Kelly. 'Christ, you don't hang about.'

'He was going to spend it on his own otherwise.'

'What is he, some kind of sexpot orphan?'

Emily glanced over, hoping Jamie wasn't listening. 'Seriously, will you keep your voice down? He's got some family issues. It's complicated.'

'Does he have a brother?' asked Kelly.

'He does,' said Emily. 'But you definitely wouldn't.'

Kelly narrowed her eyes. 'Why do I feel like there's something you're not telling me?'

'I have loads to tell you, but now isn't the time.'

Kelly nodded, mollified for now. 'Are you here for New Year?'

'Yeah,' said Emily. 'Can I come over?'

'Sure. We'll get Beth off to bed and have a party for two.'

'Why do I have to go to bed?' asked Beth. 'I want to have a party.'

'What about a hot chocolate instead?' asked Emily.

Beth thought about it for a moment, chewing the end of her grubby finger. 'Can I have a hot chocolate AND a party?'

Jamie wandered over after a few minutes, putting his arm around Emily in a boyfriendly way. It instantly made her feel a bit anxious, but she couldn't deny that it felt nice.

'You must be Kelly,' he said, giving her a kiss on the cheek. 'I've heard a lot about you.'

Kelly gave him her best smile. 'I haven't heard nearly enough about you, but the day is young.'

Emily glared at Kelly, but Jamie seemed unfazed. 'I've been invited to the pub with your family,' he said to Emily. 'Is that a good idea?'

'It's a very bad idea,' interrupted Kelly. 'They'll almost certainly meet my parents in Mulligan's and they'll all be absolutely hammered on Guinness by teatime.'

'Are your family Irish?' asked Jamie.

Kelly grabbed a hank of her dyed scarlet hair and held it away from her head. 'What, you think this isn't real?'

'It's up to you,' said Emily, trying to imagine how she might behave if Jamie was her actual boyfriend. 'We're just going to mooch about the shops for a bit, so you're welcome to come with us. Or you can go to the pub. You can always leave if it's getting heavy, say we've arranged to meet up.'

'Good idea,' said Jamie. 'I'll do that.'

He gave Emily an awkward kiss on the cheek, then turned to Kelly. 'By the way, I'm definitely putting "sexpot orphan" on my CV.'

Kelly hooted with laughter as he walked away.

'I like him,' she said. 'Right, let's go shopping. Have you bought my present yet?'

'There's a whole bag for you and Beth in the car,' said Emily, 'I'll give it to you later. I'd quite like to get something for Jamie.'

'What does he like? Other than you butt-naked on horseback like Lady Godiva.'

'Jesus, Kel,' laughed Emily. 'But yes. He likes horses.'

140

'OK. So something outdoorsy, then. Maybe a nice scarf?'

'Fine, but it needs to be a posh one.'

'Why?' asked Kelly. 'He doesn't seem that posh.'

You have no idea, thought Emily, dragging her friend off in the direction of a shop that sold men's designer labels. Maybe Ted Baker would work, something a bit fancy but still OK to get splattered with mud and shit.

Jamie reappeared a couple of hours later, very obviously a bit drunk, but also happy to give Beth a shoulder ride back to the car. Emily offered to drive Kelly and Beth home so they didn't have to get the last bus on Christmas Eve, trying not to care what Jamie might think of Kelly's battered mobile home on a caravan park on the outskirts of town. If he was surprised or shocked he said nothing, instead helping them inside with their bags of presents and shopping before wishing them both a Merry Christmas.

'You love those two a lot, don't you?' he asked as they drove back towards town.

Emily nodded. 'Kelly's been my best friend since the day we started primary school. She's smart and funny and the kindest person I know. She's just had a shit time of it.'

'What happened?' Jamie asked.

Emily shrugged. 'The usual. Her dad left when she was little, Kel and her brother got passed around a lot. No money, not much love either. She spent a lot of time at our house when we were kids. Left school at sixteen and trained as a hairdresser. Her mum's remarried and in a much better place, so she helps out with Beth when she can.'

'Is Beth's dad still around?'

141

Emily shook her head. 'He did a runner when Beth was a blue line on a pregnancy test. No great loss.'

'Wow, that's tough.'

'She works hard and she's a great mum. The caravan isn't much but it's hers, and it's a nice little community down there. She looks after her money and doesn't owe anybody anything, there are plenty worse off. I just wish she had a bit more time for herself, a chance to meet someone amazing.'

Jamie nodded but didn't say anything.

'Are you up for some carols?' she asked, keen to lighten the mood.

Jamie looked at her and nodded. 'I'm ready to ding dong merrily on high.'

'Talking of ding dongs, the traditional Christmas Eve Indian versus Chinese debate can get quite heated. You might want to think about which team you're on.'

'What's going to earn me the most brownie points?'

Emily thought about it for a second. 'Dad, Jo, Billy and I will choose Indian. Mum, David and Charlie love a Chinese. So you can either score me a chicken pasanda or send it to deadlock.'

'Oh God, this is too much responsibility.'

'Which one do you actually like best?'

'I've grown up in a house with a half-Indian/half-Chinese chef. It's an impossible choice.'

Emily laughed. 'Aww, you poor baby.'

On the walk back from the church carol service, Jamie took Emily's hand and didn't let go. It gave Emily that feeling again, a mix of nerves and a radiating warmth in the pit of her stomach that she didn't want to end.

'I'm not sure you should do that,' she said, looking straight ahead.

'I thought we were pretending to be a couple. This felt like a couply thing.'

She stopped and looked at him, gently pulling her hand away. His face was pink from the cold and his pupils were still dilated from an afternoon in the pub and mulled wine in the church hall. He really was unfeasibly handsome.

'I'm really glad you're here, Jamie. But I haven't changed my mind.'

'I know,' he said quietly. 'This isn't a big Christmas seduction thing, that wouldn't be fair. It just feels like a nice thing to do.'

'OK,' she said with a shy smile. 'Then I'll allow it.'

He smiled and carried on walking, taking her hand again and keeping hold of it all the way home.

The dinner decision was ten minutes of intense drama, where everybody argued good-naturedly and tried to change everybody else's mind, knowing that they would all pick the same thing they always did but enjoying the fun anyway. Jamie added a new dimension to the battle, and various stories were told of poor kitchen hygiene and a dead wasp in the chow mein to attempt to sway his decision. In the end he went for Chinese, letting the chocolate coin flip decide. Indian won, so Emily was happy.

Everyone pored over the menu, then Emily used the phone in the kitchen to order everything, since her parents refused to pay for Deliveroo when the Taj Mahal was a five-minute walk away and you could just pick it up. Emily and Jamie walked up to the restaurant together, Emily's pocket stuffed with £100 in cash that her mother had saved for the occasion.

'I'd like to pay,' said Jamie, getting out his card as the owner, Amrit, gave them the final bill. Amrit and Emily had been in the same class at school, and his family had run this restaurant for the best part of fifty years.

'Mum and Dad always pay,' said Emily. 'It's a family tradition.'

'Still, I'd like to pay,' said Jamie stubbornly. 'As a way of saying thank you. I won't say anything, you can just give them the cash back after I've gone.'

Amrit looked at Jamie, then at Emily. He raised his eyebrows in question, and she nodded. He took Jamie's card and processed the payment, then handed over two huge carrier bags of food. 'Free poppadoms and naans,' he said. 'It's Christmas.'

'Thanks, Amrit,' said Emily with a smile. 'You're an angel.'

Amrit grinned. 'Merry Christmas, beautiful Emily. And to you, Emily's even more beautiful friend.'

'You can't have him, Amrit,' laughed Emily. 'Even though it's Christmas.'

'I am destined to be alone for ever,' said Amrit dramatically.

Dinner was what the Wilkinsons called 'open combat', where all the dishes were dumped on the table and everybody piled in. If you stood any chance of eating what you'd actually ordered, you had to get in quick and not be afraid to use your elbows.

Emily watched as Jamie joined in with the fun, pretending to wrestle Charlie for a naan bread and batting away David's spoon as he tried to annexe the lamb rogan josh.

'What do your family normally do on Christmas Eve, Jamie?' asked Carol, earning her a glare from Emily. 'What?' she said. 'I'm just asking.'

'We don't really have a fixed tradition,' he said. 'It depends where everyone is.'

'So last year, for example,' said Carol, refusing to let it go. 'Where did you spend Christmas then?'

Jamie chewed his food thoughtfully. 'With my mum and my sister,' he said. 'We saw my dad too, but only on Christmas Day.' Emily remembered reviewing all the arrangements for last year when she'd been making bookings for this year's trip – Jamie had spent Christmas in Switzerland with Tanya and Catherine, but Mr Hunter had only been able to join them for twenty-four hours before he flew to Cape Town to spend a week with an old school friend who was terminally ill. Adam and Victoria had skipped Verbier last year and taken the children skiing in Colorado instead.

'Oh, that's nice,' said Carol, looking round the table, her face arranged into a caring smile. 'Where does your dad live, then?'

'Mum, can we leave it?' said Emily, feeling a bubble of panic.

'Is he in prison?' asked Carol, patting Jamie's hand. 'I did say to Martin that he was probably in prison. It's all right, my love. You mustn't be ashamed. Your parents' bad life choices are not your fault.'

Jamie smiled bleakly at Emily, whose shoulders were shaking with laughter. Her mum might have the subtlety of a sledgehammer, but you had to admit she was comedy gold.

CHAPTER NINETEEN

'I've got you a present,' whispered Jamie in the early hours of Christmas Day. They were alone in the lounge, enjoying the window of peace and quiet between two days of festive chaos.

'I've got you two,' Emily replied with a smile. 'Shall we open them now?'

'Don't see why not.'

He rummaged behind the sofa and pulled out a small gift bag decorated with snowmen. Inside was a pair of riding gloves in the softest brown leather and suede, a perfect fit on her pale hands.

'They're beautiful, thank you.'

'Nothing worse than being cold when you're riding.'

'My thinking was on similar lines,' she said, handing him the first tissue-wrapped parcel. In the end she'd chosen a soft lambswool scarf in classic Paul Smith stripes, not too big or bulky. Jamie unfolded it and immediately wrapped it around his neck.

'Oh, this is lovely. I don't actually own a proper scarf, my chin is always cold.'

'Is having a warm chin considered unmanly in the equestrian community?'

'Probably, but I'm going to wear it anyway.'

Emily smiled happily and handed over the second parcel, already feeling shy and uncertain about it. It was the second selfie she'd taken the previous weekend, of her and Jamie framing Rupert's dopey face, both of them grinning into the camera. She'd ordered a print online and put it in a pale wooden frame, not sure if it felt a bit personal considering she'd rejected his advances a few hours before it was taken. But it was such a great picture of all of them, and she wanted him to have a copy.

'I love it,' he said. 'We look like proud parents of a giant horse baby.'

Emily laughed, feeling like maybe things were going to be OK. Lustful feelings for Jamie aside, she realised how much she liked him. Maybe she could separate that from the physical attraction and they could make this work. Or maybe she was just kidding herself.

Carol's Christmas lunch was dished up at 12.30 p.m. sharp, and by 2 p.m. everyone was stuffed with turkey, roast potatoes and all the trimmings, with paper hats askew. Pudding would be served in a couple of hours, but in the meantime everyone was free to find a corner of the house to nap or watch TV. Billy and Charlie had commandeered the TV in Carol and Martin's bedroom to play on their new Xbox, which David confessed to having bought from a guy at work who couldn't say exactly where it had come from. But it was brand-new and considerably cheaper than in the shops, so he hadn't asked too many questions. Carol and Martin were watching a Bond film in the lounge with a bottle of Baileys, while David and Jo headed upstairs for a nap.

Emily and Jamie offered to tackle the washing-up. He admitted privately to Emily that he'd never actually had to wash dishes by hand before, but it was really no different from scrubbing tack in a bucket of soapy water. Considering the day had started at 5 a.m. and had been absolute chaos ever since, she was impressed with how he was bearing up. But even she felt like the walls were closing in, so maybe it was time for some fresh air.

'Do you fancy getting out for a bit?' she asked, putting a pile of dry plates in the cupboard.

'I'd love to,' replied Jamie, pulling the plug out to empty the sink for the umpteenth time. 'Where shall we go?'

'We could go to the beach.'

'Sounds great,' he said, drying his hands on a tea towel. 'I'll get my new scarf.'

'And some shorts you can swim in,' said Emily with a grin.

Jamie stopped and stared at her. 'You want me to get in the sea? On Christmas Day?'

Emily shrugged. 'You don't have to. You can just watch from the beach and hold my flask of tea.'

'Absolutely not,' said Jamie, shaking his head determinedly. 'If you're swimming, so am I.'

The beach at West Wittering was cold but calm, with a light breeze ruffling the marram grass along the dunes. There were a few couples and families out walking dogs and flying kites, but most people were sensible enough to be at home in front of the telly. It would be dark in an hour, but for now the light was a golden glow in a beautiful rose-pink sky.

Emily led Jamie through the hedge from the sandy car park and along the short row of beach huts, stopping at one painted in blue and white stripes. It had a wooden deck at the front with a short slope down to the beach, and at high

148

tide it was only twenty metres or so to the water. She put the flask of tea on the deck and draped her towel over the rail.

'So how does this work?' asked Jamie.

'We leave our towels and clothes here, then get in the water. Swim about for a bit, then come back and get dressed again.'

'You're insane,' he laughed.

'It's invigorating,' she said, kicking off her trainers. 'The cold will burn off all those pigs in blankets and make room for trifle.' She took off her jumper, her arms prickling with goosebumps. She already had her swimsuit on underneath. 'Make sure you turn your clothes the right way out so they're easier to put back on.'

Jamie took a deep breath and pulled off his sweatshirt. His chest underneath was bare, dusted with pale hair. He was tall and lean but with broad, strong shoulders. Emily tried not to stare as he removed his jeans, revealing fitted black boxer shorts and strong thighs.

'Hurry up,' she laughed. 'Last one in's a rotten egg.'

He grabbed her hand and started to sprint down the beach, his head thrown back with laughter.

'Don't stop or you'll never get in,' shouted Emily. 'Just keep running.'

They hit the icy water and kept going, shrieking from the shock of the cold. The water was shallow, and they were a good distance out before it covered their thighs and they couldn't run any more. Jamie took a deep breath and dived in, gasping like a fish as he resurfaced.

'Jesus fucking Christ!'

'Just try to breathe,' said Emily, swimming in short strokes around him as all the air was shoved out of her lungs. 'Don't think about it, you'll be fine in a second.'

He stood up in water up to his chest, watching her swim. 'How do you make that look so easy?'

'Years of practice,' she said. 'Swim with me for a minute, then we'll head back in.'

Jamie pushed off and swam beside her, unable to manage anything more than a gasping breaststroke.

'Any warmer yet?' she asked after a couple of minutes.

'Yeah,' he squeaked. 'But I don't think I'll ever father children.'

Emily laughed. 'Come on, let's get out.' They waded back towards the shore until it was shallow enough to start running again. It felt colder out than in now, so they said nothing other than the occasional swearword until they'd both frantically towelled off and pulled their clothes back on.

'Better?' asked Emily, handing Jamie a plastic cup of hot tea from the flask.

'Much,' he replied, hugging it with pink hands as his teeth chattered. 'What kind of masochist are you?'

'I used to come here all the time,' she said. 'Somewhere to swim away all my teenage angst. I hardly ever do it now.'

'I'll take you to Holkham or Brancaster,' he said. 'But maybe in the summer.'

Emily sat on the deck next to him and hugged her knees, her wet hair coiled into a heavy bun and tucked into the hood of her sweatshirt. Her skin tingled under her clothes, although it was hard to know whether that was the cold or how close Jamie was. He wrapped his scarf around both of them and hugged her close, passing her the cup so she could take a sip.

The time between her turning her face to smile at him and him kissing her was probably only a few seconds, but it felt like whole minutes of wondering if it was going to happen, seeing the blazing look in his eyes and knowing it was going to happen, then simply giving in to the inevitability of it and closing her eyes to wait. It was the softest, gentlest kiss – not hard or passionate, more tentative and curious. His lips tasted of salt and tea and wind.

Jamie pulled away and brushed his fingers across her cheek, tucking a loose strand of wet hair behind her ear. 'There. That wasn't so bad.'

Emily smiled, pushing away all the tangled, complicated thoughts. She'd deal with them later. 'You trapped me with your scarf.'

'I have no regrets.' He buried his face in her wet hair and kissed her head. 'I have to go back to Norfolk soon,' he said. It was his way of saying *let's not talk about this now, just enjoy the moment*, which was fine with Emily.

She nodded and took his hand. 'I'm going to stay here for New Year, but I'll be back on the second.'

'Do you want to carry on with the riding lessons?' Another unspoken question – *have I completely messed this up?*

'Yeah, definitely. Do you want more sea-swimming lessons?'

Jamie furrowed his brow. 'Hmm. Can I think about it?'

'Well, talk about a catch,' said Carol as Jamie drove off in the VW Golf, waving at the assembled family out of the window.

Martin nodded. 'You've done well there, Moomin. He's a nice lad.'

'Good at chess too,' said David. 'Gave me a run for my money.'

Emily didn't say anything as they trudged back inside, only half-hearing David saying something about a family game of Monopoly. She peeled off into the lounge and fell on to the sofa next to a sleeping Rudy, grabbing the blanket that Leon had given her for Christmas and dragging it over her legs. It was made from a hotchpotch of rainbow-coloured knitted squares; judging by the dropped stitches and the generally wonky nature of the whole thing, Emily suspected that Leon had knitted it himself. The idea of his huge hairy fingers tackling such an intricate project made her want to cry, and then feel sick about how devastated he would be if he found out she'd kissed Jamie.

She picked at the blanket as she tried to unravel her emotions – sad that Jamie was gone, but relieved that she no longer had to pretend that they were a couple. Was it still pretending if he'd kissed her on the beach? It was just one kiss, there weren't even any tongues. Did that count? She wished she could speak to Kelly, but she was at her mum's and would be five drinks deep by now. And anyway, it felt too messy to explain. She'd talk to her at New Year, get everything out in the open.

Her phone buzzed, a WhatsApp message from Jamie.

Just pulled over to say thanks for my best Christmas ever. Jx

Emily thought about her reply, her heart pounding. *Loved every minute. See you next year. Ex*

Rudy turned over on to his back, demanding belly rubs. Emily stroked him absent-mindedly, her head full of thoughts of Jamie and the beach and the kiss and what would happen when she got back to Bowford Manor. *The absolute state of you*, she thought. *You've gone and done it again. Do you NEVER learn?*

152

CHAPTER TWENTY

'You need to make a decision, Moomin,' said Martin. 'The weather forecast isn't going to change.'

It was the morning of New Year's Eve, and Emily stood by the kitchen window watching the snow fall in fat, heavy flakes from a leaden sky. There were already several inches on the ground and the Met Office website had released a weather warning for the next two days.

'We're going to head off in a bit,' said David, his face grim. Jo was already retrieving toys from every corner of the house with Billy and Charlie; Emily could hear her exasperated yelling about putting stuff IN THE BAG and not taking things back out to play with. 'I've been looking at the traffic reports, clockwise round the M25 is much less snowy. We could drive in convoy as far as the A1; you'll be fine after that. There's no snow forecast in Norfolk until tonight.'

'It's going to get bad up there, though,' said Martin. 'The woman on breakfast telly said the whole of the east coast was going to be snowed in. But if you get back today you should be fine.'

'I was going to see in the New Year with Kelly and Beth,' said Emily, who'd been so looking forward to a night drinking cocktails in Kelly's mobile home with a bag of party poppers and a tube of Pringles, watching all the New Year celebrations on TV while she offloaded all her personal baggage. She hadn't seen Kelly at all since Christmas Eve; her friend had been flat out in the salon since the twenty-seventh. They'd pinned everything on their New Year girls' night in.

'I know, Moo,' said Carol, wringing her hands, 'but if you wait until tomorrow you could get stuck. I once read this book about two men who were trapped in a Ford Cortina for days, then they found their way to a farm in the arse end of nowhere and one of them ended up marrying the farmer's daughter.'

Everyone looked at Carol in silence.

'I know it SOUNDS like a happy story,' she snapped. 'But they nearly died. He had no fingers left to put the ring on.'

Emily stared out of the window gloomily. Her parents were right, obviously. It made way more sense to go now and get ahead of the weather, rather than getting stuck in Sussex for what could be four or five more days. 'Fine. I'll call Kelly, then pack. Can we leave in an hour?'

'I'll do you sandwiches and a flask,' said Carol, opening the much-depleted fridge. Emily had given her back the takeaway cash, but her mum refused to go shopping until they'd eaten every last scrap of leftovers. There was a good chance Emily's sandwiches would include week-old turkey and the remains of a Tesco cheese selection box that should have been laid to rest days ago. She would give them a proper send-off in the first bin she encountered.

'I'll check your car over,' said Martin. 'Put a shovel in the boot. You never know.'

'Thanks, Dad.' Emily headed into the lounge to pack. She considered dropping Jamie a WhatsApp letting him know she was driving back, but she had no idea how long it would take, or if she'd get as far as the ring road and have to turn back. There was no point worrying him.

The journey was tedious in the driving snow and poor visibility, but the motorways had been heavily gritted and the traffic kept moving, albeit at a snail's pace at times. She stopped at the services on the M25 to have lunch with David, Joanne and the kids, before they headed north on the A1. It was a longer route than the M1, but it meant they'd been able to stay with her for longer. Having David and Jo in the car behind had relieved a lot of her anxiety about driving in these conditions, and she was sorry to say goodbye.

By the time she turned on to the M11 the snow was thinning out to light flurries, and half an hour later there wasn't a flake to be seen, although the sky felt heavy and ominous. She wondered if Leon and Anna had returned early too, or if she'd find Bowford Manor deserted. The charter company had confirmed that the return trip from Switzerland was still scheduled for the day after tomorrow, so clearly the Hunters hadn't felt the need to cut their holiday short.

Driving through the familiar gates of Bowford Manor felt like a relief after such a long and stressful drive, and even more so when it became clear that neither Anna nor Leon had returned. The lights were on in Jamie's apartment above the stables, however, so she spent ten minutes lugging her bags up to her room and freshening up her pale and tired face before heading over to say hello. She found him in the yard, stroking a beautiful black horse over the stable door.

'I thought you weren't back until Wednesday,' he said, looking surprised but gratifyingly happy to see her. He pulled her into an awkward hug, then hustled her into the relative warmth of the tack room.

'I decided to beat the snow,' she said with a smile.

'Yeah, I saw on the news we've got some heavy weather coming. I'm just going to take a spin around the estate and make sure everything's secure.'

'Can I help?'

'No, it's fine, you're better off indoors.' He paused for a second. 'What are your plans for this evening?'

'I was supposed to be getting hammered with Kelly, but that's gone out of the window.'

'Do you want to come over for supper? I was planning to light a campfire out the back and watch the snow.'

Emily hesitated, then nodded. Avoiding Jamie wasn't the answer, particularly on New Year's Eve. And if she was honest, spending time with him was the only thing she wanted to do. 'Sounds good. Can I bring anything?'

Jamie thought for a second. 'You could raid the freezer for a couple of Sam's dinners?'

'No problem. I'll see you later.'

Jamie smiled. 'Wrap up warm.'

She headed back to the house, thinking that if the heat between her legs spread through her body much further, she wouldn't need a coat at all.

Emily lay in the bath, steam billowing around the cold room and condensing on the tiny windows. The hot water was blissful, even though it felt strange to be in such a huge house alone. Usually there were voices or doors closing or the distant hum of a vacuum cleaner; Bowford Manor was never silent.

She supposed she could have used one of the family bathrooms – they probably had huge sunken Jacuzzis and gold toilets. But knowing her luck Anna would come back from whatever troll bridge she'd stayed under for Christmas and catch her shaving her legs in Mr Hunter's bathtub. And anyway, her little attic bathroom was perfectly fine even though the pipes clanked and the windows were draughty. She'd lit a scented candle and added some fancy bubble bath to the water, both Christmas presents from David and Jo. It all felt quite decadent.

Her phone rang, and a glance at the screen told her it was Kelly. She smiled, knowing that Beth was probably having a nap and her friend was ringing to check she was back in one piece.

'Hey, Kel.' She put the phone on speaker and balanced it on the side of the bath.

'Where are you?' asked Kelly. 'You sound like you're down a well.'

'I'm in the bath. Got back an hour ago.'

'Have you seen Norfolk's answer to Jamie Dornan yet?'

Emily smiled. 'I have. I'm going over there later.'

'I can't believe you've abandoned me in favour of shagging in the New Year with a hot man.'

'I can't imagine that's going to happen,' said Emily, who had already imagined it happening in multiple scenarios, all of them steamier than this bathroom. 'Is it still snowing?'

'Yeah,' said Kelly, undeterred. 'Coming down in sheets. Have you shaved your bikini line?'

'No,' lied Emily. Her stomach squirmed with guilt, and she wished she could be more honest, tell Kelly about how she'd messed things up by falling in love with Mark, and was now on the cusp of repeating history with Jamie. But it felt like too big a conversation to have on the phone.

'Have you got any New Year's resolutions?' she asked, keen to change the subject.

'I've got two,' said Kelly. 'First I'm going to take advantage of Beth being at school and actually look into opening my own salon, rather than just thinking about it.'

'Good for you, Kel,' said Emily, and she really meant it. She thought about the money she was stashing away for a future deposit on a house, and whether instead she could use some of it to help Kelly get things off the ground. She'd give it some more thought before she floated the idea and got Kelly's hopes up.

'I've got a bit of money saved, and Mum says she and Dad will help if they can.' Emily pulled a dubious face and was glad Kelly couldn't see her – her mum and stepdad didn't have two pound coins to rub together and were constantly sponging off their daughter.

'We'll all help,' she said, keeping the details of that offer vague for now. 'What's the other resolution?'

'I'm getting back on the dating horse, Em. Relaunching myself like Cher in the nineties.'

'Okaaay,' laughed Emily. Carol had always said that Kelly had been born a decade after her time; her love for comeback Cher knew no bounds. 'What's the plan?'

'It's in two parts,' said Kelly, doing her official TV presenter voice. 'Part one involves no-strings sex with men who have their own teeth and hair. Part two is about longterm love with someone who isn't a total fuckboy or a ghosting shit.'

Emily raised her eyebrows. 'Wow. That's a pretty low bar you've set there, Kel.'

'I'm a thirty-year-old single mum who lives in a caravan park. I can't afford to be fussy.'

'Bullshit. You're a successful woman of independent means with your own home and a beautiful daughter. You can definitely afford to be fussy.'

'See, this is why I love you,' squealed Kelly. 'What are your resolutions? Other than learning to ride a horse and also Jamie.'

Emily honked with laughter. 'The usual, I suppose. Be good at my job, save as much money as possible, keep up my fitness.'

Kelly yawned. 'God, how boring.'

Emily smiled sadly. 'I need to go. How about we do New Year all over again, next time I'm back in Chi?'

'Can I still have party poppers?'

'Course.'

'Then yes, definitely. Happy New Year, mate.'

'Happy New Year, Kel. Love you.'

CHAPTER TWENTY-ONE

Emily walked over to the stables clutching two defrosted dinners, her stomach fizzing with jittery anticipation. The snow had started – just gently falling flakes for now, but with a heavy, bone-cold feeling in the air that suggested the sky might crack open at any moment.

Aside from the portentous weather, every one of Emily's instincts was telling her that this was a bad idea. It was like Dubai all over again, knowing that something was going to happen and feeling entirely powerless to stop it. She felt like she was in a car on an icy hill, sliding inexorably towards the pile-up at the bottom. She'd keep stamping on the brakes until the very last second, just to say she'd tried. But the collision was inevitable.

Jamie appeared at the door in his black padded coat, running his hand through his hair and smiling nervously. She wondered what he'd been thinking about for the past few hours; whether he'd also played out this evening in his head. He took the containers of food and put them upstairs, then came back down in his Paul Smith scarf and a blue woolly hat, carrying a bottle of champagne and two wine glasses.

'I'm afraid I don't have any champagne glasses,' he said.

'I'm not sure I can drink it without the appropriate glassware,' replied Emily in a fake posh voice.

Jamie laughed. 'Come on, it's warmer over here.' He led

her to the paddock at the back of the stables, where a crackling fire had been lit in a shallow pit. A low wooden bench was set against the wall just a few feet from the flames, forming a cover for a neat stack of logs. Jamie sat down and grabbed a couple from between his legs, then tossed them on to the fire.

The snow was falling more heavily now, settling on the hard ground like someone had shaken out a white blanket, but the swirling fat flakes fizzled out long before they reached the flames. Jamie popped the champagne cork, sending it soaring off into the darkness of the paddock, then poured it into the glasses and passed one to Emily. She took a sip and leaned against the wall, stretching her legs out towards the fire as a wave of heat washed over her. It was a feeling of pure contentment, like a cat in front of a radiator.

Jamie's arm pressed against hers as he sat back, both of them lost in the moment and not feeling the need to say anything. She let her head fall on to his shoulder as he wrapped her cold hand in the warmth of his, entwining his fingers with hers and rubbing his thumb from her wrist to her knuckle. Everything about it felt so right, like the simple satisfaction of fitting two jigsaw pieces together.

'Remind me again why we can't be together,' he asked quietly.

Emily smiled sadly, staring into the flames. 'Because I work for your dad, and when you break my heart I'll have to leave.'

Jamie turned to look at her, his expression curious. 'Why would I break your heart?'

Emily shrugged. 'Because that's what always happens to women like me. I've had six proper boyfriends since I was fourteen, and every one of them has dumped me.'

Jamie sat forward so he was fully in her eyeline. 'Are you serious?'

'Yep,' she nodded.

'How is that possible?'

Emily leaned forward, peering into the flames. 'Let's see. The first one called me frigid when I wouldn't wank him off on the school bus, then told everyone at school I'd done it anyway.' She held out her thumb, then her index finger. 'The second one dumped me by text message on a school trip to the Isle of Wight, no explanation given. The third one took my virginity, then slept with one of my friends the next day.'

Jamie's eyebrows were off the charts. 'Do you want more?' she asked, and he gave a tiny nod, clearly not sure whether he did or not.

'I had my first serious boyfriend at nineteen, and he binned me off after two years because it felt too heavy and he wanted to see other people. Then I was seeing this guy in London for about six months, we even went for a weekend to Amsterdam together. One day he completely ghosted me, just completely disappeared. I thought he was dead and got proper panicked about it, but he was just a massive stoner who hadn't realised the conversation in his head hadn't happened in real life. After that I stayed single for a while, did the casual Tinder thing, but it just made me hate myself. And then I met Mark who I was crazy about for two years until he went back to his wife.'

'Fucking hell. How do you remember all this?'

'Kelly and I each made a list a few years back, which we then set fire to.'

Jamie stared into the flames thoughtfully, saying nothing.

'OK, what about you?' asked Emily, folding her arms.

He pulled a face like he'd rather not go there, but Emily stared him down until he gave in. 'Fine, OK. I went to an all-boys school and I was shy and spotty, so no joy there. Went out with a few girls at agricultural college, but nothing serious. I've never been hugely confident with women and am not the casual-sex type, so no Tinder dates or flings with the stable girls. One serious relationship before Louisa. In both cases the issue was . . . this place.'

'What do you mean?'

'The girlfriend I had before Louisa, her name was Naomi. Worked in TV, really smart and beautiful. They filmed a period drama here; it gets used as a TV location quite a lot. Anyway, she was here for ages and we started seeing each other. Then she was off filming for weeks at a time. She wanted me to go with her, but this place is my priority. The horses, the estate, the house, they're important to me. She called Bowford 'my other woman'.'

Emily nodded but said nothing.

'Louisa went the same way, wanting me to live in London. But it's not my scene, it's all parties and beautiful people. My mother's place in LA is just as bad – I've been to visit and it's awful. Don't get me wrong, I love getting away from here sometimes, seeing new places and having fun. But I need to be able to be myself, which is a bit quiet and serious sometimes. I don't fit in anywhere else. Not the way I fit in here.'

'So out of all of those, how many times have you been dumped, and how many times have you been the dumper?'

Jamie thought about it, then dropped his gaze to the fire. 'I've always been the dumper.'

'My point exactly,' said Emily, finishing her champagne. 'Men like you do the dumping, women like me get dumped.'

'Maybe neither of us has met the right person yet,' said Jamie, warming to the subject. 'Maybe we haven't found the right fit.'

'I thought this place was the right fit.'

'It is. But your house at Christmas felt like the right fit too. I hadn't expected it to, but it did.'

Emily smiled at him, wondering if he realised what a huge compliment that was. 'They liked you a lot.'

'Yeah, well. I like you a lot.'

Emily's stomach swooped as his eyes met hers. She swallowed. 'Why?' she asked. 'I'm nothing special.'

Jamie laughed. 'Oh, is it ego hour? Fine, I'll play along. You're beautiful, but you have no idea. Do you know how rare that is? And you're kind. I heard about how gently you let Leon down. He told Sam and Sam told me, there aren't many secrets in this place. That poor guy is crazy about you.'

'But that's the problem, isn't it?' she replied. 'There are no secrets in this place. If we start seeing each other on the quiet, eventually we'll get caught. And if your dad finds out about it, I might have to leave. That's the worst possible outcome for me, I can't risk it.'

Jamie nodded, then shrugged. 'So maybe I should ask him.'

Emily laughed, then realised he was serious. 'What, like asking his permission?'

'Sure, why not? Just hypothetically.' He made quote marks with his fingers. ' "Would you have a problem if I asked your assistant out on a date, I really like her." He doesn't need to know I've already kissed you on a cold beach.'

'It sounds stupid now you've said it.'

164

'It is stupid. You're twenty-nine and I'm thirty. We're single, consenting adults. But if it makes you happy, I'll do it.'

Emily thought about it for a moment, wondering if Jamie even asking Mr Hunter might reflect badly on her. She couldn't see how. 'Fine,' she said. 'But just hypothetically. You can't tell him I know you're asking.'

Jamie fished his phone out of his pocket and swiped the screen.

'What, now?' said Emily, her heart thumping.

'No, three weeks on Tuesday,' replied Jamie drily. 'I'm very much hoping to kiss you again before midnight, so let's get this done.'

He pressed a button and put the phone on speaker. Emily could hear the long, single note of the international dial tone, followed by a click of connection.

'James!' exclaimed Mr Hunter's voice. 'We were all just talking about you. Why aren't you here with us?'

'Sorry, Dad,' said Jamie with a smile. 'Maybe next time. I'm just ringing to wish you a Happy New Year.'

'Well, that's very thoughtful. Do you want to speak to your mother? We're all going to a party shortly, but I think she's still sober enough to speak.' Emily heard a short scream in the background, followed by the sound of a slamming door.

Jamie pulled a face. 'I'll call her tomorrow, but give her my love.' He smiled reassuringly at Emily. 'I actually have a question for you.'

'Of course, fire away.'

Emily felt a bit panicked. What if he was furious, or upset, or horrified that Jamie would consider somebody as ordinary as her?

'It's about Emily.'

'Emily?' said Mr Hunter, sounding surprised and concerned. 'What about Emily?'

'I wondered how you'd feel if I asked her out on a date.'

Mr Hunter was silent for a moment, and Emily felt like she might be sick. 'My assistant? That Emily? You want to ask her on a date?'

'Yes,' said Jamie emphatically. 'I really like her.'

'Good lord, James,' laughed Mr Hunter. 'Absolutely not. I forbid it.'

Emily pressed the heels of her hands into her eyeballs as Jamie's face fell. Tears weren't far off, and she tried to push them back. 'Can I ask why?' Jamie asked, his voice wavering.

'Because she's far too good for the likes of you. If you start courting Emily, she'll realise how entirely worthless my family is, then leave.'

Jamie laughed nervously. 'You're kidding, right?'

'Of course I'm kidding,' roared Mr Hunter. 'You're both adults and can do whatever you like. Although don't be surprised if she tells you to bugger off; she can do much better than you.'

Jamie met Emily's gaze as her insides did cartwheels. 'Thanks, Dad.'

'Is she there?' asked Mr Hunter knowingly.

Jamie chuckled. 'She is, actually.'

Mr Hunter chuckled. 'Happy New Year, Emily. And to you, James.'

Emily couldn't speak, so Jamie did it for her. 'Happy New Year, Dad.'

He pressed the button to end the call and turned to Emily, picking up a snowy tendril of hair and tucking it back inside her bobble hat. 'Better?' he asked.

'Much,' said Emily, feeling like she was unravelling with a hundred different emotions. The realisation dawned that Jamie could be her boyfriend, and they wouldn't have to sneak around, and this was happening for real.

The second kiss began like the first – curious and tentative, just a gentle touching of lips. She could feel herself trembling, the heat in her stomach drawing down into a warm, pulsing throb between her legs. She made an involuntary noise, just a tiny out breath that lived somewhere between a sigh and a gasp, but it seemed to light a fire under Jamie. Suddenly his hands were in her hair and his lips were on her neck and the zip of her coat was slowly heading south so he could slide his hands around her waist and up her jumper, trailing his fingers across the bare skin of her back. He tasted of champagne and woodsmoke, and Emily couldn't imagine ever wanting him to let go.

They came up for air, both of them breathing heavily. The snow was now coming down in a heavy white curtain, making tiny hissing noises as it touched the flames.

'Shall we go inside?' he asked, a question steeped in promise and possibility. Emily nodded and took his hand.

CHAPTER TWENTY-TWO

'Holy shit,' said Jamie, standing at the window. 'Have you seen this?'

Emily propped herself up on one elbow, admiring his naked backside. 'It's very impressive.'

'Very funny,' said Jamie, scurrying back to the warm bed. 'Go and look.'

She sighed and threw back the covers, pulling on her long jumper from last night. Jamie might be fine parading around the room naked, but Emily wasn't nearly confident enough to put her bum on show.

She walked over to the window, hoping he wasn't looking at her thighs. 'Oh my God.'

The window of Jamie's bedroom overlooked the paddock where they'd had a fire last night. It was a blanket of white, with the bottom rail of the fence buried below the snowline. She couldn't see the bonfire as it was immediately below them, but it was reasonable to assume it had well and truly gone out.

'I've never seen this much snow before. Have you?'

'Not in this country.'

Emily felt momentarily stupid, remembering that Jamie was the kind of person who went skiing in the Alps. He smiled sleepily at her, a come-back-to-bed look that took in her morning bed hair, her tugged-down jumper and her long legs. 'Stop looking at me like that,' she said shyly.

'I can't help it,' he said. 'You're lovely.'

'You're sleep deprived,' said Emily, shivering as she snuggled in next to him. 'What's your plan for today?'

'I should probably take a trip around the estate, make sure there aren't any fences down. Maybe check in on Derek.'

'The Estate Manager?'

'Yeah, he looks after the dogs when Dad's away. His cottage is in the far corner of the estate down a rough track – we keep offering to tarmac it, but he's a miserable old bugger who prefers not to have visitors. He'll be cut off right now, and he only turns his phone on when Dad's around. Do you want to come?'

'Sure,' said Emily. 'I need to go back and get changed first. Shall I grab the key to the Land Rover?'

Jamie shook his head. 'I think we should take the horses; I can cover more of the estate that way.'

'Is it safe in the snow?'

Jamie laughed. 'Horses are naturally four by four.' He smiled at Emily's doubtful face. 'They'll already be ploughing the main estate roads, and we'll take it really slowly.'

'OK. Does that mean I have to get up now?'

'Why?' said Jamie, stroking his finger down her arm and kissing her shoulder. 'What else did you have in mind?'

'Ha ha,' she replied, feeling her skin break out in goosebumps. 'That's quite enough for one night. It's only the first day of the year.'

'Oh yeah,' said Jamie. 'Happy New Year.' They had been far too busy doing a comprehensive audit of each other's bodies to celebrate when the clock struck midnight.

'Happy New Year,' said Emily, wanting to kiss him but conscious she hadn't cleaned her teeth for over twelve hours.

'I'm going to go back and have a shower and change, get some breakfast.'

Jamie put his hands behind his head and watched her pull on her clothes. Emily had no idea what he was thinking, but the smile playing on his lips suggested it was post-watershed. She remembered the way he'd touched her last night, the feeling of the cold air on her skin as she rode him, the look on his face as he reached the point of no return. Her skin tingled, like every touch of his fingers and tongue had left an indelible print.

'Put some extra layers on and a double pair of socks,' he said, snapping her back into practical mode. 'It's going to be cold out there. And take some boots from the tack room, you can't walk back in those.' He nodded at the trainers Emily had worn last night, which looked woefully unsuitable for knee-deep snow.

'OK.' She gave Jamie a smile and a tiny wave from the doorway before heading down the stairs and out into the yard.

Despite the riding boots, walking back to the house was still unexpectedly challenging. The paths and the road had entirely disappeared under a vast white tablecloth, making it impossible to know where to walk. The heavy skies didn't help, providing a flat light that took away any kind of definition on the snow blanket and made Emily feel dizzy.

But she wouldn't have given two hoots if there was a tornado on the driveway, because she was still buzzing after the best New Year's Eve of her life. It had been everything a first night with somebody should be – romantic, intimate, fun. Neither of them had racked up scores of partners, so there was no pressure to pull out all their best moves. They'd taken their time, laughed a lot, taken breaks for food and more wine and messaging family to wish them Happy New Year. Emily felt like she was on cloud nine, with no immediate plans to come back down.

There was still no sign of Anna or Leon, but that was no surprise – nobody was due back until tomorrow, and even that was looking shaky with the weather like this. She felt the same elation you got when there was a school snow day, knowing she had at least another twenty-four hours with Jamie before she had to return to the real world.

Her phone rang as she picked her way across the delivery yard, and she wasn't surprised to see it was Kelly. There were no lie-ins when you had a four-year-old, even on New Year's Day.

'Happy New Year!' sang Emily as she answered the phone.

'WOW,' replied Kelly. 'Somebody got some last night. Am I right?'

Emily giggled, looking around to check nobody could hear her. 'Fine, you're right. I definitely got some last night.'

'YES,' shouted Kelly. 'Was Jamie Dornan any good?'

'He was pretty fucking great, actually.'

'Ah, shit. I'm so jealous, but also proper chuffed for you.'

'Thanks, Kel. How's the snow?'

'Tons of it, and the sun's out. Beth and I are going outside to build a snowman.'

'Tell her to send me a picture, and I'm sorry I'm not there to help.'

Kelly chuckled. 'To be fair, you had a better offer.'

'Yeah, but I still love you guys.'

'I know. Happy New Year, Em, let's make it a good one.'

171

'Definitely.' She blew Kelly a kiss down the phone and ended the call, dreaming of a hot shower, some fresh clothes that didn't smell of bonfire and sex, and a huge quantity of tea and toast.

Emily got back to the yard an hour later feeling fully revived, wearing two pairs of leggings over some tights and two pairs of socks, with a fleece headband and matching neckie covering her ears and chin. Jamie had tacked up Rupert and Luna as usual, but with an extra fleece-lined waterproof cover under their saddles. She stroked Rupert's velvety nose and gave him a kiss as Jamie came out of the tack room, his face pink from the cold and his chin wrapped in his new scarf.

'All ready to go?' he asked. He was holding a double-sided canvas saddle bag over each arm.

Emily nodded. 'What's in there?'

'Tools in one side,' he replied, slinging it over Luna's back behind the saddle, a bag on either side. 'Just in case we need to bodge a fix on any of the fences or dig anything out. And some food in the other side in case Derek is marooned. Just bread and milk, stuff he can eat if his power has gone down.'

Emily strapped on her helmet and put on her new gloves, then jacked her left foot into the stirrup, pushing up as hard as she could and using a handful of Rupert's mane to help her keep her balance as she swung her right leg over. She was determined not to use the mounting block again, even if the muscles in her thighs ached from a night of overuse.

'Absolute pro,' muttered Jamie with a smile, doing a quick check of the girth and stirrups. He leapt up on to Luna's back and headed out of the yard, Rupert following close behind.

'We'll take it slowly,' Jamie said. 'It's not icy yet, so they'll be fine.'

'I'm in no hurry,' said Emily, feeling the pommel of the saddle push against the tender area between her legs and wondering if this was why women liked riding. Other than the creak of hooves on snow and the breaths and snorts of the horses, all the sound seemed to have been sucked away, leaving a muffled silence that echoed in Emily's ears. It felt strange and unsettling to see nothing but monochrome for miles in every direction, and she could see how easy it would be to lose your bearings if you didn't know exactly where you were going. Luckily Jamie had ridden this estate all his life.

After an hour of the main roads, following the ploughed path of the estate tractor, they picked their way down a lane to Derek's cottage. Jamie dismounted on the snowy path to knock on the door, and a veiny-faced man appeared flanked by Bailey, Murphy and Lily, Mr Hunter's three black Labradors. They all threw themselves at Jamie, barking and dancing in excited circles, then diving into banks of snow until Derek called them all back. Derek's Norfolk accent was so strong that Emily could only work out every third word, but the general gist seemed to be that he was fine; he still had power and plenty of logs for the wood burner. He took the milk and bread with a nod of thanks and gave Emily a polite wave as they headed slowly back up the track.

By the time they were back on the main path it had started to snow again, an ominous darkness gathering despite it only being late morning. 'The wind's picking up,' said Jamie, frowning at the heavy sky. 'I think we should head back.'

Emily nodded, feeling a frisson of worry. It felt like they were at a distant corner of the estate and it had taken them well over an hour to get here; what if there was no shortcut back? She pulled the neckie over her nose and mouth as they turned into the wind on the path, the biting cold of it making her eyes sting. The two pairs of leggings had been warm and cosy when they left, but they weren't remotely waterproof and already she could feel her thighs getting wet and itchy with cold.

Ten minutes later the weather had worsened to the point that Emily couldn't see anything other than the back of Jamie's jacket; Luna had disappeared into the white-out entirely. The snow was drifting at the side of the path, and it was clear the horses were struggling with the wind and the soft, fresh powder on the ground.

'We need to stop,' shouted Jamie, turning round in his saddle so she could hear him over the whistling wind. 'There's a shelter off to the right here, just stay close and follow me.'

Emily nodded and watched as Jamie slid off Luna's back and heaved open a metal gate, the snow pushing through the bars and piling up behind it. He climbed back on and left it open as they continued at a slow plod, the wind now blowing what felt like shards of ice into the side of Emily's face. Panic bubbled in her chest, so she focused on her breathing and kept her eyes on Jamie's jacket between Rupert's ears. She thought about her mum's story about the two men in a Ford Cortina and reminded herself that at least that had ended with a wedding, even if the groom didn't have any fingers.

CHAPTER TWENTY-THREE

The shelter loomed into sight after what was probably only another five minutes but felt like hours in the confusion of the blizzard. It looked like a large, single-storey wooden shed with three sets of double doors on the front, all with drifting snow banked up against them. Jamie jumped down and pulled a folding shovel from the saddle bag, then began to dig the snow away from the first set of doors. Emily dismounted too, taking hold of both sets of reins and turning the horses so their backs were to the wind. She watched Jamie battle the drifting snow with the shovel, wishing she could help but also knowing how important it was to keep the horses still and calm. One of the doors creaked open a foot, then more shovelling, then a foot more, then finally a big enough gap for Emily to lead the horses into the dry.

'Tie them up on the rail,' said Jamie urgently, 'then fill that bucket. There's a tap round the back.'

Emily didn't ask questions, instead securing the two sets of reins and grabbing a black plastic bucket from inside the door. She waded through the snow to the back of the building, her icy breaths being whisked away on the wind. The tap was stiff but working, but it was much harder carrying a full bucket through knee-deep snow with ice chips blowing into her face. Everything about the experience was horrible, and she'd never been more relieved to be indoors.

'Help me shift these bales,' said Jamie.

Emily put the bucket safely in the corner, then grabbed a straw bale from the stack and passed it to Jamie. He had closed one door and was building a wall in the space left by the other, stacking two side-by-side then two across, like a Jenga tower. She thought about why, then realised it was about stopping the snow from coming in without closing the door – if he closed it, the weight of the drifting snow might make it difficult to open again. But the bales could be removed inwards, then they could dig their way out.

After a few minutes the final two bales were wedged into the top of the doorway, shutting out the whistling wind and the last flurries of snow, along with most of the light. Jamie rummaged in the saddle bag until he found a torch, poking it between two bales so it cast a ghostly glow on the roof. They both fussed the horses for a while, wiping the snow from their ears and faces and talking softly to them. Rupert and Luna both seemed fine after their ordeal, and happy to nuzzle their riders and accept a few treats from Jamie's pocket.

'That definitely wasn't in the weather forecast,' said Jamie, his breathing finally returning to normal.

'No,' said Emily. 'Thank God for this place. What is it?'

'It's a field shelter. In the summer we turn the horses out all day and night if it's warm and dry, but they need somewhere to shelter. In the winter we use it for extra storage.' Emily looked around in the torchlight and saw bales of hay and bags of feed alongside the straw, along with a stack of buckets and a wheelbarrow. It felt surprisingly warm and cosy considering the storm outside, which was still battering the wooden cladding.

'We could be here for a while,' said Jamie, lifting the saddle bags off the horses and moving the water bucket so Rupert and Luna could both have a drink.

'Can we call anyone?'

Jamie shrugged. 'If we have to, but I'd rather wait to see if this blows through. Once it stops snowing we can lead the horses back to the road – they'll be fine from there.'

'How long will it take us to get back?'

'We've done three quarters of a loop, so the house is only twenty minutes away. We'll be fine.' He smiled at her reassuringly, and she relaxed a little. Emily wasn't used to all this countryside weather; in her world roads and paths were gritted and snow was fun, not something that could kill you.

She took her gloves and helmet off and raked her fingers through her hair where it had stuck to her head with sweat and snow. Jamie pulled some hay from a bale and stuffed it into a string net, which he hung on a hook on the wall so Luna and Rupert could chomp away at it. Then he sat on the straw and pulled a thermos flask out of the saddlebag.

'Holy shit, did you bring tea?' said Emily, her eyes wide.

Jamie smiled. 'Of course.' He rummaged around in the bag a bit more and pulled out a shiny blue bag. 'Also chocolate buttons.'

'Oh my God, I could kiss you,' said Emily.

'Well, that's a huge coincidence,' said Jamie, 'because that's exactly what I need to give me the strength to open this bag.' He held out his hand and tilted his head, his eyes challenging her to play along.

Emily took his hand and sat astride him, pressing her groin into his as she undid his riding helmet and ran her hands through his hair. Her heart was pounding as she buried her

177

face into his neck and breathed in the familiar smell of sweat and hay and horses. It reminded her of the day she arrived at Bowford, eating dinner next to him in the kitchen, then lying in bed later that night and imagining what it might be like to be this close to him. She'd never considered for a second that two months later they'd be in a barn in a snow-storm, Jamie's hands roaming her body under her jumper as he whispered everything he was thinking into her ear.

In Emily's world sex in hay barns was something that only happened in her mum's books; usually involving chiselled country squires and winsome milkmaids in poorly secured underwear. But fuelled by lust and adrenaline, she was out of her boots and leggings and on her back on the hay bales, guiding Jamie's head between her legs so he could loosen the knots on all the stress and tension of the past couple of hours. She could feel him urging her on, his fingers matching the tempo of his tongue as he coaxed her to the finish line, then plunged inside her without missing a beat. The soft glow of the torch, the whistling of the wind, the feeling of the cold air on her thighs and the rough straw on her back – all of it gave the experience a more intense edge, as if all her senses had been dialled up to eleven. Emily hadn't realised that sex could feel like this, and as Jamie cried her name and buried his face in her hair, she promised herself never to settle for anything less.

Emily's mum had once told her that the best cup of tea you will ever drink is the one the midwife brings you after you've had a baby. But even if she one day pushed out twins, Emily couldn't imagine a cup of tea ever tasting better than the one she drank out of a thermos cup after she had strug-gled back into her cold, damp leggings.

'Do you want a chocolate button?' asked Jamie, holding out the bag.

'Who eats them one at a time?' She tipped out a handful and pushed them all into her mouth. Jamie grinned, then stood up to slide one of the straw bales out of the stack. A bright light illuminated the barn, making Emily squint.

'Looks pretty calm out there now. We should make a move.'

'Can't we just live here for ever on tea and chocolate buttons?' asked Emily, not hugely relishing the prospect of getting back in the saddle.

'I can't think of anything nicer,' said Jamie, 'apart from taking you home for a shower and a proper dinner.'

'OK, that also sounds nice.'

He reached out and took her hand, pulling her to her feet. Her legs felt like they'd been put on backwards from too much riding. The journey back was going to hurt, and tomorrow was going to be a lot worse. She should go back to her room in the attic and have a hot bath and good night's sleep, but she also knew that she wouldn't be able to resist if Jamie asked her to stay.

'Will you stay with me tonight?' he said, as if he could read her mind. He tucked her hair behind her ears and kissed a trail down her neck to her collarbone.

'Stop that,' she said breathlessly. 'Of course I will.'

'Then let's get home so I can get you out of these wet clothes.'

Emily laughed, wondering if she'd ever walk normally again.

They guided the horses slowly out of the field on foot, Jamie going first to mark a safe trail through the snow. It was an inch or so deeper than when they'd arrived, but the sky was now clear and the sun was casting long shadows across the fields. Emily quickly pulled out her phone and took a photograph of the shelter behind her, wanting to have a memento that would remind her of one of the most intense hours of her life.

Once they were back on the estate road, she executed a painful mount on to Rupert's back and once again followed Jamie as Luna carved a path through the powder. She kept her phone out this time, taking pictures of the snow-laden trees and the sun making the fences look like they were coated in white glitter. She took a picture of Jamie's broad back through Rupert's ears, then captured his questioning expression as he turned to ask if she was OK. He rolled his eyes, then smiled for another one.

Emily sent the photo to Kelly with a winking emoji, wondering when she'd get the chance to tell her about today, and whether she could possibly do the story justice. She thought about whether she'd ever have the confidence to put the photos on Instagram or Facebook and show her old schoolfriends and colleagues what had become of Emily Wilkinson. Nobody from Emily's old school had been expected to amount to much, and she'd always felt like one of the few who'd made something of her life. Maybe she hadn't gone to university and got a top job as a lawyer or a doctor, but she'd embarked on a career and she was making a success of it. Jamie thought she was his equal, and so did Mr Hunter. Right now, that counted for a lot.

Her phone buzzed to announce a message from Kelly, which made her laugh. *Fucking hell, he's definitely Jamie Dornan. You lucky mare.*

'What's so funny?' asked Jamie turning around.

'Kelly thinks you look like Jamie Dornan.'

'Who's Jamie Dornan?'

'He's an actor from Northern Ireland.' There was no point mentioning *50 Shades of Grey*; it was hardly a film that Jamie would have watched. Also he might ask her to explain the plot, and who wanted to go there?

'Should I be flattered?'

'You really should. She says I'm a lucky mare.'

He laughed. 'Luck didn't have anything to do with it. I was a goner the minute Luna ate your job offer.'

A warm feeling spread through Emily's chest, which unexpectedly made her think of Mark. She'd thought she'd been in love with him, but he'd never made her feel like this. She'd assumed the secrecy was to protect her job and his reputation, but now she wondered if it was simply about Emily being the kind of girl a man like him had sex with but didn't actually date. She'd thought she'd been his equal, but he'd always been her boss, even in bed.

This, though. This was something else.

CHAPTER TWENTY-FOUR

'I think we need to agree some ground rules,' said Emily, taking a bite out of a slice of toast. She was sitting in Jamie's bed with the duvet tucked under her armpits, alternately eating toast and swigging from a mug of tea.

'What kind of rules?' asked Jamie, stealing her toast and taking a bite. Emily savoured the moment of comfortable domesticity and hoped this conversation wouldn't feel like she was taking things too fast.

'For this,' she said, waving the toast between them. 'Us.'

'And that requires rules,' said Jamie, clearly amused. He was already fully dressed, having got up early to see to the horses.

'Just to separate when I'm at work from when I'm with you.'

'Right. I'm all ears. Should I take notes?'

Emily pulled a face. 'Fuck you. Rule number one – definitely no flirting with me during working hours.'

Jamie nodded, pretending to be serious. 'I wouldn't dream of it.'

'And we should be discreet. Everyone's going to find out eventually, but I'd rather not make it obvious.'

'Absolutely.'

'If we spend the night together, it has to be here, not in my room.'

'Fine by me. Anna next door is definitely a passion-killer.'

'Weekends only.'

Jamie stared at her, his eyes wide. 'You're kidding.'

Emily shook her head. 'I'm not. In the week I need to work and get my beauty sleep. I can't have you keeping me up half the night.'

Jamie laughed, and Emily still couldn't help but wonder how on earth she'd ended up in bed with this beautiful man. She finished her toast and swept the crumbs off the duvet and on to her plate, then scrambled out of bed and hastily wrapped herself in a towel.

'Right. Shower, then I'm going back.'

'What's the hurry?' asked Jamie. 'It's not even lunchtime.'

'I need to do some life admin. I came back two days ago with a bin bag of dirty clothes, I need to do my nails myself since I can't drive to Norwich in all this snow, and your family are back later so I should probably get my shit together.'

'Fine,' said Jamie. 'At least it's Wednesday so I get to see you in a couple of days.'

'That's true,' said Emily. She thought for a second, then smiled sweetly at him. 'Would you call yourself an environmentalist?'

Jamie frowned. 'What kind of question is that?'

'I mean, do you recycle and do stuff to save the planet, that kind of thing?'

Jamie shrugged. 'I suppose. Why?'

'Because showering together is apparently a really good way to save water.' She turned off the light in the bathroom and dropped the towel in the doorway, then grinned at the noise of clothes being hastily removed and a mug and plate being abandoned on the windowsill.

★

183

Emily trudged back to the house with an end-of-school-holidays cloud hanging over her, adjusting to the idea that time with Jamie was going to have to take second place to work from now on. The snow had formed an icy crust overnight, making it treacherous to navigate, and the trees were already dripping in the sunshine. By the weekend the biggest snowstorm in Norfolk in decades would be reduced to a wet, grey slush.

The Hunter family were due back from Switzerland in a few hours, and she'd already had an email from the charter company to say that everything was on schedule. She could see Leon's car outside the garage and Anna's in the yard, so they'd both arrived back at some point since yesterday evening. She'd be glad to see Leon and say thank you for the blanket, and there was always a chance that ten days of rest and festive spirit had made Anna a bit more friendly. Then again, pigs might fly.

She found them both in the kitchen, Leon sitting at the table looking mutinous, and Anna standing by the kitchen island with her arms folded and a face like thunder. As Emily came through the kitchen door Leon turned and looked away, which prompted Anna to give her a look of purest loathing.

'I'll leave this to you,' she hissed in Emily's direction, then stalked out of the kitchen and up the back stairs.

Emily approached Leon with a creeping sense of doom, pretty sure she knew what this was about. She sat in the chair opposite him and laid her hands flat on the table. 'Hi.'

Leon glanced up at her, then looked away again.

'Is everything OK?' she asked.

'You said it wasn't me,' whispered Leon croakily. He

wasn't crying or anything, but he looked bereft, like someone had just died.

'What do you mean?'

'You said you didn't want to go out with anyone.' His tone had an edge of bitterness. 'But you stayed with Jamie last night. Anna said your bed hasn't been slept in.'

Fury bloomed in Emily's chest. How could Anna rat her out and make Leon feel like this? And aside from anything else, what was she doing in her room?

'I'm sorry,' she said. She wasn't sorry about Jamie, but she was sorry for hurting Leon's feelings.

'Why did you lie to me?' he demanded.

'I didn't lie to you, Leon,' she said gently, turning her palms upwards. 'When you asked me out I definitely wasn't looking for a boyfriend. But even if I was, it wouldn't have been you. You're my friend, but I've never felt more than that. I'm sorry.'

'But you do feel more for Jamie?'

Emily nodded. 'Yes. I didn't plan it that way, but that's how it is.'

Leon sagged. 'He doesn't deserve you,' he mumbled.

Emily raised her eyebrows. 'Why not? Is he a bad person?'

'No, he is a good person. I like him very much.'

'Then why doesn't he deserve me?'

Leon said nothing for a moment, looking sick and guilty. 'I don't know. I guess I just said that because I'm sad. He is lucky. If he hurts you I will kill him.'

Emily smiled. 'Thanks, Leon.' She reached out and took both his rough, hairy hands in hers. 'I'm sorry if I hurt your feelings. Your Christmas present was the nicest thing anyone has ever given me. I hope we can still be friends.'

Leon gave the tiniest nod and squeezed her hands in return. 'It's OK,' he said. 'You are good person. Jamie is lucky man.' He took a deep breath and stood up to leave, giving Emily a watery smile.

'Tell him. Tell him I will kill him if he hurts you.' He held his hands in a circle and pulled a face, like he was strangling someone.

She laughed. 'I will. Thank you.'

Emily stomped up the stairs feeling wrung out over Leon, and livid with Anna for stirring up trouble. She briefly considered having it out with her but decided to not give her the satisfaction of seeing how rattled she was.

If Anna had been poking around in her room there was no sign of anything having been moved, and nothing of interest for her to find anyway, unless you counted a superquiet vibrator that Kelly had bought her as a 'men no longer required' going-away gift. Hopefully she wouldn't be needing that for a while.

She spent five minutes gathering dirty laundry and organising it into lights and darks, then stuffed the darks into a carrier bag and headed downstairs to the laundry room at the back of the kitchen. None of it was particularly dirty, so she set it on a half-hour wash and returned upstairs to paint her nails. She'd do one hand, then come back down to move everything into the dryer and put the light wash on. By the time her nails were done, she'd be ready to go for a swim.

Emily was sixty lengths in before she caught sight of a pair of feet in brown leather brogues on the side of the pool. She stopped and pulled off her goggles, trying to catch her breath. Her stomach sank when she saw it was Adam. He glared at her, his eyes as cold and dark as flint, but said nothing.

'Did you want the pool?' she asked. She wondered if Mr Hunter had told him about her sneaking photocopies of his plans, or if he'd found out about her and Jamie. In that moment, she wasn't sure which would be worse.

'No I fucking don't,' said Adam, his voice dripping with malice.

Uh-oh, this is bad. Emily tried another tack. 'How was your trip?'

Adam folded his arms, ignoring the question. 'I hear you've been getting your feet under the table while we've been away.'

He knew about Jamie, then. *Oh, yippee.*

She eyed him carefully, feeling exposed and vulnerable in her thin swimsuit, but far enough away that he couldn't touch her without getting in the water. She'd also seen him swim, and she was faster.

'I'm not sure what you mean.'

Adam shook his head, a sneer on his lips. 'I said you were a piece of work weeks ago, turns out I was right. But I've got bad news for you, Little Miss Gold Digger. If you were planning on getting your hands on the family fortune, you've picked the wrong brother.'

Emily could feel her anger rising. 'I wasn't planning anything, and I didn't pick anyone.' *I wouldn't pick you if you were the last man on earth*, she thought. *I'd rather poke my eyes out with a chopstick.*

'You say that,' said Adam, inspecting his fingernails, 'but I've met women like you before. Crawling out of nowhere, wrapping men like my father around your little finger. You may have flashed your tits at my brother . . .' His eyes drifted to her chest, and he gave a sly smile. 'Actually, forget that, you don't have any. But I've got your number.'

Emily's face burned at Adam's slight on her background and her body, but she held her head high, refusing to be cowed by him. 'I have no idea what you're talking about.'

He pointed a finger in her face and narrowed his eyes to snake-like slits. 'I'm watching you, Emily. You've picked the wrong family to fuck with.'

Emily hurried back through the crusty snow to the house, her wet hair freezing to her head, feeling furious and upset in equal measure but refusing to shed any tears over that arrogant piece of shit. She'd dealt with intimidating men before; it came with the job. And she was no stranger to having her character or her body criticised either, that was just part of being a woman. But calling her a gold digger was completely out of order, particularly when she'd tried so hard to do the right thing.

The big question was, should she say anything to Jamie or Mr Hunter? Jamie would be furious, and she definitely didn't want to be responsible for a family rift. For one thing, it might change how Mr Hunter felt about the relationship between her and Jamie. Adam was better off thinking that Emily was too scared of him to say anything; nothing more than a stupid woman who had caught his brother's eye but posed no threat.

She looked at her watch. Four hours ago she'd left Jamie's bed after their snowy New Year mini-break, and in that time she'd upset Leon, elevated Anna's hatred of her to a new level, and been threatened by Adam. What else was today going to throw at her?

She detoured to the laundry room to put her second wash into the dryer, only to discover that one of the navy blue penguin socks Kelly had bought her for Christmas had crept in with the lights, so everything was now a patchy tie-die turquoise. Emily took a deep breath and decided that today could absolutely do one.

CHAPTER TWENTY-FIVE

Mr Hunter smiled at Emily with the joy and relief of a man who'd finally offloaded his family after ten days of festive disharmony. Tanya and Catherine had flown back to LA directly from Switzerland, and Adam and his family had headed back to London last night. Emily was relieved; after yesterday's showdown in the pool she was very happy not to be swapping killer death stares with Adam in the corridors. She'd arrived in the office early today, getting the coffee machine going and opening the stack of post so everything was ready for Mr Hunter to kick off a new year.

'I hear you and James are now an item,' he said jovially, sipping his coffee and putting on his glasses. 'Isn't that what the young people call it?'

'I believe so,' said Emily, trying and failing not to blush.

'I'm pleased for both of you; he's a good chap. I'm sure he'll take good care of you, but if you have any problems let me know and I'll have him shot.'

Not if Leon strangles him first, thought Emily.

Mr Hunter steepled his hands under his chin and gave Emily a penetrating look over the top of his glasses. 'I'm sure I don't have to remind you that everything related to this estate, my business interests and what's discussed in this office is strictly between us.'

Emily met his gaze. 'You definitely don't have to remind me of that, Mr Hunter.'

'I thought not,' he said, shuffling the papers on his desk, 'but I feel better for having said it. So, main thing for today is for us to catch up on all the admin this morning, and then we need to plan a trip.'

'What kind of trip?' she asked, wondering where Mr Hunter was off to. He'd only got back from Switzerland yesterday.

'Admin first,' he said. 'We'll do travel this afternoon.'

Emily nodded and handed over the correspondence folder, organised into tabbed sections by business, estate, charities and personal. She uncapped the pen he'd bought her for Christmas, then opened her notebook.

Emily was pleased to see Sam back in the kitchen at lunchtime – he was a welcome relief from Anna throwing daggers in her direction, and Leon moping about like a teenage boy who'd had his PlayStation confiscated.

'You look like the cat who got the cream, or the handsome horseman,' said Sam with a chuckle, passing over a bowl of spiced seafood bouillon with noodles. It was one of her favourites, despite her initial reservations over bok choy, which looked a lot like cabbage. It turned out to be nothing like the kind of cabbage she'd eaten at school, although maybe that was just the way Sam cooked it. Perhaps one day he could teach her mum.

'Shame not everybody shares my joy,' said Emily with a shy smile. Both Anna and Leon had left not long after her arrival, so it was just her and Sam.

'Ah, you'll be a long time waiting if you're trying to please everyone,' he said sagely. 'Leon will get over it, and Anna is just . . . Anna.' He raised his eyebrows as if to ask who else had passed comment, but Emily gave a tiny shake of her head and carried on eating. Sam was the biggest gossip on the estate, and much as it would be nice to offload, she definitely wasn't telling him about Adam.

'How was your Christmas?' she asked, wondering how he celebrated with all his extended family so far away.

'Just at home with Gabrielle and the kids and grandkids,' he said. 'I don't cook on Christmas Day – Gabrielle and my youngest son do a wonderful turkey. We talked to the family in Mauritius on FaceTime; the kids love seeing all their cousins.'

'Have you ever taken them over for a holiday?'

'No,' he said. 'It's a long way and too expensive for a big family. I'm going over in June; my niece is getting married.'

'That's lovely. What are Mauritian weddings like?'

'Ah, this one will be wonderful. There'll be a party on the beach by my old restaurant; my sister Jessie runs it now, but it's still called Sam's Café. There'll be a mix of traditions – Chinese, Indian, Creole. A big bonfire and food and music as the sun sets, dancing into the night.'

Emily tried to imagine the tropical heat and the music, but she had no frame of reference other than scenes from films. 'It sounds amazing.'

'England is home; it has been for a long time,' said Sam. 'But my heart is six thousand miles away.'

Emily checked through her list of Mr Hunter's travel plans. Two days in London next week – Leon would drive him down on Sunday night, she just needed to let the London housekeeper know. A charity dinner in Edinburgh at the end of the month; there were direct flights from Norwich so that was easy. A potential trip to San Francisco in May to receive some kind of lifetime achievement award for his work in the gaming industry, although he'd asked her to check if there was any way he could accept the award by video because 'it's a bloody long way to fly for a round of applause'.

'Anything else?' she asked.

'Actually, yes. I'd like to go and look at a hotel at the end of next week,' said Mr Hunter. 'It's an interesting concept and I might want to invest.'

'OK,' she said, turning to a fresh page in her notebook.

'I'd like to get a feel for it first, see if it's the real deal. But the owners know who I am, and if I stay they'll give me the VIP treatment.'

'Hmm,' said Emily. 'Can you get someone else to stay there for you and report back?'

'Well, yes. I thought you might be interested, actually.'

Emily looked up from her notebook. 'Me?'

'Yes,' said Mr Hunter. 'It's an all-inclusive resort for young travellers, mostly designed with Instagrammers in mind.' He said the word like he wasn't entirely sure what an Instagrammer was, and definitely didn't trust it. 'Much more your kind of thing than mine.'

Emily tried to imagine what kind of world Mr Hunter thought she lived in, where an all-inclusive Instagram hotel was more 'her thing' than a static caravan in Dorset.

'Where is it? The hotel?'

'It's in Mauritius.'

Emily pressed her lips shut, worried she might make squeaky noises if she said anything. She wrote 'Mauritius' in shorthand in her notebook like this was a perfectly normal

193

conversation to be having with your boss on a Thursday afternoon in January.

'I also wondered if my son would like to come.'

The blood drained from Emily's face at the thought of being trapped in a tropical island hotel with Adam. 'Which one?'

'That's very funny,' said Mr Hunter drily. 'James, of course. You can both be my spies. I can book you separate rooms if you'd like, all above board.'

Emily blushed, not sure how to respond. She'd leave that for now, let Jamie deal with it.

'So if we're in the hotel, where will you stay?'

'I have a house on the west coast of the island. I'll stay there, deal with some other business matters. You and James can do three nights in the hotel, then come back and join me. We'll be there and back in a week.'

A million thoughts rattled in Emily's head, but 'oh my God it sounds amazing' just sounded stupid and trite.

'Sam has told me a lot about Mauritius,' she said. 'I'd love to see it, and I'm really happy to help you decide on the hotel.'

'Good,' said Mr Hunter, clearly satisfied with her answer. 'Let's go through dates and travel arrangements today, so you can get everything booked tomorrow. You might want to speak to James sooner rather than later, see if you can lure him away from the stables for a week.'

'I'll do my best.'

Mr Hunter smiled knowingly. 'I'm sure you will, Emily.'

'You're going to Mauritius with Dad?' asked Jamie, holding up a red blanket. She'd found him in the tack room after work, folding freshly washed horse laundry.

'Yes. Next Friday.'

'Shit. Come upstairs.'

He put down the blanket, then hurried upstairs to his apartment and put the kettle on.

'Why is Dad going to Mauritius, and why does he want me to come?'

'He's thinking of investing in a resort and wants us to stay there for a few days. Like mystery shoppers.'

'Why can't he do it?'

Emily explained about the Instagram angle and him wanting to get a proper idea of what it was like.

Jamie laughed. 'This sounds like a dastardly plot where you lure me out of the country for a romantic holiday.'

'Yes,' said Emily, rolling her eyes. 'Because I definitely have that kind of power. It was your dad's idea.'

'Just for a week.'

'One week. Of very hard work.'

'And cocktails and palm trees.'

Emily shrugged. 'I've never been to Mauritius; it could be a shithole for all I know.'

Jamie laughed. 'It's not.'

'I know,' she said with an excited smile. 'I have Google. Also Sam talks about it a lot.'

'You'll get to meet Jessie, Sam's sister. She and her family run the best beach café in the world.'

'Will it be warm enough for the beach in January?'

Jamie chuckled gently. 'It's in the southern hemisphere; it's high summer there right now.'

'Oh,' said Emily, feeling her face redden as she kicked herself for being so stupid.

'Hey,' said Jamie, taking her hand and pulling her towards

him. 'There's no reason why anyone would know that if they hadn't been there.'

'My geography isn't the best,' mumbled Emily. 'Haven't been around much.'

'Well, then you're perfect for dad's mystery hotel guest. I suppose I should speak to the grooms about some extra cover.'

Emily tried to stay cool, even though her stomach was doing somersaults. 'Does that mean you're coming?'

Jamie laughed and rolled his eyes. 'It's a week in the sunshine in January watching you parade around in a bikini. Of course I'm coming.'

'I don't even own a bikini,' said Emily, her brow furrowed. 'Where do I buy a bikini in January?'

'I thought you had Google?'

Emily could feel her excitement building, and she was itching to start making lists of things she needed to do. 'It means I won't be around this weekend.'

'How come?'

'It's my mum's birthday next week; I'd planned to go home the following weekend but now we'll be away. So I need to go home this weekend instead.'

'That's fair enough,' said Jamie, opening the fridge and peering into the abyss.

'You could come if you like,' she added, feeling like she should offer even though he'd only been there less than two weeks ago.

Jamie smiled. 'Emily, go and see your family. Have a night with Kelly, make up for New Year. You don't need me hanging around. And anyway, sounds like we've got a week away to look forward to.'

'I can't wait,' she said, imagining the two of them swaying in a hammock under a palm tree.

'Yeah, me too.' He pulled her in for a kiss, sliding the clip out of her hair so it fell loose around her shoulders.

'I'm going to have to tell Mum and Dad and Kelly who you are,' said Emily. 'I'm not sure how else to explain your dad taking the guy who looks after the horses on a trip.'

'Hmm,' said Jamie, kissing her neck. 'Might be tough to explain.'

'It felt weird lying to them anyway.'

He undid the top button of her blouse and kissed her collarbone. 'I'd like to think it won't make any difference.'

Emily laughed. 'I'd like to think that too, but this is my mum we're talking about.'

'Well, you can tell them my intentions are honourable.'

Emily tilted her head, eyeing him suspiciously. 'Is that true?'

'Right this second, absolutely not.' He undid the next two buttons on her shirt and slid it off one shoulder.

'We agreed no weekdays,' said Emily, her breath catching as his fingers trailed down to her waist.

'I know, but you're here now. And you're away this weekend, how long do you expect me to wait?' His left hand cupped the back of her head as he kissed her, whilst his right hand deftly undid the top button of her jeans and disappeared inside.

'I'm not sleeping here,' said Emily, her eyes closing in ecstasy as his fingers slid inside her and began a slow and steady rhythm.

'I certainly hope not,' whispered Jamie, 'sleeping was very much not on my agenda.'

'Oh God,' she gasped, fumbling with the zip on his jacket. 'You have far too many clothes on.'

Jamie smiled and gently removed his hands, his eyes full of mischievous intent. 'That's easily fixed,' he said, taking her hand and leading her to the bedroom.

CHAPTER TWENTY-SIX

'Gin and tonic,' said Emily's dad, putting a drink down in front of her, 'in a glass the size of a baby's head.'

'They're all like that these days,' said Carol. 'There's about fifteen ice cubes in there.'

'Not like the old days,' continued Martin. 'Ten years ago this place would have given you a Gordon's and Schweppes in a half-pint glass. You'd have to beg and plead for a slice of lemon.'

'There's too much choice now,' muttered Carol. 'Two whole shelves of gin, all those flavours. Rhubarb and ginger, for Christ's sake. Tastes like a boozy crumble.'

'Six different tonics,' added Martin. 'Bloody pink grapefruit slices. My car's got a lower spec than that drink.'

Emily rolled her eyes at Kelly, who drained her pint and picked up the second one. Every visit to the White Lion now evoked nostalgia for the old days when you'd come for a cheap pint, a game of darts and the inevitable fight at closing time. Emily had drunk her first illicit cider in here, bought by Simon when she was fourteen. They'd celebrated decades of birthdays, anniversaries and graduations in this corner by the window, but Emily had no problem with a bit of gentrification if it decreased the odds of being stabbed.

'Happy birthday, Mum,' she said. 'Sorry I can't be here on the day.'

'Ah, that's OK,' said Carol mistily. 'It's nice to see you so soon after Christmas.'

Emily glanced at Kelly, who gave her a nod of encouragement. She'd spent the afternoon with her best friend and offloaded the truth about Jamie's parentage and the upcoming trip, although she didn't bother mentioning the Christmas charade. What was the point? She and Jamie were together now, so all that was old news.

Emily cleared her throat. 'So, I have something to tell you all.'

Carol's mouth fell open in horror. 'Oh my God, you're pregnant. I told you, Martin. I told you this would happen if she moved to that place.'

'What?' howled Emily. 'I'm not pregnant.'

'What is it then? Are you getting married?'

'Don't be daft.'

'Has Jamie dumped you? Your brothers will kill him.'

'Jesus, Carol,' hissed Martin. 'Can you let the girl speak?'

Carol sat back in her seat and pressed her lips together as Kelly's shoulders shook with silent laughter.

'I told you that Jamie worked in the stables at Bowford Manor,' said Emily. 'Which he does. But there's something else you need to know.'

'Is he part of a crime family?' shrieked Carol. 'Is that why his dad's in prison? Oh my God, Moo, what have you got caught up in? Is it drugs, or people-smuggling? I read this book about a woman who swallowed all this cocaine in rubber johnnies and then . . .'

Emily held up her hands. 'Mum, please. Just stop. Jamie is Mr Hunter's son.'

Carol was silent for a moment while she processed this

new information. 'What, Mr Hunter who owns the house? The multi-millionaire? Jamie is his son?'

'Yes. Well, actually Mr Hunter has two sons. Jamie is the younger one.'

'Ooh, so close,' said Martin, grinning at Kelly.

'Oh my God,' said Carol, covering her face with her hands. 'This is terrible. He stayed in our house. He used our wonky shower. He saw the state of my oven.' Each statement became increasingly loud and shrill, until nearby tables stopped talking to check somebody wasn't having a medical emergency.

Emily laughed. 'Don't be daft. He's not like that. He said it was the best Christmas he's ever had.'

'Did he really?' asked Martin.

'Yeah,' said Emily, smiling at them both. 'He doesn't get on very well with his brother or sister. Or his mum, for that matter.'

'Poor love,' mused Carol, taking a huge swig of her white wine. 'They say that about privileged children, don't they? I read a book once about a rich boy who was raised in this massive house without love. Murdered his parents in the end; stabbed his father with a gold letter opener and cracked his mother's skull with a glass paperweight.'

Emily snorted into her drink, setting Kelly off again.

'Why didn't you tell us, Moo?' asked Martin.

'Because you'd have got in a right state about it, it was such short notice. I wanted you to be normal around him.'

'And why wouldn't you,' said Kelly drily, gesturing at the assembled group, 'when normal looks like this?'

Emily and Kelly leaned against the bar, waiting to be served. It was three deep in places, packed with a mix of locals and groups from across town who came for the craft beers, the cocktail menu and the Saturday live music. Emily spotted a guy they'd gone to school with – Chris? Craig? He held his drink up and nodded towards Kelly, who was too busy pushing her boobs together with her elbows in the hope of catching the barman's eye to notice.

'You've got an admirer,' said Emily. 'Didn't we go to school with him?'

Kelly looked up and squinted across the bar. 'Oh God, Craig Nicholas,' she muttered. 'I'd rather sprinkle pollen on my tits and staple them to a beehive.'

Emily laughed. 'Wow, that bad?'

'He's known locally as Plague Syphilis. He's a walking STD.' She turned back to the bar and scowled. 'Honestly, what's the point of having a body like this if I can't even use it to get a drink?'

'I wouldn't know,' said Emily, who'd always been envious of Kelly's petite frame and bombshell curves, although she sometimes wondered if big boobs would get in the way of her swimming and running. Also it was nice to be able to wear a dress without a bra occasionally, which was definitely not an option for Kelly.

'I thought your mum and dad took that well,' said Kelly, having secured a nod from the barman that communicated *I've seen you, and you're next.* 'Ready for round two?'

'Weirdly, this bit feels harder,' replied Emily.

'Why? It's your job, they always knew there might be some travelling. Not that I'm not insanely jealous, obviously.'

'I know, but I don't want them to think I've got all fancy. Like this place. They actually preferred it when the furniture was screwed down and the barmen wore knuckledusters.'

'But you like it better like this?'

'Don't you?'

'Fuck, yes. It's OK to want more than this place, Em. You can aspire to nicer bars and rich boyfriends and posh trips. How much money your family have, the school we went to, none of that counts for shit.'

'I know.'

'You're like Julia Roberts in *Pretty Woman*. You want the fairy tale.'

'She was a prostitute, Kel.'

'Oh yeah. Sorry.'

Kelly put the tray of drinks on the table and sat back down with her pint, smiling expectantly at Emily.

'You OK, Mum?' asked Emily.

'I'm still reeling, Moo,' said Carol, gulping her wine like she'd just finished a triathlon. 'That's quite a lot of news for one night.'

'Actually that's only half the news,' said Emily.

'Oh, good lord,' said Carol. 'What else is there?'

'Mr Hunter is going on a trip on Friday,' said Emily, 'and he's asked me and Jamie to go with him.'

'What kind of trip?' Carol asked suspiciously, clearly still convinced that Mr Hunter was some kind of East Anglian drug kingpin.

'He's going to look at a hotel. He's thinking of investing in it.'

'He should come and look round here,' said Martin affably. 'There are some lovely hotels that could do with a bit of cash.'

'Where is it, Moo?' asked Carol. 'The hotel?'

Emily took a deep breath. 'It's in Mauritius.'

Martin's pint froze on the way to his mouth. 'Where the bloody hell's Mauritius?'

'It's in the Indian Ocean.'

Carol's eyes were on stalks. 'You're flying there? How long will that take?'

'About twelve hours.'

'Twelve hours?' squawked Martin. 'You're going to be on a plane for twelve hours? Each way?'

'I've seen pictures of Mauritius. Remember, Martin?' said Carol. 'Linda went there on her third honeymoon, she showed us the photos.'

'Linda went on three honeymoons?' asked Kelly, revelling in the drama.

'Well, she's been married three times,' Carol explained. 'I think the first honeymoon was in Hove and the second in Llandudno, so she's come a long way. How long are you going for, Moo?'

'A week,' said Emily, relieved that this was all finally out in the open. And excited, having said it out loud. *I'm going to Mauritius on Friday. I've ordered a bikini and a sarong from a fancy swimwear website and Kelly's going to trim my hair tomorrow. I'm off on a big adventure.*

Emily sat on the bench with her mum, watching Kelly dance with her dad. The band were good, with a female lead vocalist who could really sing. Right now she was doing a very decent job of 'Murder on the Dancefloor' by Sophie Ellis-Bextor, and the place was heaving with writhing bodies. Kelly was giving it both barrels as usual, her scarlet hair flying as she waved her arms around her head and twirled her hips in Martin's direction. He looked slightly terrified but was gamely trying to keep up.

'Hey, Emma. It is Emma, isn't it?' Plague Syphilis had appeared in front of their table, clutching a pint and an unlit cigarette.

'Emily,' she replied. 'Close enough.'

'You look hot,' he said, swaying a little on his feet with an appreciative ogle. Emily assumed this was a compliment, although you never knew with men around here. There was always a possibility he was telling her she looked a bit pink and sweaty. 'Do you fancy a dance?' he added, even though he could barely stand.

'I can't, sorry,' she said cheerfully. 'My mum can't be left alone, it's a condition of her day release.'

The man glanced at Carol, who crossed her eyes and bared her teeth, then snapped at him like a rabid dog. He nodded awkwardly and scurried off.

'Thanks, Mum,' said Emily.

'No trouble,' said Carol. 'Look at the state of those two.' She nodded at Kelly and Martin, who were now doing some kind of tango to Cheryl Cole's 'Fight For This Love'. She rested her head on Emily's shoulder and did a tiny burp.

'Have you had a good birthday party?' asked Emily.

'Epic, thank you.'

'Sorry about all the news.'

Carol sighed. 'It's fine.'

Emily turned to look at her. 'What's wrong, Mum?'

Carol took another swig of wine and gave Emily a watery smile. 'Oh, it's nothing. I'm just being daft.'

'Come on, what is it?'

Carol sighed and patted Emily's arm. 'You're the last of

my babies, and you've all moved away, but you feel different from the boys. This job, riding horses, now a rich boyfriend and fancy holidays.'

'It's not a holiday, it's work.'

'I know, but still. It feels like you've got a different life now.'

Emily took her mum's hand and ducked her head so she could look her in the eye. 'Don't be daft. It's my job, but you're my family. You and Dad and David and Simon. And Kelly too. This will always be home.'

Carol's eyes swam with tears, although Emily couldn't tell whether they were prompted by wine or genuine emotion.

'And what about Jamie?' sobbed Carol. 'What if he offers you a new kind of home? One with horses and a fancy swimming pool?'

'We've been going out a couple of weeks, Mum,' Emily said softly. 'But even if he does, it won't change anything. You'll still be my mum. In fact, you'll probably end up being his mum too, because the one he's got is a bit shit.'

'Poor soul,' said Carol. 'He seems like a nice lad.'

'He is, Mum. I like him a lot.'

Carol squeezed Emily's arm and emptied her glass. 'All right, then. You're a good girl. Send me a postcard and buy me something swish from the airport.'

Emily laughed. 'No problem. What do you fancy?'

Carol thought about it for a moment, then broke into an excited grin. 'Get me one of those massive Toblerones.'

CHAPTER TWENTY-SEVEN

Half an hour after leaving the airport in a sleek silver Lexus driven by Paul, Mr Hunter's Mauritian driver, Emily decided she could live a thousand lifetimes and never see anywhere as breathtakingly beautiful as Mauritius. She'd read a Lonely Planet guidebook on the plane and looked at hundreds of pictures of white sand beaches and crystal blue waters on her phone, but nothing had prepared her for the rolling green landscape, the mountains and the bustle and colour of cars and villages and people.

But all of that faded into the background when she saw Mr Hunter's beach house on the west coast of the island; a five-bedroomed, white-painted villa with a grey tiled roof and a thatched poolside terrace. She stood at the end of the path just a few metres from the lapping waves, her bare feet warm on the flagstones, and couldn't even begin to find words for the dazzling tableau of gold layered over turquoise layered over white.

Jamie appeared at her side and stroked her arm, bringing her out in goosebumps despite the heat of the afternoon sun on her skin.

'What do you think?' he asked.

'I mean, it's no Bognor, is it?'

Jamie laughed and took her hand. 'Come on, Madeleine has a drink for you.'

Emily let him lead her up to the terrace, where Mr Hunter was helping himself to a green coconut from a tray held by the housekeeper. She was the local equivalent of Anna, but considerably more friendly. She also smiled, which Emily had never seen Anna do.

'*Merci*,' said Emily, taking a green coconut and sipping the water inside through a straw. It was unexpectedly tepid, but still refreshing.

'We can speak English if you prefer,' said Madeleine with a warm smile and a sing-song accent.

'It's OK, I speak French,' said Emily with a shy smile. 'Maybe we can do both.'

Jamie raised his eyebrows at his father. 'Did you know Emily spoke French?'

Mr Hunter shook his head. 'I must have missed that on her CV. Clearly dazzled by her many other accomplishments.'

'I'm not really fluent,' said Emily, blushing a little, 'and it's pretty rusty. My first proper job after college was working for a French building contractor, and I might have slightly exaggerated my language skills at interview. So I did online classes in the evenings for two years while I worked there.'

Mr Hunter laughed. 'I can see you're going to put us both to shame.'

'Never been to France though,' added Emily, laughing at the ridiculousness of it.

'Well, this is the next best thing. Everyone here speaks French, lots of people speak English, and the locals speak Creole, which is a rather wonderful language. Lots of French influences, but it has its own unique style.'

Emily nodded, having learned a few basic phrases of Creole from her guidebook on the plane. Despite the overnight flight and the huge business class seat she'd only managed a few hours' sleep, but that was the last thing she cared about right now.

'Is there any work you need me to do this afternoon?' she asked, reminding herself that it was currently 3 p.m. on a Friday, so 11 a.m. in the UK.

'Good lord, no,' said Mr Hunter, glancing at his watch. 'It's technically the weekend, and the best part of the day to be on the beach. You two go and enjoy yourselves, I'm going to have a dip in the pool and a nap. We'll go to Sam's Café for dinner just after five, catch the sunset.'

Emily smiled her thanks, trying to contain her excitement and remain totally cool about this whole situation. She followed Jamie to their rooms, which had a shared terrace with a stunning sea view. She'd booked them a double room at the hotel they were staying at from tomorrow, but insisted it was more professional if they stayed in separate rooms in his father's house. Jamie said he thought she was charmingly old-fashioned, but hadn't minded.

The two rooms were identical, with white-painted shutters framing the windows and a ceiling fan that spun lazily over the wooden bed. She opened the doors and stepped out to join Jamie, who consented to posing for a selfie with the beach and the turquoise water in the background.

'Kelly is going to be spitting,' said Emily, sending it to her friend, then adding it to the family WhatsApp group with the message *Arrived safely, wish you were here!* 'What shall we do now?'

'Let's go to the beach,' said Jamie. 'It's late enough that you won't burn.'

'Fine by me,' she said excitedly, itching to have time alone with Jamie after days of being in work mode. 'I'll just get changed.'

Jamie disappeared next door while Emily emptied the contents of her suitcase into neat piles on the bed. She'd limited herself to hand luggage since they were only here for one week and summer clothes didn't take up much room. She grabbed her new rainbow-striped bikini and quickly put it on, wishing her skin was less pale; Kelly would have got a spray tan for the occasion, but Emily hadn't had time. She wrapped herself in a pink sarong and slid her feet into flip-flops, then piled her hair on top of her head in a messy bun and grabbed a pair of sunglasses. It was hardly catwalk beach glamour, but it would have to do.

'This is my kind of sea swimming,' said Jamie, floating on his back in the warm, crystal water. 'Christmas Day was great and everything, but this is more my style.'

'I've never seen anything like it,' said Emily, watching silvery fish dart around her feet. 'I'm trying to be super-chilled about it all, but oh my fucking GOD. I can't believe I'm here.'

Jamie grinned at her, clearly delighted. 'We've got a whole week of this.'

'It's like something out of a film. Girls like me don't come to places like this.'

Jamie gave her a stern look. 'Don't say that. Mauritius isn't at all exclusive; all kinds of people come here.'

'Does this beach belong to your dad?' she asked, looking back at the house in the middle of the pretty cove. There was nobody around.

'No,' said Jamie. 'All the beaches are open to the public here. There's no such thing as a private beach.'

'Oh, wow,' said Emily in surprise. 'That's really cool.'

'It's one of my favourite things about this place. All the locals go to the beach at weekends, it's like a big family party. We'll go on Sunday.'

Emily grinned happily and slid her arms around him, pulling him towards her for a kiss. They were waist deep in the warm water with the late-afternoon sun on her back, and she couldn't imagine anywhere she'd rather be. Jamie's hands disappeared below the waterline and stroked the curve of her hips, and she flinched and pulled away.

'What's wrong?' he asked, lifting his sunglasses on to his head.

Emily immediately felt stupid, but decided she might as well be honest.

'I feel a bit self-conscious, sorry,' she muttered. 'There's more of my body out in public than I'm used to.'

'You're kidding, right?' said Jamie, pulling her back towards him. 'You have a fabulous body.'

'Hardly,' she said. 'I've got no boobs and a big bum.'

'You have perfect boobs and a magnificent bum,' laughed Jamie. He paused, his eyes widening. 'Holy shit, you're not kidding, are you?'

Emily shook her head. 'Not really. I've always felt out of proportion, I guess.'

'Wow, this is mad,' said Jamie, running his hand through his hair. 'Women spend a fortune for a shape like yours. That bikini fits you perfectly; you look strong and fit and gorgeous.'

Emily looked at him, with his flat stomach and broad shoulders and strong thighs, effortlessly handsome, and wished she could be so at ease with her body. Too many years of being teased and mocked for having too much of one thing and not nearly enough of the other.

Jamie sighed. 'What was it you said to me that day we went riding? After the Christmas party?'

'I don't know,' she said, wincing at the memory of how uptight she must have sounded. 'I said a lot of things. Something about conflict of interest?'

'You said you fancied me rotten,' he said, sliding his hands back on to her hips, his thumbs disappearing inside the waistband of her bikini. 'Well, guess what? I also fancy you rotten.'

Emily smiled and pulled him into a tight hug, wondering what she'd done to deserve all this, but determined to make the most of every moment. 'Come on,' she said. 'We might be away, but Friday is still a swimming day.'

Sam's Café was exactly as he'd described it, with mismatched tables and chairs spilling off the wooden terrace into the soft sand. Fairy lights were strung haphazardly through the palm trees, filling the air with a soft glow as the sky worked its way through every shade of pink and orange and red. She and Jamie and Mr Hunter watched in reverent silence until the sun finally dipped below the horizon and the hubbub of music and chat returned.

'Mr Charles!' A woman appeared at the table with a tray of drinks. 'They told me you were here, I'm so happy to see you.'

'Ah, look at you, Jessie,' said Mr Hunter, standing up to kiss her on both cheeks. 'You're more lovely every time I see you.' Emily would have known anywhere that this was Sam's sister; they looked like twins. She was a beautiful woman in her late fifties, wearing a pale blue linen dress with sandals, her dark hair hanging loose down her back.

Jessie smiled as she put a tall cocktail in front of each of them. 'Piña coladas on the house,' she said, smiling at Jamie and Emily. 'Mr James, you are still too handsome.'

Jamie laughed and gave her a hug. 'This is Emily, Jessie. She's dad's assistant, and also my girlfriend.'

'My God, look at you,' said Jessie, shaking Emily's hand. 'So beautiful. Your skin is like porcelain, be careful in the sun.'

'It's lovely to meet you, Jessie,' said Emily, still reeling from Jamie introducing her as his girlfriend. 'Sam has told me a lot about you.'

'Ah, I miss my brother,' said Jessie. 'I hope you're looking after him.'

'Of course,' said Mr Hunter. 'He said he's coming over later in the year?'

'My daughter's wedding in June,' said Jessie, smiling indulgently. 'Delphine. You must come.'

'If I can, I definitely will,' said Mr Hunter.

'I'll leave you to eat,' said Jessie. 'Shall I send out the usual?'

'Of course,' said Mr Hunter, smiling happily.

'What's the usual?' whispered Emily to Jamie, sipping her drink. It was ice cold and tasted one hundred times better than the piña coladas she and Kelly had drunk in both of Chichester's most sophisticated cocktail bars.

Jamie grinned. 'Wait and see.'

★

'The usual' turned out to be more types of food than Emily had ever eaten in her life, mostly different varieties of fish and seafood and fruit that she'd never seen before, let alone tasted. The dishes came slowly, as though Mauritius operated on a different concept of time to everywhere else. Emily had grown up in a family where mealtimes were a battle to clear your plate and claim seconds, so this lingering over tiny plates felt entirely alien to her. But it was also wonderful to try new things and talk about the flavours and treat a meal like an experience rather than some kind of armed warfare.

'Tell us about the hotel, Dad,' said Jamie, waving at the waiter and holding up his glass and three fingers for more cocktails. 'What do you need us to find out?'

'It's called the Lapis Lagoon and it's an interesting concept,' said Mr Hunter. 'It's not been open long. It's all-inclusive, which is nothing new. But this one isn't a big resort; it's more boutique and minimalist. They're targeting young travellers on a budget; it doesn't cost much more than a hostel, really. You can get a double room there for the equivalent of fifty or sixty pounds a night.'

Emily raised her eyebrows – that sounded cheap, even by her standards. 'What's the catch?'

'That's a very good question. Meals are included, but there's no menu or buffet. You eat whatever the chef is cooking, so there's no waste. All vegan, so everybody eats the same. No alcohol, but plenty of bars along the beach if you want a drink. They make their money offering experiences for guests, but not the usual tourist stuff. Trips to hidden waterfalls, sunrise mountain climbs, that kind of thing.'

Jamie nodded. 'It sounds pretty great. Are you thinking of buying it?'

'They want to expand,' said Mr Hunter. 'Take the concept to other locations. Thailand, Indonesia, all the places young people travel. But first I want to know if it's the real deal, what it's like to stay there.'

Emily had been chewing her lip in silence for the past few minutes, but she couldn't stay quiet any longer. 'Mr Hunter, can I say something?' she asked. 'I understand what you're asking, but I can't give you a proper opinion on a place like that. I've got nothing to compare it to – the last holiday I had was in a static caravan.' She held her head up, not wanting him to think she was ashamed, which she absolutely wasn't. 'How would I know whether this place is decent or not?'

Mr Hunter smiled. 'I understand that, Emily, but with respect, what's stopping you coming to a place like this? You could get a flight for £500, and ten nights in this hotel for the same amount, all your food included. Do I not pay you enough?'

Emily considered this and realised there was nothing holding her back other than her own perception of the kind of place where women like her belonged. 'Of course, I didn't mean . . .'

'I don't want a comparison to every other place you've ever stayed, I just want you to tell me what it's like. Do a few experiences, eat the food, hang out by the pool, then report back.' He smiled kindly. 'Is there any reason why you can't do that?'

Emily thought about all the times she'd been scared of stepping out of her comfort zone, that she wouldn't fit in. But she'd taken the plunge and left Chichester, moved to London and got a job, made new friends. She'd found this job, got on a plane yesterday, and today swam half a mile in a bikini that fit her perfectly. It was stupid to think she wasn't good enough, or that being somewhere like this was some kind of betrayal of her working-class roots.

She was twenty-nine with a good job and no kids. People her age travelled all the time, so what was she afraid of? Nobody here was judging her, looking at her like she didn't belong. Quite the opposite, actually – there were a couple of guys at the bar whose eyes had been on stalks all evening (although that might be for Jamie, to be fair.) She could be a Chi girl AND a woman in a beach café in Mauritius.

'There's no reason,' she said. 'I can absolutely do that.' She looked at Jamie, who squeezed her hand and smiled, like he knew that something important had just happened.

'That's very good to hear,' said Mr Hunter, passing her another cocktail.

CHAPTER TWENTY-EIGHT

Jamie drove Emily to the Lapis Lagoon Hotel on Saturday morning, in an ancient Suzuki Jimny that Mr Hunter kept at the beach house. The hotel was on the east side of the island, so Emily had another opportunity to see a bit of the landscape inland. She hadn't expected it to be so lush and green; somehow tropical islands manifested in her head as nothing but sand and palm trees. There were signposts to interesting-looking things at every turn – an old sugar plantation, a nature trail that Jamie told her led to the island's only volcano, a beautiful colonial mansion that was now a museum. She wished they had more time to do some hiking and sightseeing, and tried not to get lost in fantasies about a time in the future when she and Jamie might come back.

The hotel was exactly as Mr Hunter had described it – simple and not at all fancy, but spotlessly clean and beautifully designed. The other guests were a lot like them – twenty- and thirty-something couples or groups of friends, mostly French or British, no designer handbags or high heels in sight. It felt fun and relaxed and effortlessly cool, and Emily instantly loved it.

They joined a tour of the hotel before lunch, led by a member of staff in khaki shorts and a pale blue polo shirt. She showed them the pool, set in a garden of citrus trees and fragrant flowering shrubs, and the winding path to the pretty beach. Then she led them to the palm-roofed terrace where meals would be served three times a day, with large communal tables laid out like a school cafeteria. They took a brochure of activities and the key to their room, then headed off to settle in. It was simple and clean, with a tiny bathroom and a small balcony overlooking the gardens and the sea.

'What would you like to do while we're here?' asked Jamie, flumping on the bed and handing Emily the brochure.

She flicked through the pages of options – hiking tours, waterfall swimming, quad biking, sunset fishing trips, diving with sharks.

'I'd really like to go snorkelling,' she said. 'I've seen pictures but I've never done it.'

'No problem,' he said, looking at the list of timings. 'There's a boat trip out to a nice bit of the reef after lunch, we can do that today.'

'What about you?' she asked. 'What's top of your list?'

'I'd really like to take you horse riding on the beach.'

'Oh, wow,' said Emily, wishing she'd picked something a bit more romantic than snorkelling. 'What will the horses be like?' She felt completely safe with Rupert, but the idea of riding a new and unknown horse felt a bit unsettling.

'The riding centre they use here is good, I've been there before. We can let them know you're a beginner – it will be fine.'

Emily paused, a thought nagging at the edge of her brain. She tried to put a lid on it, but Jamie noticed anyway.

'What's wrong?'

'Nothing's *wrong*,' she said breezily. 'I was just wondering if you'd ever brought other women here.'

He said nothing for a second, then smiled awkwardly.

'Naomi came here once. She'd been filming in South Africa and I met her here for a few days at the end of her shoot.'

'OK,' said Emily with a forced laugh. 'Did you take her riding on the beach too?'

'No,' he said, a little defensively. 'She was knackered and just wanted to lie by Dad's pool all day. I went riding on my own.'

Emily said nothing, wishing she was generally better at saying nothing.

Jamie shrugged. 'Naomi was great, and we were good for a while. But we weren't right for each other.' He rolled over so his face was close to hers. 'Emily, I don't know how many ways I can say it. I like you. I like spending time with you. I'm really glad you're here. Will that do for now?' He took her hand and kissed it.

Emily smiled, wishing for the hundredth time she was less insecure. 'Yeah, it definitely will.'

'So, snorkelling and riding. We can do both of those today. Anything else?'

'I'd like to see the island for real. Like, where the locals go. Maybe a market or something.'

'Oh, that's a great idea. I'll take you to the Sunday market in Flacq tomorrow, then we'll go to the beach on the way back, spend the day hanging out with the locals.'

'Sounds like a plan,' said Emily, bouncing off the bed and into action. 'Can I have some lunch now?'

Jamie smiled. 'Can I take you to bed first?'

She gave him a fake stern look. 'We're in Mauritius. I'm not sure doing something we can do in the UK is a good use of our time.'

'Well, I'm only asking for ten minutes.'

219

Emily laughed. 'Ten minutes?'

'There's a lot you can do in ten minutes. Why are we still talking about this? We're wasting valuable time.'

Emily thought for a second, then pulled off her T-shirt and undid her shorts. After everything they'd talked about yesterday, it was time to stop being ashamed of her body. She pulled the hairband out of her bun and shook it free.

'You look like a goddess,' he whispered, drinking in her nakedness.

'You're wearing too many clothes.'

'As always, that's easily fixed.'

Emily's horse was called Tasha, a dappled grey that felt a little more skittish than Rupert, but steady enough. Jamie's was a beautiful dark bay called Wilbur with a white stripe on his nose and white socks on his hind legs. They took a dusty path through farmland from the riding school to the beach, Emily tuning in to the unfamiliar sounds of tropical birds and the muggy warmth in the air. Having only ridden in a Norfolk winter, it felt wonderfully freeing to wear nothing but leggings and a T-shirt. Emily had taken a riding helmet when it was offered, but Jamie hadn't bothered.

'Aren't we supposed to be part of a group?' she asked as they rode past a wall covered in delicate pink flowers. She reached out and picked one, inhaling the sweet fragrance.

'Yeah,' said Jamie, 'but I paid extra and asked if we could go off just the two of us. As long as we book through the hotel and they earn their commission, they don't care.'

'It's beautiful here,' said Emily as they emerged from the path on to the deserted beach. 'So quiet.'

'The beaches this side of the island are less busy at this time of day. No sunset.'

'Still gorgeous, though.'

'How do you like your horse?' he asked.

'She seems lovely,' said Emily, reaching down to pat her neck. 'Not as fat as Rupert.'

Jamie laughed. 'Are you fat-shaming my horse?'

'No. Yes. Don't tell him I said anything.'

He pulled alongside her on the sand and reached out to take her hand as they strolled towards the distant headland. The horses didn't seem to be in any hurry, and neither were they. Emily's head was still full of an afternoon of snorkelling. They'd taken a boat out to the reef with a small group of French girls who fluttered their eyelashes and giggled at Jamie until Emily gave them a killer death stare and asked them in her most sarcastic French if they were OK.

Once the boat stopped, Jamie and Emily had headed off in a different direction from the girls, spending a blissful hour watching tropical fish and turtles swim around in the rainbow of coral. It was a spectacle Emily had only ever seen on TV, and she couldn't wait to go again. A storm had come in when they got back, so they'd spent an hour sitting on the balcony with a coffee while the rain lashed down and thunder rumbled. It was Emily's first experience of a tropical storm, and she couldn't help but be drawn to the power and drama of it. Within an hour the heavy clouds were gone and the sun was out again, baking the wet landscape and making everything steam.

'Did you burn today?' asked Jamie, looking with concern at her pink shoulders.

'Only a bit,' said Emily, 'but I'm OK.' She'd slapped on

tons of factor fifty, but still managed to catch the sun on her shoulders. The cooling evening breeze felt blissful.

'So,' said Jamie with a smile. 'Are you ready to learn to canter?'

Emily smiled nervously. 'I don't know. Am I?'

'Can't think of anywhere better.'

'What do I have to do?'

'Firstly, sit up straight, like when we're walking, and keep your heels down. Don't slump or arch your back, and don't forget to breathe.'

'OK,' she said, straightening her back and lowering her heels. She was too nervous to breathe.

'We're going to start in a walk, then move into a trot. When you're nice and comfortable there, you're going to sit nice and deep in the saddle and give Tasha a squeeze with your heels to take her up into a canter.'

'Right,' said Emily, feeling a bit sick.

'You need to relax, which will feel really unnatural at first. Heels down, back straight, let your hips move with the motion of the horse. It's like a waltz.'

'A waltz?'

'Yeah. A horse in canter moves to a three-time beat. When I learned to ride as a kid my instructor used to make me sing "My Favourite Things" from *The Sound of Music* to help get a feel for the rhythm. RAIN-drops on RO-ses and WHI-skers on KI-ttens.'

Emily snorted with laughter, imagining an adorable child version of Jamie singing Julie Andrews.

'Can you show me?'

'Sure.' Jamie nudged Wilbur into a walk, then a rising trot, then another nudge into a loping canter. He rode fifty metres

222

down the beach then made a wide U-turn and came back, Emily examining everything about his stance as he passed by. He did a couple more loops, then gently pulled the reins to tell Wilbur to slow back to a trot, then a walk. He pulled up beside her and stopped, Wilbur snorting and shaking his head.

'You make it look so easy,' said Emily with a nervous smile.

'It's definitely not easy. It takes practice, so don't worry if you don't get it straight away. When we're back home we'll do this in a big circle in the riding school; it's easier for the horse to know what you want it to do. But these horses don't really do circles.'

'What if I fall off?'

'You won't fall off if you sit up straight. People fall off when they panic and lean forwards, then slide off sideways.'

'How do I make her stop?'

'By gently pulling on the reins and bringing her down one gear at a time. But I'll ride alongside you so you can both follow my pace.'

Emily took a deep breath. 'OK, I'm ready.'

She clicked her tongue to start Tasha walking, then followed Jamie into a rising trot. *Back straight, heels down.* Then she gave the horse a squeeze with her heels and felt the change in rhythm as they moved into a gentle canter. She tried to relax but there were too many things to think about and it all just felt disconnected and out of sync.

Jamie's horse slowed to a trot, then a walk, and Tasha did the same.

'That was a good first try,' Jamie said encouragingly. 'As I said, it's not easy, but now you know what it feels like. This time try not to over-think it. Forget about the horse, just keep your back straight, heels down and focus on the movement. RAIN-drops on RO-ses and WHI-skers on KI-ttens.'

Emily laughed and relaxed a little as they set off again. By the time they reached the far end of the beach, they'd had lots of tries and Emily had sung the whole of 'My Favourite Things' apart from the bits about dog bites and bee stings. She was getting much better, although there were still times when she pulled the reins too hard and Tasha put on her handbrake, causing Emily's pelvis to slam into the saddle and make her teeth rattle. Jamie stayed alongside her the whole time, shouting encouragement and reminding her to sit up straight and keep breathing.

They stopped for a break, letting the horses cool off in the gently lapping surf as the sun set behind the mountains.

'You're definitely getting it,' said Jamie. 'I'm really impressed. You've got a strong core, you'll be good at paddle boarding.'

Emily grinned. 'Can we do that tomorrow?'

'How about a sunrise paddle?' suggested Jamie. 'It's the best time of the day on this side of the island.'

'I'd love to,' laughed Emily. 'When do we sleep?'

'Meh.' Jamie shrugged. 'You can sleep on the plane home. Ready to head back?'

Emily nodded and kicked Tasha off first this time, leaving Jamie for dust. She mentally checked her posture and hummed the song, feeling the motion through the saddle as her hips fell into step with the horse. Tasha's hooves pounded into the hard sand as Emily kept going, her skin tingling in the warm air. *I'm doing it*, she thought, *I'm really doing it*. She'd been so tired before they left the hotel this evening, but right now she felt unstoppable.

CHAPTER TWENTY-NINE

The moment Emily arrived at Flacq Sunday market, she wished her mum was here to see it. It was exactly the kind of place Carol loved – bustling with people and noise, with stalls selling everything from brightly coloured fruit and veg to seafood and textiles. It wasn't fancy or expensive or just for tourists; there was a kind of joyful chaos as locals in a hurry dodged around the dawdling visitors, the air full of sweat and shouting and the smell of spicy street food. She took loads of photos on her phone to add to the family WhatsApp later, knowing that Carol would get far more excited about this than she would about white sand beaches and sunsets.

'What do you think of this?' she asked Jamie, showing him a scarf in swirling shades of fuchsia pink and purple. 'I think my mum would really like it.'

'It's lovely,' said Jamie. 'It's cashmere, you should get one for yourself too.'

'They're about fifty pounds,' said Emily, doing the mental exchange rate maths and wondering if that sounded like a lot of money to Jamie. Probably not.

'Yeah, but you're not going to pay that. You have to haggle.'

Emily looked at him uncertainly. 'Really?' The market trader hovered impatiently, grinning expectantly at them both.

'Of course,' Jamie said. 'He doesn't expect you to pay full price – haggling is all part of the fun.'

'So how much should I offer to pay?'

'How much are you actually prepared to pay?'

'I don't know,' Emily whispered. 'Maybe twenty-five pounds each?'

'So offer him one thousand rupees for both.'

Emily thought for a second. 'That's only about twenty quid.'

'I know. You're not going to pay that, obviously. It's just a starting point.'

Emily laughed. 'How is this fun?'

Jamie rolled his eyes. 'Yeah, I'm sure haggling with a beautiful woman is a HUGE drag for him. Come on, you can be fearsome when you want to be.'

She took a deep breath and approached the man, who initially looked like he'd been stabbed in the chest when she proposed her price. She feigned equal horror at his counter-offer, getting into the good-natured theatre of it all and embracing the role of hard-nosed English bargain hunter. They wrangled over the price happily for a few minutes, until Emily had three beautiful cashmere scarves for the equivalent of fifty pounds. Kelly could have one too, whether she wanted one or not.

They browsed the alleyways for another hour, picking up souvenirs and enjoying the hectic chaos of it all, until the temperature climbed to a point where they both needed air and space and water to cool down in. Jamie drove a few miles down the coast to the public beach at Belle Mare, parking under the trees at the edge of the sand. The beach was scattered with tourists and big family groups – kids playing in the water, parents unpacking lunch from coolers or cooking on barbecues under the trees, beach vendors selling slices of pineapple dusted with chilli. There was a cooling breeze off the coast that took some of the heat out of the day, although the humidity had turned Emily's hair into a frizzy nest.

They stripped down to their swimwear and wandered hand-in-hand into the water, swimming for a while to rinse off the heat and stickiness of the market. The water felt like a cool bath and was so clear that Emily could see the red polish on her toes. Tiny glittering fish swam in circles round her feet, scattering whenever she moved.

'Did you get enough photos this morning?' asked Jamie, who'd teased her for taking close-ups of giant crabs and piles of tropical fruit.

'They're for my mum. She loves a market, absolute bargain queen. She'd have paid half what I did for those scarves.'

'You haven't taken many pictures of us since you've been here,' he said. 'I thought I'd be posing for a thousand selfies a day.'

Emily shrugged. 'I don't know,' she said, leaning her head back into the water to flatten down the frizz a bit. 'I'm not sure any photo could ever do it justice. It might show what it looks like to be here with you, but not how it makes me feel.'

Jamie smiled and took her hand. 'That's quite profound for a Sunday. How does it make you feel?'

Emily gave a tiny laugh. 'Happy, excited, a bit scared.'

'What are you scared of?'

Messing everything up. Getting dumped again. The usual shit insecure women worry about. 'Perhaps scared is the wrong word. A little apprehensive, maybe. Like I've found a side to myself that I didn't know existed.'

'Ah, I see,' said Jamie. 'The Emily who rides horses, swims with turtles and doesn't hide her body under a tablecloth.'

Emily poked him in the arm. 'It's a sarong, but yes.'

'Well, if it's any consolation, I've discovered a new side too.'

She looked at him curiously. 'What do you mean?'

He took a deep breath. 'When I asked you out before Christmas, I'd never done that before – actually decided to tell a woman I liked her. With Naomi and Louisa and the other women I've gone out with, I've let them take the lead and gone along with it, even when I knew it wasn't quite right. I'm not proud of it, but I guess sometimes it's easier to live in the moment.'

Emily thought about Mark, all those moments. Two years of them, not thinking about where it might lead, pretending the future didn't matter. Not a very healthy way to live, with hindsight.

'I'd been trying to pluck up the courage to ask you out since Louisa left, but couldn't get the words out,' he continued. Emily thought about all that time Jamie had spent hanging around her office, offering to wrap hampers and dispense sticky tape. 'And I knew you'd probably turn me down that day, but I did it anyway. I decided it was time to stop waiting for things to happen. I was pretty proud of myself, actually.'

'I'm really glad you did.'

'Me too,' said Jamie. 'Your shoulders look a bit pink. Are you burning?'

'I'm always burning,' said Emily. 'The only way I tan is out of a bottle. I'll sit in the shade for a bit.'

'Kiss me first,' said Jamie, gently pulling her towards him. She slid her arms round his waist and leaned in, wondering if there would ever be a moment more romantic than this, when she felt a sharp pain in the ball of her foot. She jumped in agony, and the pain was repeated further towards her heel.

'What's wrong?' Jamie asked, grabbing her arm as she hopped up and down, squealing with pain.

'Something's stung me, OW OW OW!' squealed Emily, her eyes filling with tears as further stabbing pains repeated across the arch of her foot. She scrunched her eyes shut and clung on to Jamie as she hobbled out of the water, keen to distance herself from whatever evil sea creature was attacking her.

A middle-aged woman sitting with her family on the sand spotted Emily hopping about and hurried over. 'Let me look, let me look,' she said in heavily accented English, grabbing Emily's leg and holding it off the sand.

'Jellyfish or sea urchin?' asked Jamie.

'No jellyfish here today,' said the woman, peering closely at Emily's foot. 'Sea urchin. *Ayo, to bizin fer atansion la. Sa bann zafair la mari bézer.*' She smiled at Emily, then stood up. 'I will be back, stay there,' she said, then hurried off back to her family, her patterned dress flapping in the breeze.

Emily tried to manage the pain by doing short panting breaths like she was giving birth. 'What did the Creole bit mean?' she asked.

'Something along the lines of you needing to be careful because those things are really wicked.'

'Brilliant. Wish I'd known that ten minutes ago.'

Jamie helped her on to her towel in the shade at the edge

of the beach. She lifted her foot on to the opposite knee and could clearly see lots of tiny black spines embedded in the skin, which was already red and inflamed. She tried to breathe through the pain, but it felt like she'd been stabbed by a hundred tiny burning knives.

'Are sea urchins poisonous?' she asked, wondering if a terrible gangrenous infection was already creeping up her leg.

'Not if you pull the spines out,' said Jamie calmly.

'Is that going to hurt?'

'Does it hurt now?'

'Fuck yes,' said Emily, jiggling her foot.

'Well, you'll just have to be brave. Here comes our friend again.'

Emily looked up to see the woman jogging over the sand waving a tiny pair of metal tweezers. 'Every island mama keeps these in her bag. You stay still now.'

Emily tried not to move, wincing as the woman pulled out the spines one after the other. It felt like the same sharp pain followed by a dull ache you get when you have a splinter removed, and it made Emily feel like she might throw up. Finally the last tiny spine was yanked out, and the woman went back to her handbag to find a tube of antiseptic cream. She rubbed it gently into Emily's foot, then patted her leg.

'Ayo, you will be fine now. Rest a little, the pain will go soon.'

'Thank you,' said Emily, her eyes full of tears of pain and gratitude. The woman smiled warmly and went back to her family.

'You OK?' said Jamie, passing her a cold can of Sprite from the cooler.

'Yeah,' said Emily, trying to ignore the dull throb in her

foot as she looked at all the families up and down the beach. 'I can see why people like deserted beaches, but this is much more my cup of tea. Lots of helpful people.'

'More like Bognor.'

'Exactly like Bognor. Hard to tell the difference, really.'

Jamie sat with her in the shade for as long as it took to drink a can of Coke, but Emily could see he was restless. Eventually he stood up and grabbed a football from the boot of the car, then wandered back on to the sand.

'Since when did you play football?' she asked, wondering what else she didn't know about him.

'I almost signed for Norwich City.'

Emily snorted. 'You're kidding.'

'Of course I'm kidding. I played rugby at school, and I wasn't very good at that either.'

'So why the football?'

Jamie grinned. 'It's the best way to make new friends. Watch and see.'

He carried the ball a little further down the beach, stopping a few feet from the water and tossing it up and down in his hands, like he was waiting for something. Within seconds a teenage boy from the family of the woman with the tweezers stood up and walked towards him with a smile. Jamie dropped the ball on to the sand and kicked it to him, and the boy kicked it back. An older man from a different family joined them, then a teenage girl who whipped the ball from between them and dribbled it back to Jamie. The boy called out something indignant in Creole, and the game was on.

Emily lay on her front on the towel, comfortably warm

231

and relaxed in the shade of bird-filled trees, the pain in her foot having now retreated to something more like a stubbed toe. She watched the group organise themselves into vaguely defined teams and throw down some towels as makeshift goalposts. Jamie ran and gesticulated and shouted in a mix of English and French and occasional Creole, his hard body shining with sweat and already turning brown after a few days in the sun. She remembered Kelly calling him 'hunky' and grinned to herself, feeling like she'd won the lottery.

'Hey,' whispered a gentle voice.

Emily dragged herself out of a groggy sleep to find Jamie lying on the sand next to her, propped up on one elbow. She rubbed her face with her hands, hoping it might smooth out the fuzzy towel imprint on her face.

'Hey. I fell asleep.'

'Over an hour ago. You looked so relaxed I didn't want to wake you up.'

'Oh God, I'm sorry.'

'Don't be silly. You clearly needed it.'

'I think these past few days might have caught up with me. What have you been doing?'

'Playing football, swimming, making new fish friends.'

Emily sat up, swiftly bundling her crusty salt hair into the hairband round her wrist. 'I'm starving.'

'Me too. How about we go back to the hotel, have a late lunch, then camp out by the pool for the afternoon? I think we're both pretty shattered.'

Emily thought about lying on a sun lounger under an umbrella, or maybe sitting in the shallows of the pool with a book and a cold drink. It sounded like bliss.

'Sounds good. Can we go snorkelling again later? I've got a second date with a turtle.'

Jamie laughed. 'Whatever makes you happy.'

You make me happy, thought Emily, already feeling sad that they'd be going home in a few days.

CHAPTER THIRTY

On Tuesday Emily and Jamie reluctantly checked out of the Lapis Lagoon Hotel and headed back to the Hunter beach house. It had been three nights of honeymoon-level bliss, and Emily felt sun-kissed and rested and happy. They'd done sunrise paddle boarding and another snorkelling trip, made the most of the pool, and even the vegan food had been great. Emily had eaten more fruit and done more exercise in the past few days than she usually managed in a month, and she felt all the better for it. They'd both fallen in love with the hotel – it wasn't anything fancy, but it was welcoming and fun and had a nice buzz about it.

They'd also had a great deal of sex, which had also been fine by Emily. She'd enjoyed sex with Mark during the two years they were seeing each other, but he had liked to dominate proceedings and there'd always been an element of urgency to it, like they didn't know when they'd get a chance to do it again. Jamie was a lot less assured but considerably more tactile, and never missed an opportunity to remind her how much he fancied her. Sometimes it was nothing more than a glance, but it was enough to give her a warm feeling that she carried around for the rest of the day.

By the time they arrived back at the beach house the Jimny had developed an audible rattle, so Jamie dropped her off outside the front door and headed to the garage in town.

Emily grabbed a cold bottle of water from the fridge, then went in search of Mr Hunter. She heard him in the office before she saw him, on a speakerphone call with a male voice that she quickly identified as Adam. She hovered in the corridor for a moment to see if the call was wrapping up.

'And since we're talking about property,' said Adam in his usual sulky drawl, 'I can't believe you're looking into property investments in Mauritius when you're totally uninterested in the suggestions I gave you for investments in the UK.'

'It's a completely different proposition, Adam,' said Mr Hunter, sounding tetchy and bored. 'It's a hotel.'

'I've come to you with two hotels.' Emily rolled her eyes; Adam was such a manbaby. It was clear this conversation wasn't ending any time soon, so she turned to head back to the kitchen.

'And what are Jamie and your floozy secretary doing there?'

Emily stopped in her tracks, her heart thumping.

'That's enough, Adam,' said Mr Hunter, a note of warning in his voice. Emily wondered if this was the first time Adam had stuck the knife in about her since New Year, and decided it probably wasn't.

'You know I don't trust her, Dad,' Adam said petulantly. 'She's been at Bowford for five minutes and she's got both of you wrapped round her little finger. She's an absolute nobody, and suddenly she's bagging free holidays and screwing members of the family. Not very professional, is it?'

'I said that's enough,' shouted Mr Hunter, making a thumping noise on the desk, presumably with his fist. 'How dare you talk about my staff that way? Who do you think you are?'

'I'm your firstborn, Dad,' spat Adam, 'and for better or

worse Bowford will one day be my responsibility. You can't keep cutting me out like this, it's not fucking fair.'

'Oh, grow up, for God's sake,' Mr Hunter said. 'You sound like your mother.'

Adam gave a hollow laugh. 'Me, grow up? I'm the one who went out and built my own business. Your other son is still playing My Little Pony.'

'He's hands-on with the estate, Adam. Something you've never been interested in.'

'You've never offered,' said Adam huffily.

'Because you'd have to do some work,' said Mr Hunter impatiently. 'Planning, maintenance, liaising with tenants and staff, being respectful to people. I'm not sure it plays to your strengths, to be honest.'

Adam said nothing for a few seconds. Emily could hear the cogs in his brain whirring from six thousand miles away and wondered what evil scheme he was plotting. 'I need to go,' he said briskly.

'Fine. Give my love to Victoria and the boys.'

The line went dead, so Emily quickly tiptoed to the other end of the corridor, trying to organise her thoughts. Adam calling her names was nothing new, but it was clear that he'd moved into a new phase of actively trying to get her fired, apparently just out of pure spite.

She gave it a couple of minutes, then noisily opened and closed the front door and walked back to Mr Hunter's office. He was leaning over his desk, deep in thought with a face like thunder.

'Is now a bad time?' she asked.

'Emily, you're back,' he said with a warm smile. 'Of course not. Come on in. Where's James?'

'At the garage with the car, it's got a weird rattle. We've just got back.'

Mr Hunter smiled. 'Then let's ask Madeleine for lunch on the terrace when he gets back, so you can both tell me all about it.'

Jamie arrived back in the Jimny, mysterious rattle fixed, and Madeleine served a delicious crab salad with a huge plate of fruit, which they all piled into while Emily and Jamie shared their experience of the Lapis Lagoon Hotel. Mr Hunter asked lots of questions about the staff and the facilities and the food, and they told him all about the activities they'd signed up for. Jamie had a few suggestions for small improvements, but Mr Hunter seemed encouraged by the positive review.

'Thank you both, that's very helpful,' he said, dabbing his mouth with a linen napkin. 'I'll revisit the financials and make my decision. Emily, I wonder if I can borrow you for a few hours this afternoon? I have some contracts that could do with your eye for detail.'

'No problem,' she said, standing up. 'I'll go and get my stuff.' She picked up her plate and glass, unable to let go of the habit of clearing up after herself. Jamie gave the tiniest smile, so she put them back down again. However hard she tried, Emily couldn't imagine ever being comfortable with somebody being paid to wash her dirty dishes.

'James, what are your plans?' asked Mr Hunter.

'I might head south on the paddle board,' said Jamie, looking through the trees to the beach beyond. 'The weather's due to pick up later so now would be a good time.' He stood up and gave Emily a chaste kiss on the cheek. 'I'll see you both later.'

'We'll go to Sam's for dinner at six,' said Mr Hunter. 'Jessie has some new specials she wants us all to try; she'll keep us a table inside if bad weather comes in.'

Jamie nodded and waved, then headed down the path towards the beach, and Emily hurried to her room so she could change into a dress. She watched him from the window for a minute as he pulled a red and white paddle board out of a shed and checked it over, then she grabbed her notebook and pen and laptop.

She found Mr Hunter back in his office, looking troubled and preoccupied. It wasn't hard to guess why, but Emily didn't ask. They worked through a pile of contracts over the course of the afternoon, closing all the windows in the office when the rain started to hammer down just after 4 p.m. Half an hour later Emily finished her work and went to sit under the cover of the terrace to wait for Jamie, watching the trees bend double in the wind and leaves scatter all over the garden. Presumably he'd ended up a fair distance from the beach house and was now having to carry the paddle board back, no doubt soaked and grumpy.

By 5.30 p.m. the rain had stopped and Emily was officially worried. Jamie had been gone for hours, and there was no way he would still be out on the water. He could have taken shelter somewhere, but he knew they were due to leave for dinner soon. Surely he would have called? She walked to the headland at the end of the beach, but it was deserted.

When she got back, Mr Hunter was waiting on the terrace. 'No sign of James?' he asked, his brow furrowed with concern.

'No,' said Emily. 'I'm assuming he was caught out by the

storm, but it seems weird that he hasn't called. Do you have any idea where he might be?'

Mr Hunter was silent for a moment, his lips clamped together and his eyes fearful and distant. 'I have no idea,' he said quietly. 'But it's nowhere good.'

CHAPTER THIRTY-ONE

'Let's think about it rationally,' said Emily, trying to get a hold on Mr Hunter before he drifted off to a very dark place. 'Could he have got chatting to some locals and lost track of time?'

Mr Hunter considered the possibility. 'If he did, it would be at Sam's Café,' he said. 'Maybe he paddled there and thought we were meeting him for dinner?'

'You should call Jessie,' said Emily, following him to his office. It sounded like an unlikely theory, but she didn't have any better suggestions and the alternative didn't bear thinking about. A knot of anxiety flickered in her stomach – Jamie wasn't the type not to message if he changed his plans.

Mr Hunter put his desk phone on speaker and called Jessie's number. She answered after a few rings.

'Jessie, it's Charles Hunter. I'm here with Emily.'

'Hey, Mr Charles, hey, Emily,' said Jessie cheerfully.

'Is James there?' asked Mr Hunter.

'Mr James? No, we haven't seen him today. We were expecting you all for dinner soon.'

Mr Hunter was silent.

'Mr Charles?' asked Jessie. 'Is everything OK?'

'We don't know where he is, Jessie,' said Emily. 'He went paddle boarding earlier, he should have been back by now.'

The cheerfulness drained out of Jessie's voice. 'We had some big swells earlier, before the rain.'

Mr Hunter leaned on the desk and hung his head, his eyes tight shut. 'What should we do, Jessie?'

She was silent for a moment, clearly thinking. 'Which way did he paddle?' she asked.

'South,' said Emily quickly. 'I definitely remember him saying he was going south.'

'Drive down the coast road and ask the locals if they've seen him,' said Jessie. 'If something's happened, they'll know. I'll make some calls from here, so take your cellphone.'

Mr Hunter thanked her and pressed the button to end the call, then looked at Emily with the bleakest expression she'd ever seen. It was now nearly six, and Emily's worry had turned to a churning feeling of panic. What if he'd been in an accident or got into trouble in the water? He wasn't wearing a life jacket; the water had been like glass when he'd left.

'You take the car,' she said. 'I'll walk along the beach to see if there's anyone around.'

'No, come with me in the car,' said Mr Hunter. 'You speak French and I'm afraid I don't.'

Emily nodded, deciding that enquiries into how Mr Hunter could have owned a home on this island for over forty years without learning basic French or Creole could wait for another day. She ran upstairs to grab her bag, stuffing her phone and a stack of Mauritian rupees into it. She added some US dollars and Jamie's passport, since that was the easiest way to show someone a photograph of him. Mr Hunter was waiting by the car when she got back, shuffling nervously from foot to foot. Madeleine was with him, looking equally anxious. 'I will wait by the phone,' she said, and Mr Hunter nodded.

He turned south on to the coast road and drove slowly, both of them scouring the landscape for people or police cars or ambulances or something that might indicate some kind of incident. After a couple of minutes they spotted a pick-up truck full of locals parked on the side of the road, so Mr Hunter pulled alongside them and Emily leaned out of the window.

'*Bonsoir*,' she said, praying her French lessons wouldn't let her down. '*Nous cherchons un homme sur un SUP.*' Christ knew if that made sense – funnily enough they hadn't covered 'We are looking for a man on a stand-up paddle board' in her French evening classes. She also couldn't remember the French word for 'storm', so she went with 'he hasn't returned after the rain' instead.

The men frowned and chatted in Creole amongst themselves, pointing and gesticulating. Emily had no idea if she'd been understood or if they were just bitching about the weather or stupid foreigners.

'You are English?' said the man in the driving seat, leaning out of the window so he was barely a foot from Emily. He was younger than the rest, probably not much older than her.

'Yes,' she said, relief washing over her. 'He went out paddle boarding hours ago but hasn't come back. An English man, wearing red shorts.'

The man nodded and translated for the other men, prompting more discussion and shaking of heads.

'We have not seen him, but you are doing the right thing,'

said the man. His English was heavily accented, but good. 'Keep asking on this road, someone will know.'

'Will you come with us?' asked Emily. 'To help us ask questions? We can pay you.' She reached into her handbag for cash, but the man wafted her away.

'Yes,' he said, getting out of the truck and climbing into the back of the Jimny. He wound down the window and yelled some kind of explanation to the men, then waved as Mr Hunter pulled back on to the road and left them in a cloud of dust.

'I am Joseph,' said the man. 'I am a gardener at the Coral Reef Hotel.'

Emily turned and forced a smile. 'I'm Emily, and this is Mr Hunter. We are looking for his son, Jamie.'

'The weather was bad today,' said Joseph ominously. 'It can change very suddenly.'

They drove for another mile along the coast road, Emily and Joseph's gaze fixed on the glimpses of beach and water between the properties and the trees. The sun was beginning its descent, making Emily's eyes water; she hadn't thought to bring sunglasses.

'Stop here,' said Joseph suddenly, prompting Mr Hunter to slam on the brakes and hurl Emily's shoulder into the dashboard. This wreck of a Jimny had seatbelts, but they hadn't worked in years.

'Sorry,' said Mr Hunter, pulling over into a lay-by. Joseph jumped out of the car and ran across the road to a group of fishermen tending their colourful boats on the narrow beach. *Pirogues*, thought Emily, remembering Jamie telling her the name of the traditional craft used by generations of Mauritian fishermen, repaired and repainted a hundred times. They watched carefully as Joseph asked a question, then received nods and excited responses in reply – nothing like the men in the truck.

'They know something,' said Mr Hunter, throwing open the door to the Jimny and hurrying across the road to the beach. Emily followed, the knot in her stomach ballooning into her chest.

'What is it?' asked Mr Hunter.

'They heard about a man,' said Joseph. 'He was found on the rocks. Not by these men, some other fishermen. Further up the coast, near where we met.'

'Where is he now?' asked Emily. Jamie must have been heading back if he was that close to home, so it couldn't have been long ago.

'They think he was taken to the hospital, but I do not know if . . .'

Mr Hunter's phone rang, and he quickly fished it out of his pocket. 'It's Jessie,' he said, prodding it frantically to connect the call and put it on speakerphone. Emily chewed the end of her thumb and leaned in to listen.

'I've found him, Mr Charles,' said Jessie. 'He's in the community hospital. I don't know what happened, but he's hurt.'

'Why didn't anyone call?' asked Mr Hunter.

'They got his name before he passed out, but the address he put on the immigration form was for the Lapis Lagoon Hotel, and they said he checked out of there this morning.'

My fault, thought Emily. She'd filled in the forms on the plane and put the hotel address because she happened to have it to hand. Mr Hunter and Jamie were both asleep and she didn't want to wake them up to ask for the beach house address.

'Dear God,' said Mr Hunter. 'Is he conscious?'

'I don't know,' said Jessie, 'but I know he's not dead. That's the best I can do right now.'

Mr Hunter started to walk back towards the car. 'We'll go now.'

'I'll meet you there,' said Jessie. 'You may need some help.'

CHAPTER THIRTY-TWO

Emily took the wheel of the Jimny this time, dropping Joseph back at the truck in a flurry of thanks and then following Mr Hunter's directions to the hospital. His face was pale, and Emily's emotions were in turmoil. But she was glad to have a reason to focus and do something useful.

She dropped Mr Hunter by the main entrance and sped the car round to the parking lot, resisting the temptation to dump it across two spaces in case clamping was a thing in Mauritius and they needed the car later. She grabbed her handbag and ran back as fast as she could, finding Jessie and Mr Hunter waiting for her by the main doors. 'I've spoken to some people,' Jessie said quickly, resting a reassuring hand on Emily's shoulder. 'Nothing official, just a nurse I know. He's got some kind of leg or back injury. He's conscious but confused. They think he might have hit his head.'

The sick feeling in Emily's stomach intensified. How badly had he hit his head? What kind of leg or back injury? She followed Jessie and Mr Hunter into the hospital and was hit by a wall of noise. The waiting area was crowded and chaotic, with some people queuing and others waiting around in various states of injury. Several babies were crying, and the sound felt like daggers in Emily's scrambled brain. 'Follow me,' said Jessie, weaving through the crowd towards some swing doors. Emily felt like this probably wasn't the official route to visit a patient in the hospital, but Jessie didn't seem to care. She hurried down corridors and up a flight of stairs, then through some more doors into a quieter, less frantic space. Jessie stopped and searched the faces of the staff, then saw somebody she knew and waved. A woman wearing green surgical scrubs hurried over to meet them.

'This is my cousin, Celeste,' said Jessie.

'Follow me,' said the woman, not bothering with pleasantries. She led them down a corridor to a row of identical cubicles, all of which seemed to be occupied with the curtains drawn. Emily heard low moaning from behind one, like a cow or someone in labour, and the sound of a crying child in another, accompanied by someone making gentle sssh-ing noises. A world of human odours hung in the air – the place smelled like a school changing room that had just been rinsed down with antiseptic. It made Emily feel sick, but she took deep breaths and swallowed it down.

Jamie was behind the fourth curtain, looking pale and battered with cuts and scrapes all over his face and shoulders and chest. A bandage was wrapped around a wound on his arm, the skin around it stained yellow with iodine spray. He looked like he'd been beaten up, then thrown to the sharks. His right leg was immobilised in some kind of splint.

Mr Hunter sat in the chair by the bed and gently took his son's hand. Emily walked round to the other side of the bed and looked at the IV drip in his arm. There were a couple of bags of clear liquid hanging off it, but that was it. If he was badly injured or his life was at risk, surely he'd be hooked up to beeping machines?

'I'll find the doctor,' said Celeste, hurrying off and pulling the curtain shut behind her. Jessie followed, leaving Mr Hunter and Emily alone with Jamie.

They both sat and watched him for a while, not sure if he was unconscious or just pumped full of heavy-duty painkillers. The fact that he was entirely unsupervised suggested the latter, but Emily had no idea what was normal in Mauritian hospitals.

His eyes flickered, then opened. 'Hey, Dad,' he croaked blearily.

'Oh, thank God,' muttered Mr Hunter, breathing out like he'd been holding it in for some time.

'Where's Emily?' Jamie tried to turn his head and winced.

'She's here,' said Mr Hunter. 'Don't move. We'll get you out of here as soon as possible.'

Jamie groaned. 'I think I've fucked my leg.'

Emily walked round the end of the bed and stood next to Mr Hunter. 'What happened?' she asked, brushing his hair gently out of his eyes.

Jamie gave her a weak smile and tried to swallow. 'Not sure. I was paddle boarding, then there was a wave and everything went dark. Guess I hit the rocks.'

'My God,' said Mr Hunter. 'You could have been killed.'

'Don't let them cut my leg off,' said Jamie dramatically, before drifting away again.

Mr Hunter patted his hand. 'Don't worry. Emily and I will sort everything out.'

The doctor appeared a few minutes later, looking like he'd been strong-armed down the corridor by Jessie. He was in his fifties and looked about as exhausted as Emily felt.

Mr Hunter stood up and shook the doctor's hand. 'I'm Charles Hunter,' he said, 'James's father.'

'I'm Doctor Ramsamy,' said the doctor. 'We've been trying to find you. It helps a great deal if you put the correct information on your immigration form.'

Emily gave a guilty cough. She'd apologise properly for that later.

'I've had a look at your son's X-rays,' said the doctor, flipping through some pages on a clipboard. 'He has several broken ribs and multiple fractures in his right leg and ankle, plus some likely ligament damage in the knee. And he has concussion, but nothing to suggest a more serious head injury.'

'Is he going to be OK?' asked Mr Hunter.

'Yes, of course,' said the doctor, looking at Mr Hunter like he was an idiot. 'It's a broken leg and ankle. It will need surgery to pin it, but it's a routine operation.'

'Does it need to be done here?'

The doctor looked up from his notes and glanced at Mr Hunter's expensive watch, before smiling thinly. 'He shouldn't be here at all; only locals use this hospital. But it was closest and they thought he was going to die. He should be moved to a private clinic as soon as possible.'

Mr Hunter slumped in the chair and rubbed his hands across his face. 'Thank you.'

The doctor smiled. 'He was very lucky. Some local fishermen witnessed the accident and dragged him off the rocks, then had the common sense to call for help rather than trying to move him any further. If they hadn't seen him, he would almost certainly have drowned.'

Emily cleared her throat. 'Will he be able to fly?' she asked.

'Yes, but not for at least two weeks. He will need to recover after the surgery, and the swelling will need to go down before he will be signed off to travel.'

Emily nodded, feeling like she should be doing something useful, but not sure what. 'He'll be fine,' said the doctor. 'The private clinic will look after him – perhaps it would be best for us to make those arrangements.' He stared pointedly at everyone, letting the unspoken 'get out, you're taking up a much-needed bed' hang in the air like a toxic fart.

'I'll go and get that all sorted,' said Emily, grabbing her handbag. Mr Hunter said nothing, happy to let Emily do what she did best. Jessie disappeared into the corridor with her phone, presumably to check in with the café and let them know what had happened.

Emily followed the doctor through the rows of curtained beds to a horseshoe-shaped desk manned by nurses. The doctor handed over the clipboard and said a few things in French. Emily got the general gist – call the clinic, get him picked up in a private ambulance as soon as possible.

The nurse turned to Emily. 'Do you have his passport?' she asked, still in French. Emily nodded, rummaging in her bag and handing it to the nurse. She picked up the phone and made a call.

'He will go to the Darné Clinic,' said the doctor, switching back to English. 'It's the best on the island, and not far from here. He will be in the care of an excellent orthopaedic surgeon. Very experienced.'

Emily nodded, feeling slightly disconnected from everything. This morning they'd woken up in a beautiful hotel, gone swimming, taken a lazy drive back across the island to the beach house. Now Jamie was in a hospital with multiple fractures, having nearly died in an awful freak accident. She felt herself start to shake and wondered how she could feel so cold when this hospital was so stifling.

'What is your name?' asked the doctor, looking at her properly for the first time.

'Emily,' she whispered.

'It's OK, Emily.' He put his hand on her shoulder to steady her. 'It's a shock, I know, but please don't worry. I have seen many injuries like this, and I'm sure Mr Hunter will make a full recovery.' Emily tried to filter this through her addled brain, then realised he was talking about Jamie and not his father.

'OK,' she said, still not feeling very OK at all. She gave the doctor a weak smile.

'It will be fine,' said the doctor, his attention drifting to some panicked movement and shouting from a room behind some swing doors. 'The nurse will tell you when the ambulance is here.' He gave her a nod, then disappeared through the doors and out of sight.

Emily waited silently at the desk until the nurse finished her call and gave her back Jamie's passport. 'They are on their way,' she said. 'Twenty minutes.'

Twenty minutes in Mauritian time is more like an hour, but it felt like several weeks to Emily, waiting with Jessie and Mr Hunter at Jamie's bedside for something to happen. Whatever painkillers he was on had knocked him out cold, which she was glad of – leg and ankle fractures and three broken ribs sounded incredibly painful, never mind all the cuts and scrapes. But eventually a team of paramedics arrived, checked

251

Jamie's notes and spoke to the nurse, then swarmed around his bed with purposeful efficiency. He was hooked up to a different drip, hopefully with better, more expensive pain-killers, then transferred carefully to a trolley. They stabilised his right leg, signed some forms, then wheeled him off down the corridor without a backward glance.

'Emily,' said Mr Hunter. 'Can you go back to the house and get some things for James? You'll know what he needs. Also let Madeleine know what's happened, she'll be worried. I'll get a taxi to the clinic and make sure James gets the best care.'

'I will take you,' said Jessie, gathering up her belongings.

'Thank you, Jessie,' said Mr Hunter, putting his hand up to stop her for a moment. 'I have one last favour to ask.'

'Of course, Mr Charles,' said Jessie. 'Anything.'

'Can you find the fishermen who rescued him? And a man called Joseph, he is a gardener at . . .?' He looked at Emily with his eyebrows raised.

'The Coral Reef Hotel,' said Emily.

Jessie processed the request for a second, then nodded. 'Yes, I'm sure I can find them all.'

'Will you speak to them, find out what they need? Money, new boats, something for their community. Whatever will best express our gratitude.'

Jessie nodded, her eyes filling with tears. 'I'm glad Mr James is going to be OK.'

'You've been such a help,' said Mr Hunter. 'We can't thank you enough.'

'You keep looking after my brother,' said Jessie. 'That is thanks enough. And come to Delphine's wedding in June.'

'I will, I promise,' said Mr Hunter. 'We'll come with Sam and Gabrielle and the children.'

Jessie's smile faltered. 'Ayo, I don't think they are all coming.' Emily heard the unspoken words on her lips – *it's too expensive.*

Mr Hunter shook his head and patted Jessie on the arm. 'Don't worry, Jessie. We will all be there.'

CHAPTER THIRTY-THREE

Jamie stayed at the clinic for a week, during which Emily juggled work for Mr Hunter with daily visits to the hospital. Mr Hunter had secured the best room available, which had an en-suite bathroom and a separate area where Emily and Mr Hunter could work so they'd be there when Jamie woke up. The surgery had been declared a success, and Jamie's right leg and ankle were now a bionic limb of metal rods and plates, immobilised with a plaster cast from his toes to above his knee. His broken ribs and various cuts and scrapes were left to heal on their own, and even the smallest movement prompted a wince of pain.

Once Jamie was taken back to the beach house, his physiotherapist came every day to help him mobilise and get used to walking around on crutches, but the polished floors in the beach house were treacherous, and he got tired quickly with all the painkillers and antibiotics. He spent a lot of time in a wheelchair with his leg elevated, which meant he could manoeuvre around the house on his own, mostly getting under Madeleine's feet.

Emily had taken to getting up early and going swimming before work, giving herself a much-needed hour of headspace before the day started. Mr Hunter insisted that his driver Paul went with her for safety, so he waited in the car at the edge of the beach, sipping a coffee and watching the mad English girl swim. The water was calm and safe inside the reef, but Emily bought some rubber rock shoes to protect her from sea urchins. She soon became a familiar sight with the locals as she ploughed back and forth across the lagoon at sunrise, emptying her mind of everything but the water and the rhythm of her arms and legs.

A few days after Jamie returned to the beach house, Emily got back from her swim to hear him having a lively conversation with Mr Hunter on the terrace. She hung back in the kitchen to avoid interrupting and made herself a coffee.

'Please, Dad, tell them not to come. I'm begging you.'

'I can't, I'm sorry. They're both on their way. Adam called me from the plane. He'll be here after lunch.'

Emily's heart sank. It sounded like Adam and his wife were coming to Mauritius, which was pretty much her worst nightmare.

'But why?' said Jamie, clearly frustrated.

'To see you and keep you company, apparently,' said Mr Hunter. 'They're both worried about you.'

'No, I'm sorry,' raged Jamie. 'I'm not buying it. Neither of them gives a damn about me.'

Emily raised her eyebrows as she poured milk into her coffee. She could understand Jamie being furious about Adam, but it felt a bit harsh on Victoria.

'Catherine was very shaken by the news, according to Adam. You could have died.'

Emily nearly dropped the milk on the kitchen floor. There was definitely a worse nightmare than Adam and his wife, and it was Adam and his sister. *Oh, dear God, please no.*

'OK, fine, Adam's coming. But please, can you at least stop Catherine?'

'She's on her way too, via Dubai. Absolutely hellish flight from LA, she'll be here later tonight.'

'Then book me back into the hospital, I'm begging you.'

Mr Hunter laughed. 'Come on, James, I know they're both difficult, but they're making an extraordinary effort for you. At least give them a chance. Maybe your near-death experience has opened their eyes to the importance of family.'

Jamie was quiet for a moment. 'Then we need to protect Emily,' he said quietly. 'Send her off to look at another hotel, ask Jessie if she'll have her to stay. Adam and Catherine will treat her like shit.'

'Don't be silly,' said Mr Hunter briskly. 'I need Emily here. And don't underestimate her; she can take care of herself. Tough as nails, that one.'

Emily leaned against the kitchen counter and sipped her coffee. It felt like a compliment, kind of. But now Mr Hunter had said it, she had to live up to it. She lifted her chin and mentally shook off the feeling of impending doom, then crossed her fingers that they wouldn't stay long.

Adam arrived after lunch, wearing a linen suit with deck shoes and a Panama hat, as if he had a lunch date in Monte Carlo in 1930. Emily heard him arrive from her desk in Mr Hunter's office and found various reasons to work through lunch so she didn't have to be anywhere near him. He swept off to his room for a nap in the afternoon, so Emily made herself a sandwich and ate it on the terrace with Jamie. He was quiet and moody, particularly as the cuts on his arms and chest were scabbing over and itched like mad in the heat. She spent half an hour trying and failing to rally his mood, then went back to work.

When she finished for the day at five, Emily took a deep breath and headed out to face Adam. She couldn't put it off any longer, so she might as well rip the plaster off. He was keeping his brother company on the terrace, drinking a G&T as he tapped into a laptop.

'Adam,' said Emily, with as much bonhomie as she could muster. He glanced up briefly and smiled, then returned to his work like she was a scrap of nothing who wasn't worthy of his notice. Jamie rolled his eyes in apology, as Mr Hunter appeared in shorts and a polo shirt, carrying a towel.

'I'm off for a swim,' he said. 'What would you like to do for dinner this evening, Adam? Catherine won't be here until much later, so it's just the four of us. Do you fancy Sam's Café?'

Adam pulled a face as though there was a bad smell nearby. 'Can we go somewhere a bit more upmarket? Sam's is a bit . . . basic, don't you think?'

Mr Hunter pressed his lips together. 'Well, perhaps we can go further afield. James, what about you?'

'I'm really happy with Sam's,' said Jamie quickly. 'It's not far in the car and easy for the wheelchair.'

'Well, perhaps you and Emily can go there, and I'll take Adam somewhere a little more haute cuisine.'

Jamie gave him a look of heartfelt thanks, missing the disgusted glare that Adam threw in Emily's direction, like she was dragging his beloved brother to a pigsty and forcing him to share her trough.

★

257

By the time they'd been at Sam's for half an hour, Emily had decided that having Adam on the island might be worth it if it meant that she and Jamie got the chance to dine alone. They'd eaten here several times since they'd arrived, but always with Mr Hunter – Emily had no objection to his company, but he was still her boss and it was lovely to have a romantic dinner for two. Neither of them was drinking – Jamie because of his medication, and Emily because she was driving – but Jessie made them some delicious non-alcoholic cocktails and served them up a feast.

'This is nice,' Emily said, looking out at the moonlight over the water.

'I'm sorry about Adam,' said Jamie. 'I know he ignores you.'

Emily laughed. 'Ignoring me is FAR preferable to the time he called me a flat-chested gold digger.'

Jamie looked shocked. 'What the hell?'

Emily smiled and shrugged, like it was no big deal. 'He cornered me in the pool after New Year and gave me a mouthful about me "getting my feet under the table". I also heard him on the phone to your dad the day of your accident, calling me a floozy. I don't think I'm Adam's favourite person.'

'I don't know what to say,' said Jamie. He looked genuinely shocked.

'I mean, at least he has an opinion,' she said. 'In some ways that's better than him not caring about me one way or the other, like your sister. I get an odd kind of pleasure from knowing my existence pisses him off.'

'I have to say, you're taking this far better than I would.'

Emily shrugged. 'I honestly don't care what Adam thinks of me. All that matters is what you think, and what your dad thinks. As long as you both know who I really am, Adam is irrelevant.'

Jamie shook his head and took Emily's hand. 'He's still a bullying arsehole.'

Emily smiled. 'Yeah, but bullies are always cowards. They pick on the weak, or at least people they think are weak.'

'My dad said you were tough as nails earlier,' said Jamie. 'He's right.'

Emily laughed. 'I grew up in a house with two brothers and went to the kind of school where you have three choices – to be a bully, to be bullied, or to find the right friends and keep your head down. Kelly and I chose the third option – we stuck together and didn't draw attention to ourselves.'

'I know you probably won't believe me,' said Jamie, 'but my school wasn't all that different. You learn to blend in and become invisible.'

'Exactly,' said Emily. 'Unfortunately it hasn't worked on Adam. But he's just piss and wind.'

'Piss and wind?' said Jamie, clearly amused.

Emily shrugged. 'It's one of my mum's favourite sayings.'

'It's very apt,' said Jamie. 'Can I also apologise in advance for Catherine?'

Emily grinned at him. 'Yeah. I'm not scared of her either.'

There was a commotion on the terrace behind them, so both Emily and Jamie twisted round to see what was going on. Catherine was trip-trapping across the terrace in pink capri pants and kitten heels, carrying an enormous baby-blue handbag and wearing sunglasses despite it being dark.

'Oh, thank God I've found you,' she said loudly, making the family on the table next to them freeze with their forks halfway to their mouths. 'Madeleine said you were here.

259

The place Daddy's gone to sounds nicer but I literally couldn't face any more travelling.' She kissed the air in the vicinity of Jamie's cheeks, then turned to Emily. 'We haven't met, I'm Catherine.'

Actually we have, thought Emily, but decided not to mention it. 'Hi, I'm Emily,'

'Oh my God, I'm like, so exhausted,' said Catherine, falling dramatically into a chair. 'Who do I have to fuck to get a drink around here?' She snapped her fingers and waved at one of the waiters, who hurried over.

'Vodka and tonic. Slimline. No ice, slice of lime. And food, I need food.' She surveyed the leftovers on the table and decided nothing Jamie and Emily had eaten was to her taste. 'I'll have a green salad, no dressing, no onions.'

'Just a green salad,' said the waiter, his brow furrowed with confusion.

'Yes. Get a salad bowl and put in anything that's green. Lettuce, cucumber, green peppers. But not avocado.'

The waiter looked doubtful. 'You sure you wouldn't like chicken with it? Or shrimp?'

'Are either of those green?' said Catherine rudely, like the man was an imbecile. 'No. Just the salad. Although actually, what other kinds of fish do you have?'

Emily stared at Catherine and cringed, wondering what level of privilege it took to be this obnoxious. Jamie was scarlet, watching her with his mouth opening and closing like one of the many fish the waiter was currently listing.

'Fine, I'll have some kind of white fish, but grilled, not fried. And filleted, I literally can't do bones. Next to the salad, not on it. Remember, no dressing.'

The waiter nodded and scuttled off, no doubt to instruct

the kitchen to dress Catherine's salad with every type of body fluid they could muster. She took off her sunglasses and reached over to squeeze Jamie's arm, acting for all the world as if Emily wasn't even there. 'Isn't this fabulous?' she said, then plucked her phone out of her handbag with a perfectly manicured hand and took a selfie.

I am in hell and I can't even drink, thought Emily, as Jamie mouthed an apology and sank further into his wheelchair.

CHAPTER THIRTY-FOUR

After a week with Adam and Catherine occupying the two remaining bedrooms in the beach house, Emily was beginning to wonder if they ever planned to leave. She'd become expert at staying out of the way, blending into the furniture whenever Adam or Catherine passed by, and reverting to her teenage norm of being dull and invisible. She'd also never worked so hard in her life, just for an excuse to stay in Mr Hunter's office and out of everyone's way. On the upside, Adam was now ignoring her entirely, which Emily was absolutely fine with.

Time alone with Jamie was scarce, but they'd got into the habit of having breakfast on the terrace together when she got back from her swim, which was still a good hour before everyone else got up. Then Adam and Catherine would appear to spend some token time with their brother, usually bickering about something that Jamie didn't care about, and Emily would quietly merge into the background and slink away to the office.

She and Jamie had also managed a few dinners alone, because Jamie preferred to eat at the beach house or go to Sam's, whereas Adam and Catherine expected to be fed in the best restaurants the island had to offer. Mr Hunter had started to look haunted, and Emily really hoped they would leave him in peace before he had a nervous breakdown.

She had always suspected that the two older Hunter children had an ulterior motive for visiting Mauritius, because they definitely had nothing more than a passing interest in their brother's injury or recovery. She frequently came across the two of them whispering in corridors, and pieced together enough snippets to establish that they were trying to get a clearer picture of their father's business interests. Presumably their main priority was protecting their inheritance, whilst keeping a close eye on anyone who might get in the way. No doubt Emily's name was at the top of that list.

One morning Adam took Mr Hunter off for a drive to Grand Baie in the north of the island, ostensibly to look at a house he and Victoria were thinking of buying, even though non-Mauritian citizens hadn't been able to buy beach-front property on the island for years. Adam seemed to think there were loopholes he could exploit to get round that, and Mr Hunter was humouring him. Jamie was having a session with his physiotherapist in the garden, and Emily was enjoying the peace and quiet of time alone in the office to catch up on Mr Hunter's emails.

'Hey, Emma,' said Catherine from the doorway, her voice disconcertingly friendly.

'Hi,' said Emily. She didn't bother to correct her.

'There's nobody in the house, I was feeling super-lonely,' said Catherine in the same whiny baby voice that Adam used. She wandered over to the desk and idly picked up a glass paperweight with a piece of pink coral inside. 'Thought I'd, like, come and keep you company.' Emily was immediately suspicious of this unlikely girl chat.

Catherine flopped into the chair by the window, and

Emily had the opportunity to look at her close up for the first time. She must be in her early thirties, presumably a few years older than Jamie, but her face had been tweaked and moulded to a point where she could be any age between twenty and fifty. Her features were childlike, with big eyes and an adorable button nose, but the Botox and fillers had left her looking blank and expressionless, like a doll.

'That's such a pretty dress,' said Catherine. Emily was wearing a halterneck cotton sundress that she'd bought for the equivalent of six pounds from the local market. It had large purple flowers on it and had been chosen for comfort rather than style.

'Thanks,' said Emily. 'It's vintage Pucci.'

'It's super-cute,' said Catherine. 'What are you working on?' Her hybrid accent was pure Valley girl on the 'sooper' but the hard T in 'cute' was classic British upper class. It made her sound like a robot.

'Just admin,' said Emily blandly. 'Your dad gets a lot of emails.'

'What does he, like, actually do?' asked Catherine, inspecting her manicure. 'I know about the gaming business and stuff, but I have no idea what he's been doing since he sold it. I mean, what has he done with all that money? Isn't it, like, crazy that I don't know?' She gave a ridiculous fake laugh, and Emily had to force herself not to roll her eyes. If this was a plot she and Adam had cooked up, it was pathetic. Catherine might live in LA, but she definitely wasn't destined for a career in Hollywood.

'Perhaps you should ask him,' Emily said airily. 'I'm sure he'd love that you're interested.'

Catherine did the stupid laugh again. 'I feel so dumb, though. Not knowing anything. Maybe you could give me the highlights, just so I can, like, ask the right questions?'

Emily tilted her head and studied Catherine. It was too good an opportunity to miss, and God knows there wasn't much fun in her life right now.

'Well,' she said. 'Right now he's investing a lot of money in animal rescue.' She'd watched a video on Facebook earlier about a scrawny stray dog who'd been found living in a storm drain, but he'd been nursed back to health and found his furever home. Those videos always made her cry.

'He's what?' said Catherine, her eyes wide.

'Animal rescue. There's a dog rescue centre in Crete that your dad funds, and a refuge for retired horses in Spain, and a stray cat hotel in Cornwall. Right now he's thinking about funding a donkey sanctuary in Norway.' Emily wondered if that was an example too far – did they even have donkeys in Norway?

Catherine's mouth was hanging open. 'Wow, I had no idea. Do these places, like, make money?'

Emily laughed. 'No, of course not. They're charities. Mr Hunter covers the cost of all their work, it's such an amazing use of his money. I mean, you can't take it with you, right?'

'No, I guess not,' said Catherine, her eyes glazing over as she tried to process this new information. 'Are you serious? Dog rescue centres and a cat hotel in Norway?'

It took everything Emily had to keep a straight face. 'No, the cat hotel is in Cornwall. It's a donkey sanctuary in Norway.'

'Wow,' said Catherine. 'Thanks, Amelia. Maybe I'll go and, like, lie by the pool.'

Stay out of the sun, thought Emily. *Your face might, like, melt.*

Mr Hunter appeared in the office later in the afternoon, leaning on the doorframe with his arms folded. His face was unreadable, but Emily thought she could detect a trace of a smile. In that moment he looked unsettlingly like Jamie.

'Emily, do you have any idea why my daughter thinks I'm burning her inheritance on some kind of dog rescue in Norway?'

'It was a donkey sanctuary in Norway,' said Emily, 'the dogs were in Crete.'

Mr Hunter smiled and shook his head. 'I'm guessing you were under interrogation.'

Emily nodded. 'It was easier than saying nothing, and the first thing that came to mind. Sorry.'

'It's not you who should apologise,' he said, wafting her away. 'I've reassured her and Adam that I'm not selling the family silver to fund a donkey hotel.'

'Fine, but the hotel was actually for cats.'

Mr Hunter chuckled and sat down at his desk. 'They've both decided to head home tomorrow, so it will just be the three of us again until James can fly.'

Emily closed her eyes and said a silent prayer of thanks. 'It must be nice for you to have all your children together for a while.'

Mr Hunter thought about it for a second, his brow furrowed. 'Yes, I suppose it has been, in some ways. I might take them all out for a final dinner tonight, maybe somewhere special.'

Emily thought about how much Jamie would absolutely hate that, but there was nothing she could do to save him. She could, however, save herself. 'I'm very happy to do my own thing,' she said quickly. 'Give you guys some space.'

'Thank you,' said Mr Hunter. 'I'll get Madeleine to organise a taxi to take you to Sam's. Jessie will look after you.'

Many hours and several piña coladas later, Emily was propping up the bar with Jessie and her daughter Delphine, who was in her mid-twenties and just as beautiful as her mother. Dinner had been mostly cocktails, along with a selection of tiny taster plates that had been delivered by the chef at regular intervals. It felt great to relax and laugh after the stress of the past couple of weeks, and Emily realised how much she'd missed a girls' night out.

'So Mr James taught you to ride a horse, then asked you out on a date?' asked Jessie.

'He did,' said Emily, slurping the dregs of her drink through the straw. The barman took the glass away and immediately replaced it with another.

'Man, that boy is smart,' said Jessie. Delphine nodded sagely.

'What do you mean?' asked Emily.

'Everyone knows that riding a horse gets a girl in the mood for love.'

Emily shook her head and waved a finger in the air. 'Jamie gets me in the mood for love. I don't need a horse.'

Jessie and Delphine both cackled into their drinks. 'Good that he's taught you to ride though,' said Delphine with a wink. 'Because with his leg the way it is, you're going to be on top for a loooong time.'

Emily inhaled some piña colada up her nose and realised she was absolutely hammered. She looked around at the groups of friends and families on the terrace and wished Kelly was there with her. She'd love this place so much – the drinks, the music, the food, the warm tropical air. It was the longest Emily had gone without seeing her best friend in years, and it made her heart hurt.

'I need to make a phone call,' she said, tumbling off her stool. She wobbled to the edge of the sand and fell into a low wooden beach chair, pulling her phone out of her pocket and fumbling with the screen. It was 6.30 p.m. in England; Kelly would have just finished Beth's dinner.

'Kel, s'me,' said Emily with a hiccup as her friend answered the phone.

'I know it's you, you daft cow,' said Kelly. 'Your name's on the screen.'

'Well, maybe you know 'nuther Emlee.'

Kelly laughed. 'Oh my God, you're smashed.'

'Absolutely wankered,' said Emily. 'Girls' night with Jessie and Delphine. Soooo many cocktails.'

'I'm jealous,' said Kelly petulantly. 'You've made new friends.'

'Yeah, but being with them made me miss you,' said Emily. 'So I wanted to call and tell you you're 'mazing.'

'Aww, that's so nice,' said Kelly. 'You're amazing too, you absolute pisshead. When are you coming home?'

'Not sure. Shoon, I hope. Jamie can't fly yet, he's still all swollen up.'

'I bet he is, looking at you in a bikini.'

'Veh funny,' said Emily. 'None of that business at the moment, I'm all about the self-love.'

'Oh God, now I know you're pissed,' said Kelly. 'Go back to your new friends and bring me home a nice present.'

Emily kicked off her flip-flops and buried her toes in the cool sand. 'Wotchoo want?'

'I don't know,' said Kelly. 'Something fancy. Maybe one of those massive Toblerones from the airport.'

Emily laughed. 'Mum arshed for the same thing.'

'What can I say?' said Kelly. 'The women in your life are really easy to please.'

CHAPTER THIRTY-FIVE

In the end it was three weeks after Jamie's accident before the orthopaedic surgeon at the clinic gave him a full examination and pronounced him well enough to fly. His wounds were healing well and the swelling had subsided enough for the doctor to provide a letter confirming fitness to travel, with some additional medication and advice on getting through a twelve-hour flight. Emily was relieved for Jamie's sake – even though the beach house was quiet again now Adam and Catherine had gone, the heat and humidity made life uncomfortable for him. He was keen to manage his recovery in the blissful cold of an English winter, ideally in the company of his horses.

Emily ran her pen down her to-do list – she'd already called the airline to confirm their upgrade to First Class seats and book extra assistance at both ends of the journey, and she'd given Jessie a quick ring to discuss plans for their final evening. Now it was time to call Anna to make arrangements for their return. She sighed heavily, feeling like she'd rather pull her own teeth out. She pressed the button to dial the house number, listening to it ring several times before the housekeeper answered.

'Anna, it's Emily.'

Anna said nothing; Emily could hear her sucking a lemon from six thousand miles.

'Jamie has been approved to fly tomorrow evening, so we'll be home on Wednesday,' continued Emily. 'I just want to talk about arrangements for when he gets back.'

'Fine,' said Anna, with a tone that suggested she'd rather shit Lego.

'The main thing is he needs step-free access.'

'We can make up one of the rooms in the house,' said Anna. 'The green drawing room would work.'

'He'd like to be moved to the pool house.'

'I don't think that's suitable,' snapped Anna dismissively.

'It has a bedroom and a wet room, both on the ground floor, a kitchen of its own, and it's close to the pool so he can start hydrotherapy,' said Emily, who'd done a great deal of reading about this kind of injury. 'What's not suitable about it?'

'If he's in the house, we can give him proper care,' said Anna.

'Well, he'd like the pool house,' said Emily.

There was twenty seconds of silence, during which Emily doodled a picture of a witch in her notebook. It had a big pointy hat, crooked teeth and crossed eyes. 'If you say so,' said Anna grudgingly. 'I'll have it cleaned and made ready tomorrow.'

'Thank you,' said Emily sweetly. 'I'll email you our flight details so you can pass them on to Leon. I've organised a private ambulance for Jamie – he can't sit in the car for that long with his leg cast. Can you ask Leon to liaise with the driver at the airport?'

'Why haven't you organised a helicopter?' asked Anna, like Emily was a colossal moron. 'It would be so much quicker and more comfortable for Jamie.'

'Because the weather forecast for Wednesday morning is high winds and heavy rain,' replied Emily. 'It's not safe, and it won't be comfortable. I'll call you tomorrow if anything changes.'

Anna hung up without saying goodbye, which prompted a weary eyeroll from Emily. Every conversation with the housekeeper made her feel like she'd been pushed through a mangle, but all household arrangements had to be funnelled through her. She looked at her watch, then walked through to the kitchen to fetch the tray that Madeleine had prepared with lunch for her and Jamie. She'd left him in the shade of the terrace with a book earlier, and he'd be going out of his mind by now.

'On a scale of one to ten, how bored are you?' she asked, plonking the tray down on the table and pouring some iced water from a jug. Jamie was tapping away on his phone but slid it into his pocket when Emily appeared.

'Twenty,' he said with a tired smile. 'Which, coincidentally, is how many days it's been since we last had sex.'

'Uh oh, somebody's feeling better.'

'My ribs don't hurt so much today, I can breathe properly. I think we could make it work.' He picked at one of the many scabs on his arm until Emily swatted his hand away.

'I'm more concerned about your blood pressure, to be honest. Can we at least get you home first?'

Jamie made a 'humpf' noise and sipped his water. 'We need to sort out some cover at the stables.'

'Already done it,' said Emily. 'For six weeks, to start with.'

'And I can't manage the stairs to my apartment for a while.'

'It's all sorted.'

Jamie looked at her in amusement. 'Anybody would think you did this kind of thing for a living. Where am I sleeping?'

'Anna's going to turn the green drawing room into a bedroom for you, and she's hired a nurse to tend to your every need.'

'Jesus,' said Jamie, his face aghast. 'Are you serious?'

'Of course not,' said Emily with a grin. 'I suggested the pool house and told her it was your idea when she got all pissy about it.'

Jamie looked relieved. 'But the nurse is real, right?'

'Haha, no. You'll have to make do with me.'

'Do you have a special outfit?'

Emily rolled her eyes. 'Sadly not. You're quite frisky for a man with a broken right leg.'

'My left leg is fine. As is the middle one.'

Emily laughed. 'I think I need to call the doctor and check your medication.'

'I like the medication here,' said Jamie. 'I'm pretty sure they don't do painkillers this good in the UK.'

'You'll be on two paracetamol every four hours when we get back. That's your lot.'

'Oh God,' said Jamie. 'Can we stay here?'

Jamie's physio arrived after lunch, so Emily went to check in with Mr Hunter. He was on the phone and held up his hands to indicate ten minutes, so she went and sat on the edge of the pool with her feet in the water and called her mum. Carol had a tea break at 10.30, so there was a good chance she might pick up.

'All right, Moo,' said Carol. 'It's Emily,' she said to whoever else was in the room. 'Calling from Mauritius.'

'Are you at work?' asked Emily.

'In the break room,' said Carol. 'Cottage pies are all made,

273

just got to go in the oven. Still got the pink sponge and custard to do.'

'Sounds delicious,' Emily lied. She could taste that exact lunch – the greasy mince, the powdery mashed potato piped into uniform swirls, the rubbery skin of the custard. She swallowed down a dry heave and focused on the lovely lunch she'd just eaten. 'I just wanted to let you know we're flying home tomorrow night. Jamie's been signed off.'

'Oh, that's lovely news,' said Carol. 'How long have you been there now?'

Emily swished her feet around in the cool water. 'Nearly a month.'

'You haven't sent us any photos for a while. I was telling Parminder who does the veg all about your holiday and showing her the pictures of that market you went to.'

'It's not a holiday, Mum. I've been working and looking after Jamie.'

'Is he being a misery? Men are the worst. When David broke his wrist on that bloody skateboard you'd have thought they'd cut his arm off.'

Emily laughed. 'He's fine. The heat makes him itch, but he's getting better.'

'You're like Grace Kelly in *Rear Window*.'

'I haven't seen that one.'

'Ooh, you should. It's Hitchcock. Jimmy Stewart is stuck in a wheelchair with nothing to do but spy on his neighbours with a pair of binoculars, and he convinces himself that one of them has committed a murder.'

'Where does Grace Kelly fit in?' asked Emily.

'She's his girlfriend, but much richer and fancier than him. The other way round from you two, now I think about it.'

'I'm sat with my feet in the pool right now, feeling pretty fancy. And I've been going for a swim in the sea every morning. I've seen loads of turtles and tropical fish.'

'Crikey, Bognor is going to be a bloody shock after that.'

'Yeah, I know. I miss you guys, though.'

'We miss you too. Oh, Geraldine's giving me evils, I need to go and make the custard. Give Jamie our love.'

'I will, Mum. Give Dad a hug for me.'

When Mr Hunter pushed Jamie on to the terrace of Sam's Café in his wheelchair, a party was in full swing. It took a few seconds for Jamie to realise it was all for him, and he gave Emily and his father the biggest smile he'd managed since the accident. With Emily's planning skills and Mr Hunter's money, Jessie had laid on a farewell dinner with drinks and live music, with a path of rubber wheelchair matting running from the terrace to the water's edge so Jamie could access the beach for the first time in weeks.

Emily and Mr Hunter had invited all their friends on the island, as well as the medical staff from the clinic who'd managed Jamie's surgery and recovery. The biggest surprise for Jamie was that Emily had invited Joseph the gardener and the group of fishermen who'd rescued him, along with their families. Jamie had no recollection of the accident or these men, and he shed a bucket of tears as he thanked them in French and halting Creole for saving his life.

It was an eclectic collection of people, but the food and drink flowed freely and the atmosphere was one of thankfulness and celebration. Emily mingled and helped Jessie with drinks, then sat on the terrace with Jamie for a while, keeping an eye on him while he chatted with a stream of well-wishers.

By 10 p.m. he looked exhausted, so Emily quietly sidled up and squatted down next to him. 'Ready for bed?' she asked.

'Yeah, soon,' said Jamie, taking her hand. 'Thank you for organising all this. It's been amazing.'

'My pleasure,' said Emily. 'You look knackered. Let me get Paul to take us home.'

'Take me down to the water first,' he said.

Emily stood up and pushed the wheelchair through the crowd, manoeuvring it down the hastily constructed wooden ramp without landing him face first in the sand. She took the rubber matting slowly so it didn't jolt around too much, putting the brakes on when the wheels were in the water. Nobody followed them, and it felt blissful to have a few minutes alone to watch the moon glittering over the water. Tiny waves lapped over her bare feet, which had finally gone brown after a month of carefully managed time in the sun.

'I know this has been a bit of a nightmare,' said Jamie. 'But I'm really glad we came.'

Emily bent down so he could see her. 'Me too. Can we come back one day?'

Jamie gave her a smile that made her stomach do somersaults, exactly as it had when they'd first met. She realised how much she cared about him but felt too scared to say it.

'I'd really like that,' he said, cupping the back of her neck as he pulled her in for a kiss.

CHAPTER THIRTY-SIX

Despite the first-class seats and the calm, efficient attention of the cabin crew, Emily had never known a night drag on for so long. While the rest of the plane slept, she kept an eye on Jamie, waking him up every hour to help him change position or take his medication, and asking him about any unusual pain or discomfort. In between she watched a couple of movies, neither of which she paid much attention to. Mr Hunter woke up about four hours before landing and ordered Emily to leave him in charge. She put her eye mask on, stretched out on her flatbed seat and passed out in minutes.

Their flight landed on time at 0530 UK time, and the Gatwick ground staff were waiting on the air bridge to transport Jamie through the airport in his wheelchair. Leon was at the arrivals gate, having stayed in a hotel at the airport the night before, and Emily let him give her a much-needed hug. With him was Darren, the paramedic who would drive Jamie home by private ambulance, and he quickly whisked away the wheelchair to get him settled in for the journey.

The weather was wet and windy and it made Emily's chest hurt as they left Gatwick and turned north for London rather than south for Brighton. It was only an hour to Chichester from here, where breakfast and her crappy bed in her mum's abandoned craft graveyard would be waiting. But instead they drove for three hours back to Bowford Manor, Emily's mood mirroring the dark, heavy clouds.

Anna was waiting outside the front door when they arrived, wrapped in a black wool coat that made her look like a malevolent crow. The ambulance was a few minutes behind, so Mr Hunter said his goodbyes before hurrying out of the cold, reminding Emily that he didn't need her until this afternoon. While Leon unloaded the bags, Emily watched as the ambulance trundled down the drive and parked up behind the Audi.

She moved to open the sliding side door, but Anna stepped in her way. 'I'll take things from here,' she said, like some kind of nightclub bouncer.

'But I . . .' said Emily, outraged.

Anna turned her back on Emily and opened the door. 'Welcome home, Jamie. I've made some breakfast for you; I'll drop it over in half an hour and do your unpacking.'

Jamie looked exhausted. 'Thanks, Anna.'

'Leon, can you show Jamie round to the pool house,' Anna continued. 'It's all ready for him.'

Leon nodded and climbed into the passenger seat of the ambulance.

'Everything's in hand now, Emily,' said Anna, her tone icy. 'You should get some rest.'

Jamie reached out and took Emily's hand. 'Anna's right, you've been up half the night, you must be shattered. I'll see you later.'

Emily nodded and chewed her lip, not wanting to make this situation all about her. Right now all that mattered was Jamie.

'OK, I'll pop over at lunchtime.' She smiled and waved as the ambulance drove away.

'He's in good hands now,' said Anna, a slight emphasis on the word 'good'. 'His physiotherapist will be here tomorrow.'

'His physiotherapist?' said Emily. 'We didn't . . .'

'Jamie's friend Louisa is coming to help,' said Anna. 'I believe they've been messaging while you were away. She's an expert in this kind of rehabilitation, so she'll be staying in the stable apartment for the time being.'

Emily's mouth hung open, her vocal cords paralysed with shock.

'You should go home at the weekend,' said Anna, turning on her heel and stalking back into the house. 'You look terrible.'

Emily plodded up the stairs to her room with her suitcase, feeling like she was wearing concrete boots. Her head felt foggy and jumbled, and she couldn't remember the last time she'd felt this exhausted. She tried to compute the news that Louisa was arriving tomorrow and work out if it was next-level malice from Anna, or actually the best solution for Jamie's recovery. She remembered him telling her about Louisa's job, how she worked with soldiers injured in Afghanistan. Maybe she was the ideal person to get him back on his feet and Anna had his best interests at heart. Or maybe the evil cow had seen an opportunity to stick the knife into Emily and grabbed it with both hands. Probably it was a bit of both, but it still hurt to think about it.

She unpacked her clothes, putting her bikini and sarong and summer dresses in the back of a drawer as an icy wind rattled the window frame; she wasn't going to be needing them for a while. Then she messaged Kelly and the family WhatsApp to let them know she was back safely and turned off her phone. Finally, she wrapped herself in the blanket Leon had knitted her for Christmas, then lay on the bed and fell asleep.

When Emily walked over to the pool house at lunchtime, Jamie was up and about and practising navigating the small space on his crutches. He seemed pleased to see her, and it was clear that Anna had gone to every effort to make the space more accessible for him. There was a new ramp up to the front door and a couple of handrails had been fitted in the wet room, along with a plastic chair so Jamie could sit down and have a shower. Emily wondered if she'd consulted with Louisa over what he would need and felt an irrational stab of jealousy.

They chatted about nothing much for a few minutes, until it became abundantly clear that Jamie wasn't going to mention Louisa without some prompting. 'Anna said that Louisa is coming tomorrow,' she said casually, checking inside the pool house fridge to make sure it was fully stocked.

'Really?' said Jamie. 'Anna didn't say when she came over to unpack.' His voice sounded high and slightly musical, like he was fudging a response. He did a final lap of the sofa, then headed back into the kitchen, wincing at the pain in his ribs as he landed heavily in the chair.

'But you're not surprised?' said Emily.

'Louisa's an expert in this kind of injury; she offered to come but I said it wasn't necessary. I'm sure she just wants to help.'

'I'm sure she does,' said Emily with a thin smile, trying not to sound snippy. 'How did she even know you were injured?'

'I messaged her when I was in the hospital,' he said airily. 'It seemed like a good idea to get her advice.'

'You never said.' Emily thought of all the conversations they'd had about his injury, the treatment, the set-up he'd need at home, the plan for his recovery. Not once had he mentioned Louisa.

Jamie sighed, blowing out his cheeks. 'I guess I didn't.'

'I get that Louisa is an expert,' said Emily tightly, 'but I've spent over three weeks running back and forth to the hospital, reading every bit of information I could find about your injury, talking to your doctors, liaising with the private hospital in Norwich. If you were getting advice from somewhere else, it would have been nice of you to mention it. Perhaps I could have saved myself some time and effort.'

'It wasn't like that,' said Jamie, anger flaring briefly in his eyes.

'It was like that for me,' said Emily. 'But we'll have to talk about it later. I need to get back to work, there's a month's worth of post to sort through.'

'Adam's coming over tonight,' Jamie said moodily. 'He's staying in Wedmore Cottage and wants to play devoted brother for a couple of hours.'

'Well, tomorrow then,' said Emily. She leaned over and gave him a light kiss. 'Let me know if you need anything.'

Jamie gave her a bleak look as she turned to leave, feeling like all the warmth she'd carried home from Mauritius was slowly draining away.

★

'Well, if it isn't Little Miss Sunshine,' sneered Adam, blocking the path through the walled garden. 'Enjoy your month-long holiday grift?'

'What do you want, Adam?' asked Emily, trying to sound more confident than she felt. She was reasonably sure that he wouldn't dare touch her, and she was determined not to get upset about his verbal abuse. *He's just piss and wind.*

'I'd like a lot of things,' said Adam, looking her up and down like he was deciding where to stab her first. 'But mostly I'd like you to leave this house and never come back. I don't think you're good enough for it.'

'Well, that's interesting,' she said, feeling overwhelmed by tiredness and jetlag and absolute fury that she had to put up with this obnoxious wanker on top of everything else. 'Because your father doesn't agree, and neither does your brother. So that just leaves your opinion, which I don't give a flying shit about.' She stepped up on to the hard soil of the raised planter and walked around him, then strode off down the path without looking back. Her heart remained in her mouth until she was on the main driveway, when she finally breathed out slowly, leaning forward with her hands on her knees.

'Are you OK?' called Leon, jogging over from the garage.

'I'm fine,' she said with a weak smile, never more glad to see her friend. 'Just ran into Adam. He doesn't like me very much.'

Leon's brow furrowed with concern. 'Did he do something?'

'No,' said Emily quickly. 'Nothing physical. Just the usual insults, a reminder to know my place.'

'He is mean bastard,' said Leon, clenching his fists. 'We

have many words in Croatian for men like him. Does Mr Hunter know?'

'No, and nor does Jamie. Please don't say anything, I can handle Adam.'

'OK,' said Leon with a gentle smile. 'I am glad Jamie is OK, and I am glad you are back.'

'Me too,' lied Emily, very much wishing she was back on the beach in that first week in Mauritius with Jamie, snorkelling and horse riding and having sex. But in the absence of that, she'd settle for lunch, a cup of tea, and tackling a mountain of post in the quiet solitude of Mr Hunter's office.

CHAPTER THIRTY-SEVEN

Emily walked the road way round to the pool house at lunchtime the following day, just in case Adam was lurking in the walled garden waiting to strangle her with a rubber hose. There was no sign of him, but the trill of laughter from the kitchen when she knocked and opened the door was more than enough to dull her enthusiasm for hanging out with Jamie for half an hour.

'Hi,' said Emily, smiling half-heartedly. Louisa was sitting at the kitchen table, tapping away at an expensive laptop. She was wearing a kitten-soft green cashmere rollneck that was very similar to the one Emily had worn on her first visit to Bowford, but probably fifty times more expensive. Emily clocked the piled-up hair and immaculate make-up, which was artfully done to look entirely natural, but had very likely taken hours. Only another woman would spot this, but it was obvious to Emily that she'd made a huge effort to look like she'd made no effort at all.

'Hey,' said Jamie, 'you remember Louisa? She's here to help with my physio.' Obviously Emily already knew that, so this conversation was clearly for Louisa's benefit, to make her feel less awkward. Jamie hadn't messaged or called following their conversation yesterday – no apology, no explanation, no nothing. His face begged for mercy, but she realised she was furious with him. Couldn't Jamie see how upsetting it was to walk into his kitchen and find his ex-girlfriend sitting there like she owned the place?

Emily said nothing, so Jamie turned to Louisa. 'This is Emily, she's dad's assistant.' Emily waited for *and also my girlfriend*, just as he'd introduced her to Jessie a month ago, but there was nothing but silence and tumbleweed.

'Hi,' said Louisa, glancing briefly in Emily's direction before turning back to whatever she was doing. It was the same trick Adam had pulled in Mauritius, giving a clear message of *You're not worthy of my attention, I'm far too busy and important.* The arrogance made Emily even more furious, and it took everything she had not to slap the laptop off the table.

Instead she folded her arms and raised her eyebrows in Jamie's direction, hoping her expression went some way to communicating her growing list of grievances. 'I just came to ask if you need anything.'

'No, I'm fine, thanks,' he replied, looking at her helplessly. He knew he'd messed up, but on top of jetlag and Adam and the parade of people yelling at her on the phone this morning, this was more than Emily's fragile emotional state could handle. It was clear Louisa wasn't going to leave them alone, so she needed to get out before she started to cry.

'Well, you know where I am,' she said quietly, then turned and left.

Louisa caught up with her a minute later, doing a theatrical jog down the path in skinny jeans and heeled ankle boots, the sleeves of her jumper pulled down over her fists. Emily heard her approaching and waited for her; even though she felt too numb to muster much curiosity about what Louisa wanted, it seemed rude to blank her entirely.

'Sorry to hold you up,' said Louisa, clutching her hand to

her chest like she was out of breath. 'I just wanted to say thank you for looking after Jamie. He's in really good shape considering what he's been through.'

'Oh,' said Emily. 'You're welcome.' *Actually you're not welcome at all, bugger off.*

'I know you're super-busy with Charles,' added Louisa, resting a perfectly manicured hand on Emily's arm, 'so don't feel like you need to play nurse to Jamie as well. I'll take care of him.' The accent was cut-glass perfection, and she was heartbreakingly pretty up close. If Louisa was a Michelin-starred meal, Emily would be one of her mum's lumpy school dinners.

She wondered if it was possible that Louisa didn't know that she and Jamie were a couple. If so, this might be perceived as a genuinely kind gesture towards an overworked staff member. But if she DID know, Louisa had just declared a battle for Jamie's attention, and made her intentions quite clear. Which was it?

'What's the plan for his recovery?' asked Emily, tucking her hands into her armpits against the cold.

'A trip to the hospital tomorrow morning for some X-rays, see if he can swap the cast for a boot. Thank you so much for organising that.'

Emily nodded. She'd spent ages on the phone from Mauritius last week, getting Jamie's X-rays emailed from the island clinic to a private hospital in Norwich so there were no issues with his ongoing care. The orthopaedic surgeons in both hospitals had spoken to each other, and Emily had confirmed the follow-up appointment before they'd left the island. It was fascinating to discover what could be achieved when money was no object.

'If that's all fine,' continued Louisa, 'we'll start in the pool and get his leg muscles working again. All being well, he'll be able to do some weight-bearing exercises in a few weeks.'

'It sounds like a lot of work,' said Emily, trying not to imagine Louisa in a tiny swimsuit, touching bits of Jamie's body. Then she remembered that Louisa had seen and touched the same bits of Jamie's body as she had. She put her hands in her pockets so she didn't poke out one of her huge green eyes.

'He's lucky I was available,' said Louisa with the same twittering laugh Emily had heard earlier, 'but obviously I'd have found a way to be here, one way or another.'

'Obviously.'

Louisa looked away, her confidence waning. 'Well, I'd better get back. Just wanted to say thank you, and let you know I'll take it from here. You've done so much.'

She gave Emily a dazzling smile, then turned and jogged back along the path. Emily scowled, trying not to hate Louisa for her pert bum and skinny thighs when there were so many other, better things to hate her for.

Questions rattled around in her head as she walked back to the house to find solace in a mug of tea and one of Sam's lunches. How long was Louisa going to stay? Why hadn't Jamie warned her? And most importantly, how on earth was she going to manage to not be a jealous, snarky bitch about it?

By the end of the day Emily had turned the situation over in her mind a thousand times. She made a decision and caught Mr Hunter after they'd finished work and she was collecting documents for filing from his desk. He liked to start the day with a clear space, so this was always her final job of the day.

'I wonder if I could take a day off tomorrow,' she asked. 'I'd really like to go home and see my family for the weekend. I know it's short notice.'

'Of course,' said Mr Hunter, putting on his jacket. 'You've worked so hard over the past few weeks. Take Monday too, spend some time at home. There's nothing that can't wait until Tuesday.'

'Thank you,' said Emily, already feeling the heaviness lifting from her shoulders. There was nothing she could do about Jamie; he needed to decide for himself how he was going to handle Louisa. But she could look after her own emotional well-being, and for that she needed to go back to the comfort and safety of her family home.

When she wandered downstairs to find some dinner, Anna was on the kitchen phone. She heard her say 'Louisa' and stopped outside the door to listen.

'Jamie's dinner is ready if you want to pop over and collect it,' said Anna. 'I've prepared some for you too, I thought you and he might like to eat together.'

What a fucking cow, thought Emily, clenching her fists. She counted in her head for two minutes, then nipped into the kitchen and grabbed the tray from the table. Anna was in the pantry and didn't see her, so she hurried back up the stairs to the entrance hall and out through the front door.

She took the route through the walled garden, betting that Louisa was currently walking along the road to the delivery yard. Sure enough, she arrived at the pool house to find Jamie sitting at the kitchen table alone.

'I've brought you dinner,' she said cheerily.

Jamie looked up in surprise. 'Oh, I thought Louisa was getting it.'

Emily gritted her teeth as she dumped the tray on the table. 'Well, you'll just have to make do with me instead.'

Jamie looked at her for a few seconds, visibly worried and uncertain of her mood. 'I'm glad you're here. It's nice to see you.'

Emily forced a smile. 'I just wanted to let you know that I'm heading home tomorrow morning to see my mum and dad.'

'Oh,' said Jamie, grabbing his crutches and standing up. 'Are you upset with me?'

'Why would I be?'

'Well, just with Louisa being here and everything,' he said. 'I really wasn't expecting her to come.'

Emily looked at him, wondering if this was true and deciding it probably was; Anna obviously had a hand in this whole plot. But whilst Jamie hadn't overtly lied about chatting to Louisa in Mauritius, he hadn't been entirely honest with her either. It made the ground under her feel uncertain.

'It's fine,' she lied. 'It's great that you have a physio on hand, you'll recover more quickly.'

'Well, yes,' he said. 'That's the idea.'

'But I figured since you've got someone looking after you, I can get home for a few days without worrying.'

Jamie looked at the floor. 'I'm sure that's a good idea,' he said quietly, then looked back at Emily. 'I'll miss you.'

'I'll be back on Monday,' she said. She walked over to kiss him and caught a whiff of an unfamiliar perfume in the air.

Something soft and floral and expensive. Tears and anger bubbled up inside her, and she knew she had to get out before Louisa returned.

'See you soon,' she said, giving him a half-hearted smile from the doorway.

'OK,' said Jamie as she walked away. She didn't look back, but she could hear the sadness in his voice.

CHAPTER THIRTY-EIGHT

'We're going to the pub,' said Carol on Saturday evening. 'You and me, right now. Get yourself ready.'

Emily rolled over from her recumbent position on the single bed in her old bedroom. She'd been looking at the paper stars on the ceiling, thinking about Jamie and picking at the peeling suntan on her arms. Bowford Manor felt like it was on the moon, but Mauritius felt like another planet entirely. Maybe the one over by the wardrobe, being nudged through the universe by a rogue spaceship.

'I really don't fancy it, Mum,' she said with an exaggerated yawn. 'I'm absolutely knackered.'

'Bollocks,' said Carol, her lips pursed so tight they'd practically disappeared. 'Get up, put your coat on, we're leaving in five minutes.' She closed the door with no-nonsense force and stomped down the stairs. Emily had seen her mum in this kind of mood before, and resistance was futile. Her dad would be hiding behind his newspaper somewhere, but there was no point begging him for help. Nobody messed with Carol Wilkinson when she was a mum on a mission.

Emily yawned again and sat up, glancing at her phone. Nothing from Jamie since a WhatsApp this morning saying he hoped she had a nice day. They'd exchanged a few messages about his cast coming off and his first session in the pool yesterday, and he'd asked her to pass on his regards to

291

her parents and Kelly. She'd had three missed calls from her best friend today and hadn't yet called her back. Kelly asked too many questions, and Emily didn't have nearly enough answers. She'd go and see her tomorrow before she headed back to Norfolk on Monday.

She dragged herself over to the mirror and ran a brush through her hair, wondering what Jamie was doing now, whether Louisa was with him, and whether her healing hands had eased her way back into his bed. Emily hated how things between them had gone sour so quickly, with them both feeling wronged and angry and unable to see each other's point of view. She'd assumed that two hundred miles might give her more perspective, but right now she just felt worse. Obviously her claim of being exhausted and jetlagged wasn't cutting it with her mum any more, so maybe it was time to drink gin and offload.

Emily shouldn't have been surprised to find Kelly sitting at their usual table in the White Lion, but somehow it still managed to give her a jolt. Clearly this was by previous arrangement, and a drink with her mum had now been upgraded to a two-pronged ambush. She hadn't really wanted to do the former, and the latter was definitely more than her fragile state could handle. But there was no escaping now.

Carol went to get drinks while Kelly stared silently at Emily, her arms folded over her yellow dungarees. They clashed horribly with her bright red hair, making her look like Ronald McDonald. Emily avoided her gaze, worrying away at a section of dry skin on her forearm with her fingernail until it peeled off in a satisfying strip.

Carol came back from the bar with a round of drinks,

then sat next to Kelly. The silence continued as they both glared at Emily, like any minute Carol would shine a spotlight in her eyes while Kelly administered electrodes to sensitive parts of her body. Emily sweated it out, knowing that she could stay silent far longer than her mum could.

'So, what's the deal?' asked Kelly.

'About what?' replied Emily, folding her arms.

'I told you,' said Carol. 'She's been like this ever since she got home. Moping around, saying she's tired, face like a dog's arse.'

'I can hear you both, you know,' said Emily, unable to stop herself from smiling.

'What's happened with Jamie?' asked Kelly. 'You sounded like you were super loved-up while you were away, even after the accident. So what's happened since you got home?'

Emily's eyes unexpectedly filled with tears. There was no point pretending; these two weren't going anywhere and they had ways of making you talk. 'His ex-girlfriend has turned up.'

'WHAT?' yelled Carol. 'The little shit. I knew this would happen.'

'No, it's not his fault,' said Emily. 'She's a physiotherapist.' She sighed deeply, blew her nose on a cocktail napkin, and told them everything.

'So let me get this straight,' said Kelly, her eyes wide and her glass empty. 'Jamie's ex-girlfriend has gone up to Norfolk to give him hands-on rehab in a skimpy swimsuit and you've LEFT THE FUCKING COUNTY.'

Emily nodded. 'I know it's mad, but I just needed to get away. Everything felt too intense.'

Carol pressed her fingers to her lips, her brow furrowed thoughtfully. 'Did she finish with him or did he finish with her?'

'He finished with her. He said they weren't right for each other.'

'Right,' said Carol, holding up her finger like she'd just cracked the Enigma code. 'So clearly she wants him back and has decided playing Florence Nightingale is the answer. I read this book once where this nurse got her patients to fall in love with her, then killed them one by one using this syringe full of poison. Sometimes she'd inject them while they were having sex, then watch them die while she had an orgasm. Like a black widow spider.'

Emily and Kelly both looked at her in silence, their eyebrows raised. 'And was this fiction, or a true-life story?' asked Kelly.

'Good question,' said Carol. 'I can't remember. But I do remember the nurse turned out not to have any actual nursing qualifications.'

'OK, this has taken a weird turn,' said Emily. 'Louisa definitely isn't a psycho nurse. She's actually really nice, and incredibly beautiful. And really good at her job. She helps soldiers injured in Afghanistan.'

'I don't care if she's Motherfucking Theresa,' said Carol. 'She's a schemer. I read this other book once where . . .'

'Not now, Carol,' said Kelly quietly, putting a restraining hand on Carol's arm.

'It's not just Louisa,' said Emily. 'It's the housekeeper too. I think she was the one who asked her to come.'

'Why would she do that?' asked Kelly.

Emily shrugged. 'She doesn't like me. Never has, no idea

why, but it's been a whole new level of horrible since Jamie and I got together.'

'Oh my God,' said Carol, leaping to her feet. 'You're Mrs de Winter.'

'Who's Mrs de Winter?' asked Emily.

'She's the new wife in *Rebecca*; it's a book and a film with Laurence Olivier. She gets bullied by an evil housekeeper.'

Emily shook her head in confusion; she had no idea what Carol was talking about and it wasn't really helping.

'I never liked that woman much,' Carol added. 'What was her name? Anna? She got her knickers in a right piss about my plan to save the Christmas party dinner.' Emily wondered how many times her mum had told that story, and how much embellishment she'd added over time. In Carol's version she'd probably put out a fire and saved somebody from being trampled by a horse.

'Do you love him?' asked Kelly, fixing Emily with her stare.

Emily shook her head. What kind of question was that? 'What do you mean?'

'What am I, speaking German?' said Kelly. 'Do you love him?'

Emily thought about it for a minute. About the horse riding and the snowstorm and the hotel in Mauritius, and how she had felt when she thought something terrible had happened to him. 'Yes.'

'Then get back in your car and go and act like it,' said Kelly, her face burning with fury.

'What, NOW?' asked Emily incredulously, staring at them both.

'No, next fucking Thursday,' snapped Kelly. 'How do you think Jamie feels? He nearly DIED a few weeks ago, he's got weeks of recovery ahead of him, his ex-girlfriend turns up out of the blue and then his current girlfriend fucks off. What the bloody hell is wrong with you?'

Emily was silent for a second, then she crumbled into heaving sobs, her hands over her face. 'Oh God, I've really messed this up, haven't I?'

'Yes, you have,' said Carol, giving Kelly a chance to catch her breath. 'So go and fix it. Go home, get your stuff, get your silly arse back to Norfolk and don't let Florence Nightingale or Mrs Danvers try to TAKE AWAY THE MAN YOU LOVE.'

'Christ, Carol,' said Kelly, clearly impressed. 'You should be on the stage.'

'Who's Mrs Danvers?' asked Emily.

'Oh, bloody hell, never mind,' said Carol, wafting her away. 'Go.'

'What are you going to do?'

'Stay here with Kelly,' said Carol. 'Drink your G&T, drink my wine, probably get hammered and get a kebab on the way home.'

Emily laughed through her tears. 'I love you both so much.'

'Yeah, we know,' said Kelly, waving Emily away. 'Now fuck off.'

It was almost 1 a.m. when Emily pulled up outside the pool house. The drive had flown by, fuelled by strong coffee and her foot jammed on the accelerator on an empty motorway. The conversation with her mum and Kelly had cleared her head, and the need to resolve things pulled her towards Jamie like he was the Earth and she was the moon. She'd been a selfish, insecure idiot, and she hoped it wasn't too late to fix things.

The door to the pool house was unlocked, although she'd have happily thrown rocks at the window if she'd had to. She crept through the kitchen to Jamie's bedroom, then stood in the doorway for a minute, watching him sleep. He was alone, and she hated herself for how much she'd doubted him. After everything that had happened between them, after he'd bared his soul about his previous relationships and told her what it had taken for him to ask her out, how could she have thought he'd go back to Louisa?

A sliver of moonlight shone through the gap in the curtains and across his face, making him look more handsome than ever. She tiptoed over to the bed, trying to work out the best way to wake him without scaring him half to death and risking him breaking the other leg. In the end she sat on the edge of the bed, gently stroking his arm until he stirred. 'It's Emily,' she whispered. 'Hi.'

Jamie squinted at her blearily, reaching up to push his hair out of his eyes. 'I thought you'd gone home,' he said, leaning up on his elbows.

'I did,' she said quietly. 'But then I realised I'd forgotten something important.'

Jamie smiled at her for a long moment, then folded back the covers, pulling off his T-shirt and slowly shuffling his plastic boot over to make room for her. Emily stripped off her clothes, not caring that she'd been in a car for four hours and needed a shower, not caring that she was buzzing on coffee and probably wouldn't sleep. It was the first time they'd shared a bed in weeks, so she snuggled into his arms, feeling entirely certain that this was where she belonged.

'I'm glad you're back,' whispered Jamie. She could hear the relief in his voice.

'Me too,' said Emily, trailing her hand across the hard muscles of his stomach. 'I love you.'

Jamie gave a deep sigh of happiness. 'I love you too.'

CHAPTER THIRTY-NINE

'I'm really sorry I left,' said Emily, putting a tray of tea and toast on the bed. 'It was a shitty thing to do. I just felt a bit overwhelmed by everything.'

'You and me both,' said Jamie, pushing himself upright with a wince. 'I genuinely didn't think she was coming. You do believe me, right?'

Emily nodded. 'You messaged her while we were away, though.' It was a statement, not a question. 'Why didn't you tell me?'

'I . . . I don't know,' said Jamie. 'It was nothing other than advice about my treatment, I can show you the messages if you like.'

'I don't need to see the messages,' she said. 'I just wish you'd been honest.'

'I'm sorry,' said Jamie. 'You were working so hard and doing so much for me, I didn't want to say "Louisa says this" and "Louisa says that" and spoil our little bubble. I didn't think you'd like it.'

'I wouldn't have liked it, but I'd have understood. Better that than finding out from Anna.'

'I'm really sorry,' he said.

'It's fine,' said Emily, because right now it felt like it genuinely was fine. The fog had lifted, and she felt much clearer

299

about the way forward for both of them. 'What are you going to do now?'

'I'll talk to Louisa this morning, make it clear that you and I are together and nothing has changed between me and her.'

'Why didn't you tell her about us before?'

'Because it's none of her business,' said Jamie, raking his hair in frustration. 'And anyway, she already knows, presumably from Anna. She's done some fishing, tried to find out how I feel about you.'

Emily smiled. 'And how do you feel about me?'

'Now who's fishing?' said Jamie with a grin. 'I told you that last night.'

'I wasn't sure you'd remember. You were half asleep.'

'Well, the important half was still awake.'

'I noticed.'

'Fine, I'll say it again. I love you, and you're the best thing that's ever happened to me.'

Emily's heart sang; she hadn't realised how much she needed to hear that.

'Don't tell Louisa that, she'll probably leave.'

Jamie nodded. 'All things considered, I think it's best if she does leave. I really appreciate her offering to help, and I hope we can stay friends. But it's never going to be more than that, and her being here isn't ideal for any of us.'

'You'll lose your physio,' said Emily, feeling like she should at least table a small objection. 'If you really think she's the best, I will totally understand if you want her to stay.'

'She's not the only physio in the world,' said Jamie, grabbing his crutches and levering himself out bed. 'I believe Norwich has several. Even she admitted that my rehab is quite straightforward; I just need someone to keep an eye on my progress and help me with the hydrotherapy, check I don't drown.'

'Maybe we should book you in at the local leisure centre, get you a slot between Aquafit and toddler splash time.'

'You're very funny.'

Emily left Jamie's a few minutes before Louisa was due, walking back to the house through the walled garden. She didn't care if she met Adam or Anna or the local axe murderer, frankly – today she would melt them all with the power of her fuck-you killer death stare. The last time she'd felt this good was the day she'd wangled a month's paid leave off Mark and set herself free from the pain of looking at his face every day. She'd wrestled back control of her life for the second time in four months, and it felt pretty great.

Leon was under the bonnet of the Audi when she walked past the garage, so she wandered over to say hello.

'I thought you had gone home,' he said, clearly confused.

'I decided to come back,' she said breezily.

Leon was quiet for a few seconds, twisting a spanner in his hands. 'I don't like the way you are being treated,' he said. 'By Adam and Anna and the other lady. It is not nice.'

'Thank you,' said Emily. 'But I've got things under control.'

'I am glad,' said Leon. 'Jamie is very lucky to have you.'

Emily rested her hand on his arm. 'You're a good friend, Leon. Thank you for looking out for me.'

His eyes looked a bit watery. 'Is no problem,' he said. 'I don't suppose you have a twin sister?'

Emily shook her head and laughed. 'Two brothers, I'm afraid.'

'Ah well,' said Leon. 'What is it the English say – you can't win them all?'

'You can't,' said Emily, heading off into the house to find Anna. She felt like she was on a winning streak today, and she wasn't done yet.

She found Anna in the kitchen reading the *Sunday Telegraph* on the sofa, an empty cup of coffee on the table. She looked up as Emily came in, her eyebrows raised in annoyance.

'I thought you weren't back until tomorrow,' she said, with a tone that suggested Emily had just pissed in her slippers.

'I came back last night,' said Emily cheerfully, boiling the kettle for a cup of tea. 'I realised I was in the wrong place.'

Anna said nothing, her mouth set in a grim line as she returned to her newspaper. Emily could hear the cogs turning in her evil mastermind brain as she tried to formulate a new plan.

Once she'd made her tea, Emily didn't take it straight upstairs as she normally would. Instead she carried it over to the sofa and sat down. Anna froze and glared at her, clearly unsettled by this turn of events and the implacable expression on Emily's face.

'Did you want something?' she asked.

'What have I done to upset you, Anna?' Emily asked calmly, sipping her tea.

Anna stared at her for a few seconds, then looked back at the paper. 'I don't know what you mean.'

'You've never taken to me, since the day I came for an interview. I've tried really hard; I'm good at my job, I'm respectful of this house and your space. So what's your problem?'

Another silence, which Emily waited out patiently. She wasn't moving until she got an answer, even if that meant sitting there all day.

Anna snapped the paper shut and briskly folded it. 'You're not Andrea,' she said. 'She was my best friend for nearly twenty-five years.'

Emily said nothing, waiting for Anna to continue.

'I thought she might come back when her mother was over the worst, but she's decided to stay in Somerset. But even if she wanted to come back she couldn't, because Mr Hunter's got YOU now.' The 'you' was delivered with as much venom as Anna could muster, but Emily could tell that her heart was no longer in it.

'Why did you want her to come back?' she asked gently.

Anna looked up, her expression bleak. 'Andrea and I were a partnership. We ran this place like a military operation. George is gone, Andrea is gone, and now I've got nobody.'

'Who's George?' asked Emily.

'He was my husband,' snapped Anna, like Emily should have known this. 'He was the head gardener here. So much of the Bowford gardens was his design; I still see him everywhere.'

'When you say he's gone, do you mean he . . . died?' Emily knew she had to tread carefully if she was going to have this out with Anna without her storming off.

Anna nodded, her eyes filling with angry tears. 'Seven years ago, we were married over thirty years. Andrea helped me through that, but now she's left me too.'

'I'm sorry,' Emily said.

Anna made a huffing noise, like she didn't really believe her. 'And I absolutely don't approve of you and Jamie,' she added. 'We're staff, we shouldn't get involved with the family. It's not right.'

Emily said nothing as Anna stood up. She thought she was going to leave, but instead she went to the kettle and made herself another coffee, then returned to the sofa and sat down.

'Tell me about when you met George,' said Emily.

Anna eyed her suspiciously. 'Why?'

Emily shrugged. 'Because I'm interested.'

Anna said nothing for a while, clearly torn between wanting to talk about the love of her life, but also wishing Emily wasn't the one asking. 'It was my first week here,' she said with a sigh. 'Forty years ago, nearly. We had a lot more staff then; old Mr Hunter was in charge.'

'It must have felt very different.'

'It did. The house was always full of people, not like now.' She glared at Emily, like she was somehow responsible for reduced visitor numbers.

'Were you the housekeeper then?' asked Emily, desperately trying to keep Anna talking.

'Of course not,' snapped Anna. 'I was younger than you. I did a bit of everything then – laundry, cleaning, cooking, helping out with the children when they came along. One of my jobs was to collect vegetables from the walled garden, so I used to see George every day.' She gave a misty-eyed smile, lost in memories. 'I knew he was for me the first time I met him.'

'What did that feel like?' asked Emily.

Anna looked at her suspiciously, like she was being led into a trap. Emily kept her expression soft, wondering how long it was since Anna had last had a proper woman-to-woman conversation. 'I thought about him all the time,' she said quietly, a faraway look in her eyes. 'I couldn't wait to go out to see him. I started doing the flowers in the house, so I could see him more often. George loved roses most of all, he spent hours in the rose garden. It's still a special place to me.'

Emily smiled. 'And what if he'd been family?'

Anna's head snapped round to glare at Emily. 'What do you mean?'

'If George had been part of the Hunter family rather than the gardener. What then?'

Anna looked affronted, like the idea was impossible. 'I'd have stayed away from him.'

'I'm sure you would. But would you have felt any differently about him?'

Anna stared at Emily for a long moment. 'I don't know.'

'Because what you've just described about meeting George,' said Emily, turning up her palms like she had nothing left to hide, 'that's how I felt the first time I met Jamie. I had no idea who he was, I thought he worked in the stables.'

Anna dropped her head and stared at her coffee. 'I didn't know that,' she said quietly.

'When I found out he was family, I did my best to stay away from him. But it was no good. The heart wants what it wants.'

Anna said nothing, so Emily continued. 'I'm sorry about George, and I'm sorry about Andrea. She sounds like an amazing woman, and she's made my job here so much easier. Her filing was incredible.'

Anna half-smiled, clearly proud on behalf of her friend.

'But I can't bring her back. All I can do is try to be as good at the job as she was. And I'd like for us to be friends. I love this house, and I think you do too.'

'It's been my life,' whispered Anna bleakly. 'I worry about that too.'

'What do you mean?'

'Adam. What he'll do when he's in charge. He doesn't care about this house at all. I'll be long gone by then, but I still worry about it.'

'Yes. You and me both.'

'I'm sorry,' said Anna. 'You coming here has put me in a very bad place, and I haven't behaved well.'

Emily wasn't quite ready to let Anna off the hook just yet. 'No. Telling Leon about me spending the night with Jamie was pretty low, not to mention getting Louisa here.'

Anna stared at her in silence for a moment, her expression impassive. 'I told Leon your bed hadn't been slept in; I went to check because I was a little worried about you, what with all that snow. He worked the rest out for himself.'

'Oh,' said Emily, feeling her cheeks flush.

'And Louisa wasn't my doing either. Adam was the one who called her; I was just told to make her welcome and take over Jamie's care until she arrived. I accept my behaviour hasn't been friendly at times, but I'm really not that cruel.'

Emily felt the blush of shame creep down her neck to her chest. 'Ah, OK. I just assumed . . .'

'Perhaps neither of us has judged the other particularly well.'

Emily gave her a weak smile. 'No, it seems not. Well, maybe we can try again?'

Anna looked at her like she was seeing her for the first time. 'Maybe.'

Emily nodded and took her tea upstairs. It was a start, and today was very much about fresh starts.

CHAPTER FORTY

On Monday morning Emily turned up in Mr Hunter's office at 9 a.m. as usual, and wasn't remotely surprised to discover that he already knew she was back from her trip home. There weren't many secrets at Bowford Manor.

'I heard you'd returned early,' he said with a warm smile. 'You look very well on it.'

Emily supposed that Anna or Leon had told him this particular titbit of gossip over dinner the previous evening, which she'd spent in the pool house with Jamie. She'd stayed out of his way all day so he could resolve things with Louisa; apparently she'd taken it all extremely badly and fled back to London in tears. Seemingly Adam had weaved some bullshit tale that gave her reason to hope for a reconciliation, at least until Jamie spoiled everything.

'I'm very happy to be back,' she said, having had her best night's sleep for a week. Anna hadn't exactly been friendly over breakfast, but she sensed that something had shifted between them. They might never be best mates, but she'd settle for a mutually respectful truce.

'That's good to hear,' said Mr Hunter. 'I've got some things to talk through with you; how about some coffee before you do the post?'

Emily nodded and headed through to the tiny kitchen, pressing buttons on the coffee machine while she fired up her laptop and retrieved her notebook from the drawer. Within a few minutes she was back in Mr Hunter's office with two steaming mugs.

'So,' said Mr Hunter. 'I've been giving some thought to the plans you showed me before Christmas. A lot of thought, actually.' Emily looked blank. 'The ones Adam left on the photocopier.'

'Ohhh,' said Emily as the penny dropped. So much had happened since then, and she'd pretty much forgotten about the papers she'd copied in a moment of madness. 'Do you know what they are?'

'I have my suspicions,' said Mr Hunter, unlocking one of the drawers in his desk, 'but I would welcome your thoughts. Adam isn't back here until later in the week, so now seems like a good time for us to take a look.'

He unrolled the photocopies and spread them out across the desk, weighing down the corners with various heavy objects – a photo of his three children flanked by dogs and horses, a pen pot, his coffee mug. Emily had only glanced at them for a few seconds at the time, but she could see that they were topographical maps of the Bowford Estate, with several areas shaded in different colours.

'A little bit of background information first,' said Mr Hunter. 'Adam is due to inherit the Bowford Estate when I die, the eldest child of the eldest child.'

Emily nodded, not entirely sure if she was supposed to be making notes. She decided she probably wasn't and sipped her coffee instead.

'It's not a legal entail or anything like that,' continued Mr Hunter, 'they got rid of those a long time ago. But it's how this estate has worked for four hundred years. I have every intention of being around for a while, but I suspect Adam is thinking ahead to a time when this place might be his to do whatever he likes with.'

'What do you mean?'

'He's a property developer, Emily. Conservation is of no interest to him, he likes to build new things, not look after old ones.' He held the corner of a sheet down while he sipped his coffee, then pointed to an area shaded pink on the plan. 'These coloured areas are parcels of land around the estate. Currently farmland – they're the higher points on the estate that never flood in winter. Prime development spots, perfect for new housing.'

'You think he's planning to sell bits of the estate for housing?'

'None of it is his to sell, at least not yet. So we're safe for the time being, as long as I don't pop my clogs tomorrow. But it wouldn't surprise me if he's laying the groundwork for the future.'

Emily stared at the plans for a moment, scanning the margins for tiny details. 'Did he draft these plans himself, do you think?'

'I have no idea,' said Mr Hunter, his brow furrowed. 'What are you thinking?'

'It looks to me like he's had the estate fully surveyed and had someone make recommendations on the best sites for development. Unless he's a qualified surveyor and has the right equipment, he'd definitely have needed help.'

Mr Hunter raised his eyebrows. 'Is this a field of expertise you didn't mention on your CV?'

Emily gave an awkward smile. 'I was PA to an architect for three years; lots of plans like these passed over my boss's desk. Could he have brought land surveyors here without you noticing?'

'I suppose he could,' said Mr Hunter thoughtfully. 'I'm away all the time; when I interviewed you back in October I'd been in London for over a week. James and Leon were with me, James was staying with a, uh . . . friend.' He tripped over the final word, and Emily realised he meant Louisa. It wasn't important, so she moved on.

'What about Anna? Would she notice a team of surveyors with all their gear?'

Mr Hunter shook his head. 'There's no reason why she would. Anna rarely leaves the house and garden, and the estate workers mind their own business.'

Emily thought for a moment, her eyes narrowed. 'So I guess it would be good to know if this is just Adam messing around with a wild idea, or if he's already laying concrete plans.'

Mr Hunter nodded and smiled. 'That, my dear, is the killer question. We need to find out if he's in cahoots.'

'Who would he be in cahoots with?' The word felt unfamiliar on Emily's tongue; she was pretty sure she'd never used it before.

Mr Hunter sat back in his chair. 'Adam calls himself a property developer, but actually he's a fixer. He finds the investors, influences the powerful and makes things happen. He greases the wheels of the property industry but doesn't actually build anything.'

'So he could be working with a developer?'

'Yes. Probably not one of the big ones; it will be somebody who doesn't have to answer to board members and shareholders, easier to keep everything under wraps. But they'll be an established firm; this could be a very long game for them. I might go another twenty years if Adam is unlucky.' He removed his glasses and chewed the arm thoughtfully. 'Any ideas how we find out, without my son getting wind of it?'

Emily didn't hesitate. 'Yes.'

Mr Hunter raised his eyebrows in surprise, like he'd just been musing to himself without any expectation that Emily would answer. 'Really?'

'Yes,' she said. 'I know a man with a lot of connections, who also owes me a favour. His name's Mark Thompson.'

Emily walked through the walled garden, enjoying the early signs of industry in the vegetable beds and the greenhouse. Sadly there wasn't time to stop and chat with the gardeners as she was carrying lunch for her and Jamie on a tray. Sam had made them bean curry flatbreads that were as close as he could get to Mauritian street food with the limited access he had to authentic ingredients.

An uncomfortable feeling had been sitting like a brick in the pit of Emily's stomach since she'd messaged Mark to ask if they could meet for dinner on Wednesday. He'd replied almost immediately with a yes, without asking any other questions. She definitely didn't want to keep the dinner secret from Jamie, but she also couldn't tell him why they were meeting. Which meant she now needed to tell a white lie, or at least fail to mention relevant information. It didn't feel right, particularly in view of the conversation they'd had about honesty yesterday. But the alternative was saying nothing at all, which felt even less right.

She'd always known that something like this might happen – when she'd told Jamie that having a relationship with him was a conflict of interest, she hadn't been joking – but she hadn't envisaged Mark somehow being involved in the sub-terfuge, and she didn't like it one bit. But there was no way round it that she could see, so she was just going to have to go with it.

'Lunch delivery,' she sang as she opened the door. Jamie flew across the kitchen on his crutches, showing off how fast he was now. She put the tray on the counter as he pulled her into a passionate kiss.

'Steady on,' she laughed, 'I'm only on my lunch break.'

'I've missed you,' said Jamie. 'It's lonely here on my own.'

'I'm afraid you can't have Louisa back.'

'Very funny,' he said. 'I spoke to three physios in Nor-wich this morning; one of them sounds perfect and is coming over tomorrow.'

'Good news,' said Emily, pushing the plate towards him. 'Eat.'

They were both quiet for a few minutes as they ate their lunch. 'I'm going to London on Wednesday,' she said cas-ually, getting two cans of Diet Coke out of the fridge.

'With Dad?'

'Yeah. He's got some meetings.'

Jamie laughed. 'So you've come back and now you're abandoning me again.'

'You're doing really well now. Super-speedy on those crutches. I'm going to have dinner with a friend while I'm there.'

Jamie looked up at her. 'Ah, that's nice. Anyone I know?'

'It's Mark, my old boss,' she said, sitting back down at the table.

'Oh,' said Jamie. 'Any particular reason?'

'I don't know the details,' she lied. 'He wants a favour, a

professional one. I know he's had two PAs since I left and they haven't worked out, so I'm guessing he wants my help with the job spec.'

'Is sleeping with him part of the job spec?'

'Very funny.'

'You know you can do this kind of thing by email, right?'

'Yes, but he asked if I was in London anytime soon, because it would be nice to meet in person. And since I am in London on Wednesday and have no other plans, I said yes.'

Jamie pursed his lips. 'Is this you punishing me for Louisa?'

'No, of course not,' she said. 'He's asked for my help, and I thought you wouldn't mind since we're all grown-ups.'

'You're definitely punishing me.'

'I'm not,' said Emily. 'If you really have a problem with it, I'll cancel. I don't care enough for us to fall out over it.'

Jamie pouted. 'No, it's fine.'

Emily smiled, wishing she could be honest but knowing her job depended on keeping her work and personal lives separate. 'What if I promise to call you as soon as I get back and tell you I love you?'

'What if you tell me now,' said Jamie, unable to stay annoyed at her for long.

'Fine, I love you.'

'Mmm, I'm not convinced. Maybe you should show me.'

Jamie watched as Emily walked out of the kitchen to turn the heavy key in the front door, then pulled the blinds in the kitchen, plunging them into a dim light. She stood in front of him, already feeling the warmth and anticipation building in the pit of her stomach. 'You want me to use my valuable lunch break to show you how much I love you.'

'Yes,' breathed Jamie, lifting her jumper and burying his face in her stomach.

Emily gasped as his hands stroked her back and his lips kissed a trail from her hip bone to her ribcage. She really needed to get back, but sometimes Jamie made it incredibly hard to leave. 'Maybe I'll show you first,' he whispered, as his fingers found the zip of her jeans and slid them down over her thighs, taking her underwear with them. She moaned and buried her hands in his hair as his tongue and fingers found their mark, knowing that this wouldn't take long. When Jamie took charge, it never took long.

CHAPTER FORTY-ONE

Mark was waiting in the bistro when Emily arrived, a bottle of red wine and two glasses already on the table. It was hard not to be annoyed by his assumption that she would happily drink his choice of wine, and Emily was tempted to order an umbrella-festooned cocktail just to remind him that she was her own woman. But she pushed the irritation aside; she was here to solicit Mark's help, not start a fight over something that really didn't matter.

She'd chosen a place in Soho, mostly because it was within walking distance of Mr Hunter's house in Mayfair, and she really couldn't be arsed to slog across town to Mark's usual haunts in the City. It was dark, cosy and French, but not to the extent it had those odd half-curtains in the window and Edith Piaf on a loop. It had good online reviews, and most importantly it wasn't crazy expensive, because it was her intention to pick up the bill this evening. She'd invited Mark to dinner, so the least she could do was pay. Mr Hunter would obviously reimburse her, but Mark didn't need to know that. She wanted it to feel like an Emily kind of place; cosy and not too stuffy. The kind of place where friends might meet for a relaxed dinner and offer to help each other out.

He stood up as she arrived and kissed her on both cheeks, his aftershave achingly familiar in a way that she felt in every fibre of her body. Two years of horizontal encounters flashed through her mind like a near-death experience, but she brushed them aside. It was history, and she needed to focus.

'You look amazing,' said Mark, holding her at arm's length so he could look at her. It reminded her of the way her grandparents had admired her when she was twelve and had grown four inches since they'd last met. 'Have you been away?'

'No,' lied Emily, not wanting to get waylaid by lots of questions about her travels. 'It's all out of a bottle.' She put her coat on the back of the chair and sat down. She'd chosen her outfit carefully – jeans, her favourite jumper over a shirt, almost no make-up, hair in a tidy bun. Nothing sexy or provocative that might distract Mark from the reason she was there.

'Well, you look great.'

'Thanks, so do you.' This wasn't strictly true, actually; Mark looked pale and tired, and next to Jamie, he looked old. Emily knew it wasn't fair to compare them – Mark was forty-five, compared to Jamie's thirty. There was no question that Mark was an attractive older man, still with all his hair and a smattering of silver around the ears, but for the first time she realised that he was closer in age to her dad than he was to her. That said, he'd clearly made an effort this evening – a just-showered scent, a clean shirt, product in his hair. She wondered where he'd told his wife he was going.

Mark poured wine into Emily's glass, and then topped up his own. The waiter hurried over and laid two menus in front of them, then rattled off some specials in a French accent so heavy Emily wondered if he was actually a struggling actor from Croydon. Mark waited for him to leave, then steepled his hands under his chin and gave Emily his best twinkly smile. 'So was there a reason for summoning me to dinner, or were you just missing me?'

'There was a reason.'

Mark laughed and clutched his chest. 'Ouch. That hurt.'

'Sorry, we'll talk about it later. How are things at the office?'

'Fine,' said Mark with a shrug. 'I actually really miss working with you. Your replacement is very efficient but not nearly as easy on the eye.'

Emily smiled. 'I still think it was the right thing to do. I like my new job, it was a good move for me.'

Mark sipped his drink and regarded her for a while, clearly trying to work out why he was there and what Emily was thinking. 'I've been trying to find out where you're working,' he said casually, 'but I'm not having much luck. LinkedIn says nothing, and you've been very quiet on Instagram lately.'

Emily rolled her eyes. 'I'm taking a break from social media. I know it's weird for someone my age not to slap their entire life online, but I thought I'd brave the wilderness.'

Mark ignored the 'someone my age' dig and continued with his interrogation. 'So where ARE you working?' he persisted. 'I'm pretty sure it's not for one of our competitors, I'd know by now.'

Emily shook her head and laughed. 'Can you stop stalking me? Fine, I've had a change of direction. I don't work for a firm; I work for a private individual.'

Mark's eyes widened. 'How fascinating. Anybody interesting?'

'I'll tell you later, when we get to the reason why I invited you to dinner. Let's just hang out for a bit.'

Mark nodded as they browsed the menu, then ordered the same steak frites as Emily. They sat in companionable silence and sipped their wine for a few minutes, checking out the other diners and admiring the copper light fittings and the black-and-white arty photos on the walls. Mostly vintage shots of stick-thin French models, which made Emily want to call the waiter back and cancel her order in favour of a black coffee and a pack of Gauloises. It was quiet on a Wednesday, but the place still had a nice buzz about it. Emily recalled how easy Mark was to spend time with, and she realised with a jolt of surprise how genuinely glad she was to see him.

'How are your family?' he asked.

'Fine,' said Emily. 'How's your wife?'

Mark roared with laughter. 'My God, I've missed you.'

'What?' she said innocently. 'That isn't a reasonable question?'

Mark sighed. 'She's fine, we're fine, kids are great, blah blah blah.'

Emily watched him carefully. 'I mean, you don't sound very happy.'

'I'm not,' said Mark matter-of-factly. 'The reasons Kay and I split up first time round are still there, but I made my choice to be a proper dad to the kids. That decision hasn't changed, I just have to find a way to live with it.'

Emily nodded and sipped her wine. 'Fair enough.'

'What about you?'

'What about me?' she asked. She'd known the inevitable question was coming and was prepared for it. There was no reason to lie, and for the first time in a while she had nothing to hide. Kind of.

'Are you seeing anyone?'

Emily smiled awkwardly, then looked down at the table in her best attempt at Lady Diana-level coyness. 'Yes.'

Mark looked visibly shocked, like somehow he expected her still to be pining for him, or taking orders as a nun. *Honestly, men and their egos.*

'Wow. That's great news,' he lied, his eyes casting round in various directions as he tried to process this bombshell. 'Are YOU happy?'

'Actually, yes I am,' said Emily. 'It's somebody I work with, but a bit more legitimate this time round.' No doubt he'd want more information, but this was all he was getting.

Mark gave a hollow laugh. 'Just give that knife a twist, why don't you.'

'You don't want me to be happy? You'd rather I was alone and miserable?'

'Absolutely. Then I'd stand a better chance of persuading you to come back to me.'

Emily tilted her head in amusement. 'Professionally or personally?'

'Personally. My new PA is perfectly competent, but I miss hanging out with you in a naked context. Aside from your excellent shorthand, you were a spectacular fuck.'

Emily shook her head and smiled. This was all a game to Mark; the same one he'd played over lunch in October. She'd turned down his advances then, but he wasn't a man who gave up easily. It was a matter of male pride now, a test of his manliness to establish if he still had what it took to seduce a woman sixteen years younger than him. He was going to be sorely disappointed. 'It's never gonna happen,' she said, suddenly remembering the last time she'd heard someone say

319

that. It was Jamie, the day after the Christmas party when he told her how he felt about her. Look how that turned out.

'Never?' said Mark, doing puppy dog eyes.

'No. You and I had a good time, Mark, but I don't want to be your bit on the side. I'm in a much healthier relationship now.'

He sighed, then picked up his wine glass and raised it to Emily grudgingly. 'Fine, you win for now. But you can't blame a man for trying.'

Once their plates had been cleared away, Mark poured the remainder of the wine into their glasses and rested his chin on his hands. 'So, why am I here?' he asked. 'You've already rejected my sexual advances, I'm not sure what else I have to offer.'

Emily laughed. 'OK, fine. Have you ever heard of a man called Charles Hunter?'

Mark thought for a second, then shook his head. 'I don't think so.'

'He made a fortune in software and online gaming, sold his company a few years ago for gazillions.'

'Oh yeah,' said Mark. 'I remember reading about that. Isn't he some kind of viscount or duke or something?'

'Something like that. He's who I work for.'

Mark looked impressed. 'Wow. I bet that's really interesting.'

'It is. He has a son, Adam Hunter.'

'Ah, now him I do know,' said Mark, holding up a finger. 'He's in property, very well connected, not very well liked.'

'Hmm. Why am I not surprised?'

Mark eyed her expectantly, clearly wondering where she was going with this.

'Look, I need some information about Adam Hunter, but it needs to be top secret. It's really important that he doesn't find out that anyone is sniffing around. Like, my job depends on it.'

'OK,' said Mark, twiddling the stem of his wine glass.

'It's a big ask, so feel free to say no. And there might not be anything to find, but I didn't know who else to ask. I need someone I can trust.'

'It's fine,' he said softly. 'I'm glad you thought of me, even if it wasn't in a wanton fucking capacity.'

Emily smiled. 'Thank you.'

'Tell me everything.'

Emily crossed Regent Street towards Grosvenor Square, enjoying the thrill of being back in the midst of London's traffic and noise. She was glad she'd seen Mark, although she was pretty sure he'd have booked them into the nearest hotel if she'd given him half a chance. But actually it now felt like she'd laid that ghost to rest – she'd enjoyed Mark's company, but the physical attraction had waned with time and distance, and this time it had been easy to say goodbye. She'd given him Mr Hunter's details to call when he had information, so she didn't expect to hear from him again any time soon.

Mr Hunter had also gone to dinner with friends, so the Mayfair house was blissfully empty. Emily found herself checking for Adam around every corner these days, knowing he could turn up at any time, but he had his own place in London so there was no reason for him to rock up here.

And if he did, she'd see his bastard piggy-eyed face on the CCTV and just pretend she wasn't in.

She hurried upstairs to her room and sat cross-legged on the bed so she could call Jamie. He answered after a couple of rings, which made her wonder if he'd been waiting for her call. 'Hey,' she said. 'I'm just calling to say I love you, as promised.'

Jamie laughed. 'You're home early.'

'Not really,' she said vaguely. 'It was just dinner.'

'Did you have a good time?'

Emily smiled, wondering why men asked questions they really didn't want to hear the answer to. 'It was nice to see him, and I was able to offer some staffing advice. How was your physio?'

'He was great, don't change the subject. Did you tell Mark about me?'

'He asked if I was seeing anyone, so I said I was. He didn't ask for details, so I didn't offer any.'

'That's it?'

Emily sighed. 'He also asked if I was happy, and I said I definitely was.'

'Hmm,' said Jamie. 'Sounds like he was trying to get back in your knickers.'

Emily laughed. 'Well, unluckily for him, my knickers are off limits to everyone but you.'

'I'm very glad to hear it.'

They were both quiet for a moment. 'I'll be back tomorrow,' she said, wishing she was there already.

'I'll think about your knickers until then.'

'Maybe I'll buy some new ones while I'm here,' she said playfully. 'Pop to Selfridges tomorrow, get something fancy.'

'Interesting,' said Jamie. 'Do you take requests?'

Emily laughed, all thoughts of Mark wiped clean from her mind. 'Maybe. What were you thinking?'

She lay back on the pillows and closed her eyes while Jamie told her exactly what he was thinking.

CHAPTER FORTY-TWO

Emily woke up in Jamie's bed on Sunday morning feeling like all was well in her world, allowing herself a smile at the discarded scraps of black lace on the bedroom floor. She'd popped to Selfridges during her lunch break on Thursday and selected a triangle bra and a matching Brazilian thong – neither was remotely practical or suitable for everyday wear, but they made her feel like a completely different woman. The set had cost more than the cumulative amount she'd spent on underwear in her entire life, especially considering how little there was of it, but Jamie's enthusiasm last night had made it worth every penny.

She stared at the clear blue sky out of the window as he clattered mugs in the kitchen, thinking about how Jamie's leg injury had changed things between them in the bedroom. Aside from the obvious logistics of Emily having to be on top, it required them to communicate more, for Jamie to tell Emily exactly what worked and what didn't. They needed to slow everything down and take their time, which definitely wasn't a bad thing. It was an unexpected level of intimacy so early on in their relationship, but things still had all the intensity of their first few weeks together.

It was hard to believe it had already been over a month since Jamie's accident – his ribs and knee had healed well, he was doing daily physio in the pool, and expected to be able to start putting some weight on his leg in the next couple of weeks. With any luck the boot would be off by the time the weather started to warm up, and he'd be able to ditch at least one of his crutches and get back on a horse. His physio had advised against it for a few more weeks, so instead he was spending a lot of time getting under the feet of the grooms and stable hands.

Emily jumped out of bed and pulled one of Jamie's T-shirts over her head, then padded through to the kitchen.

'Good morning,' she said, wrapping her arms around his waist.

'I've made tea,' said Jamie, twisting round to kiss her. 'Let's go back to bed.'

Emily picked up both mugs and carried them back to the bedroom, Jamie following on his crutches. He leaned them against the wall and sat on the edge of the bed, then swung his legs round, punching the pillow behind his back to make himself comfortable.

'I've had a message from my dad,' he said. 'Do you fancy going riding today?'

Emily looked at him in surprise. 'With your dad?'

Jamie nodded. 'He's going out and asked if you wanted to go with him. It seems a shame for you not to go because I can't. You've been making such great progress.'

'What about Adam? Is he going?' Emily knew that Adam was back at Bowford; she'd seen him prowling the corridors yesterday like a hungry Dementor.

Jamie shook his head. 'I shouldn't think so. Adam rarely rides these days.'

She tried not to let the relief show on her face. 'What will you do while I'm out?'

'Hang out with the horses, fold blankets, get insanely jealous that you're out riding, wait impatiently for you to come back.'

Emily snuggled into his shoulder. 'You'll be out with me soon.'

'I know,' said Jamie with a smile. 'But in the meantime you can practise your canter so we can do lots of weekend rides this summer.'

'That sounds nice.'

'We can do a tour of all the local pubs.'

Emily smiled at the memory of their first ride together. 'Maybe just the ones with valet horse parking.'

Emily sat on Rupert's back waiting for Mr Hunter to arrive; apparently he'd been held up by a phone call with Tanya, who was no doubt demanding more money to fund her LA lifestyle. His horse was a beautiful light bay called Chester, who was currently tied to the rail and waiting patiently. Jamie sat on the mounting block, his booted leg stretched out in front and his crutches hanging loosely on his arms.

'I'm going home next weekend,' said Emily. 'It's my birthday on Sunday.'

Jamie looked up in surprise. 'I had no idea. Why didn't you say?'

'I don't know, I guess there's been a lot going on and I kind of forgot. Now it's crept up on me.'

'Is it your thirtieth?'

'Yeah. I think Mum is planning family drinks at the pub on Saturday night. Nothing fancy, probably just me and Kelly and Mum and Dad.'

'Am I invited?'

'Of course, if you want to come. But it's going to be in a crowded pub and I'm worried you'll get knocked about.' Emily had given it some thought and decided it really would be best if Jamie didn't come, but she hadn't worked out the best way to word it without offending him.

Jamie thought about it for a moment. 'I'd really like to be there, but to be honest I'm not sure I can handle that long in a car. Would you be upset?'

'Of course not,' said Emily. 'We can celebrate when I get back on Sunday. That's my actual birthday anyway.'

'It's a deal,' he said. 'I'll cook you something fancy, get some tips from Sam. It's not every day you turn thirty.'

'How did you celebrate yours?'

'Oh,' said Jamie, blushing furiously. 'Um, Dad took me out for dinner.'

'Where?'

'New York.'

Emily snorted with laughter. 'I'm a much cheaper date. The kitchen will be just fine.'

'You have good posture,' said Mr Hunter, walking alongside Emily towards the large paddock at the south end of the estate. They'd been heading that way for ten minutes, after Mr Hunter suggested it would be a good place to practise cantering. 'You've taken to riding very quickly.'

'I really enjoy it,' said Emily with a smile. 'I never thought I would.'

'I'm sorry this isn't quite the beach in Mauritius.'

'It's still beautiful though,' she said. 'It must be lovely to have all this space to yourself.'

'I suppose it is,' replied Mr Hunter. 'I've never really thought about it.'

Emily heard a distant clip-clop noise and twisted around in the saddle to see a figure on a black horse approaching at a trot. 'Who's that?' she asked.

Mr Hunter turned, then sighed. 'Ah. Looks like Adam has decided to join us.'

Emily felt all her positivity and enthusiasm drain away. Nothing good ever came from being anywhere near Adam.

'Hello,' he huffed grumpily, pulling his horse to a walk beside his father. Every part of his riding outfit was black, including the sleek, shiny horse he was sitting on. Emily remembered Jamie telling her it was called Lucifer, which seemed appropriate – against his pale, waxy skin it made Adam look like one of the four horsemen of the apocalypse. 'I thought we were going riding this morning?' There was a tiny emphasis on the 'we', just in case Emily was under any illusion about how welcome she was to this little party.

'We were,' said Mr Hunter. 'Two hours ago. But luckily Emily offered to accompany me instead.'

'So I see,' said Adam, turning to look at Emily like she was a nugget of shit on his boot.

'Are you ready?' Mr Hunter asked Emily. 'I've had all the gates opened, so we have a clear run all the way to Chapel Farm.' Emily gave a nervous nod as she picked out the farmhouse on the horizon. 'We'll go nice and steady,' he said reassuringly, kicking Chester into a trot, then a canter. Emily followed, pretending not to notice Adam's narrow-eyed glare.

Mr Hunter kept a comfortable pace along the line of the fence – a little faster than she was used to, but still a gentle canter that gave her the time and space to focus on her posture. She kept Chester in sight between Rupert's ears and enjoyed the buzz of adrenaline in her veins and the wind in her face.

She wasn't aware of Adam overtaking on her left-hand side until she heard the swish of his riding crop and the change in rhythm of Lucifer's hooves as he rose out of his saddle into a gallop. Rupert surged forward to follow him, taking Emily to a pace that felt entirely alien and terrifying. The rhythm was all wrong and she struggled to maintain her balance, clamping her lips together to stop herself screaming as fear and panic set in.

She clung to the pommel of the saddle for dear life as Adam overtook Mr Hunter, Rupert in hot pursuit. It took a few seconds for Mr Hunter to realise what was happening, and he immediately pulled ahead of her, putting Chester between Rupert and Lucifer. 'Pull back on the reins!' he shouted, gently slowing Chester down as Emily urged Rupert to do the same. Rupert slowed to a canter, then finally a trot.

'Are you OK?' asked Mr Hunter, bringing Chester down to a walk and coming alongside her. 'What happened?'

Emily quickly wiped the tears off her face with the back of her glove, forcing a weak smile as she tried to catch her breath. 'Rupert followed Adam's horse.' She strongly suspected that Adam had whacked Rupert with his riding crop, but there was no point telling Mr Hunter. She had no proof and Adam would almost certainly deny it.

'He's an idiot,' said Mr Hunter furiously. 'You could easily have come off.'

'I'm fine,' said Emily, trying to stop her knees from shaking. 'Just a bit faster than I'm used to.'

'You did very well. Kept a cool head.'

'Thank you.'

He looked at her for a long moment; no doubt she looked white as a sheet and her hands were visibly trembling. 'Do you want to head back?'

Emily nodded. 'I think I need a cup of tea. You carry on and join Adam, I'll be fine walking back on my own.'

'Are you sure?'

Emily nodded, so Mr Hunter gave her a smile and trotted off towards the barn. She watched him move seamlessly into a canter, then rise into the gallop. One day she'd be able to do that, and then Adam could go fuck himself.

She clicked her tongue to get Rupert moving, then turned back towards the house. The day was still and silent, other than birdsong and the thunder of Chester's retreating hooves. The realisation of what could have happened struck her, and a sob broke free from her chest. Another followed and she let them flow, releasing all the fear and tension until her face was streaked with snotty tears and her trauma was replaced by cold, hard fury. One way or another, Adam had it coming.

CHAPTER FORTY-THREE

'Surprise!' yelled Carol, clapping her hands like a performing seal as Emily stood in the doorway of the function room out the back of the White Lion. The shock on her face was entirely genuine – she'd been expecting a couple of drinks with her parents, maybe a club with Kelly then a dirty pizza on the way home, but this was an actual party with *Happy 30th Birthday* balloons and everything. 'I've been busting to tell you,' Carol babbled on. 'It's been a bloody nightmare, to be honest.'

Emily looked around, taking in the applauding people and the bunting and the DJ who appeared to be an actual professional with decks, rather than some random with a wireless speaker and a premium Spotify account. With hindsight she should have guessed something was up – her parents had been out for most of the day, claiming they needed to pick up Emily's present because of some delivery issue or other. Emily had hung out with Kelly instead, getting her hair done at the salon then picking Beth up from Kelly's mum's and taking them both to Nando's.

Emily squealed as she spotted her brother Simon and his husband Eric, who she now realised were the present her parents had needed to pick up. She hurtled across the room and hugged them both, unable to believe that they'd travelled all the way from Hamburg just to celebrate her birthday. She hadn't seen either of them since the previous summer, and it felt like the best present she could have hoped for. David and Joanna were there too, their boys already doing knee slides on the dance floor while Beth ran around in frantic circles trying to get their attention.

The rest of the party was made up of Kelly, Beth and her parents, along with a scattering of old school friends, neighbours and relatives. But the biggest surprise was when the crowd parted briefly and Emily spotted Jamie and Leon at the bar. Her heart soared as she ran over and hugged them both.

'Nice dress,' said Jamie, leaning forward on his bar stool to give her a kiss. She was wearing the same sparkly number she'd worn to the Bowford Christmas party, figuring that only her parents would have seen it before. Jamie had put on a pale blue shirt and a grey jacket for the occasion and looked more gorgeous than ever. Even Leon had scrubbed up nicely; with a beard trim and a tight white T-shirt and leather jacket, he looked like a *Faith*-era George Michael.

'Thank you,' said Emily, giving them both a twirl. 'I thought you weren't coming.'

'I didn't want to spoil the surprise,' said Jamie. 'Your mum invited me weeks ago.'

'How did you manage the drive?'

Jamie blushed and shuffled awkwardly on his bar stool. 'OK, please don't tell anyone because it makes me sound like a massive wanker, but Dad insisted we fly down by helicopter.'

Emily snorted with laughter, looking from Jamie to Leon to see if they were joking. 'You came to my birthday party by helicopter?'

'Sssh,' said Jamie, looking horrified. 'It was the only way I could get here with this stupid leg. I can't sit in a car for that long without the Mauritian happy pills.'

'How long did it take?'

'About an hour. Leon is going to drive your car back tomorrow night so you can fly back with me on Monday morning.'

She looked at Leon, her eyes boggling. 'Are you serious?'

Leon nodded and grinned. 'Mr Hunter thought it would be a nice birthday present.'

'Wow,' said Emily. 'I don't know what to say. But just so you know, there are people here who will beat the shit out of you if they find out, so don't tell anyone.'

'Don't tell anyone what?' asked Kelly, muscling her way to the bar, Beth clutching her hand. 'Surprise!' she added, giving Emily a hug.

'I was genuinely shocked,' said Emily, picking Beth up and giving her a big kiss. 'How's my favourite goddaughter? Your dress is very pretty.'

'You're a fish,' said Beth, picking at one of the sequins with her finger. Emily put her down and she immediately ran back to the dance floor to find Billy and Charlie.

'Hey, Jamie,' said Kelly, leaning over to give him a kiss on the cheek. 'Those crutches have made your arms super-hench.'

Jamie laughed. 'What does that actually mean?'

'Like, fit. Built. Hunky.'

'Oh,' said Jamie, as Emily rolled her eyes. 'Thanks.'

Kelly looked at Leon with evident interest.

'Leon, this is my best friend, Kelly,' said Emily. 'Kelly, this is Leon. We work together.'

'Hi, Leon,' said Kelly, giving him her most becoming

smile. 'Shall we leave these lovebirds alone while you buy me a drink?'

Leon opened and closed his mouth like a goldfish, then nodded and followed Kelly to a gap further down the bar.

'Uh-oh,' said Emily with a grin.

'Match made in heaven,' said Jamie.

'Thanks, Dad,' said Emily, leaning her head against Martin's shoulder as they watched Carol dancing enthusiastically with Simon, David and Eric. The song was 'I Wanna Dance with Somebody' by Whitney Houston, and Carol had chosen some dance moves that made her look like she was shaking out a picnic blanket. It was a heartfelt thank you, because Emily couldn't remember the last time she'd had this much fun with so many people she loved.

'Ah, your mum did most of the work,' said Martin.

'I know, but this must have cost a bit.'

Martin shrugged. 'Not really. The DJ is one of David's old school mates and your mum did the buffet with Janet next door. Kelly sorted the decorations, so everybody chipped in.'

'I've had such a great time,' said Emily. She'd had a bit too much to drink but was still in the happy-drunk phase. Later would herald the arrival of the over-emotional drunk phase, followed by the final I-need-a-pizza blotto phase.

'I think your man needs rescuing,' said Martin, nodding towards the bar. Emily looked over to see Jamie being chatted up by a woman in a red dress that elevated her boobs to about three inches below her chin, creating a convenient place for the saliva to pool. It was Stacey Connor, an old friend from school who she and Kelly used to go clubbing with occasionally, mostly because she'd shagged

334

every doorman in Chichester and they never had to queue. Emily watched her beadily as she repeatedly touched Jamie's arm and giggled, to which he responded with a polite but dead-eyed smile that offered her no encouragement whatsoever. God, he was amazing.

'Back in a bit,' said Emily, weaving her way over. Jamie looked relieved to see her and slid his hand around her waist, prompting Stacey to beat a hasty retreat towards the loos.

'You look happy,' said Jamie, giving her a kiss.

'You look tired,' she said.

'I'm going to head off soon,' he said. 'But don't let me drag you away from your birthday party.'

'Don't be daft,' said Emily. 'The DJ wraps up in ten minutes, everyone will leave then.'

'Kelly said she wanted to take you clubbing,' said Jamie. They both looked over to where Kelly and Leon were grinding against each other to 'Naughty Girl' by Beyoncé. Her mum and stepdad had taken Beth home hours ago.

'I think Kelly has a better offer right now,' said Emily with a grin. 'Will you dance with me? I said no last time you asked, but I've changed my mind.'

Jamie hauled himself to his feet and propped himself up on one crutch so he could wrap his other arm around Emily's waist. They swayed on the spot in time to the music, Emily feeling the heat of his skin through his shirt. The smell of him still made her feel a little heady, even though tonight it was aftershave rather than sweat and horses.

'Is there any chance I can take you to bed?' he whispered in her ear. 'Much as I love that dress, I'd really like to get you out of it.'

'Where are you staying?' she asked.

335

'Leon and I are both in the Goodwood Hotel, I needed a double bed and a big shower.'

Emily smiled at him. 'Is there room for one more?'

'At least,' said Jamie.

'Very funny. Can I get room service food? I'm starving.'

'Whatever you want.'

Emily weaved her fingers into his. 'Let's get to end of this song, then start saying our goodbyes.'

Emily sat cross-legged on the four-poster bed in Jamie's room at the hotel, wearing a giant fluffy bathrobe as she drank room service champagne and ate a gourmet cheeseburger. It was 1.30 a.m. and officially her thirtieth birthday, and she couldn't imagine a better start.

Jamie hobbled out of the bathroom on his crutches, wearing nothing but a white towel around his waist. He flumped on the bed and grabbed a handful of chips from the bowl on the tray then drained Emily's glass before reaching for the bottle in the ice bucket to fill it up again.

'Happy birthday,' he said.

'Thank you,' said Emily, polishing off her burger. 'Thirty is proving to be pretty awesome so far.'

'I got you a present,' said Jamie, leaning down the side of the bed and picking up a large box wrapped in blue paper covered in birthday balloons. Emily squealed and got up to wash her hands, then carefully pulled away the wrapping. Inside was a tissue-lined Smythson of Bond Street box holding a tote bag in the same sea-green leather as the notebook Mark had given her exactly one year ago.

'I took a peek at your notebook,' said Jamie. 'Saw where it was from and got you the matching bag.'

'It's beautiful,' said Emily, slightly breathless at the feel of the bag and the tissue and the cloth dust bag nestling underneath. She'd never owned anything this lovely in her life. 'This must have cost a fortune.'

'There was a brief moment when I wondered why you couldn't have gone notebook shopping at WHSmith,' Jamie joked.

'It's the best present ever,' said Emily, reaching over to kiss him. 'Thank you.' The kiss deepened and the box was pushed to one side as Jamie slid his hand under her bathrobe, but his progress was interrupted by a shriek and a thump in the corridor outside their room, followed by a cackle of laughter.

'That sounds like Kelly,' said Emily, her eyes wide.

'Leon's staying in the room next door,' said Jamie. 'Indications are that Kelly is too.' They heard a door close, then more laughter and a piece of furniture falling over.

'She sounds wasted,' said Emily.

'Leon's a gentleman,' said Jamie. 'I don't think he'd have brought her back if it wasn't Kelly's idea.'

There was quiet for a few minutes, during which Emily used the bathroom, cleaning her teeth and brushing out her freshly cut and coloured hair. It had been pinned up all evening and now it fell in soft blonde curls down her back. She checked her phone for a message from Kelly and hoped she was OK.

Jamie was waiting in bed when she came back, the duvet folded back so she could snuggle into his arms. He kissed her hair and trailed his fingers down her shoulder, making her shiver with anticipation.

Oh yeah, come on, squealed Kelly's voice from the other side of the wall.

Jamie's hands stopped their steady path southwards. *Right there, don't stop*, continued Kelly.

'Oh my God,' whispered Emily, 'are we going to listen to Kelly and Leon having sex all night?'

Up a bit, yelled Kelly. *Oh yeah, that's it. Harder.*

'She sounds like a foreman on a building site,' laughed Jamie. 'I'll put the TV on.'

He scrambled for the TV remote as Leon's enthusiastic grunts joined Kelly's incredibly specific directions. Emily turned up the volume on a repeat of *Gogglebox* and nestled back into Jamie's shoulder, both of them shaking with laughter as a rhythmic thumping penetrated the wall behind their bed.

CHAPTER FORTY-FOUR

Emily and Jamie were eating breakfast in the hotel restaurant when Kelly and Leon appeared, both of them looking rough as old boots. Even though Emily loved Kelly like a sister, it was hard to ignore that she and Jamie had been kept awake half the night by their incredibly vocal shagging. But on the flipside, Kelly hadn't had a man in her bed for far too long, so Emily couldn't begrudge her what had clearly been a very satisfying evening. Leon at least had the decency to look a little sheepish, but Kelly was entirely impervious to any judgement.

'Happy birthday, gorgeous,' she said to Emily, pulling her into a hug before grabbing a triangle of toast from the rack and plonking herself down in one of the two spare chairs. Jamie nodded to the waiter, who scurried over with a fresh pot of coffee.

'Sleep well?' asked Emily sweetly. Leon glanced at Jamie and blushed.

'Like a log,' said Kelly. 'What a great party. Your mum and dad absolutely smashed it.'

'They're on their way over,' said Emily. 'I think they want to have a nosy at the hotel.'

Kelly's slice of toast froze halfway to her mouth. 'Oh crap, I need to leave,' she said. 'They'll think I'm a right slapper if they know I stayed the night.'

'We can get a taxi later if you're not in a hurry,' said Leon quickly. 'Do you need to get back to your daughter?'

'No,' said Kelly with a coy smile. 'She's at my mum's. I said I'd go for lunch, so I'm free all morning.'

Emily couldn't help but smile at them both, even though the 3 a.m. memories of Kelly demanding that Leon spank her with a rolled-up copy of *Sussex Life* were still vivid.

'Might take breakfast back upstairs then,' said Kelly. 'Don't tell your mum and dad I'm here.'

'Won't say a word,' said Emily. 'Enjoy the rest of your morning.'

Kelly winked at Emily, before giving Jamie a wave and following Leon to the buffet. They watched them both fill a tray, giggling and nudging each other like schoolchildren, before disappearing back towards the stairs.

'Unbelievable,' said Jamie. 'Do you think she'll be embarrassed when you tell her we heard everything?'

Emily laughed and shook her head. 'Kelly doesn't do embarrassment. She is entirely without shame.'

'This is a bit posh,' said Carol, looking up at the lantern window in the roof of the restaurant. She poked the flowers in the vase on the table to check they were real and admired the modern artwork on the walls. 'I've always wondered what this place was like. Maureen almost had her wedding here but ended up getting a marquee at the football club instead. I don't think Nigel had as much money as she thought. Do you remember, Martin?'

'Why don't you join us for breakfast,' said Jamie quickly, before Carol launched into further stories about random acquaintances. He signalled to the waiter, who came over with his pencil poised. 'Can we have some more toast and pastries?'

'Well, don't mind if I do,' said Carol. 'I've only had a SlimFast.'

Martin took the fourth chair and smiled indulgently at his daughter. 'Happy birthday, Moomin.'

'Thanks, Dad,' said Emily. 'It was such a great party.'

'We got you a present,' said Carol, rummaging in her handbag for a tiny box. Emily excitedly pulled off the ribbon and the wrapping and opened the lid; inside was a delicate silver bracelet with three hearts hanging from it.

'One heart for each decade,' said Carol.

'I love it,' replied Emily, her eyes filling with tears. 'Thank you.'

'Also that birthday roast I told you I was cooking,' said Martin conspiratorially, 'is actually a family pub lunch. Your brothers are treating us all.'

'That sounds perfect,' said Emily, holding out her wrist so her mum could do up the clasp on the bracelet. She was relieved that Jamie wouldn't have to suffer Martin's cooking, and wondering if she could fit in a couple of hours' sleep before they headed off to the pub.

'When are you two heading back?' asked Carol. 'Is that nice driver going with you? What was his name? Croatian, he said he was, like Nina the cleaner from work, but I asked and he didn't know her.'

Emily rolled her eyes at Jamie, who covered his mouth to hide a smile. 'Leon,' she replied, feeling like her friendship with Mr Hunter's driver had moved into a new phase. It wasn't every day you heard a man detail all the things he loved about your best friend's body like he was providing audio description for the blind.

'Kelly was all over him last night, poor chap looked scared to death.'

'Actually he's popping over to yours later to pick up my car,' said Emily. 'He's going to drive it back to Norfolk for me tonight.'

'How are you getting back?' asked Martin.

Emily cleared her throat and looked at Jamie, not quite able to find the words.

Jamie twiddled a spoon between his fingers. 'I can't sit in a car with my knee bent for that long, so my dad organised a helicopter. Emily is going to fly back with me first thing tomorrow.'

There was a heavy silence before Carol responded in a voice that had somehow risen several octaves. 'In a helicopter? You're going back to Norfolk in a helicopter?'

Jamie smiled awkwardly. 'Think of it more as an air ambulance.'

Carol looked at her husband. 'Martin, did you hear that? They're going back by helicopter.'

Martin shook his head in amazement. 'I can hear perfectly well, Carol. Can we come and watch you take off?'

'Of course,' said Jamie, clearly relieved that Emily's dad wasn't going to make a fuss. 'We fly from the aerodrome at seven thirty a.m. tomorrow. Takes about an hour to get back to Bowford.'

'We'll be there,' said Martin, pouring a glass of orange juice and grinning at Emily.

'Your brothers are going to be sick as pigs,' said Carol, scooping marmalade out of a tiny jar with a buttery knife.

'Don't make a big deal out of it, Mum,' said Emily. 'It's just because of Jamie's leg. He wouldn't have been able to come otherwise.'

'Still, travelling about by helicopter,' said Carol dreamily. 'It's like *Fifty Shades of Grey*. Remember Charlie Tango?'

'It is nothing like *Fifty Shades of Grey*,' said Emily firmly, as Jamie snorted into his coffee. Maybe he did know the plot, after all.

Emily's birthday lunch was held in a village pub outside Chichester that offered a fabulous Sunday roast for fifteen pounds a head, with a selection of local ales that made Martin and his sons extremely happy. They were a happy party of ten – Emily and Jamie, Carol and Martin, Simon and Eric, David and Jo and their two boys. Emily sandwiched herself between her brothers, taking the opportunity to have a proper catch-up with them both before they headed home. She glanced over to check on Jamie every now and then, but he was deep in conversation with Eric and Jo, presumably learning about museum curation and inner-city teaching. Or maybe they were wondering how on earth they all got involved with this unhinged family and were plotting their escape.

He looked up and caught her eye, giving her a smile that made her wish it was just the two of them again, out riding or back on paddle boards in Mauritius. The ten weeks they'd spent together had made her realise what being in love actually felt like, and how much she wanted to make this relationship work. She knew it was early days, but it was hard not to think about what life might be like if she and Jamie lived together, or maybe one day got married and had babies. Perhaps it was tempting fate to imagine herself as Emily Hunter, or even Emily Wilkinson-Hunter, which sounded even more fabulous, but what woman didn't do that? Obviously she'd never say any of this out loud, even to Kelly.

She watched Jamie lean over to chat to her mum, his face and hands full of animation. She could see how hard he was working to fit in, but it was also obvious that Jamie felt more at home here than he did with his own family. He'd never exploited the Hunter family's wealth and status the way Adam and Catherine had; none of that seemed to interest him at all. It didn't take a genius to see how much he preferred this – pub lunches, chatting with people who weren't looking over his head to see if someone more impressive was approaching, lots of love and laughter in the room. It occurred to Emily that Jamie's family might have money, but her family were richer in a million other ways.

When they got back to the hotel after lunch, both of them took the opportunity for an hour's much-needed nap, then went for a swim in the hotel pool. Emily wanted to do fifty lengths in the hope of making a dent in the two slices of caramel and chocolate birthday cake she'd eaten, and Jamie needed to do his daily physio, which mostly involved stretching exercises and walking backwards and forwards across the shallow end. It felt nice to know they had the rest of her birthday free to spend together, and the prospect of a night without listening to Leon and Kelly bang each other senseless.

Talking of which, Emily noticed she'd missed two calls from Kelly while she was in the pool, so she sat on the bed in her fluffy bathrobe to call her while Jamie was in the shower.

'Hey, birthday girl,' said Kelly. 'How's your day been?'

'Fab,' said Emily. 'Pub lunch with the fam, now we're back at the hotel. How was last night?'

'Oh my God, Em,' said Kelly. 'We had the best time.'

'Yeah, we heard,' laughed Emily.

'What do you mean?'

'Jamie and I were on the other side of the wall. Sounded like Leon was really good at taking direction.'

Kelly hooted. 'Fuck me, he was incredible. Best shag I've ever had.'

'It sounded like it. What did you do today?'

'We went back to bed this morning; God, I can barely walk, he's hung like a horse. Then we got a taxi to your place so he could pick up your car. Then he dropped me at my mum's for lunch and picked me and Beth up a few hours later. Now we're back at mine.'

'What, Leon is there now?'

'Yeah, I've come outside. He and Beth are playing Guess Who?'

'Shit. Is he going to stay there tonight?'

'Christ, no. He's got to drive your car back in a bit, and anyway I don't want Beth waking up and finding him in the kitchen in his pants.'

'Fair enough. But you like him?'

'Yeah, he's great,' said Kelly. 'Not going to come to anything though, is it? He lives two hundred miles away.'

'I guess. A shame.'

'I'm fine with it,' said Kelly matter-of-factly. 'We had a great time, and it was nice to be hot and sexy again, rather than a knackered mum. Definitely got me back on the horse.'

Emily laughed. 'Talking of which, Jamie's finished in the shower. I need to go.'

'Give him one for me.'

'How about I give him the one I was going to give him last night, until we listened to you in stereo instead?'

'Yeah, sorry about that. Love you, mate. Happy birthday.'

'Thanks, Kel. Love you too.'

CHAPTER FORTY-FIVE

Emily waited with her parents outside Hangar 3 at Goodwood Aerodrome, all of them hugging their coats around
them in the morning cold. Emily's stomach was fizzing with
nerves and excitement, along with relief that it wasn't windy
or raining. She supposed Plan B would have been a private
ambulance again, which seemed like a lot less fun.

Jamie was over by the hangar talking to the pilot and a
woman from the helicopter charter firm, who was simultan-
eously checking paperwork on a clipboard and talking into
her phone. The collar of his coat was turned up against the
cold, and she could see his white knuckles against the grey
of his crutches.

'Never thought I'd see the day,' mused Martin. 'One of
my family travelling by helicopter.'

'It's only because of Jamie's leg,' said Emily. 'It's not like
his family travel like this all the time.' She conveniently
failed to mention the private jet to Switzerland at Christmas,
or the helicopter transfer to the ski resort.

'Still, it's a bit of a step up for a Wilkinson,' said Carol. 'I
don't know anyone who's been in a helicopter. Your cousin
Judith did a skydive once, but that was out of a rickety plane.
Do you remember, Martin? She puked up a blueberry muf-
fin after the parachute opened and it all blew back in her
face.'

Jamie returned to the group, an absolute pro on the crutches now. 'We're ahead of schedule, so the pilot has offered to take us all for a spin, before Emily and I leave.'

Martin's mouth fell open. 'All of us? Now?'

Jamie nodded happily. 'Just for a ten-minute trip round town.'

'Oh, my good lord,' said Carol. 'Can I text the Grove Street WhatsApp group first? Make sure they're all out watching?'

'Mum,' beseeched Emily. 'Please don't make a big fuss.'

Carol ignored her, fishing her phone out of her bag. 'Have I got time for a quick wee before we go?'

'Sure,' said Jamie. 'They're in the hangar. We'll get our bags loaded and let the pilot know we'll be good to go in five minutes.'

Carol and Martin both scurried off into the hangar as Emily grabbed her weekend bag and carried it across the grass. The helicopter was black and silver and sleek with a pointed nose, and much bigger than she expected. 'This is really kind of you,' she said.

Jamie smiled. 'It's no trouble.'

'No, really. It means a lot. To them, and to me.'

'Dad chartered a six-seater so I could put my leg up. Might as well make the most of it.'

Emily handed her bag to the pilot and climbed into the cabin, which had two rows of three cream leather seats facing each other. She took the furthest seat by the window opposite Jamie, who angled his leg so his boot could rest on the seat next to her. They grinned at each other until Carol and Martin appeared, both of them chuntering excitedly.

'Ooh, it's so POSH,' said Carol, putting her seatbelt on as the pilot closed the doors. 'It's like a stretch limo.'

'When have you ever been in a stretch limo?' asked Martin, as a whining noise told them the main rotor was starting to turn. The cabin began to vibrate as the speed of the rotor increased, and Carol gave another series of squeaks.

'Margaret's second hen night,' said Carol indignantly. 'We went to Brighton.' She pulled out her phone and started taking photos, presumably to be shared with every WhatsApp group she was a member of.

They waited in excited anticipation for a few minutes, until the pilot's voice came over the tannoy to tell them that all the flight checks were complete and they were ready to go. They'd be heading south over Chichester to the coast, then circling back over the west of the city before returning to Goodwood. Carol whooped as the helicopter left the ground, tilting and bouncing a little as it rose high above the aerodrome, then dipped to one side as it turned and headed south west.

Emily took in the view in awed silence, unable to believe that she was doing a tour of her hometown in a helicopter. It was a clear day and as they gained height she could clearly see Hayling Island and the Isle of Wight beyond. 'There's the cathedral,' said Carol to nobody in particular, unable to sit in silence for a second longer. 'And the market cross. You can see all the streets laid out. Ooh, it's a smooth ride, isn't it? I expected it to feel like a rollercoaster.'

'There's West Wittering beach,' said Emily a minute or two later, pointing at the stretch of sand. 'Our Christmas Day swim.' Jamie smiled at her, no doubt also thinking about the sweetness of that first kiss, and how far they'd come since then. The pilot headed out to sea, then swung the helicopter in a big U-shape over the thousands of tiny boats anchored in Chichester harbour before returning back up the west side of the city. He descended a little and flew the helicopter directly over the estate where Carol and Martin lived, sending Carol into spasms of excitement about the possibility that their neighbours were standing in Grove Street right now, looking up at them. She waved out of the window pointlessly, then alerted Jamie to the exact location of Emily's old school and the 24-hour Tesco.

Five minutes later they were flying low over Goodwood, back to the helipad outside the hangar. The pilot kept the propellers going, giving Carol and Martin instructions over the tannoy on how to leave the aircraft safely.

'That was brilliant,' said Carol with a beaming smile. 'Thank you, Jamie.'

'Really great,' added Martin, reaching out to shake Jamie's hand.

'No problem,' said Jamie. 'I've had a lovely weekend.'

'Me too,' said Emily. 'Thanks for a fab birthday party.'

Carol looked at them both, her eyes full of tears. 'We'll see you both soon,' she said with a wobbly lip, giving them both a hug. The woman with the clipboard opened the door so Carol and Martin could step down on to the grass, ducking down to avoid the idling rotor blades until they were well clear. They turned to wave furiously as the helicopter took off again and headed north.

'This will be the talk of Chichester,' said Emily, waving until her parents were just specks against the green expanse below.

'It was fun,' said Jamie, as the helicopter set a steady course north-east. 'We should be back at Bowford in an hour.'

'I could definitely get used to this,' said Emily, kicking off her shoes. She lifted her socked feet into Jamie's lap and he rubbed them gently, just enough to relieve the residual aching from all the dancing on Saturday night. It felt entirely blissful, to be relaxing in a warm and comfortable leather seat as the villages of the South Downs whizzed by below, a handsome man giving her a foot massage. In another life she'd be sat on the M11 right now, cursing every broken-down lorry and bad driver. This was infinitely more like it.

Arriving at Bowford Manor made Emily feel like a pop star arriving at Glastonbury. They set down on a helipad behind the hedge at the far end of the lawn, but this time the pilot turned off the rotors so he could unload their luggage while they made a more sedate exit. Leon appeared to take their bags, and by the time they were back at the house the helicopter had taken off again, the pilot giving them all a salute before turning east to his home base at Norwich Airport.

'I had no idea you had a helipad,' said Emily, looking back at the lawn. It was impossible to see the concrete pad set into the grass from the terrace.

'Mum used to use it a lot,' said Jamie, 'for shopping trips to London. Dad isn't usually in that much of a hurry. Although it's useful in the summer holidays when the roads are jammed with holidaymakers.'

'But the helicopter isn't his?'

Jamie shook his head. 'He doesn't use it enough to justify having one of his own. It's cheaper to charter as and when; we've used a local firm for years.'

Emily smiled, acutely aware of what a ridiculous conversation this was, and wondering what other things rich people did to avoid the inconvenience of holidaymakers clogging up Norfolk during the summer. Perhaps the Hunters had their own private ice cream van so nobody had to queue for a Mr Whippy.

She said her goodbyes to Jamie in the yard, then headed up to her room to dump her bag and freshen up before going to work. By the time Mr Hunter arrived at 9 a.m., she had a coffee on the go and was halfway through opening the morning post.

After welcoming her back and asking about her party and the helicopter ride, he went through to his office and closed the door behind him. She could hear him talking quietly on the phone and waited until he'd finished his calls before carrying through a coffee, her notebook and today's file of post.

'That was Mark Thompson on the phone,' said Mr Hunter. 'He has some information.'

Emily sat down. 'What did he find out?'

'I'm not sure yet,' said Mr Hunter, his brow furrowed. 'He insists on meeting in person.'

How very Mark, thought Emily. *Can't resist a grand audience.* 'When are you next in London?'

'He's coming here, actually,' said Mr Hunter. 'Tomorrow morning. He absolutely insisted. Apparently he has other business in this part of the world, so it's no problem.'

The cogs in Emily's brain started to whirr. Mark had never had a single client in Norfolk, so unless he'd picked one up recently, this was complete bullshit. It was much more likely that Emily's announcement that she was dating a work colleague had touched a nerve, and he wanted more information about who it was and whether he was worthy competition.

Mr Hunter took off his glasses and looked at Emily pointedly. 'I'm not ready to tell James about all this just yet, Emily. So if you could find a way to deal with this situation that doesn't leave my son asking questions, I'd appreciate it.'

Emily nodded, already feeling a headache starting to set in.

CHAPTER FORTY-SIX

Emily cornered Anna and Leon over breakfast, having lain awake for several hours trying to work out the best way to manage the whole Mark situation. In an ideal world she'd tell Jamie he was coming to Bowford, but there was no way she could do that without making up a massive lie about why. The truth was also a no-go, which meant the best-case scenario was that Mark arrived and left without Jamie ever knowing. Emily was banking on Anna seizing an opportunity to make amends for past crimes and agreeing to help her out.

The other problem was Mark himself – clearly he was coming to sniff out the competition, presumably to perform some weird male mating ritual that would establish his alpha supremacy. Perhaps he planned to challenge the interloper to a duel, using their dicks as weapons. Under different circumstances it might be pathetic enough to be funny, but somehow it felt important that Mark didn't know that she was dating Charles Hunter's extremely handsome son. Mark's pride bruised easily and this information would eat away at him; who knew what he would do next? But now she had a plan for Leon to save her.

She put down her toast and cleared her throat. 'I wonder if I could ask both of you for some help.'

Both Anna and Leon stopped eating and looked up at her expectantly.

'There's a man coming to visit Mr Hunter today.'

Leon nodded and swallowed his toast and Marmite. 'Mr Thompson, he's coming on the train. I'm picking him up from Norwich station at half past eleven.'

Emily turned to Anna. 'I wonder if you could keep Jamie busy, make sure he doesn't come to the house while Mr Thompson is here.'

Anna raised her eyebrows but said nothing.

'And Leon, I need you to pretend to be my boyfriend.'

Anna quietly put down her coffee mug, her eyes narrowed with suspicion. 'These are very strange requests, Emily. Is there any chance you could explain?'

'Not really. It's a bit complicated.'

Anna smiled thinly. 'Is it reasonable to assume you know Mr Thompson?'

'Yes,' said Emily with a sigh. She had to tell them something, so maybe they'd settle for the bare bones of this sordid mess. 'Mark Thompson is my ex-boyfriend, but he's also assisting Mr Hunter with a business matter. They could have met in London, but Mark insisted on coming here. I think he wants to see where I'm living and working.'

'You mean he's trying to get a look at Jamie,' said Anna. Emily had never been more grateful that Anna didn't miss a trick.

'Yes. He knows I'm seeing someone, but not who. I've got nothing to hide, but it's the principle. My life is none of his business any more.'

'So you'd rather not give him the satisfaction of getting what he wants,' said Anna.

'Exactly.'

'Fine,' Anna said, taking her mug and plate to the

dishwasher. 'I'll go and see Jamie while Mr Thompson is here, take some lunch for us both. It's long overdue – we can catch up on all his news.'

Emily could have hugged her, but maybe it was too soon for that level of friendliness.

'Explain my job again,' said Leon. 'You want me to tell him I'm your boyfriend?'

'Not exactly, no,' said Emily. 'But I'm pretty sure he'll ask you questions in the car, try to fish for information. So if you could just drop a few hints, let him fill in the gaps for himself.'

Leon nodded and gave a sly smile. 'So we make sure he doesn't get what he wants, but also make him think he has.'

Emily nodded and smiled nervously. 'That's the plan.'

As plans went, it was riddled with holes. But right now it was the best she could come up with.

Emily spent the rest of the morning holed up in her office, keeping busy and trying to relax the nervous tension in her shoulders. She made Mark a coffee when he arrived, unable to resist asking him how he took it, even though she knew exactly. A flicker of annoyance passed across his face, and she could see he was intimidated by the splendour of his surroundings. Mark had ventured out of his normal territory, and he looked entirely out of place in his expensive London suit and his shiny City-boy shoes.

During the meeting Emily kept herself busy in the filing room and watched her phone for a message from Leon, who was pretending to wash the cars so he could keep an eye out for any sign of Jamie. But there was nothing, and when Mr

Hunter opened her office door to ask if she could let Leon know it was time to bring the car round before showing Mark out, she dared to think she might get him off the premises without a man-on-man showdown.

'I met Leon,' said Mark as they walked down the grand staircase to the entrance hall. 'I'm guessing he's the guy you're seeing.'

Emily did her coy Lady Di smile again. 'What makes you think that?'

Mark looked pleased with himself, like he was some kind of crack detective. 'I asked if he lived on the estate and he said he did, but it was OK because his girlfriend did too.'

Emily laughed, being careful not to confirm or deny either way. 'What did you think of him?' she asked.

'I liked him,' said Mark. 'Polite, clearly good at his job. Down to earth, you know.'

Oh Mark, thought Emily. *You're such a snob. You're happy because you think I've traded down, so you don't need to feel threatened. But Leon is ten times the man you'll ever be.*

'I'm glad,' she said, opening the front door. 'It was good to see you, and thanks for everything.'

'Good to see you too,' said Mark, giving her a kiss on each cheek. Leon was waiting outside by the Audi, the rear door open so Mark could climb in. Emily gave Leon a furtive smile and a nod, as if to say *your task is complete*, and he winked in return.

She watched the Audi disappear down the driveway and breathed out, unclenching her jaw for the first time since waking up. Jamie was none the wiser, and Mark was leaving Bowford with the information he'd come for, and hopefully having helped out Mr Hunter too. Knowing Mark as she

357

did, she was reasonably confident he'd leave her alone now, comfortable in his own male supremacy.

It was almost lunchtime, so she headed for the kitchen and found Sam cooking up a delicious-smelling stir fry. Emily sat on a stool at the counter and sipped a Diet Coke from the fridge until he slid a bowl over for her to try. It was packed with fat prawns and vegetables and sweet and spicy flavours, which made her long to be back in the tropics with the sun on her face, rather than dealing with jealous, petty ex-boyfriends.

Anna appeared through the door from the delivery yard and gave her a conspiratorial nod, before heading upstairs with Mr Hunter's lunch on a tray. She returned a few minutes later and gestured to Emily to join her in the pantry where they could talk away from Sam's gossip-mongering ears.

'Was everything OK?' whispered Emily.

'Jamie was fine,' said Anna. 'We had a good catch-up. I can't say I approve of all the secrecy, but I'm sure you had your reasons.'

Emily breathed out slowly. 'Thank you, Anna.'

'He's very happy, you know,' said Anna, her face softening.

Emily blushed, slightly disarmed by the all-new caring version of Anna who wasn't trying to make her life miserable. 'I'm really glad. He makes me happy too.'

'He reminds me of George sometimes. So gentle and easy to talk to.'

'Mr Thompson is gone,' whispered Leon, bustling into the pantry like an old woman who needed to be in on the action. 'I watched the train leave, just to make sure.'

'Thank you, Leon,' said Emily.

He pulled a face. 'I didn't like him very much. He seemed like . . . I cannot think of the English word.'

'Smug?' Emily suggested.

Leon shrugged. 'I don't know that word. He seemed kind of an asshole.'

Emily laughed, trying to be generous to Mark in view of the huge favour he'd just done her, but also incredibly glad he was gone. 'That too.'

'So,' said Mr Hunter, peering at Emily over his desk. 'Mark Thompson did a very thorough job, for which I have you to thank. It seems Adam is working with a property developer called Milburn Scott. Do you know them?'

Emily nodded as she dug through her memory for the details. 'I've heard of them, yes. Timber-framed homes and lodges, right? Pretty high end. My previous company pitched for some design work with them, but I don't think it came to anything.' She scribbled shorthand notes so she didn't forget anything.

'Yes,' said Mr Hunter approvingly, as though Emily had just passed some kind of test. 'It seems Adam has a gentleman's agreement with them. Nothing in writing, obviously; he has no legal rights. But a deal in principle that once Bowford is under his control, plans can begin for development. Subject to all kinds of wrangling with the local planning department, but no doubt Adam is greasing the wheels there too.'

Emily's mind boggled, imagining how many kittens her dad would have if that planning application landed on his desk. 'Why that style of property, though? What's the benefit of wooden lodges over normal houses?'

Mr Hunter smiled. 'The wooden lodges are only part of the plan, I'm afraid. Another organisation is involved in this deal, a leisure company.'

Emily's eyes narrowed. 'What kind of leisure company?'

'The kind that turns big houses like this into hotels. With guest lodges in the grounds.'

'Oh my God,' said Emily, her eyes wide. 'He's going to turn Bowford into fucking Center Parcs.' She clamped her hand over her mouth in horror. 'Sorry.'

'Perfectly understandable,' said Mr Hunter with a smile.

Emily quickly regrouped. 'What are you going to do?'

Mr Hunter sat back in his chair, his fingers steepled under his nose. 'I'm going to finish something I started some years ago, Emily. How much do you know about the National Trust?'

She racked her brains for useful facts, but there was nothing worth mentioning. 'Not much. I've been to a few of their properties, but that's it.'

'I've had my concerns about the future of this estate for some time, so a number of years ago my people started talking to their people. You'll find a file in one of the cabinets labelled "Neil Turner"; it's where Andrea kept everything. Read the correspondence, but don't leave it lying around.'

Emily nodded and made a note.

'The plans you found before Christmas prompted me to escalate things, and the information your friend provided today has given my decision a little more urgency.'

'What decision?'

Mr Hunter took a deep breath. 'I'm going to give this house to the National Trust. It's a place of great historic interest and they'll protect it for the benefit of the nation.'

'How does that work?' asked Emily. 'Do they buy it?'

Mr Hunter stood up and walked to the window, prompting one of the dogs in the basket to open an eye, then close it again. 'Sometimes. But in this case I'm going to gift it to them, along with a substantial endowment to support the ongoing costs.'

'Wow,' said Emily, not sure what else to say. 'Where will you live?'

'I'll keep part of the estate, along with most of the outlying properties. Plus a small apartment in this house for my own use. Our respective lawyers have been drawing up the paperwork for months; it will be ready to sign next week. I was just waiting for the final confirmation I needed, which I now have.' He turned and looked at Emily. 'It's imperative that Adam doesn't find out until the deal is done. He's not going to take it well.'

'What about Jamie?' she asked.

'What about him?'

'How is he going to take it?'

'A lot better than Adam, I should think.' Mr Hunter gave Emily a penetrating stare. 'Does he know anything at all about this?'

She shook her head vehemently, mildly insulted. 'Not from me. I've never said a word.'

Mr Hunter nodded slowly. 'I think it's time he knew. I'd like him to review the proposal; it will mean big changes for him. I'll go and see him this afternoon, save dragging him up to the house.'

Emily wondered what 'big changes' meant. Did it mean Jamie was going to be jobless and homeless?

'Anything else, while you're here?' said Mr Hunter.

361

Emily looked at her list. In view of everything that was about to happen around here, it seemed like a good time to address the fact that she'd never had a three-month probationary review, and technically her contract was out of date. But it felt a bit tactless to mention it now, and it really was the least of Mr Hunter's worries.

'No, everything's fine,' she said, crossing her fingers that it would be.

CHAPTER FORTY-SEVEN

'I've brought you tea.'

Emily smiled at how pleased with himself Jamie was, having carried a mug from the kitchen to the bedroom without spilling any. He was now officially mobile on one crutch and was making the most of every opportunity to do normal things again.

'Thanks,' she said, stretching like a cat. After a long and stressful week, it felt good to have the weekend ahead.

'Are you up for a ride around the estate today?'

'Who with?' The memory of what happened when she went riding with Adam flickered in her memory; she'd mentioned it to Jamie at the time but framed it as an unfortunate incident rather than something Adam had done on purpose. It felt easier than making a fuss, and she didn't have any proof anyway.

'Me,' said Jamie with a grin. 'My physio says I can go for a gentle hack as long as I properly support my leg. One of the grooms who works with the disabled riding group has rigged something up.'

'That's amazing.' Emily was delighted by the prospect of getting back on a horse with Jamie again, particularly on such a beautiful day.

'It's been a big week. I could do with a change of scenery.'

363

Jamie returned to the kitchen to collect his mug, then settled himself back in bed.

'I'm really glad you know about everything.'

Jamie nodded. 'It must have been hard for you not to say anything.'

Emily shrugged and sipped her tea. 'Not really. It's my job.'

'Ouch,' laughed Jamie. 'And here's me thinking you were losing sleep.'

Emily looked a bit sheepish. 'Sorry. I guess you just get used to being the keeper of other people's secrets.'

'Dad and I had another chat yesterday. He's asked me to be Estate Manager after this is all over. Derek is ready to retire, wants to move down to where his daughter lives in Suffolk.'

'What does that mean?' asked Emily. 'Will there even be an estate to manage?'

'Yes, we'll actually keep quite a lot of land and most of the estate properties, although this one isn't on the list, sadly.' Jamie looked forlornly up at the exposed beams, no doubt lost in memories of pool parties and teenage misbehaviour. 'The stables will need to move to a different part of the estate too. Dad's asked me to manage everything.'

'Congratulations,' said Emily, genuinely delighted for him. 'How are you feeling now you've had some time to think about everything?'

'It's the right thing to do,' he said emphatically. 'Adam will tear this place apart. I'm happy to stay on and be custodian of what's left, get the house ready for the transition.'

'I'm really happy to help.'

Jamie smiled at her. 'There'll be plenty to do; it's going to be an interesting few years. Has Dad talked to you about your job yet?'

'Not for the long term,' she said, 'but I'm assuming nothing changes for now.' The idea of leaving Bowford and Jamie made her feel sick, but there was too much at stake right now for her to think about it.

'Let's just get this all over the line first, then you can talk to Dad about it. It will all be done on Tuesday.'

Emily nodded, nerves fluttering in her stomach. In three days, Jamie and Mr Hunter had a meeting with the National Trust in a room full of lawyers and representatives from both sides. All being well, the deal would be signed and Bowford Park would be safe.

Jamie's plastic boot was propped in a special contraption that kept his leg supported under his knee and slightly away from Luna's body, so it bounced about less. It didn't look particularly comfortable, but Jamie looked happier than she'd seen him in weeks. He'd collapsed one of his crutches and secured it in a saddle bag just in case he needed to dismount for any reason, but both he and Emily were happy to walk through the paddocks towards the edge of the estate. Emily had been having occasional lessons in the outdoor riding school with one of the grooms, but it was the first time since Mauritius they'd been on horseback together.

When they reached the far paddock Jamie watched Emily canter for a while, applauding her for how much more confident she was. She practised turning in the canter, using the reins to tell Rupert what she wanted him to do and concentrating on keeping her seat during the changes in pace and direction. After half an hour of lessons, they turned and headed back via Emily's favourite route, past Wedmore Cottage and a beautiful row of blossom-filled cherry trees that lined the road.

Emily turned her head to look dreamily at Wedmore Cottage, just as she always did, and was surprised to see the silver Aston Martin parked on the driveway. 'Adam's here.'

'Fuck,' muttered Jamie. 'We could really do with him not being around right now.'

'What does he DO while he's here?'

Jamie shrugged. 'Your guess is as good as mine. Strokes a white cat and plots world domination?' He thought for a second, then turned to look at her. 'If he went to Dad's office and had a poke around, would he find anything?'

Emily thought about the password-protected laptop locked in her desk, the locked filing cabinets, the information hidden in a boring-looking file labelled 'Neil Turner' in amongst scores of other files labelled with the names of companies and tenants and properties. 'No.'

'That's good,' said Jamie.

They rode on for another ten minutes until the main house came into view, at which point their peace and quiet was interrupted by Adam driving past at high speed. Luna reared sideways and even steadfast Rupert skittered on to the grass verge.

'God, he's such a prick,' muttered Jamie.

'What does he want at the house?' Emily asked.

'No idea. Is Dad home?'

'No. He's having lunch in Holt with some friends, Leon took him.'

'Shit. I'm going to head over and see what he's up to. If we ride to the delivery yard, can you take Luna back to the stables?'

They took a shortcut through one of the paddocks to the yard just as they heard the roar of Adam's car pulling up to the front door. Jamie slid off Luna's back gingerly and pulled his crutch out of the saddle bag.

'I'll see you in a bit.' He handed Luna's reins to Emily and she led her off as fast as she could, keen to get back to the house before Adam decided to break Jamie's other leg. One of the grooms was mucking out Luna's stable, so she handed her both horses with an apology and ran back as fast as she could.

There was nobody around as she crept up the back stairs, other than a distant vacuum cleaner humming in one of the bedrooms. She hugged the wall of the corridor to Mr Hunter's office, stopping behind the open door at the sound of raised voices.

'You need to wake up, little brother,' said Adam.

'What are you talking about?'

'I'm talking about Emily. Your little whore.'

Emily pressed her hand over her mouth and reversed into an alcove in the corridor that had probably once held a suit of armour. 'Don't you dare,' Jamie snapped.

'Can't you see what she's doing?' said Adam, his voice even whinier than usual. 'She's manipulating you and Dad. You're too blind to see it.'

There was silence for a moment as Jamie's crutch clunked across the wooden floor. Emily couldn't tell if he was going towards Adam or away from him. 'What's your problem, Adam?' he asked quietly.

'She's a scrubber,' spat Adam. 'Common as muck.'

'You're such an unbearable snob. I think your problem is that she makes me happy, and you're so fucking miserable you can't bear it.'

'God, you're stupid,' Adam sneered. 'What do you see in her?'

'She's smart,' said Jamie. 'Funny, beautiful . . .'

Adam snorted derisively.

'. . . kind, emotionally intelligent. All the things you'll never be.'

'At least my wife has breeding.'

'Victoria is a woman, Adam. Not a horse. Have you EVER asked her if she's happy?'

'I give her everything she wants,' shouted Adam.

'Do you, though?' said Jamie. 'Do you make her laugh? Do you tell her you love her? Or do you assume that money and a nice house is all she needs to get through the day? You should find out before she takes half your cash and both your sons.'

'She wouldn't dare,' seethed Adam.

'Don't be so sure, Adam. Lesser women than Victoria have made their escape from pieces of shit like you. Oh, and one more thing. If you ever talk about Emily that way again, I will beat the living crap out of you.'

There was silence for a moment, then Adam stormed out of the office and down the corridor without noticing Emily. She stayed where she was until Jamie had clunked away too, her heart pounding out of her chest.

CHAPTER FORTY-EIGHT

Emily checked her watch for the third time in half an hour. Jamie and Mr Hunter would be on their way to the National Trust's Head Office in Swindon by now – she'd waved them off at the helipad earlier. They'd have the meeting, sign the documents, then have lunch with some important people before flying back. It was incredibly complicated, the culmination of years of discussions and negotiations and legal wrangling. The text of the agreement had been checked and re-checked, and now it was just the formalities. All being well, they'd be back by 4 p.m.

She made herself her third coffee of the morning and wandered through to Mr Hunter's office. Adam had returned to London on Saturday after his run-in with Jamie, so the house was blissfully quiet, other than the rumble of the gardener giving the lawn its first proper mow of the year and a distant door closing on one of the other floors. She stood by the floor-to-ceiling sash window behind the big walnut desk and watched the ride-on mower carving perfect green stripes in the grass. It was calming to watch and gave her something to do other than look at her watch and flap about things that were out of her control.

'Where have my father and brother gone?' said a loud voice, making Emily jump and slop coffee down her jumper.

Adam stood in the office doorway, giving her a glare that would melt tarmac from fifty yards.

'They're at a meeting,' she said, trying not to panic. What was he doing here? He must have driven up this morning. What the hell did he want?

'What meeting? Where? With who?'

Emily gave him her best resting bitch face, hugging the coffee mug to stop her hands from shaking. 'Obviously I'm not going to tell you that.'

Adam bared his teeth and strode across the room towards her. She backed away, suddenly aware how alone she was. There was nobody in the house to help her – no Mr Hunter, no Jamie, no Leon. She could see that Adam's face was red and sweaty. What had he heard?

'Don't give me that shit,' he snarled. 'Where are they?'

Emily looked at him coolly. 'You can shout at me all you like, Adam. I don't work for you, and I'm not going to tell you.'

Adam cast around Mr Hunter's desk for papers or a diary, like Emily was stupid enough to leave evidence of Mr Hunter's whereabouts lying around. He huffed in frustration, then marched into her office. She quickly followed, confident that he'd find nothing there either – Mr Hunter's diary was entirely digital and her laptop was currently a screensaver of Rudy the dog. So unless Adam planned to torture her for her password, he wasn't getting access to any emails or appointments. Every document relating to today's meeting had been carefully filed under Neil Turner, hidden in a nondescript filing cabinet. Adam could turn the place upside down for hours and remain entirely ignorant.

He spotted her notebook on the desk and gave a triumphant smile. She reached out to grab it but he got there first, holding it out of her reach as he riffled through the thin blue pages. Emily's heart leapt into her mouth – she'd made hundreds of notes in there.

'What is this shit?' demanded Adam, waving the open book at her.

'It's shorthand,' said Emily, taking deep breaths as she put her mug in the kitchen and mopped the coffee off her jumper with a tea towel. *Stand your ground, tell him nothing, don't let him think you're scared of him.*

'What does it mean? It's fucking hieroglyphics.'

'Yeah, I'm not going to tell you that either.'

'You think you're so clever,' said Adam, bearing down on her. 'But you're nothing. You're not fit to lick my brother's boots. He's just using you as a convenient fuck. He told me the best thing about common girls is they like it dirty.'

Emily didn't mean to laugh, but she couldn't help it. The idea that Jamie would ever say those words, particularly to Adam, was completely ludicrous.

Adam had been teetering on the edge since he came into his father's office, but Emily's reaction sent him into orbit. 'Don't you dare fucking laugh at me,' he spat, grabbing Emily's wrist and pushing her shoulder against the wall of the kitchen. She could smell his aftershave and the cigarettes on his breath and thought she might be sick.

'What on earth is going on?' said a voice. Adam dropped Emily's wrist like a hot poker and stepped away. Anna was standing in the doorway to the office, her mouth hanging open in horror.

'What do YOU want?' boomed Adam, his face purple with rage.

'Get away from her right now,' said Anna. 'Before I call the police.'

He walked to the window and took a few deep breaths, clearly aware that this situation was no longer in his control. 'It was nothing,' he said briskly, straightening his jacket. 'Just a misunderstanding.'

'Are you OK?' said Anna, looking at Emily.

She nodded, her knees shaking and her lips pressed together to stop herself throwing up.

Anna turned to Adam. 'Get out.'

Adam laughed. 'You can't tell me to get out, it's my fucking house.'

Anna put her face six inches from his. 'It's your father's house,' she said quietly, 'and if he was here right now he'd be chasing you down the drive with a shotgun.'

Adam's face turned scarlet. 'But he's not here, so I'll leave when I'm fucking ready,' he snarled.

'I will be happy to show you out,' said a male voice. Leon's frame filled the doorway, his fists clenched. He was twice the size of Adam and could snap him like a wishbone.

Adam looked at the three of them, his nostrils flaring, then shoved past Leon and fled. Emily waited until she could hear him running down the stairs, then clamped a hand over her mouth as she let out a sob. Anna gathered her into her arms and nodded towards the kitchen at Leon, who walked through and put the kettle on. She held Emily tight and stroked her hair, whispering sssh-ing noises as they stood by the window and listened to Adam's Aston Martin burning rubber down the drive.

'He's gone,' said Anna, handing Emily a lace-edged handkerchief.

'Thank you.' Emily honked her nose into the hanky and took a few deep breaths. 'I don't know what would have happened if you hadn't come.'

'What did he want?' asked Leon, handing her a mug of tea and patting her gently on the shoulder. She'd never seen him look so upset and angry.

She shrugged. 'Information. I wouldn't give it to him.'

Anna stared at her for a moment. 'I'm not going to ask what Mr Hunter is doing,' she said quietly. 'I know better than that. But tell me one thing – is it going to make Adam miserable?'

Emily paused for a second, then nodded.

'Good,' said Anna, with a smile of grim satisfaction.

Mr Hunter summoned Jamie and Adam into the office at 5 p.m., along with a woman called Moira, who was one of Mr Hunter's many lawyers. She'd travelled back from Swindon with him and Jamie, and when Emily took in a tray of tea she was sitting at Mr Hunter's desk making brisk notes on a sheaf of paperwork. Mr Hunter leaned against the front edge of the desk, his arms folded, whilst Jamie and Adam sat on the sofa, as far away from each other as possible. Catherine was on speaker phone from LA, no doubt with her mother close by.

'Thank you, Emily,' said Mr Hunter. 'Perhaps you could close the door.'

Emily nodded and scuttled back to her office, closing the door quietly behind her. It was their secret code, giving her permission to listen in on this momentous family conversation if she wanted to. Somehow this made her feel quite emotional, like it was a sign of how much Mr Hunter trusted and valued her.

She sat at her desk and rubbed her wrist absently. It wasn't bruised, but she could still feel Adam's fingers on her skin. She hadn't had a chance to tell Jamie or Mr Hunter yet, but she would. The verbal abuse was one thing, but putting his hands on her for doing her job was something else entirely.

'A decision has been taken,' said Mr Hunter on the other side of the door. 'About the future of Bowford Manor.'

Nobody said anything, so he continued.

'It's now been passed into the ownership of the National Trust; they will take responsibility for it in perpetuity. It's no longer owned by the Hunter family.'

Emily wished she could see Adam's face right now; presumably he was opening and closing his mouth like a ventriloquist's dummy. Catherine's face would no doubt look the same as it always did, because it no longer had the capacity for expression.

'Adam, I'm inviting you to make a choice. Moira has redrafted my will, leaving you the London house and the chalet in Verbier. There is a condition, that after today you never set foot on the Bowford Estate again until the day I die. If I hear that you've so much as eaten a scone in the National Trust café or put a sticker on your car, you will forfeit everything.'

'What about him?' bleated Adam. 'What does he get?' Presumably he was talking about Jamie.

'James will inherit what's left of this estate and the Mauritius house, and Catherine will receive the New York penthouse and the apartment in LA. All of you will receive a great deal of money, and there is a substantial trust for your sons and any other Hunter children that may arrive before I die.'

'My God,' said Adam. 'I can't believe you'd break a four-hundred-year tradition out of spite.'

'Out of respect for this house and our family's hard work,' bellowed Mr Hunter. 'You conspired with a property company to turn this estate into a holiday village – don't you dare deny it.'

Adam said nothing.

'How could you think I wouldn't find out?' said Mr Hunter. 'Are you really that stupid? People talk, Adam. People always talk.'

Emily breathed out. Adam didn't know about the photocopied plans, and now he probably never would.

'What if . . .?' Adam began.

'No,' said Mr Hunter firmly. 'The deal is done, and it can't be undone by anyone. I've made absolutely sure of that. Your choice is either to accept the terms of my will and get out of my sight, or kick up a legal fuss and lose everything. It's up to you.'

Emily locked her notebook in her desk and picked up the bag Jamie had given her for her birthday. She knew what Adam's decision would be, just as Mr Hunter did. A line had been drawn under four hundred years of Bowford Manor's history, and tomorrow the next four hundred years would begin. She left quietly through the door from the tiny kitchen to the corridor and headed up the back stairs to her room. She needed a cup of tea and a KitKat; maybe she'd have them both in the bath.

When she opened the door to her bedroom, there was a small blue cake tin on her bed. Inside was a batch of home-made chocolate biscuits and a note that read *Andrea would have been exceptionally proud of you today, and so am I. Give yourself a night off, tomorrow is a new day. Anna.*

CHAPTER FORTY-NINE

'How are you feeling, Emily?' asked Mr Hunter, his face filled with concern. It had been a week since the ugly show-down with Adam, and she had hoped it was now behind them. Apparently Mr Hunter was still worried.

'I'm fine,' she said breezily. 'Really.'

'With everything that's happened, I would completely understand if you wanted to leave us.'

Emily's heart sank. She'd wondered if this conversation might happen at some point – encouraging her to leave so he didn't have to make her redundant. Just when everything was looking so great, too.

'Mr Hunter, I totally understand if you need to let me go. I won't make a fuss, it's just how it goes sometimes.'

'Sorry, what?' said Mr Hunter. 'You think I want you to leave?'

'Isn't that what you're saying?'

'Good lord, no,' he laughed. 'Quite the opposite. Where on earth did you get that idea?'

Emily didn't bother trying to explain how women's minds worked; it was too complicated. 'I just thought, with all the changes and everything, you might not need me any more.'

Mr Hunter smiled at her. 'It's true I'd like to slow down a little, take things a little easier. James will run what's left of the estate; I think he'll do an excellent job. That will give me more time.'

'But you still need an assistant?'

'More than ever, I should think. There's less estate work, but my business dealings don't change and there is much work still to be done. I was actually wondering if you'd consider a promotion.'

'A promotion?' Emily's brain was struggling to keep up. This was absolutely not how she'd expected this conversation to go.

'I'd like you to be my executive assistant,' he said. 'It would involve taking on more of the management of my affairs, and there are some charitable trusts and foundations I'd like to set up before I shuffle off, make sure my money goes on to do good things. The role may require you to undergo some training. Finance, project management, law. Or of course you could study part-time for a degree. Business and Economics, something like that.'

Emily looked up. 'Really?'

'If you'd like to. I'd hate for that brain of yours to be wasted typing up an old man's memoirs when you're clearly capable of so much more.'

Emily blinked back tears, reminded of the day her maths teacher had begged her to apply for university. *You have so much potential, Emily. Don't waste it making tea for men who are stupider than you are.* She'd assumed it was all too late to go back to studying, but Mr Hunter had just opened the door to a whole world of possibilities.

'I'd love to stay, and that all sounds amazing,' she said. 'Thank you.'

'I've also been giving some thoughts to where you might live,' said Mr Hunter.

Emily looked up at him, having not really given it any consideration. She'd convinced herself she wouldn't be staying at Bowford, so assumed she'd find a new job and rent a flat somewhere else. Ideally locally, so she and Jamie could still see each other all the time. 'Oh,' she said. 'What are my options?'

'Well, you can rent one of the estate cottages, if you'd like to. There are several small ones that are currently empty, although they might need a bit of a spruce up. A proper tenancy, all above board.'

Emily covered her mouth to stop herself sobbing. A proper place of her own, maybe even with a garden.

'Oh goodness, please don't cry,' said Mr Hunter, wafting her away with his hand. 'It's the least I can do. You've done more for Bowford Manor in four months than some members of my family have done in a lifetime. And I'm fairly confident I'm not the only one who would like you to stay.'

Emily sat at the kitchen table with Anna and Leon, eating a soup with dumplings that Sam had prepared for their lunch. He listened in on the chat at the table while he chopped onions and peppers for Mr Hunter's dinner.

'What will you do, Sam?' asked Leon. 'Has Mr Hunter spoken to you?'

'He has,' said Sam mildly. 'He won't need a cook and a cleaner and a housekeeper any more; I expect he'll find someone to do all three. But that's OK, I've been here a long time. Maybe I can work in the National Trust café instead, just for a few more years until I retire. Mr Hunter will put a word in.'

Emily laughed. 'Can you make scones, Sam?'

He shrugged. 'It's a scone. How hard can it be?'

'Rock hard,' muttered Anna in a stage whisper, 'if you don't know how to make scones.'

Sam grinned and kept chopping. 'What about you, Anna? What are you going to do?'

'I'm ready to retire,' she said. 'Andrea has invited me to spend some time with her and her husband in Somerset. I'm going to see what it's like, maybe buy a little place down there. I have savings and a good pension.'

They all looked at Leon expectantly.

'Mr Hunter has asked me to stay on,' he said, 'but it would only be part-time. I would need to find other work as well, so I think maybe I will find something new.'

Emily nodded, sad that Leon might not be around any more. 'Any ideas?'

'I have been speaking to the charter company, the one Mr Hunter uses for jets and helicopters. They use drivers to transfer passengers, very nice cars. They have offered me a job.'

'So you'll stay in Norfolk?' said Emily hopefully.

'No, there is not enough work here. I will have to move closer to London.'

Emily stared at him, her eyes narrowing suspiciously. Leon said nothing, focusing intently on his lunch.

'How much closer to London?' she asked.

Leon smiled and gave a tiny shrug. 'South of London. Somewhere easy for Gatwick or Farnborough.'

'Or Goodwood,' said Emily.

'Goodwood is very nice too.' Leon caught Emily's eye and they both smiled.

'I'm going down there on Saturday, just to see,' he said casually.

'Are you?' said Emily, making a mental note to give Kelly a call as soon as possible. It sounded like her best friend had been keeping important information from her.

Emily and Jamie sat on a green tartan picnic blanket on the grass, leaning against the same sunny stone wall where they'd warmed their hands in front of a New Year bonfire. It was still only March, but the wall sheltered them from the wind and created a blissful little sun trap in the late afternoon. Jamie removed his boot and wiggled his toes, the skin pale against the shiny pink scars. His leg was getting stronger and the scars would fade.

All three of Mr Hunter's dogs had joined them – Bailey was asleep next to Jamie, and Murphy was watching Lily wrestle with a stick, trying to decide if he could be bothered to join in. Instead he mooched over to Emily's side and rested his head on her lap, his eyes closing happily as she stroked his head. The warm weight of him felt calming and reassuring.

'Your dad has asked me to stay on,' she said, taking Jamie's hand. 'He offered me a promotion and the tenancy on an estate cottage.'

Jamie grinned. 'Congratulations. That makes two of us. How do you feel about it?'

'I'm a bit overwhelmed, to be honest. What do you think I should do?'

Jamie said nothing for a few moments. 'I think you should take the job but not the cottage.'

Emily's head whipped round to look at him. 'Really? Are they that bad?'

'No, they're lovely, if you don't mind freezing your arse off for nine months of the year. But instead of you shivering away in one tiny cottage and me shivering away in another, I thought maybe we could take one of the bigger ones and shiver away together.'

Emily's mouth fell open. 'Are you asking me to move in with you?'

Jamie nodded. 'A joint tenancy, everything fifty-fifty. Proper grown-up shit.'

Emily could barely breathe, let alone process what Jamie had just suggested. 'I don't know what to say.'

Jamie shuffled round to face her, looking into her eyes intently. 'Listen. You once told me that if things were different, you definitely would.'

'God,' said Emily, feeling a blush creeping up from her neck. 'How do you remember stuff like that?'

Jamie laughed. 'I remember every conversation we've ever had, even the drunk ones. My point is that things ARE different. You're not the same woman who turned up in November with your life in a suitcase. You're part of the history of this estate now, part of the family. You get to help us decide what comes next.'

Emily blinked the inevitable tears away. 'It just all feels a bit much, off the back of everything else that's happened this week.'

'If you want more time, that's OK,' he said. 'I'm not going to rush you. But I just want you to know that nothing would make me happier than waking up next to you every morning in Wedmore Cottage and . . .'

'Wait,' she interrupted. 'Are you saying we could live in Wedmore Cottage?'

'Why not? Adam and Victoria have moved out. We could ask Dad for a joint tenancy there, rather than two separate ones. We may need to fumigate it, obviously.'

'Holy fuck, are you serious?' Emily could feel herself start to shake, her heart pounding.

Jamie put his hands on Emily's shoulders and looked into her eyes. 'Of course I'm serious. To be honest, I don't think I've ever been more serious about anyone or anything in my life.'

Emily looked back at him, her heart racing. 'It's just a lot to take in, Jamie. Can I think about it?'

'Oh,' said Jamie, raking his hand through his hair. 'Well, sure. Of course. I didn't mean to . . .'

'I'm kidding,' she said with a grin. 'My answer is yes. Absolutely, one hundred per cent YES.'

CHAPTER FIFTY

Emily didn't think she'd ever seen a bride as beautiful as Delphine, in a simple white dress with pink hibiscus flowers woven into her long hair. Her new husband Fabrice was so handsome it should probably be illegal, and their wedding was full of joy and laughter and music. Most of the ceremony was based on Mauritian Creole traditions, but Chinese and Indian songs and rituals were woven in too, to reflect Delphine's heritage. Jamie held Emily's hand from start to finish, and her heart felt like it might burst.

They'd been in Mauritius for two weeks already, having decided to tag on a holiday before the wedding. It was Emily's first proper time off since she'd started working at Bowford Manor seven months earlier, and she and Jamie had been determined to make the most of it. They'd spent a few days at the beach house to decompress and enjoy Madeleine's cooking, before heading across the island to the Lapis Lagoon Hotel for a week of snorkelling, riding and paddle boarding.

Back at home, Bowford Manor was now occupied by teams of surveyors and conservationists and people with clipboards making important decisions. Anna was keeping them all under control, so it felt like a good time to get away. Emily could see how difficult it was for Mr Hunter to see people swarming all over his beloved house, but he was also resigned to it. The alternative was unthinkable.

So far Adam had kept up his side of the bargain – there had been no legal challenges or fuss, and he had clearly decided to keep his head down for the time being. Mr Hunter had told Emily that any kind of father/son reconciliation would need to begin with a heartfelt apology to his assistant. Emily decided that hell would probably freeze over first, but there was always the possibility that Adam would undergo some kind of personality transplant if it meant benefitting from his father's money for the next twenty years. Either way, she wasn't holding her breath.

Emily stood at the edge of the terrace at Sam's Café, looking out over the water as she sipped a rum cocktail and felt the warmth of the setting sun on her face. The weather was cooler than it had been in January – less humid, but still glorious. Two weeks of careful sun exposure had given Emily something vaguely resembling a tan, so she was wearing a backless pink halterneck dress that made the most of her not needing a bra. Her hair was loose around her shoulders, pinned back on one side with a yellow flower. Her feet were bare, the toes painted a soft coral.

A band struck up on the terrace behind her, playing traditional Mauritian Sega. She turned to watch the dancers and listen to the song – she couldn't understand many of the words, but she could hear the love and celebration in every line. A barbecue had been lit on the beach, and the smell of charred seafood drifted on the breeze. Later they'd light a bonfire and the dancing would spread off the terrace and on to the sand.

'Did you speak to Kelly?' asked Jamie, appearing at her side and kissing her bare shoulder. He was wearing pale blue shorts and a linen shirt, his plastic boot and crutches long gone. His leg still got a little stiff sometimes, but the warm weather and swimming helped a lot.

'I did,' said Emily. 'She and Leon loved the flat, and it's on the ground floor so it's got a nice garden. Apparently Beth asked Leon for a princess bed, the kind with a pink canopy. He said no problem, so Kelly now has to get her one.'

'She totally deserves a princess bed,' said Jamie. 'If Kelly won't buy her one, we will.'

'That's what I said.'

'Dad wants to know how you feel about staying for one more week. He's not quite ready to go home yet, but we can all work from here.'

'Fine by me,' said Emily happily. 'Will the house be ready by the time we get back?'

'I'll call them on Monday, see if they can move things along a bit. It would be nice to move straight in.'

Emily nodded, excitement fizzing in her belly. They'd been to look at Wedmore Cottage lots of times in the past couple of months and agreed to wait until some repairs had been carried out. Some floorboards that needed replacing, a new guest bathroom, new carpets upstairs, fresh paint throughout. She was desperate to move in and start buying bedding and towels and kitchen stuff, and she had a ridiculous number of Pinterest boards on the go. But it would be worth the wait.

'I've been thinking about Christmas,' she said.

Jamie laughed. 'Emily, it's June.'

'I know, but I've already decided how amazing it's going to be.'

'Of course you have. What have you been thinking?'

'About whether we could invite my whole family to stay.

All of them. There's enough room for everyone. We haven't done that since we were kids.'

Jamie put his arm around her. 'I think that's a brilliant idea. But that means you'll miss out on skiing in Verbier.'

'Honestly, I think I can deal with the pain.'

Jamie laughed. 'I don't think Dad was planning on going this year anyway. I think the rift between him and Adam may take a little longer to heal.'

'Does that mean you won't be going either?'

'Definitely not. I'll spend some time with Mum and Catherine before they go, but I'd love to spend another Christmas with your family. I can teach Billy and Charlie to ride if they like. And we can always ask Dad if we can borrow the chalet for New Year. Celebrate our anniversary.'

Emily turned to look at him. 'What, just the two of us?'

He shrugged. 'Sure. Or we could invite Dad, or Leon and Kelly and Beth. I don't mind.'

'You're right,' said Emily. 'It's weird talking about this in June. My mind is already blown.'

Jamie laughed. 'Well, you started it.'

'I think Mum and Dad might want to come up to see the house before Christmas, though.'

'Emily, they're your parents. They can come whenever they like.'

'Maybe over the summer when Mum isn't working.'

'Tell them to come for a couple of weeks in August. They can do day trips to the beach, make a holiday of it.'

Emily grinned at him. 'Mum will get in a flap about the traffic.'

Jamie shrugged. 'We'll send a helicopter.'

'Whoa, are you serious?'

386

'What am I, Richard Branson? No, I'm not serious. They can bloody drive.'

Emily hooted with laughter and leaned over to kiss him. 'You're the best, have I ever told you that?'

'Not nearly recently enough, as it happens.'

Emily couldn't wait to see the transformation of Wedmore Cottage – and the garden too. She and Anna had been working with the gardeners to quietly transplant some of George's favourite flowers and shrubs over to the cottage garden, where they'd be safe from visitors and stompy children. The people from the National Trust had no plans to change George's rose garden; in fact most of the grounds would be left exactly the same, other than turning Leon's garage into a gift shop and the stables into a café. A new home was being built for the horses in a paddock twenty minutes on horseback from the house, on the site of a field shelter where Emily and Jamie had once had mind-blowing sex in a snowstorm. Luna would have had her foal by the time it was finished, and they'd already decided to call it Storm whether it was a boy or a girl.

Emily and Jamie walked hand-in-hand towards the water, others drifting in the same direction as everyone waited for the sun to touch the water and make its final descent. She could see Sam and Gabrielle with their three adult children a little further along the beach. They were only here for a long weekend because of the grandchildren, but Mr Hunter had offered to fly the entire family back in a few weeks so they could spend the school holidays with their extended family. It was Mr Hunter's farewell gift to his friend and chef of thirty years, with the option to come back every year for as long as he and Gabrielle wanted.

Mr Hunter was chatting with Jessie and her husband, a cold bottle of beer in his hand and a look of peace and contentment on his face. Delphine and Fabrice stood at the heart of the gathering, their arms around each other as Delphine rested her head on her husband's shoulder.

'I love this place,' whispered Emily.

'Me too,' said Jamie. 'I'm really glad we're here.'

'Feels strange to think that seven months ago I had no job, no boyfriend and nowhere to live.'

Jamie laughed. 'And what do you have now?'

Emily thought for a moment. 'A great job, a super-hench boyfriend and access to several beautiful houses.'

Jamie shook his head. 'Man, you work fast.'

Emily pinched him playfully on the arm. 'Hey, you asked me out. I was determined it was never gonna happen.'

'I'm very happy it did.'

They stood in silence for a few minutes, Emily's back pressed against Jamie's chest, their hands entwined as they watched the sun disappear over the horizon in a blaze of a thousand colours.

'Can we go riding tomorrow?' asked Emily quietly, not wanting to break the spell.

'Sunrise on the east coast, or sunset over here?'

'Sunset over here, I think. Sunrise might be pushing it; the party's just getting started.'

Jamie rested his head on her shoulder and stroked his hand down the bare skin on her arm. 'Everything's just getting started,' he whispered.

Emily closed her eyes, feeling the warm water lapping over her feet like tiny waves of happiness.

Acknowledgements

Never Gonna Happen was originally my third book, but to cut a long story short my publisher loved it so much they asked if it could be my second. So huge thanks must go to my editor, Bea Grabowska, and the amazing team at Headline Accent for their endless encouragement and enthusiasm. Also, my agent Caroline Sheldon, whose wise words and gentle guidance are always welcome and much appreciated. Book three, formerly known as book two, will be out later this year.

I'd also like to thank my friend Paul Choy for being my guide to all things Mauritius. Paul is an amazing photographer, and some years ago he and his wife Aideen invited my partner and I to stay in their beautiful island home. Later, I helped Paul edit a guidebook to the island – who knew how useful that would be one day? Thank you for reviewing the relevant bit of the manuscript and confirming my memory hadn't failed me, teaching me a bit of Creole, and patiently answering all my random WhatsApp questions about sunset times and hospital protocols and sea urchins. As they say in Creole, *to incroyable*.

Thanks also to my beloved friend Sarah Burr for her National Trust wisdom, to Gemma Teed for being my equine expert, and to my family for their endless support and encouragement – I couldn't have done this without you.

And to all my friends and colleagues and neighbours and total strangers who have taken the time to get in touch and say lovely things about my first book — you made this one so much more of a joy to write. Thank you.

**Have you read Heidi Stephens' hugely uplifting and laugh-out-loud funny debut novel,
*Two Metres From You?***

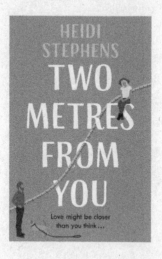

Gemma isn't sure what upsets her more.
The fact she just caught her boyfriend cheating,
or that he did it on her *brand-new* Heal's cushions.

All she knows is she needs to put as many miles between her and Fraser
as humanly possible. So, when her best friend suggests a restorative few
days in the West Country, it seems like the perfect solution.

That is, until the country enters a national lockdown that leaves her
stranded. All she has for company is her dog, Mabel. And the mysterious
(and handsome!) stranger living at the bottom of her garden . . .

Available to order

ACCENT